BEFORE IT BREAKS

DAVE WARNER

BEFORE IT BREAKS

For Nicole, shelter in the storm.

PROLOGUE

In his bright blue windbreaker the boy was clearly visible to his father, who dawdled behind, allowing the little girl the opportunity to try to walk on her own. She would manage about five steps before tumbling, her round thighs cushioned by soft grass. The boy was lead scout up the steeply rising fairway that signalled the last stretch before turning home. Summer was losing its grasp, the air significantly cooler than even a week ago but still pleasant. After a day staring at a computer screen the father enjoyed this little pre-dinner ramble with his children across broad swards of park, over the little wooden bridge where the boy would run fast to avoid the troll hiding below, through the mini forest of slender trunks ideal for hide-and-seek. Refreshed by this exercise the trio would return home where, beneath a sub-strata of television news and the delightful smell of roast pork, his wife's demands for dirty shoes to be removed would ring in their ears. There would be baths, books read, some tears from the boy wanting to stay up late, a compromise offer to read a story which involved robots and the destruction of the planet, at first rejected, later begrudgingly accepted. After around twenty minutes the boy would grow sleepy, his eyes would shut, his blond hair fanning over the pillow. Mother and father would kiss him goodnight, retreat quietly to a glass of wine and perhaps a favoured television show or some music.

The father glanced up. The boy had disappeared from sight. The father was not concerned. It was a steep rise and anybody over the crest of the hill was momentarily absent from the view of those following. Even so, he called out the boy's name, yelling for him to wait. The girl, perhaps feeling she'd lost her father's attention tripped over a little too deliberately. She was giggling, golden curls framing her angelic face. After righting her once again her father called for the boy to come back but when he did not appear at the top of the hill, the father scooped up the little girl, threw her over his shoulder and, much to her amusement, began jogging up the incline. He was still not worried, the only reason he was jogging was to entertain her. By the time he began to crest the rise however a scintilla of anxiety had worked its way into his pragmatic soul, for the boy was still invisible. Surely he had heard him?

He hit the top of the rise and immediately looked to the right, which was their route back. His heart cramped. There was nothing but a narrow strip of grass and widely spaced trees. Reflexively he threw to the left and relief swept through him. The boy stood twenty metres ahead looking at something on the ground. His father took three quick strides towards him and any mystery evaporated. It was obvious why he had not responded. His whole attention had been snared by a cute black cocker spaniel. The boy adored dogs and his father would have loved to give him one but the apartment block where they lived had rules about pets.

Now as he drew closer, however, the father saw something about the scene was not right. Tail down, fretting, torn between sitting and pacing, the whimpering spaniel was wearing a collar and lead.

His son was not even looking at the dog. A man was prostrate, a quite large man with a shock of white hair. The father put down the girl without breaking stride. His first thought was that the man had collapsed. Even as he pulled his phone from his pocket he was regretting he had not signed up for one of those CPR courses. So often he had told himself it might be critical, the kids could somehow touch a live wire, it could be the difference between life and death, but the impetus always drifted away like smoke in the opposite direction.

Then he froze as if somebody had punched a pause button.

He was looking down at the man's face. It was clear he had not suffered a heart attack. An arrow bisected his throat, the fin somewhere under his chin, the arrowhead protruding through the back of his neck. There was no question about it, the man was dead.

1

BROOME, WESTERN AUSTRALIA

Clang, clang, clang. There he was, that guy with the hammer, five fifty-five every morning. Had to be illegal. The sound of metal on metal carried any time but over water it echoed and bounced exponentially. Clement supposed he could put on some shorts, stagger down to the wharf, find the culprit, play the heavy. I'm Detective Inspector Daniel Clement and you're out of line, mate. By the time he did all that he would have to get ready for work anyway. Sure, it might discourage the guy in the future but what if the fellow kicked up, asked where Clement was living and happened to know by some chance that this apartment above the chandler's contravened the industrial zoning for the wharf?

Clement swung up and sat sideways on the mattress. He rubbed his face as if that might make the place tidier. Okay, it wasn't exactly what you wanted to wake up to but it could be worse: a bottle of white which had lasted three days; three longnecks which had lasted around ninety minutes last night, not so good. Already the air was thick and sticky, no breeze yet. Clement scooped up the empties and dumped them in a large green garbage bag. He walked to the window and stared out over the ocean, which always seemed greener here in the north-west. The place was small and devoid of luxury but it had a great view. He'd been lucky to find it, or maybe fate had handed it to him, a special token from one estranged husband to another. The chandler's marriage had broken down and he'd taken to sleeping in his office above the workshop. It already had a toilet, so one weekend the chandler had shoved in a kit bathroom and kitchen and made it his home. Unlike Clement, he had eventually patched up differences with his wife and moved back with her. Realising he had a potential earner in his bachelor quarters, he relocated the minimal office equipment downstairs and began renting the 'apartment' for cash. Clement found out about it by word of mouth and snapped it up. At night it was tranquil and isolated, but during the day it was like living inside an axle and totally inappropriate for a nine year old. Instead, for his weekends with Phoebe, Clement maintained a second property in Derby over two hundred k to the east. He loved Derby. It was open, untouched and unfashionable, and he'd found a gem of a property, a genuine stilt house looking north over mangroves, the famous Derby jetty visible in the distance. The loan to buy it wiped out any other lifestyle but what lifestyle did he desire anyway? He had a small runabout and Phoebe loved spending time with him on the water.

After dousing himself in the cold shower for all of two minutes, Clement dried himself and threw on his clothes. His system was to rotate shirts and pants, two of each, which gave him three days' wear before washing, four at a pinch. The place didn't have a machine so he handwashed in the basin or used the laundromat near the station.

A couple of months earlier, in the prime of his career as one of Perth's go-to Homicide cops, Dan Clement had brought down the cleaver and cut clean through to the bone, amputated his prospects, his professional standing, his minor celebrity even. Not that he ever wanted that part of it; the press conferences, the six p.m. news grabs, that wasn't him. He was no show pony but a smart, hard-working detective who had toiled a long time and sacrificed too much to get to the top of the heap.

And that really was the nub of it, the paradox, he thought you called it. You were good at something, you excelled, it was what you were meant to do with your life and you clawed your way to its peak losing pieces of yourself along the way, first small nips, then progressively larger chunks. There was no avoiding it, no best of both worlds. There you were, part of a crack team, clever colleagues, the latest in crime detection paid for by the trainloads of iron ore being shipped out from deserts to the north. You had pretty much a murder a week to put away. You had restaurants and bars and colleagues' patios where you could talk about the cases to the gentle click of an articulated sprinkler. You had honed yourself, you were elite. But, and here's the paradox, you discover that's not enough, that those things you had to discard were things you should have kept. Like a marriage. And no, you're not taking all the blame here but it's too late to apportion blame because it has happened and now, on the eve of your forty-first birthday, Marilyn's heading back to her ancestral home with your daughter and you have a simple choice: stay and say goodbye, or keep close to the only thing you wouldn't dare screw up.

Clement had chosen the latter. So here he was counting flies in that desolate country near where the ore was shipped, working junior cases with rookie detectives or jaded colleagues who would rather drink beer and fish.

And no washing machine.

There was nothing to eat in the bar fridge except a

block of cheese and an apple but as he had no bread, only crackers, he decided he'd leave the cheese for an evening meal. He took the apple and was halfway through it before he'd reached the bottom of the rickety external staircase at the foot of which was his car. He climbed in, put his hands on the wheel and sat there, already feeling stale. The day promised little. There was a domestic violence case going to trial tomorrow and he'd have to make sure there was nothing to let the bastard slip off. Apart from that it would be an array of minor dope charges and grog-induced assaults. He would have pushed to go north with Hagan and Lalor where there'd been some clan strife but this weekend he had Phoebe and he didn't want to risk cancelling.

Having delayed as long as he could, he turned over the engine and drove slowly out. Though it was Wednesday peakhour, there was hardly any traffic, not much more than when as a ten year old he'd ridden his pushbike around these streets with a playing card attached to the back wheel by a peg so it clattered, allowing him to imagine he was on a motorcycle. He switched on the police radio and caught Mal Gross, the desk sergeant, directing a car to a suspected break-in at the old abattoir. He was minutes away. The turn-off was dead ahead. Clement eased left. Of course he should have radioed Gross but then he'd be told there was no need for him. The approach, a pitted feeder road with low scrub either side, was not too different to how he remembered it thirty years ago. The smell which used to waft toward school on the inland breeze was there in his nostrils as if the long-dormant slaughterhouse were still operating, so real, so clear that Clement was forced to consider if the place had been reactivated. But by the time that thought had run, the smell was gone and he knew it was just memory, just a trick like those mornings when he woke and felt certain he heard

Marilyn's soft breathing beside him.

The outline of the slaughterhouse showed up ahead, nothing much more than a flat group of tin sheds. A police car was pulled up at a rusted perimeter fence, the uniforms clambering out. The dark-haired female constable he recognised as di Rivi. Jo? He'd only been there around nine weeks and his retention of names of those in the lower ranks was poor. The uniforms paused and watched his car pull in. He saw puzzlement, suspicion, then, when they identified him, a kind of vague fear that they must have done something wrong.

'Hi, sir.'

It was di Rivi who found the words. The partner, a young guy about her age, was frozen.

Clement put them at ease. 'It's okay, I was on my way in and I heard the call. You're di Rivi?'

'Yes, sir. '

She must have twigged he didn't know her partner's name and indicated him. 'Nathan Restoff.'

The men nodded a greeting. Restoff, slim for a cop up this way, filled him in.

A person from the historical society, a Mr Symonds, had driven out to take a photograph for his 'Old Broome' Facebook page, but had heard sounds inside and what might have been somebody crying in pain. He'd called the station.

While Restoff was talking di Rivi examined the padlocked gate. 'No one got in this way.'

Clement jerked a thumb. 'It's hardly Fort Knox. Let's check the perimeter.'

It took them about three minutes to find an unsecured part of the fence that had probably been used for years as a doorway. Jo di Rivi held up the wire for him to crawl under.

'You armed, sir?'

'No.'

Restoff offered him a taser. He was worried he'd use it incorrectly, look an idiot so he waved it off.

'I'll be right. I'll stay out of it.'

A gaping doorway led into gloom. Restoff and di Rivi approached cautiously and in a firm but calm voice Restoff called, 'It's the police. Anybody there?'

When there was no answer they edged inside. Already Clement was regretting his decision to reject the taser. He couldn't very well follow them now.

Standing outside he heard them call again. Both had torches but there was enough tin ripped off the roof that they wouldn't need them. Then Clement heard a quiet shuffling footfall which seemed to come from around the corner of the building where he stood. He edged over and peeked. In the middle of what had been a space between this larger shed and a smaller one was mound of dirt, as if a bulldozer had pushed everything into a lazy heap, sand, old brick, rotten wood and wire. The mound was just high enough to prevent him being able to see what might lie behind it. Arming himself with a crumbling half brick, he edged carefully around the heap.

The intruder turned and looked at him with the cold glare of one who has absolutely nothing to lose.

Clement put out his left hand to placate her. 'Easy.'

She was lean, her hair matted, her teeth bared, her wiry tail low but taut. She could have been part dingo, part shepherd, but she was fully alert.

'I'm not going to hurt you.'

His calming words had about the same effect they had on Marilyn. She snarled and sprinted at him and leapt for his throat. Only his years as a very average opening batsman saved Clement. He pivoted inside her arc and swung his right hand, the one holding the half brick. It hit the bitch's head with a crack. The dog dropped at his feet.

Restoff and di Rivi came running, weapons drawn, which only made him feel worse standing over the prone body. What kind of man starts his day by clubbing a starving dog with a brick?

•••

In what was otherwise a large open-plan space Clement had managed to secure himself one of three discrete offices. The others belonged to his boss, Scott Risely, and Anna Warren, the Assistant Regional Commander. She was on long service leave and rarely in Broome anyway, usually flying between the mining camps and far-flung communities. It was as well Clement was afforded privacy, for three hours on from the abattoir, he still sat staring at his desk. His blow had not killed the dog but it may as well have. It hadn't had much of a life but it had been something, a living organism. Maybe it was a mother trying to fend for her pups and now it had been hauled away to a pound, most likely with a fractured skull. It would be euthanised for sure. And it had all been for nothing. There had been no sign of any other intruder, just that one skinny hound which maybe had uncovered some long-buried cattle bones.

Clement was thirsty. Even in the air-conditioning the heat dried you out. He left his office and headed to the water cooler. The Major Crime section was near deserted. Mal Gross appeared to be taking a statement from an aboriginal couple. It sounded like their place had been burgled. Even paradise has its thieves. Clement drank the cold water. It made his tooth ache and he remembered that was something else he'd been putting off.

'What kind of axe?' Gross was asking.

'You know, for chopping wood,' the man answered, like Gross was an idiot. The woman, who seemed around fifty, slightly younger than her husband, said she thought she heard something Sunday night. Gross made a note. 'We didn't know it was missing till he went to chop wood this morning.'

Stolen tools, bicycles and mobile phones, this was what the crime landscape looked like all the way to the horizon. Clement ditched the plastic cup and headed out the back door to the carpark.

He thought he'd drive to the shops and get some proper food into him but once he was driving he admitted to himself he had no appetite so he kept going, no destination in mind. At some point the car began heading out of town as if of its own will. Around five k on, past the servo, he swung right. Whether he actually recognised these trees he wasn't sure but he definitely felt he did. This grove had been the boundary of his early years, the geographical zone beyond which 'home' became 'elsewhere', or more correctly, as he was heading in the opposite direction right now, where elsewhere became home. Marilyn was happy to overlook the fact he'd grown up here too. Sure his lineage was far less grand, no pearl farm, just the caravan park his mum and dad worked up from scratch but this had been his home for fifteen years. He had almost escaped it.

Almost.

...

The bush hadn't changed at all in thirty years but up the road was a different story. The caravan park started by his parents was gone and in its place was an industrial complex: two large pre-fab-type buildings, some sort of muffler centre and several smaller units, spray shops, a tyre place. He pulled in on the crumbling bitumen lip of the road and tried to remember it how it was. This was the first time he'd returned since he'd been back, first time in fact since he'd left all those years ago. His parents now lived in Albany near the southern tip of the state. He'd lost track of friends. There'd been nothing to pull him back here to the heat and dirt. He wasn't sure exactly why he'd chosen now to visit his heritage location but knew it had something to do with the dog and Phoebe and all the things in his life he'd messed up. From the look of them, the buildings were a decade old. How long after his parents had sold up had the caravan park survived, he wondered? He had expected they would have at least kept the old shower block but he couldn't spy it, not from here. It could be behind the units but he was not inclined to get out for a stroll.

Not for the first time he felt a stranger in what had been his homeland, and he sensed a swell within him to act, to turn the car onto the main road and head south all the way back to Perth. He quelled it easily enough but knew it had not left him anymore than that sour feeling over the dog, knew it would linger and eventually may prove stronger than his ability to resist.

2

JASPER'S CREEK, WESTERN AUSTRALIA

As if exhausted from an arduous day keeping itself aloft and baking the earth below the dull, rusty red of blood, the sun plummeted quickly. This was the way up here, night falling more like a guillotine than a handkerchief. Almost every night for the last thirty years he had gone to sleep alone. He could seek company and usually did, at least for a few hours, normally in a bar, sometimes in a café, very infrequently over dinner at the home of an acquaintance. There had even been the occasional night he had slept with a woman but not for a while now. Human company he had discovered was no longer effective in reducing his sense of being an island. Indeed, the opposite was true. He felt less isolated here on the other side of the world than those last years in his hometown. Solitude was the natural state here. A man could stand silent knowing no other heart was beating within a hundred kilometres. But isolation did not equate to loneliness.

Back then he'd had real friends, not just people you met in a bar, men he had gone to school with, worked with, but especially in their company he had felt a desperate loneliness. It was as if it were his avatar interacting with them while his real self skulked in a dungeon. But, you make your bed, you lie in it ... alone.

His fingertips travelled over his whiskers. If he really willed it he could remember his wife's fingers doing that. She had eventually grown tired of his detachment and struck out for a new life free of the burden of what he had become.

And why had he become that again?

The voice asking him was always there, asking in the same measured tones, dragging him back to smoky bars, leather jackets, a crackling radio somewhere in a corner. Funny, a face could slowly erase over time but not a voice, a voice did not age. He did not offer an answer to the question—what was the point? It was a long time ago and it was too late now to change anything. All life after forty was regret.

A sound that did not belong to nature pulled him from his contemplation. It was a vehicle somewhere on the other side of the creek, which really wasn't that far away. It was probably twenty metres from his little camp here to the water's edge, and no more than fifty across the span of the creek, so less than a hundred metres all up. As long as they kept to themselves, what did he care?

He set up the small tent with great facility, sat back on the front seat of the car and popped a beer can. Warm, but so what? He was after the faint buzz, not the taste. The creek was still, only shadows created an illusion of movement. He drained the can quickly and tossed it on the floor in back with the others. At the roadhouse he'd bought a cooked chicken. Now he pulled it from its foil wrapper and ripped off a drumstick. Mosquitoes buzzed around him but for some reason they never bothered with him much. There were flies but only a fraction of what there would have been in daylight. He chewed the chicken meat slowly and thought about South America. That was one place he had always wanted to visit. Another failed aspiration, along with a boat trip through Alaska and a hotel romp involving Britt Ekland. His life was a series of joined dots that drew the picture of a fat zero. It was fortunate how things had fallen into place here, remarkable in fact. He had taken a gamble which could have backfired badly but then there was not so much to lose, was there. He had owed money all over Hamburg, HSV were playing like crap, staying there was validation of his failure. Even so, at least he was alive there. His gamble could have cost him that life, miserable as it was. But it had proved the right move. This was where all the tributaries of his life were destined to pool. It was where he would die.

He turned the key far enough to ignite the CD player. Country music, what else for a single man who could no longer lie to himself he was even middle-aged?

He sat for a long time listening to the music, drifting. A memory would constitute itself: his parents, his father's braces worn even at dinner-time. That memory would crumble but reconstitute as another, and another: the street where he grew up, a school friend, a shopkeeper who was particularly generous, a girl he fancied who preferred one of his friends, the game of handball where he broke his little finger. What had become of those whose lives had intersected his? Some would be dead but others might be sitting in a little flat, or hunched over a campfire on a sweeping plain in Argentina eating roast beef, the strum of a guitar in the background floating over a starry sky like the one above him now. And they might be reflecting on their parents, generous shopkeepers and maybe even him.

...

His legs had stiffened by the time he swung back out of the car and pulled the aluminium dinghy, the tinny, off the roof of his old Pajero. Still strong, he enjoyed the weight of the boat on his arms for it confirmed he was real, not just one of his memories. He placed the boat by the muddy bank then dragged the outboard from the back of the Pajero. Fishing and drinking beer, two worthy occupations to pass the time until the next sunset. The proximity of crocodiles did not worry him though he would take no foolish risks. While he had heard stories of crocs flipping over tinnies in the Territory, nobody he knew here had ever witnessed it, and given that men exaggerate any such brush with death, he had to wonder if this absence was proof such things were myth. As he attached the outboard his thoughts meandered back to last night, those two fresh-faced women laughing with him as he spun tales. The young fellows with them were pissed off, he could tell, but that was just the way the world worked. He had what the women wanted, so they'd sat with him and drank his beer and laughed at his stories, genuinely, he believed, for he wasn't one to dissemble. He caught sight of himself in the wing mirror. The last year or so the lines had deepened, the brightness in his eyes had dulled. He was drifting inevitably towards old age and death. Not yet though, there were still beers to drink and fish to catch.

He caught a sound back in the bush towards the track down which he'd driven. He turned the radio right down and strained to hear.

Nothing. Yet he felt it out there, a presence. There were many feral pigs in these parts. He'd shot and eaten more than his fair share. In fact he'd toyed with the idea of sending them back home where boar was a delicacy but then discovered somebody else was already doing that. Whenever he came up with some exciting idea it was inevitable he would discover he was too late. His ears stayed alert for any sound but there was nothing more.

He wrapped his chicken back in the foil and slid

it into the tent. He would have it later after a spot of fishing. As he was about to zip up the tent, he heard something approaching rapidly through scrub from behind and swung around fast. Before he could identify what it was, white sizzled his eyes.

'Who's that?' he said trying to block the torch beam. The answer was something heavy and cold, slicing into his head. His knees hit hard ground, his body throbbed, his head ached yet seemed distant at the same time. Through all this he understood he was being murdered. A voice came from the darkness. The voice from before, as if like the serpent spirit of the aborigines, it had slithered over continents and through years to find him.

Reason told him it was not possible, it could not be the voice, so he must already be dead. Yet the pain was intense and multiplying. Blows rained on his body, he fell to the ground and tried to call out but it was beyond him. Hell, which he had postponed for so long, had taken him to its bosom. The choice he'd made had stalked him as efficiently as any reptile of the deep and was destroying him now. He comprehended in some distant way the absolute rightness of this.

'I'm sorry,' he heard himself gasp but that was a trick of the brain.

He was dead before the thought had moved his tongue.

3

The report of shots fired came from some adventurous tourists who had foregone ceiling fans, sachets of hair conditioner, soft sheets and high-priced grog to brave bush, crocs and mosquitoes and thereby experience the True Australia. If he'd ever had any idea what the True Australia was, Clement had long since admitted defeat in capturing it. So far as he could tell, True Australia was Maoris and Sri Lankans singing their lungs out on TV to impress a bunch of overseas judges to win a career singing American songs someplace other than here. True Australia definitely wasn't the front bar of the Picador late on Saturday night. At least he hoped it wasn't. Yet people had it in their heads that drunk losers breaking pool cues over one another's heads was a link in a chain that stretched all the way back to Anzac Cove.

'True Australia.'

He gave a bitter grunt and pushed the accelerator flat. He wished the Net had never been invented. He longed for a return to the days of high-cost air-travel when only the wealthy could afford to see another country. Then these adventurous tourists from Tokyo or Oslo or Rio would never have had a clue about the Kimberley region in the north-west of the Great Southland and he wouldn't have to worry about shots fired and the possibility somebody was illegally taking crocodiles, a job that should have been left to Fisheries or Parks and Wildlife. Unfortunately they were thin on the ground, the call had come to the station and the tourists were probably tweeting now about their 'brush with death'. Somebody had to take the trouble to check it out. He could have left it, but the uniforms were all run off their feet. Hagan and Lalor were still hours inland sorting out the tribal stoush, and di Rivi and Restoff had their hands full processing a grand final party that had got out of hand. As for his fellow detectives, his sergeant, Graeme Earle, was off fishing and his junior, Josh Shepherd, tied up in court on the domestic violence case so, senior detective or not, he was left to do the dirty work.

As well, that dog yesterday was still at the back of his mind, his tooth continued to flare, and the bloke with the hammer had been at it again before six, none of which helped his disposition. He forced himself to take a deep breath. Phoebe had taken to referring to him as Mr Cranky though he had no doubt the words were her mother's. Marilyn still hadn't forgiven him for transferring here. 'Chasing us' had been the phrase she'd used. Marilyn was angry because she believed he'd made the kind of sacrifice for their daughter he never would have for her. She was probably right but he would always love her, part of him anyway, the part you couldn't explain any more than the part of him that wedged itself between them like a crowbar. And she wasn't snow-white, this wasn't all at his feet. Surprisingly, she hadn't married that turkey, Brian, yet. Maybe Brian hadn't asked or maybe she treated him the same way she'd treated Dan, like he never quite measured up. If her old man had still been alive Clement would have had an ally. Nick might have died a rich pearl farmer but he started as a bloody boat mechanic. Geraldine was the problem, she always had been. She loved to play the Lady of the Manor, and Clement had been the stablehand, never good enough for her daughter. It had taken a dozen years, but Marilyn had eventually synched with her mother on that. Sometimes Clement toyed with the idea she might be having second thoughts, might have at least understood her role in their demise and that's why she hadn't walked down the aisle again.

He had calmed now. This wasn't so bad, getting out of the office and away from petty crap a rookie could handle. The low, dry scrub either side of the road reminded him of those baking hot days when, as a boy, he'd played at being a soldier sliding towards his imagined enemy. Experience had taught him the enemy was generally not where you thought or even who you thought.

The turn-off was up ahead. Australians signposted their roads in the same laconic style they spoke. For a hundred years nobody visited Australia except English cricket teams or Russian circus performers, and no circus performers or cricketers ever bothered to come to places like this. So signs were a waste of time. If you weren't local you wouldn't be here, simple as that. If you weren't local and you were here, you shouldn't be. You were a freak, not the kind of person desired and therefore not to be encouraged by signage.

Many things might have changed but that attitude was buried so deep in the national psyche that it persisted. Unless you knew there was a track about to come up on your left that led down to the waterhole you'd eventually be in Darwin still looking for the non-existent sign that said Jasper's Creek.

But Clement knew.

He braked and turned easily down the wide dirt track. A four-wheel drive was as necessary as insect repellent up here. Clement passed a bullet-riddled Parks and Wildlife sign showing a crocodile and the word DANGER. They couldn't signpost a road but the odd spectacular death by croc had put the wind up the bureaucrats in the Tourism department enough to get every little creek for five hundred k covered. He could see rust around the edges of the bullet holes so he knew they weren't anything to do with the shots reported as coming from here in the early hours. Over the phone the tourists had given him a precise location for where they were when they heard the gunshots so Clement drove towards a waterhole he'd always known as Jasper's. Who the hell Jasper was, nobody had been able to tell him. The waterhole wasn't named on any map, it was too small down in mangrove territory. The bush was denser here, with paperbark, blackboy, even a few big gums. Clement pulled up at the point where the car-trail narrowed.

No matter how long you lived up here you never got used to the dry blast of hot air that hit you the moment you stepped out of air-conditioning. Clement felt it now, that morbid, unfriendly heat. He began walking through bush toward the creek bank. Flies greeted him like a lost king.

Having read up thoroughly about crocs, the tourists had slept on the roof of their camper van for safety. It was a practice Clement didn't recommend. Already since he'd transferred he'd dealt with two incidents of people falling from their perch during the night and cracking bones in the dirt below. One bloke was pissed and had overbalanced. The other had woken up at dawn, forgotten where he was and rolled straight off the roof. Better to scrunch up in your car or move further away from the water. Still, they'd been wise to be cautious. There'd recently been reports of a large croc in the area that had taken a pig-dog.

It took only a few minutes to find the car tracks and the broken scrub from where the tourists had driven out. According to them the shots had come from the west side of the creek but as it was night, they'd seen nothing and simply hightailed it out of there. Clement didn't blame them. He suspected it was probably a couple of drunk hoons firing at the stars but it could have been some dickhead after a croc. Close to the creek, the trees bent in and leaned over the dark water, boughs sprawled across the muddy bank like a party-goer who'd never made it home. The light was dappled, the smell of rotting weeds and dead wood bringing to mind dragonflies and mosquitoes. Here Clement was extremely careful. Coming out of the bright light into this shadowy grove your eyes took time to adjust and you could literally trip over a big croc lazing in its muddy bed. He made sure the logs near the bank were logs then advanced close enough to be able to look west to the other bank, a distance he estimated might be a swimming pool and a half, say eighty metres. His first scan registered nothing out of the ordinary but when he looked again, he sensed rather than saw something wasn't right. His focus narrowed to a shag levitating above the water but without its wings extended. Closer inspection revealed it was sitting on something curved and silver, the bottom of an upturned tinny. It was in shallow water right near the edge of the opposite bank. Despite the proximity there was no way Clement was swimming across. Foreboding thudded in Clement's chest, not a salvo, not a flurry, just one solid thump. He started around to the other side of the creek.

'Anybody there?'

His words spun around the empty space and slapped him.

No reply.

The bush was thick and spikey through here. Sharp,

stiff foliage poked into his neck and the backs of his legs, tangled branches scratched his arms. It was as if the bush was saying, keep away, leave me alone, I don't want you here. Even pushing as quickly as he could it took him a good ten minutes to circumnavigate the creek and get to the opposite side from where he'd started. His position now was about twenty-five metres from the water, in bush but directly in line with the partly submerged tinny. A gap in the foliage surrounding the creek at this point meant there were no trees obstructing his line of sight. He guessed the easy access might be why you'd launch your tinny from here. No outboard motor was visible on the tinny, and alarms bells sounded a fraction louder. Every tinny up here had some kind of motor.

He called out again but heard only the ghost of his own voice. He continued on his arc, shoving his way through a tight screen of bush, sweating like a pig, moving sideways rather than down to the water because he was after the vehicle that had carried the tinny. About ten metres on, in a small clearing, was an early model Pajero, the driver door open. A low hum turned him around to a one-man tent that looked like somebody had poured a sack of tea over it: bush flies, thousands of them. Off the nearest tree, Clement snapped a small branch and waved its dead leaves around near the tent. The flies scattered long enough for him to recognise they'd been feasting on blood, quite a deal of it from the looks, tacky, not fresh but relatively recent, over the nylon tent and in the dark earth.

Steeling himself, Clement flipped back the tent flap.

Another dense army of flies. Fifty or so launched themselves at his eyes and nostrils, the rest remained undisturbed, clumped on what had once been a cooked chicken. Apart from a sleeping bag, a couple of utensils and plastic drinking cup, nothing else was in the tent.

No blood from what he could see. If the blood on the tent was from an animal killed on a hunt, there was no sign of the carcass. His guts tightened fractionally. Something bad had happened to somebody here.

'Hello. Is there anybody here?'

He yelled it as loud as he could but all tone was flattened by the vast emptiness around him. He yelled again. And again. There was no response. He turned his attention to the vehicle, put it at eight to ten years old, small dents in the body and paintwork, scratches spanning a few years. His guess: either bought second-hand in this condition cheap, or the owner was a drinker who preferred to save his money for grog. The roof bore racks for transporting the tinny. Through the back window he could see fishing rods and tackle, a bucket, esky, various crap, old towels and a tarp. Making sure to touch nothing he peered down at the back seat. A pair of wading boots, shoes, three empty cans of VB. He moved to the open driver door and was surprised to find the key in the ignition. Closer inspection showed the lights were switched to on but the car headlights weren't illuminated. He carefully twisted the key in the ignition with as little grip as possible already aware fingerprints might be important.

Not a kick, flat battery his diagnosis. The glove box was open and disturbed. In the crack where the hinges sat was a live cartridge, twenty-two by the looks. There was another on the floor where it might have spilled. No weapon though.

It was looking more and more like a crime-scene. No blood in the car. No obvious sign of more than one person, no women's clothing, anything like that. Clement slowly circumnavigated the vehicle. A bumper sticker extolled the virtues of Broome Anglers.

Clement used his phone to take photos of the scene and record the car's number plate and odometer setting.

A phone burst into life somewhere close by. Generic ringtone. Clement tracked the sound to the dirt a few metres from the edge of the creek. Using his shirt over his fingers, Clement carefully picked up an older model smart phone. Number Withheld flashed on the screen. Clement answered.

'Hello?'

No answer but somebody was on the other end.

'This is Detective Inspector Daniel Clement ...'

The line went dead. Clement stared at the phone. His police car was equipped with a computer that would enable him to trace the Pajero plates but to get back to it through the bush was going to take another twenty minutes slog. He scrolled through the phone's last calls. The most recent out was identified as 'Rudi'.

He dialled, using his own phone.

Voicemail. A man, foreign accent, something European. "I'm not available. Leave a message.'

Clement left a brief message asking Rudi to call him. He scrolled to the next entry which was labelled 'AngClub'. Clement had never been inside the Anglers Club but he'd passed it often enough, a small modern brick building at the industrial end of town, so indistinguishable it could as easily have been a public dunny or scout headquarters. Broome was a small town and he doubted there would be more than fifty members of the Anglers. He gave it a try. The phone rang for some time. He was about to give up when a woman answered.

'Anglers.'

'This is Detective Inspector Daniel Clement.' He ran through his spiel. He was at an abandoned vehicle he thought might belong to one of the members. After eliciting the woman's name was Jill he described the car.

'Just a sec,' Jill said. He heard her calling to somebody

in the background. She came back on. 'Sounds like Dieter's.'

'Dieter who?'

A further bout of offline consultation was followed by 'Schaffer. Don't ask me how you spell it. Is everything okay?'

That was the question, wasn't it?

Apparently Dieter Schaffer was about sixty-five, retired and unmarried. He generally fished alone. The only number they had for him was the mobile. He lived way out on Cape Leveque Road somewhere. Jill didn't know who Rudi was. Clement got off the phone and considered his options. His gut said it was a probable crime scene but there could be many explanations for what he'd found. Schaffer could have accidentally shot or cut himself, then called Rudi or some other mate to come get him. Clement rang Derby Hospital, and got Karen who had made it abundantly clear to him several times that there was always a bed ready for him there, with her in it. Karen was late forties and it showed in her face but she had the taut body of a woman half her age.

'You finally asking me out?'

Clement sidestepped.

'You have a Dieter Schaffer there? Sixty-five, German accent, emergency admittance most likely?'

'We got a twenty-something idiot who blew himself up with his barbecue gas-bottle.'

'Anybody admitted with any sort of gunshot or other wound, the last twenty hours?'

'No. And you still haven't answered my first question.'

'I'm not dating.'

'I'm not asking for a date.'

He had to extricate. 'I'll buy you a beer at The Banksia.'

'She's not coming back to you, Dan. Sooner you understand that, the better off you'll be.'

'Thank you, Karen.'

'My pleasure. I'll call you if Mr Schaffer turns up here.'

He'd never slept around on Marilyn. Once or twice he'd kissed women, a greeting or farewell, felt that jolt, knew that if he wanted it anything was on the table but he always pulled back, no matter how bad it was with Marilyn at the time. He was never sure if this was any testament to his morality, he liked to think so, but maybe he just wanted the high ground. It was eighteen months since they'd split. It took him eight months before he slept with another woman and it was strange, not unpleasant, not earth shattering, but like wearing new shoes. He slept with two other women in quick succession and knew he shouldn't compare them to Marilyn but couldn't help it. He resented this weakness in himself. She's not coming back; even if she did, it would be a mistake so you're more the fool for protracting the inevitable. Karen is right, he thought, but she's wrong too. Marilyn and he were a conundrum, a circular square, yet he was still unable to move on with his life. As a boy he'd been fascinated by the story of Scott of the Antarctic who must have known he was pushing on to his doom. Clement had not meant it to act as a template for his behaviour but sometimes he felt it did.

The buzz of the flies drummed in his ears, the bored or weak ones who couldn't get to the blood were attracted to his sweat.

Clement made his way back to his vehicle through the same unwelcoming bush and the same over-friendly flies. They crawled up your nose and were in the back of your throat before you could blow them back out. En route he tried Graeme Earle. As expected the call went dead. Earle was the kind of bloke who loved this life, fishing, drinking, blue skies, wide open space and malevolent heat. You could never reach him on a rostered day off. Clement didn't rate him highly as a detective but to be fair it wasn't like he was basing this on a great sample. They'd worked assaults, rapes and one tribal spat that turned into attempted murder. Earle's work was solid, he wasn't incompetent. It was more that while this might be a massive region of thousands of ks, the crime garden was very small and there was nowhere to hone real detective skills so they stayed unborn or undeveloped. Earle had lived here fifteen years and in him Clement saw the traits more of a small-town sheriff than a detective. He dialled Shepherd next. The detective constable answered his phone promptly.

'Guilty. Course the beak's given him a slap on the wrist. Three months.'

Shepherd couldn't finish a speech without some complaint. On this occasion Clement sympathised. They'd gone after an inveterate wife-beater. Those cases were hard to get to court and when they got a sentence lighter than a cicada shell you felt you were in the wrong job on the wrong side of the planet. The women looked at you like you were the one who had given them the black eye or split lip.

Clement explained where he was and what he'd found, or rather hadn't. He told Shepherd they'd be setting up a crime scene.

'Bring Jared. And those guys who trapped the Callum Creek crocs. See if they're available.'

He opened his car and risked his bum on the scorching seat. He tapped the Pajero's plates into his computer. Bingo. Dieter Schaffer. DOB 14.04.48. As Jill had warned, the address was a lot number on Cape Leveque Road, a strip of bitumen that ran a hundred k north–south in a wilderness of mainly low scrub. The only phone number was the mobile he had. He did all this while Shepherd whinged about how hard it was going to be to do each of the tasks set. He ignored him. 'See you soon, Shep.'

Clement called the station and asked Mal Gross if he knew a Dieter Schaffer. Of course he did. Gross knew most everybody in the Kimberley.

'Dieter. They call him "Schultz". Used to be a cop in Germany.'

So far as Gross was aware Schaffer lived alone in what was little more than a bush shack. Gross said he would get a car out there to look over the house but it was a good hundred k so Clement should not expect anything for a while.

Typical.

Clement fought his way back to the locus of his investigation. The missing outboard worried him but he began constructing plausible alternatives to murder–robbery. Dieter could have taken it with him in a mate's car. In fact he could have injured himself on it if the boat capsized. Against that, things about the scene jarred. You could lose your phone in the accident but would you leave keys in the ignition? No, surely even if the battery had already run flat, you'd take the keys. Clement wondered if he should drive out and around to the yet-to-be-pegged crime scene but he was worried about driving over evidence so he was forced to yet again retrace his steps to the other side of the creek. Before leaving he took a swig of water, you could dehydrate fast out here. On the way the flies harassed him again. They bit him this time. He flicked them off as best he could.

Using the tent as the centre of the target, Clement began searching out in bands of about five metres thick. After around thirty minutes he found an area of flattened bush as if a vehicle had recently been there. He estimated it was about sixty metres north-west of the tent and would not have been visible from it. There was a bush track leading out from there, clearly used by vehicles for access. He'd always approached the creek from the eastern side, as the tourists had, but clearly some regular traffic came this way too. He followed the path for another hundred metres calling out Schaffer's name over the incessant insect buzz but received no reply and doubled back.

Gradually he worked his way anti-clockwise around the entire creek. There was the usual kind of litter, chocolate and chip wrappers, plastic bottles, beer cartons. He took photos of everything he encountered. The only piece of recent technology he gave credit to was a phone with a camera in it. So much easier than logging everything with a biro that wouldn't write on a cheap pad. Karen's comment needled him. It wasn't like he was trying to get back with Marilyn. Was he just terrified of another relationship, the unknown?

The dissolution of their relationship had caught him by surprise even though he supposed it had all the classic pointers. They'd both let it go too far. It was like a DVD on your shelf you look over at every day still in its case, telling yourself tonight was the night you'd watch it. But you never got around to it. There was always something more at hand, more demanding of your time. Until she announced she was leaving, and of course he said that's ridiculous. That's how it starts, he thought, the end. Every grievance is dredged out. Pride flares. He offers to move out, the martyr. And before you know it, what is just bravado, a sympathy play, turns into the real thing and when you drag your sorry arse back and apologise, it's too late, she's 'discovered' herself and how much you've 'inhibited' her.

Back to where he started in more ways than one. His phone rang. Mal Gross. One of his mates had family near Dieter's shack. They'd driven over and taken a gander. Nobody was there. He had di Rivi and Restoff heading there too but he thought the sooner Clement knew, the better. Clement thanked him and looked up to see a swirl of dust announce Shepherd's arrival. Jared Taylor, the aboriginal police aide, was with him towing the trailer on which was mounted an inflatable boat. A tinny was lashed to the roof as back up. Shepherd stepped out wearing the plastic white-framed sunnies Shane Warne had made famous in the late nineties. They looked ridiculous then and worse now. Shepherd was around one eighty-eight centimetres and fit, the build of a centre-half-back, de rigueur tattoos just poking out from under short sleeves. Jared Taylor was shorter with a gut and, at forty, around twelve years older than Shepherd. Unlike Shepherd, he had a sunny disposition. They'd sparred in the ring once as part of Shepherd's training for the annual Kimberley v Gascoyne police comp. Naturally Shepherd fancied himself. Taylor's punches had nearly sent poor Shepherd through the ropes.

'What's the plan, Skip?'

Shepherd's vocabulary reduced everything to a footy match.

'I guess we need to poke around for a body.'

Both of them looked at him, hoping he was joking. They didn't need to mention the croc. If it had overturned one tinny, why not another?

'Let's get to it.'

'Serious?'

'Yeah, Shep. Come on.'

'Shouldn't we wait for the croc blokes?'

'No time for that.'

They lifted the tinny off the roof of the vehicle and walked it to the water's edge, keeping a wary eye. The creek was only shoulder-deep but too muddy to see into. Taylor had thought ahead and brought a couple of thin plastic rigid electrician's tubes, perfect as probes. He stayed on the bank, rifle ready, just in case. The little motor shattered the default static of bush noise. Clement guided the tinny to the far bank near Dieter's upturned tinny, cut the motor and they began probing the waters close to the shore. Gradually they worked their way out.

'Fucking flies,' grumbled Shepherd for the fiftieth time.

About twenty minutes in, Clement's pole struck something just below the surface firmer than mud but too soft to be a rock or tree.

'Pass me the gaff.'

While he held the position, Shepherd passed over one of two gaff hooks. Clement sank it down, let it find purchase and pulled hard. The unmistakable shape of a body broke the surface.

4

It took them a good half-hour to manoeuvre the body across the creek to the eastern side where they'd left their cars. During the time they remained vigilant. If there were a croc lurking it might not like this potential food source being dragged away. Eventually they got close enough to shore for Taylor to get the winch hook to them. Like many police vehicles the van had a winch mounted on the front. Nothing up here was simple. Had the body been under longer, winching it in wouldn't have been an option, it might have pulled the body apart and they'd have had to wait for some kind of nets. But the body was not so long in the water. Even so, trying to get the winch hook on the body while bending over from the boat, was tedious. Finally Clement managed it. Taylor set the winch motor going and in a macabre visual the body surfed up to the bank which was too high at this point, a drop rather than a slope, so Taylor had to cut the motor or the body would have ploughed into it. It needed lifting. Clement had had enough by then. Stuff the croc. He jumped from the tinny into the thigh-deep dark water and helped Taylor drag the body up over roots to scrub beyond the bank. After protesting loudly at the stink and danger, Shepherd finally abandoned the boat in shallow water and pulled the tinny up with alacrity while Taylor kept his rifle ready just in case.

Dieter Schaffer, or at least the body they presumed to be him, lay facedown. Forensically Clement's method may not have been ideal but this wasn't the city and the longer the body stayed in the water the worse it would be for the techs. The body was of a man who looked early sixties, large build but not tall, wearing shorts, boots a t-shirt and dungaree style pants. Except for where the centre of his head had been cleaved like a mandarin with a couple of pieces missing, he boasted a good shock of grey hair. He wore a Citizen watch on his left wrist. Inconveniently, unlike in the movies, it hadn't stopped or been shattered at time of death and was still ticking. After putting on plastic gloves and shoe covers and instructing the guys to do the same, Clement bent and examined the body as best he could.

'Bullet holes?' asked Shepherd keeping his distance.

'Doesn't appear to be.'

Clement was open to suggestions but couldn't resist looking for the kind of smaller holes a twenty-two might make. Taylor stated the obvious.

'Someone caved his head in.'

'Could have been an accident, couldn't it?' As usual Shepherd was trying to sound like he had some idea of what he was talking about.

Taylor shook his head. 'Man, I seen plenty of these. I reckon it's an axe done that.'

Clement had to agree with his aide. Back in the days before gas and electric heaters, every house had a woodheap and the axe had been a common murder weapon but these days in the city it was rare. Up here, an axe was a cheap available weapon sometimes used when there was clan strife. The wound may have been caused by a heavy machete but that was, to use a grisly pun, splitting hairs. Unless it had been inflicted post-mortem, Clement was sure this was the cause of death.

The blow had been severe, the skull shattered. Studying the victim's face in profile, Clement mentally matched it to the driver's licence photo on his police computer. Not the ideal conditions for a comparison but good enough to declare this was Schaffer. He took photos while the guys shooed flies.

'Let's turn him.'

They rolled the body onto its back and Clement almost recoiled. Nasty. The right cheekbone and jaw had been smashed in. The t-shirt was caked in mud now but appeared to be one of those souvenir types of a sport team. There was a photo of the team, a trophy, the words HSV 1978–79 and some other words in, he presumed, German. It looked surprisingly new compared to the dungarees, probably a reprint. It only just made it over Schaffer's belly. Taylor had called an ambulance right after they'd found the body. Once it arrived they'd load the body and it would be taken to the morgue at Derby Hospital then flown to Perth for the coroner to do the official autopsy. Western Australia was a huge state, the logistics immense. It was like the police in London flying a body to Moscow for the once-over.

For now there wasn't much to do but cover the body as best they could and tape off the whole area. The death would have to be treated as homicide. Lisa Keeble was the senior crime-scene tech who worked the region. Of all Clement's colleagues up here, she was the only one he thought could have held her own with any of the Perth crew. Smart, pretty and efficient, she preferred to live here than the city, quite likely because she had a boyfriend here. The boyfriend acted as no impediment to Shepherd. He invariably embarrassed all of them with his attempts to crack onto her. Despite her competence Clement suspected HQ might send in reinforcements for any homicide that was not a simple domestic.

Whether they would also send detectives was another matter. He was pretty sure his boss, Scott Risely, would ask for his opinion and hold the fort if he wanted. Just into his sixties, Risely, Area Commander for the whole Kimberley, had a knack of serving his political masters without alienating the local community. Up here that was a tricky business. Risely wouldn't want to palm this off to southerners at the get-go, thought Clement as he swung back to the boys.

'You called Lisa?'

Taylor said, 'Same time as the ambulance.'

'Something to look forward to.' Shepherd flexed as he spoke, as if preparing for his show of muscular strength that would knock Lisa Keeble off her feet. Not for the first time Clement wondered what went on in that brain and visualised some pinball contraption. He got Taylor to try the croc guys again. They hadn't left Derby yet.

'Tell them to get a wriggle on.'

Taylor blasted them down the line. Clement was thinking they'd need to check the creek for evidence but nobody was going to dive in there if there might be a croc about.

'These guys are good, right?'

'The best,' Taylor was definite. 'Any croc's in there, they'll trap him.'

'Yeah well I'm not going in.' Shepherd folded his arms. Clement had a good mind to order him in now. His phone rang. Number withheld on the ID.

'Clement.'

'This is Gerd Osterlund. You left a message on my voicemail, Detective.'

German accent. Rudi perhaps?

'Thank you for returning my call. Sir, are you a friend of Dieter Schaffer?'

A pause.

'An acquaintance. Why?'

'Mr Schaffer has been killed.'

'That's terrible.' It sounded like genuine shock. 'An accident?'

'We don't know. I found your number on his phone. Under the name Rudi.'

'His nickname for me. He called me yesterday morning to say he was going fishing. It's awful.'

'Did he have any family here?'

'Not that I know of. Like I say, we were acquaintances.'

Clement didn't see any value in hanging about here. He needed to know all he could about Dieter Schaffer as soon as possible. He asked if he could come and see Osterlund now. 'Sure. I'm practically retired.'

Clement asked where Osterlund lived.

'Broome. Number five Mars Place. You know it?'

'I'll find it. I'll be a couple of hours.'

He ended the call asked the guys where Mars Place was.

Shepherd jumped in. 'Private little cul-de-sac above Cable Beach, a half-dozen houses, three mill plus. I went to a pool party there for Kirsty Liriano.'

'Who is ...?'

Shepherd was waiting for a chance to trump Clement's ignorance. 'American singer. Hot.'

While Clement had faith in Taylor's competence he knew that he could feel insecure with responsibility. Shepherd would have to stay with Taylor and be ranking officer. Poor Lisa Keeble.

He pulled the card from Schaffer's phone and put it into his wallet. The phone he sealed in an evidence bag which he handed to Shepherd.

'Give this to Lisa. I want you to ring around all the banks, find out who Dieter Schaffer banked with. I want you to check any withdrawals. If he had a credit or debit card, find out. They're to call me direct if it has been used anywhere since last night, or if it is used again.'

'Got it.'

'Call me if there's anything important at all.'

...

Foot to the floor, Clement hammered down the highway, illegally calling Risely with just one hand on the wheel. He caught the boss mid-scone at a church forum where indigenous and town leaders were brainstorming how to keep local youths on the straight and narrow. What flashed through Clement's mind was a room with a couple of brand new ping-pong tables that would be trashed within a month. Best of intentions guaranteed no results. The kids needed fathers but half of them were banged up in jail or on the run. He ran through the basics as Risely munched.

'Homicide?'

'Quite likely.'

Clement explained he was trying to find out more about the victim. Risely was relaxed.

'How are we going to search the creek?'

'Jared's got a couple of croc trappers onto it.'

'Good. Hagan and Lalor are back. I'll send them to secure the site and watch it overnight. Call me if you know anything.'

That's what you wanted in a boss, though Clement wasn't getting carried away. He hadn't worked with Risely in a pressure situation yet. His years in the city had shown him that was when monsters revealed themselves. He searched about for his Cruel Sea CD, realised it must have been at his apartment and settled on Dr John because he only owned five CDs and this was one of two in the car. Just after the good Doctor had finished and the Black Crowes were being given their chance to shine along the relentlessly flat road, he passed the ambulance on its way to the crime scene. About ten minutes later Lisa Keeble followed in her old Fairlane. It had been her grandfather's but she'd retained its pristine condition. Clement figured it must guzzle half her wages in fuel but she'd told him she was sentimental and it was worth every cent. She looked like a jockey in that beast, her head just visible over the dash. She gave him the nor-west wave, a barely perceptible raise of the fingers off the wheel.

...

It took Clement a good hundred minutes to make Broome. On the road he toyed with the idea of hitting the Anglers Club first but decided to wait for the post-work 'rush'. It amused Clement the way so many people talked of Broome like it was some Valhalla. No doubt it was exotic, desert on one side, green-blue ocean on the other, a Japanese cemetery testifying to the presence of a community that began with their pearl divers over a century before and was bombed by Japanese planes in World War Two. Flicking through glossy airline magazine photos of the pristine white sand of Cable Beach, occupied only by camels and swimwear models, Europeans read of this isolated land of pearls and giant sea turtles and made it a must-see along with Tangiers, Buenos Aires and an ice-hotel in the Arctic Circle. But for all that, the town was flat with more than its share of box-like brick buildings, chain-link fences and litter. You could have been blindfolded, drugged and dumped in parts of town and woken assuming you were in one of those Perth industrial suburbs like Welshpool. What was unique was the mix of people, indigenous groups—some the original coastal clans, others whose forebears had drifted in from the desert—jumbled with money-chasing miners and old hippies, both the genuine pot-smoking Kombi van breed and affluent boomers who yearned to have been the real thing, grown tired of their well-paid government jobs to the south, on a pilgrimage to an idea. Except for the hippies and musicians travelling up from Perth for the annual Shinju Festival, nobody had paid much attention to this oasis on the tip of a desert until the 1980s when it was marketed as a kind of real people's Club Med. To Clement, the attraction of Broome had always been simple, it actually was an oasis, and when you travelled to it from whatever direction through hundreds of ks of boring, scrubby desert, all its positives were maximised. Broome was to travellers what the sight of a woman must have been to whalers returning from a long expedition. Even with teeth missing, a port whore was desirable, but a pleasantly attractive woman was glorious. Growing up here, Clement had loved the open space, the smell of the bush, the Robinson Crusoe beach; but there was a lot he was glad to turn his back on. Months out of every year you couldn't swim in the tantalising sea for box jellyfish even though the heat and humidity was smoking you through. And he hated the deadbeats that drifted here. Broome was like family: you might love it but if you stuck around long enough it grated. He felt confined and defined by it. Given a real choice, he wouldn't have chosen to return. His phone rang. It was Shepherd.

'Dieter was a Savings Bank client of Bankwest. No cards; cash transactions, a little in, a little out; a balance of nearly eight thousand. Last withdrawal was three hundred bucks over two weeks ago.'

The guy was frugal. 'He might have had one with another bank.'

'I checked them all. None of the locals have him as a customer except Bankwest.'

Clement had been hoping that if this was indeed a robbery-homicide somebody would stuff up and use Dieter's card, but that wasn't going to be an option.

'What about the croc blokes?'

'They're onto it. Say it could be tomorrow before it's safe to go in.'

It wasn't the kind of thing you could rush apparently. 'Alright.'

Clement ended the call as he broke free of the industrial section of town and struck out for the ridge overlooking Cable Beach. In the last twenty years this millionaire's row had grown gradually. The pearl farmers, like Marilyn's family, generally lived further out of town on estates overlooking the ocean but many of the town's wealthy and newly settled were dotted up around here.

Mars Place turned out to be a new strip of asphalt running between lush vegetation. Clement had never been to the Caribbean but this was how he imagined it. Each of the properties was the width of half a dozen suburban houses and all were screened in bush. Palm trees rose high in several places. Number 5 was not identified, nor was number 3, but 1 and 7 were so Clement found it by the process of elimination. A short driveway off Mars Place led to an iron gate set between white walls. The gate had been left open. Clement took the narrow drive which rose slowly before ending in a small circle, nothing ostentatious. A tile path led up between a natural, well-tendered garden of luscious grevillea and other plants unknown to Clement, and ended in low wooden steps and a veranda. The front door was open. Balinese carvings and indoor plants adorned the vestibule.

'Hello?' called Clement on the threshold.

Footsteps scuffed over a slate floor. The man he assumed was Osterlund appeared around a corner. Wiry, sixties, a grey ponytail, loose Indian style cotton shirt and pants, espadrilles. Clement automatically made him for advertising or IT.

'Detective? Come through.'

Osterlund didn't offer his hand, simply swung on his heel. One used to giving orders. Clement followed up the short hallway which gave onto a stunning wide and spacious split-level lounge. You didn't notice the expensive mix of modern and aboriginal artwork on the walls, nor the minimalist European furniture. Not at first. Dead ahead through floor to ceiling glass spanning the width of the house was the Indian Ocean and Cable Beach. It was breathtaking. Osterlund floated coffee or tea as refreshment. Clement dragged himself from the vista and accepted coffee. A sleek young Asian woman in a sarong whom Clement hadn't even realised was there, moved to oblige. She had been standing in front of a massive wall painting, camouflaged by it, her clothes being of similar colour. When she moved, the effect was of her stepping out of the two-dimensional space into the real world. Osterlund did not introduce her. Clement assumed she was a servant.

'White? Sugar?'

'Yes and yes. One.'

Osterlund didn't even glance at the woman who moved towards a galley of shining steel and stone surfaces. He gestured to a bright orange sofa on the lower level, adorned with lime green cushions.

'It gets the downdraft,' explained Osterlund pointing at the closest ceiling fan. 'I don't like air-conditioning.'

'With you there, except in a car,' quipped Clement.

Osterlund smiled. They sat. The sound of a cappuccino machine erupted in the background. Osterlund got to the point.

'Dieter is dead?'

'His body was at a place called Jasper's Creek.'

'I don't know it. I am not a fisherman.' He sighed, frowned. 'That's upsetting. You said it may not be an accident.'

'It's possible he was murdered.'

Osterlund shifted slightly in his seat, a natural reaction. 'Robbery?'

'We're looking into that. Would you know if his boat had an outboard motor?'

It bothered Clement no motor had been with the boat, people had been killed for less. Of course it could be on the bottom of the creek.

'I only went out with him once, in an aluminium runabout. That had a motor. May I ask how he died?'

'We're not certain.'

The girl arrived with his coffee and a tea in a glass for Osterlund. Clement thanked her. She had large, dark brown eyes. She didn't look more than early twenties.

'The last time you spoke was yesterday morning, you said.'

'Ja. I don't remember exactly what time but I think between ten and eleven. Poor old Dieter.'

They sipped their drinks at the same time. The coffee could have come from a café, smooth, professional, though Clement's tooth or gum twinged at the hot fluid.

'What did you talk about?'

'Nothing really. Dieter was a lonely fellow, a bit tragic. He calls every day or so and starts talking about German football or the weather, crocodiles. I don't share much with him except we are both German. Probably he just wanted to hear my wife answer.'

It was the first time Osterlund had mentioned his wife. Clement almost stepped right in and asked where she was but Osterlund continued.

'He was always going on about how lucky a man my age was to find a beautiful young woman like Tuthi.'

Osterlund gestured at the young woman who had served them. She was busy making the kitchen immaculate again. Clement felt dumb and was only pleased his gaffe remained private. He pushed on.

'Did he have any close friends?'

'Not that I know of. He was a loner really. He'd talk about the guys at the Angler Club. I think he had a few drinking mates.'

'Did he have a job? What did he do for money?'

'He told me he had a police pension.'

'Did he have credit cards?'

Osterlund cast through his mind. 'I don't remember.'

'Enemies?'

Osterlund's eyes shifted evasively. 'I don't want to speak badly of Dieter. He was okay but he gambled, he drank, he mixed with a ... how you say it, a rough crowd.'

Clement wasn't sure if Osterlund was a snob or if he was covering for his dead friend, making him sound more genteel than he was.

'Did he owe money?'

'Probably. He asked me for loans from time to time. I didn't oblige.'

'And he has no family?'

'Not here. I think he may have mentioned a sister in Germany. Actually, I am pretty sure he did but I don't think she lived in Hamburg.'

'So he was not married. Children?'

'He told me he had no children. We have none. The subject came up. He said he was sad about not being a father. He was married but divorced. He did not speak about it much. I don't think he ever mentioned his ex-wife by name.'

'Do you know when the marriage might have ended?'

'Not exactly but I think it was a long time ago. I remember him saying once something about being a bachelor for twenty years. It might have been thirty.'

Clement made notes. 'How did you meet him?'

'Where everybody met Dieter, at a pub. He heard

me talking, picked the accent and came over and introduced himself.'

'This was when?'

'Two, three years ago. He said he was from Hamburg. I grew up in Hanover. We were about the same age, so you know, we had some fun talking old times, Germany when we were growing up.'

'Is it true he was a policeman?'

'I have no idea. He claimed he was a policeman, had plenty of stories. I believed him.'

'Did he ever say why he came to live here?'

'The climate. I think he had nothing in Germany, no family, no work. The idea of crocodiles and fishing ... well Germans are suckers for that.'

'Why did you move here?'

'Actually, I lived in Bali for six years. For Germans Bali is the tropical paradise, the Holy Grail. I went there in my twenties and promise myself when I retire I will go back. Eventually I did. I met Tuthi there. But Bali became too busy, too ... spoilt. Muslims, Australians, no offence. One lot want to chop your hand off for drinking, the others get drunk and vomit on the street. We took a trip down here one time and I liked it. Like Bali used to be. Similar climate and you Aussies are better behaved at home.'

'That was when?'

'A little more than three years ago. I'm here for good.'

'So as far as you know Dieter had no enemies?'

'No.'

'And he wasn't unusually worried lately?'

'Not that I noticed.'

Clement asked the obvious question. 'Last night. You were here?'

Osterlund did not seem offended. 'Ja. We had guests for dinner, Gilbert Lucas and his wife, Sondra, across the road. Early dinner. They left around nine-thirty. We drank some wine and went to bed about ten.'

'You are retired I think you said?'

'More or less. I have a few business interests in Europe still. These days, Skype, Twitter, all this stuff, it is easy to work from anywhere.'

Clement scanned the large, sparse room, saw a laptop set up at the end of the long breakfast bar. 'What line of business? You mind me asking?'

'Not at all. IT. I got in early, made good money before the space became crowded.'

Clement awarded himself a prize for guessing correctly. Osterlund reached into what might have been a cigar box once and handed him a card which was printed in German on one side and English on the reverse. It simply read OIC with a bunch of contact numbers. Clement recognised the one for Broome.

'If you need to speak to me again, Detective, or need IT solutions.'

He said it without the hint of a smile and Clement couldn't be sure if he was serious or just being very droll. Clement found a crumpled, soiled card in his wallet and deposited it on the table to return the compliment, knowing Osterlund had got the worst of the deal.

'Likewise, if you think of anything you think might be important. And thank you for the coffee.'

Clement stood. Osterlund assured he would call him if he remembered anything relevant, and saw him to the door. His wife had vanished into thin air.

Clement took a last look back at the house and felt a pang of envy. He couldn't deny it. Imagine living like that, pretty much retired, beautiful, devoted wife, amazing house. No kids he'd said. If Osterlund had any they were probably with an early wife back in the Fatherland. Clement imagined himself at some future date, alone, a grown-up Phoebe he never saw. That hurt. He would never have this. At best there might be a modest house in the suburbs, at worst one of those caravans like his parents used to lease to losers.

He opened the car door and a dragon's breath blasted him. He'd left the window open a crack and parked as close to shade as he could but it had made no difference. He cruised slowly down the driveway feeling no more enlightened on the victim than when he'd dragged him from the creek, a loner who liked his grog and the simple life. The Kimberley was full of them. Clement had garnered all that from one glance at Dieter Schaffer's vehicle. No wallet, no outboard motor, no rifle recovered. It was looking like a robbery, either from a stranger who happened past or somebody who'd accompanied him fishing. And yet the murder in a way seemed careful, ordered. There were no signs of argument, nothing to suggest the presence of the killer other than blood and body, as if a bunyip had risen up from the creek and killed Dieter Schaffer before sinking back down. Bunyips were not myths, twenty years of policing had taught Clement that much. Bunyips were the depraved hearts, souls and minds of people given form by fury, anger, greed, envy, lust, and they could just as quickly fade into a ripple, a shy smile, a quiet sigh. Violent and careful killers were as hard to grab hold of as smoke. Clement knew he could be staring into the killer's face and see nothing more than that tranquil billabong with the reflection of his own.

5

Clement called through to Shepherd and checked on progress at the crime scene. The croc guys had just arrived and were deciding how to clear it. Lisa Keeble had done a preliminary examination of the body which had been loaded up and sent to Derby Hospital from where it would be transferred to the airport. Though not a medical examiner, Keeble had worked numerous deaths-by-trauma in conjunction with the Coroner's department. She had trained under professor Michael 'Rhino' David, an expert entomologist and head of the Forensic Science department at the University of Western Australia. She knew her stuff.

Clement's and Rhino's careers had grown in step. Clement was the first cop to make use of Rhino's abilities but it was a symbiotic relationship. Rhino helped him solve cases and Clement's support kept Rhino's numerous bureaucratic enemies at bay. Rhino's CV included stints lecturing at the FBI's US body farms, consultant on a number of international murder trials, and reigning faculty titles for piss-drinking and Donkey Kong. Politically incorrect, looking more like a roadie for a heavy metal band than a professor, Rhino scared his university colleagues and was anathema to the State Coroner, who saw him as some kind of forensic cattle baron muscling in on her turf. But his department was brilliant at identifying DNA, whether human or mineral, and earned the university a tidy sum from commercial clients, thereby coating Rhino in just enough Teflon to keep from being jettisoned. Rhino was also a teacher par excellence. His graduates could find employment anywhere in the world but Lisa Keeble's best quality was she was adaptable. There were plenty of gourmet chefs but up here you needed one who could cook on a Bunsen burner. Clement had Shepherd put her on.

'You know I can't speculate on what killed him.'

'Of course, but did you see anything other than a whopping blow to the head or drowning?'

'No ligature marks but I lifted the t-shirt and had a quick look. I'd say he took a heavy beating, rib fractures most likely. You saw the jaw, right? Curious thing was that the shirt didn't have any corresponding marks on it, that I could tell. If you hadn't dragged him up onto the shore with a mechanised winch it might have helped.'

'There's crocs around, I'm not stupid.'

'No, I'll give you six out of ten.'

'So what are you saying about the t-shirt?'

'I don't know, maybe he put it on after he was beaten.'

That was important. Maybe Schaffer got into a fight, took a beating, changed and then whoever beat him came back to finish the job?

'Anything else?'

'Sorry, that's it for now.'

'Is Shep making a nuisance of himself?'

'Of course. But I can handle him. Now the croc guys are here, he's occupied.'

'You going to need more bods?'

'I've already called Perth. Given the size of the potential area, the billabong, it's going to take a bit of time. Two techs are on their way from Perth and my guys will be here any minute.'

It was as he expected but just because they'd be sending techs didn't mean Perth was going to run the case, not if he could help it, not after weeks of nothing more exciting than petrol theft.

'Take care,' he said and swung into the small carpark of the Anglers Club. There were half a dozen vehicles in a carpark of about twenty spaces that doubled for the printing business next door. Only the late model Ford and the early model Toyota Camry had bothered to actually stick between the lines. Clement assumed they belonged to the employees. The other vehicles, pig-shooting and fishing rigs, were splayed as if the drivers were already a few sheets to the wind even though this wasn't necessarily the case. Up here people got used to space, more space than they needed. Why bother to straighten up when there were plenty more bays available?

Clement left the car, the heat not capitulating one iota. He pushed through aluminium and glass doors into heavy-duty air-conditioning. The sweat trickling down his back froze instantly. The building was no-frills, white brick walls, concrete floor. A small L-shaped bar gave onto a door presumably through to back-office and storeroom. Furniture consisted of a pool table and three round, standing bar tables with high stools. Two blokes in t-shirts and shorts sucking lager had claimed one of them. They glanced his way but did not stop their conversation. The walls were adorned with photos of future melanoma candidates holding large dead fish in their hairy forearms. A shellacked groper was mounted above the bar, which featured a colourful display of donated caps hanging like bunting. Apex Windowframes, St Mary's Football Club Darwin, Adelaide Crows were a few that caught his eye. Beneath them a blonde barmaid somewhere north of forty and south of fifty-five was chatting animatedly with three men, one in a shirt and tie, one in overalls, one in shorts and T. All had the leathery look of long-time residents. Clement had no doubt Schaffer's death was the subject. The blonde barmaid turned and caught his eye.

'Detective Clement,' offered Clement as he strode over. 'Jill?'

She grimaced as confirmation. 'Is it true about Dieter?'

She pointed behind her at a display of home snaps that showed, presumably, the regulars having drinks at this very bar. Beaming at the camera, Dieter was alongside a ruddy-faced man whom Clement recognised as the man here in the overalls.

'I am afraid so.'

The man wearing the tie rose from his stool.

'Rod Walters, I'm the Club President. This is Arko, our Secretary, and Jason.'

Arko was the one in the photo.

Clement asked, 'Would you mind if I had that photo? It might help me.'

Jill pulled out the drawing pin and handed it over.

'Can you tell us what happened?' Jill seemed the most upset of the three but it didn't look like she had been crying. Clement gave them the usual spiel about how they were trying to work that out. The two blokes at the high table were listening in. Clement asked when the last time was anybody had seen, or spoken to Dieter.

'We were just talking about that,' said Jill and the others nodded. 'He was here last Sunday afternoon. That was the last time I saw him.'

It was now Thursday. One of the men from the high stool chimed in. 'Tuesday night he was at the Cleo.'

The Cleopatra Tavern was a popular but low-grade drinking hole. Clement walked over.

'Was he alone?'

'Well, he was just at the bar joining in like. You don't remember me, do ya?'

Clement searched the face. It seemed familiar now.

The man sipped his beer and smirked, 'Bill Seratono.'

Jesus. He'd gone to school with him. It wasn't that long ago was it? Now he'd been told, he could see right away it was Bill.

'I'm sorry, Bill.'

'Mate, I don't recognise meself half the time. You haven't changed much.'

The way he said it didn't make it sound like a compliment. There was a time they'd been pretty close but Bill left school a year or two ahead of him and they'd drifted apart. Clement didn't recall any bad blood, they'd just gone their own ways.

'What are you up to, Bill?' There would be time to pursue Dieter Schaffer soon enough.

'Usual shit, working haulage down near the port. McIntyre's.'

'Married?'

'Yeah, two boys, teenagers. Fucking pains in the arse, just like we were, though actually you were always pretty good.'

'You never left?'

'Nah mate, some of us stuck it out.'

There it was again, that antagonism. Maybe it was just the natural response to one returning from one who'd stayed. Clement looked for a conversational point.

'You got a boat?'

'Eighteen footer. This is me mate, Mitch.'

The mute Mitch extended his hand and they shook. Mitch had a goatee and strong, corded forearms.

'G'day, Mitch.'

'Mitch owns the boat halves with me.'

'Did you know Dieter well?'

Bill looked at Mitch. 'We'd see him around, chat about this and that. Can't say we knew him that well but.'

'Liked his piss,' offered Mitch, breaking his silence.

'Who doesn't?' Bill drained his glass as if to emphasise this natural law.

'Did you speak to him at the Cleo?'

There was an instant where something crossed through Seratono's eyes, some evasion.

'Yeah, just the usual shit. He said he was going fishing up at Jasper's. I told him to watch out, there was supposed to be a croc round there. He just laughed. Crazy fucking Kraut, said if crocs were there, must be something to eat.'

This it turned out was around ten that night, the Tuesday. The tavern was pretty full, regulars, backpackers and some of the staff from the resorts who preferred the cheaper liquor to their own bars. Schaffer did not appear to be with anybody. Seratono had bailed out before ten thirty but Schaffer was still there. If this had been the city there might have been a chance of CCTV coverage in the carpark but up here that was a remote possibility.

'I heard Dieter hung out with a rough crowd.' Clement threw it out to the crew at the bar as well.

'Probably us!'

Mitch cracked up at his mate's joke.

Clement persisted, 'Nobody rough?'

'Nah, mate,' assured Seratono.

Again that evasion with the eyes. Clement picked up a sideways glance from Mitch too. There was something. The door opened and another customer entered, male, shorts, short-sleeved shirt, sandals. Clement ignored him for now.

'How about money?'

Jill moved automatically to serve the newcomer,

obviously a regular, she didn't even bother to ask his preference. She spoke as she poured. 'He was a shocker, always trying to run up a tab.'

'Did he have a credit card?'

Jill shook her head. 'Johnny Cash only.'

That killed that line of inquiry. The newcomer looked around, unsettled by the changes in his watering hole. The others at the bar brought him up to speed. He was shocked at the news.

'Schultz was a bad punter.' For Mitch this was loquacious.

Bill elaborated. 'He'd put the bite on but he'd pay you back. He reckoned he was going to be rolling in money soon.'

Mitch looked for a cigarette then remembered he couldn't smoke in here.

'He told you that?'

'Yeah. Not Tuesday. Before, here one time a couple of weeks ago I think.'

'Did he say where this money was coming from?'

'Nah, I just took it as the usual shit that he thought he was going to have a big win on the punt.'

'You remember his exact words?'

'Not exact but he said something like, "I'm good for it, I'm gonna be rolling in it soon."'

'And what did you say?'

'Something like, "You are rolling in it, mate, manure that's what you're rolling in."'

Now Jill seemed to recall Schaffer had also cockily mentioned about how he would be 'looking after his friends' when he became a man of means.

'I didn't think anything of it.'

'He was a bit of a bullshitter like that.' Arko threw it in as he drained his beer.

All the same, if Schaffer had just wound up with a jackpot of some kind it could provide the motive for his murder. Clement made a note.

'No enemies? No fights?'

Nobody recalled anything, shrugs all round. Clement asked them to contact him if they thought of anything. Before he left he went back to Bill Seratono.

'We should have a drink sometime.'

It was one of those things you said that was polite yet non-committal, an acknowledgment of shared times but no definite insistence they should be renewed, the kind of thing Clement found himself doing a lot more of these last couple of years.

'Come out on the boat, any time.'

Clement was surprised at the invitation. Maybe he'd been in the city too long and forgotten how put-down banter was the stuff of male friendship up here. He thanked everybody and pushed back outside.

...

Standing beside his car, he contemplated his next move. He needed to follow up on the Cleopatra Tavern, get out to Dieter Schaffer's shack and check it out, but he also needed to nail down the tourists who had called in the report. They could be halfway to Darwin by now. He fumbled in his pocket for their mobile number, found it, edged over to a thin rim of shade from the roof of the print shop and called. The man's name was Evan Doherty and he was the one who answered. Clement identified himself then asked Doherty where he currently was.

'At the Mimosa Resort.'

Perfect. After their brush with Kimberley life in the wild they'd gone running to the closest five-star accommodation they could find. Clement arranged to meet them by the pool in an hour. The Cleopatra was on the way to the Mimosa and he was hungry, a good fit.

...

The Cleopatra Tavern was a low, pagoda-style building, usually well frequented by locals and low-end tourists. Clement walked up the small brick paving entranceway to the tavern. Smoking was not allowed inside and Clement had to beat his way through a cloud of smoke supplied by three men in blue singlets gathered just out front of the doorway.

Inside in the public bar he was greeted by unflattering lighting, grey carpet with a yellow thread pattern, a generous bar and close to ten customers. A couple of blokes were playing darts, a pair of male backpackers were on the pool table. It was probably too early for trouble but when it came it nearly always involved young backpackers beating the locals on their own table. The locals would then belt them. In the smaller adjoining saloon bar the clientele appeared to consist of two couples. A barman, mid-forties, was working the bar with a perky blonde in her twenties. Clement thought of Jill at The Anglers; twenty-five years earlier this is probably how she would have looked.

He took a seat on a stool at the bar, glanced at the bar menu though he'd already made up his mind to order the fish burger which he'd had here before and considered good value. The perky blonde served him and Clement got his order out of the way. When she asked if he'd like a drink he declined. Once his order was through to the kitchen he called her over, explained he was a detective investigating the death of Dieter Schaffer. She looked blank.

'A German guy, about sixty, was in here night before last.'

It clicked. 'You mean Schultz?'

'Yes. That was his nickname.' She was already feeling sad. 'That's horrible.'

The barman, who carried himself like he was her

boss and wore a tight shirt to show his muscles, made his way across. The blonde brought him up to speed and he turned to Clement.

'What happened to him?'

'That's what we're looking into. He was found dead up at a waterhole called Jasper's Creek.'

The blonde, whose name was Michaeley, recalled now he had been talking about that on Tuesday night. Clement repeated his questions as to whether Dieter Schaffer had been with anyone. The bar manager, Justin, recalled he'd spent a bit of time with a couple of the 'girls from the resort'. Before Michaeley broke off to serve customers she ventured their names.

'Marie and Rosa I think. Marie's Polish. Rosa is South American.'

Clement made a note. Justin explained.

'The resorts get a lot of casuals drifting through. They work as maids or kitchen hands mostly.'

'Wasn't Schaffer a bit old for them?'

Clement saw Justin wondering how much to tell him.

'Schultz grew his own dope. I don't think he sold it. I think he just gave it away. I told him if I found him doing deals in here, he'd never be allowed back but you can't police it if they go outside for a walk and a smoke.'

Clement recalled Bill Seratano and Mitch's evasiveness. That's probably what it was about. Maybe Seratono had bought some grass off Dieter too? It also might explain why Schaffer was able to draw down so little from his bank account. He had a cash business going.

'You ever see him in any fights?'

'Bit of a slanging match about the soccer once. Schultz and some Pommies were going on. His team was playing Man United or Liverpool or somebody.

Otherwise he joked, kept to himself. He was liked, you know.'

'He mention anything about money coming in?'

Not to them he hadn't. Justin couldn't recall exactly what time Dieter Schaffer had left on the Tuesday night. Michaeley joined again and was more helpful.

'Just before eleven. The girls started playing pool with a couple of locals and Schultz left.' She hadn't noticed anybody follow him out.

'You have any CCTV?'

'Not for the last month,' offered Justin. 'They were supposed to fix it.'

Whoever 'they' were. Dieter hadn't been killed for another twenty hours but Clement would like to have seen how he had interacted. It was annoying.

The fish burger arrived and Clement tucked into it at a furious pace, improving his mood. It was well past five now which made it eight hours since he'd eaten. He asked Michaeley to let him know if anybody there now had been there Tuesday night. She pointed out a couple of possibles, bearded blokes in fluoro vests. Clement waited until after he had eaten before tackling them. Both said they'd been here on Tuesday but had left early for a feed in town. Neither knew Dieter Schaffer.

Clement collected his plate and carried it back to Michaeley who was serving again. He thanked her and Justin and headed out just as a new bunch of clients arrived. These were younger, backpackers or workers at the resort. Michaeley read his mind and shook her head. They weren't the ones from Tuesday.

Ever since he'd left the creek Clement had been sounding his memory on old cases, looking for echoes. Now as he reached his car, something faint pinged. A sixty-three year old former music teacher who had been found strangled and mutilated in his apartment. It was violent but the scene was devoid of the presence of anybody other than the victim. The murderer turned out to be a former male student who'd been sexually abused by the teacher thirty years earlier. The killer had planned the deed in his head for many years and left not a scrap of DNA. Had his wife not realised there was something up and talked him into confessing, Clement probably would have never solved the case.

Clement would be extremely grateful if Dieter Schaffer's killer handed himself in but he doubted very much that would happen. If it was something personal that provoked this, it was likely the only way he would solve it was to know every dark secret of Dieter Schaffer.

6

It was out of peak season and the resort was sparsely populated so Clement had no trouble spotting the tourist witnesses on the patio area adjacent to the pool. None of the other guests looked like they'd venture much beyond the resort's boundary, let alone take to the bush; for a start, they were too old. The men wore the too-neat shorts and crisp shirts of those whose idea of a holiday was a game of golf with an ocean backdrop, the women, colourful light dresses perfect for art galleries. Evan Doherty on the other hand was clothed in lived-in black t-shirt and shorts; tall, slim, studious looking, mid-thirties. The woman whom he introduced not as his wife but 'partner' was petite and dusky, maybe of Sri Lankan origin, guessed Clement. She was Marguerite Luskin and she also favoured shorts.

The sun had finally had enough for the day and the heat from the paving had dulled. Clement led them to a table away from any other guests and explained succinctly that the matter was considered serious, possibly a homicide. He saw the fear in their eyes and reassured them they were not suspects, though of course he never ruled that out. Before he could get further into stride, the barista arrived, dropping a menu on the table.

'Can I get you anything to drink?'

A lilting Irish accent. By God they were everywhere now. Down in the city the gang resurfacing the road out front of his place had all been Irish, women and men. Normally Clement would forgo a coffee at these prices but he wanted to put the tourists at ease so he raised an eyebrow their way. They indicated they were fine. Clement handed the menu back and was about to say forget it but relented and ordered an orange juice. They did good fresh juice here.

'Could you tell me what time you arrived at the waterhole?'

Evan took the role of spokesman.

'Just after the sun went down, six-thirty, maybe seven.' He looked at Marguerite for support.

'Around seven,' she agreed.

They had not seen anybody else in the vicinity though Marguerite thought she heard some faint music from a radio or iPod around the time they arrived. They had made some dinner from a small cooker they carried with them, chatted, taken a look at the waterhole but kept their distance having been warned of crocodiles. By this time it was pitch dark. They had been driving for quite a few hours and were tired so they climbed up on top of the van to sleep and had drifted off. The gunshots woke them. Evan wore a watch and was able to put the time at one-twenty. The gunshots echoed intermittently for what seemed like about ten minutes.

'We'd had enough, we decided to go,' said Evan.

'I was scared,' offered Marguerite.

They had grabbed their sleeping bags, climbed into the van and driven off quickly. They drove all the way back to Broome and spent the night sleeping near the beach, or trying to. They'd come to the resort for breakfast and decided they should notify the police just in case.

'It's a good thing you did.'

Clement was acutely aware of his own hypocrisy. Hours earlier he had been deriding them. Clement's juice arrived. He gulped it and gave himself brain freeze which wasn't helped by the bill. They were too polite to press for details on the homicide but he told them the basics, a man's body had been found in the creek and thanks to them there'd been a relatively short time lapse before its discovery. Clement took them over it all a couple more times but without any change in their recollection. Once they were off the highway on the track heading to the waterhole they had seen no vehicles, nor did they hear any voices or splashing in the water when they were camped, just that faint sound of music. Clement scooped up the bill, thanked them for their time and took address details. They were from Melbourne, which might be tricky if they were needed for any inquest, but Clement urged them not to concern themselves with that for the time being and to try and enjoy the remainder of their holiday. What he didn't mention was that he would check with Victorian police on their background but there was nothing about them that raised the slightest warning signal. Clement paid for the juice at the desk.

'How'd you like it?' asked the Irishman. Clement handed over a ten.

'Excellent. Working holiday?'

'Not much holiday.'

The young Paddy shovelled a couple of coins back. Clement followed the path around to the front of the resort and the main reception area. Just a few hire cars and a couple of vehicles bearing Perth or interstate plates were in the neat carpark. There was little breeze but the smell of eucalypt and jasmine infused the air regardless. Clement entered through automatic doors. Large runners decorated in aboriginal motifs covered the floor of polished wood, possibly jarrah. A comfortable settee for the benefit of guests faced a coffee table. The usual tourist brochures were laid out evenly. This was the complete opposite of the Anglers. A well-groomed brunette clinging to her twenties manned the desk, her skin tanned a shade darker than her skirt and contrasting with a crisp white blouse. Her sleek neck was like the stem of a flower and was adorned by a scarf matching the skirt but highlighted by a blob of bright blue. She wore it with the aplomb of an air hostess from a different era. Clement imagined she'd keep an immaculate bathroom with an array of moisturisers and perfumes and was immediately embarrassed that if she looked at him she'd see the opposite. This was the sort of resort we should have stayed in, he thought. The only holidays he could remember were up to his cousin's fishing shack in Lancelin, a spell at Rottnest when Phoebe was little and a small motel unit in Bunbury. The receptionist looked up brightly to offer assistance. A nametag designated her as Kate. Clement announced who he was and Kate blanched through her tinted moisturiser. He reassured her he was only here for some routine questioning of her staff. He gave the names of the young women.

'That would be Marie Kasprov and Rosa Figueroa. They'll be finished for the day. We could try their bungalow. The quickest route is back through the front door.'

She pronounced 'route' the American way so it rhymed with shout. She picked up the desk phone.

'Shona, could you take over for a minute.'

She led Clement back out the front door and along the paving path which curved behind the reception and office area. Evening had arrived and new fragrances were detectable even beyond Kate's perfume. They crossed a courtyard then traversed a narrow path which bisected a screen of trees and gave onto a set of bungalows, styled as if weatherboard but actually made of some flimsier material. The washing hanging on lines and the pushbikes propped against the sides of the buildings betrayed them as staff quarters. Kate knocked on the screen door of bungalow 8. A girl with a sullen, haunted look and an unhealthy grey hue to her skin came to the door. She wore small pink shorts and a grubby t-shirt.

'Hi Sherry. Are Rosa and Marie in?'

'Over at Arnie's.'

The girl's accent suggested somewhere like Wolverhampton. If she was curious what it was about, neither her voice nor eyes hinted at it. Kate led Clement around a corner to another set of bungalows.

'We separate the single males from the single females but you know they're going to mix.'

The door to 12 stood open and music was playing, not overly loud. Shoes and thongs were lined up on the step. Kate rapped the door and poked her head around it.

'Hi guys. Detective Clement is here to ask some questions.'

Clement followed her inside. The living room was a reasonable size, better than what he had above the chandler. The faint odour of marijuana hung in the air with a variety of cooking smells, Clement guessing chilli con carne. It was definitely a bachelor pad. Sneakers lay scattered on the lino floor, a wetsuit was hung off a kitchen cupboard and game consoles and cigarette packets jostled each other for room on the top of a low coffee table placed before a bamboo sofa. A blonde, small and chunky without being fat, he estimated early twenties, was sitting on the floor. He guessed this was Marie Kasprov, the Pole. At one end of the small sofa was the girl he presumed was Rosa. Even younger than her friend she looked exactly how

Clement imagined a young Guatemalan would, with curly dark hair and flashing brown eyes. At the other end of the sofa, a shirtless young guy with thick curly brown hair, sat with one foot on the floor and one curled up under him. Clement guessed this was Arnie. He addressed the girls who seemed too surprised to register an attitude yet.

'I need to ask you some questions about Dieter Schaffer.'

He saw confusion on the girls' faces. He produced the photo from The Anglers.

'This man. Tuesday night you were with him at the Cleopatra Tavern.'

Now they looked really worried. He turned around to Kate, who was torn between dashing back to her post and listening to the detail.

'It's okay. I can take it from here.'

'I'll be at reception if you need me.'

Kate vanished with the skill of somebody born to the service industry. Arnie was waiting to see if he was required or not. Clement decided to leave him there. The girls seemed very anxious but he didn't want to reassure them yet.

'You remember this man?'

The girls nodded.

'He was German,' said the Polish girl.

'Schultz they call him,' offered her friend in less perfect English.

Clement explained the man had been found dead the next day in suspicious circumstances. The girls appeared genuinely shocked. Arnie squeezed backwards into the sofa.

'You hadn't heard?'

They shook their heads. They said they'd been out diving all day the previous day, a claim supported by sunburned faces.

'We were with Arnie.'

Arnie nodded. 'That's right.'

'You work here, Arnie?'

'One of the gardeners.'

'Where are you from?'

'Brazil.'

'Were you at the Cleopatra, Tuesday?'

'For a little while. I don't know the guy.'

Clement turned back to the girls. 'Tell me how you met Schultz.'

The girls said they had gone to the Cleopatra with Arnie and his roommate for the cheap drinks. The drinks here were too excessive for their wages. Schaffer, who they had never met before, started talking to them, seemed friendly and Marie could offer a little German to chat with him. They got to playing pool and having a few drinks. Schaffer spent most of the time asking whether they had seen kangaroos, snakes and so forth. At about ten-thirty they had said goodbye, gone and got some food from the town and then come back to their rooms around eleven-thirty. It was the one and only time they had met Dieter Schaffer.

'Did you buy marijuana off him?'

The girls denied it vociferously, Arnie squirmed.

'But he offered and you smoked it with him, right? It's best you tell me the truth. Don't worry, I'm not interested in a few joints.'

'A puff or two, that's all.' Living up to the stereotype, Rosa used her hands expressively.

'How did he seem?'

Happy, fun. He was quite old but he seemed in good spirits. He told them he was going fishing in crocodile territory the next day and asked if they wanted to accompany him. They politely declined but his mood didn't change, he was still happy to talk with them.

'Did he mention whether he was expecting any money?'

Not that they could recall. He didn't seem worried about anything and nobody else spent any time talking with him, although most people in the tavern seemed to know him.

'Did any of you take photos that night?'

Clement was aware that these days young people took photos of anything. They looked at one another trying to remember. Arnie and Marie shook their heads but Rosa wasn't sure. She pulled out her phone and scanned through snaps. Her lips pushed out as if about to blow a raspberry.

'Sorry.'

Clement hadn't been expecting much but wished he had been wrong. After warning he may need to speak to them again, he took his leave, picking his way back along the paths that led around the outdoor garden setting to the dining area. There he stopped cold. Marilyn was about to be seated. She was not alone. Brian was with her. He had some job that involved travelling overseas for plastics. Though he'd admit it to nobody but himself, Clement knew some vanity in him had hoped that Brian's absence and his own presence up here might somehow tip the scales back in his favour, might awaken in Marilyn something she missed, might put them on collision course and let the Fates decide if anything came of it but since his arrival he'd rarely encountered Marilyn without her poisonous mother or Brian in tow.

He saw Marilyn make him. She glared, whispered something to Brian, who looked over, and then she started towards him while Brian took his seat and perused the menu. He was older than Clement. Had it been cooler, Clement reckoned Brian would have had a pale-coloured knit sweater draped over his shoulders.

He was that type. Marilyn glided down the terrace, a chiffon vision, all those years in private schools paying off in balance and poise. Her dress print was white with pink hibiscus. It carried echoes of early sixties but was somehow contemporary in the cut, clinging to her body just enough. Clothes liked Marilyn and vice-versa but she never ventured too far, never attempted a faux-celebrity look, she was pure style, putting the more conservatively dressed women with whom she would socialise in the shade, gliding above the nouveau riche with their gym-toned bodies the way only women born into money can.

'This is getting ridiculous.'

She wasn't happy but neither was she as angry as she might have been. Her years dealing with primary school children availed her of a number of tones to deal with him, the problem child, in any given situation. Today's was forbearance slipped into a glove of future threat but whichever day it was, whichever particular technique employed, she never lost the ability to make him feel he'd disappointed her. He was thinking all this as he studied her hair, brown, lush, obedient, natural. She would rather have died than dyed but the cut was different to last time.

'I'm working, had to interview some people.'

The answer seemed to mollify her further. 'What's the case?'

'Fisherman. Could be a homicide, can't really talk about it. Shouldn't Brian be choking on some Shanghai smog?'

She deadpanned him. 'He has some time off.'

Clement hoped Brian might go swimming and be stung to death by box jellyfish. He said, 'I like your hair. It suits you.'

Later tonight Brian would be kissing, touching her, making love to her. He tried to bury the image. It shouldn't affect him but it did.

'Thank you.'

He could tell she enjoyed the compliment. She offered no quid pro quo; instead she said, 'You still picking Phoebe up Saturday morning?'

She knew his policeman's life well enough to understand how fluid things could be.

'I'll let you know as soon as. How did she do go on that assignment about frogs?'

'Fine. She'll tell you.'

Code for this isn't the time or place and stop delaying me. Brian had made up his mind, placed the menu down and stared over. She caught the look.

'Take care.'

And with that she slid back along the path to Brian and a different future. He watched her go for as long as was polite and once again wondered at the wisdom of uprooting himself for the constant reminder of what might have been. Phoebe would only spend a year or so here before being shipped off to the city for what Geraldine would consider real schooling. Then where would he be?

He'd switched off his phone before talking with the tourists. When he switched it back on there were messages from Risely and each of his team filling him in on where they were at. Risely's was simple: if there was any news, call him, they had to work out what to do once 'Tomlinson and *The Post* came sniffing'. Tomlinson referred to Kevin Tomlinson, the editor and main reporter for the local newspaper. Graeme Earle's message announced he was back from a successful fishing trip, had heard about the investigation and was ready if he needed him urgently. Otherwise he would be a work at seven a.m. He sounded like he'd had a few beers but was totally coherent. Clement tried to work out if he needed Earle for anything and concluded he'd be better fresh in the morning. Mal Gross called to say Jo di Rivi and Nat Restoff had found nobody at Schaffer's shack and nothing untoward and he had directed them to head to Jasper's Creek. The next message was from Shepherd. He and Lisa Keeble were still at the scene collecting anything and everything. Two of Lisa's local techs had joined them. Inevitably Shepherd complained about how hungry he was. The croc guys said the creek would be ready in the morning. Beck Lalor and Daryl Hagan had arrived and would keep an eye on the scene overnight, although it was expected the Perth techs, Lisa and her team would be working it till the early hours. Clement called Shepherd back and got the latest.

'We've rigged lights. Jo and Nat are on their way back from Schaffer's. They're about a half-hour away.'

'Ask Lisa how long she needs you, then get home, get some sleep and be back there first thing to search the creek for the murder weapon, the outboard and the rifle.' He predicted Shepherd's objection and cut it off at the pass. 'I'll call the boss and see if he can get us some Fisheries boys to help.'

It seemed Risely was happy to organise Fisheries support. His concern was how they were going to handle the release of information to the media, the kind of stuff Clement tried to ignore.

'Let's keep it to ourselves as long as we can,' said Clement.

'That won't be long. News travels fast in a small town.'

They arranged to meet first thing in the morning for a briefing. If Clement came across anything else he was to call.

Clement climbed back into his car and sat to reflect a moment on the interviews. When he was interviewing he tried to listen to the answers people gave rather than let his mind explode in a fever of possibilities. Often he wasn't successful but today he'd done okay and now he'd afforded himself a moment to slow-roast scenarios.

If the outboard, wallet and rifle were not sitting on the bottom of the creek then it could be a crime of opportunity: robbery–murder. Alternately somebody might have gone to the creek with the idea of killing Dieter Schaffer and disposing of his body there. In that case they must have known his movements, either because they were acquainted personally or following him. Or Schaffer could have gone with one or more companions, they argued about something and he was killed. Schaffer had told Bill Seratono he was expecting money. His bank account wasn't showing anything just yet so either he was lying and it hadn't arrived yet, or he'd been paid cash. What might Schaffer's idea have been of 'rolling in it'? He lived very modestly. Maybe he was going to sell the outboard or the boat to somebody. That person had decided it was cheaper to just do Schaffer in and take it.

Plenty of questions without answers.

In effect, Clement had been able to eliminate nothing. He simply did not know enough about the victim. Dammit, he'd have to go to Schaffer's shack now and see what he could learn. He didn't trust leaving it to the uniforms. In the city it would be simple. You'd drive across town, forty-five minutes at most. And there would be somebody who could back you up, keep on train A while you shot off to investigate B, C or D.

Not here. He was more or less it. He fired up the car, consoling himself with one new fact learned. Presuming the girls were telling the truth, Dieter Schaffer had no inkling that within twenty-four hours of enjoying himself at the Cleopatra Tavern somebody was going to bury an axe in his head.

7

Clement drove north towards Schaffer's place in a declining mood. It might be over with Marilyn but the encounter with Brian present rankled. He flashed to himself twenty years on as Dieter Schaffer, lonely and single, still here, using pot to befriend girls younger than Phoebe would be then. The thought of another woman in his life wasn't on his radar, it was all too complicated.

The highway was straight, the night black. This part of the world ate time. In a sense it was like you were already dead, a soul passing through dark space. Igniting in his brain out of nowhere, an image, circa late 70s, early 80s, his parents sitting in those uncomfortable aluminium deckchairs with the plastic strips that pinched your bare legs.

It could have been any weekend in that span because it was their perennial occupation: a dainty wooden table between them, a large bottle of Swan Lager in a chill bucket, two frosted small glasses. Not like now with everything big, giant glasses, giant bottles of Coke. Only cars had gotten smaller. The way things were going, in a year or so a bottle of Coke would be too big to fit into the boot of your car. Back then people knew how to sip not gulp. His aunt used to do jigsaw puzzles or play Patience, soaking time. Life was cruise-liner speed compared to now, no internet, you wrote with a leaky Bic biro, you mailed, you watched for a postman, you contemplated. His parents in those uncomfortable chairs in their shorts, staring ahead into nothingness, relaxed, seemingly contented. No words. As one drained a glass the other would politely refill it. They could sit like that for hours. At the time he could not imagine how they survived these hours of flat nothing. Truth be told, he still couldn't quite grasp it but he had an inkling that at some point in life you accepted, not its pointlessness, that would be too negative, the vastness of it perhaps, the volume of it that was out of your control. You began to assess your inability to make any difference not just to other people's lives but your own.

Up here, that revelation was focused by the lack of distraction. The blackfellas had evolved to this state well before white Australians. 'Don't sweat' was the saying and how apt it was here. A hard day's work had been done, this was sufficient in itself, anything else was futile bordering on posturing. His mother and father had appreciated all of this, knew it in the pores of their skin and what's more needed no conversation to communicate this. Each was embedded in his or her own thoughts and yet at the same time aware of their partner, considerate. He marvelled now at such intimacy. Did he and Marilyn ever have that? Not that he could recall. They had to find events to entertain them, movies, dinner. Neither of them would have lasted five minutes in those deckchairs. Perhaps that was it, they just weren't robust enough together in the first place, so when his work challenged him, seduced him, and the same for her, they really had nothing left except Phoebe.

Even though Clement was prepared for the turn-off to Schaffer's, he nearly missed it. It was not bitumenised, just a wide dirt entranceway between bending trees.

About twenty metres in, the trees thinned and he found himself on a rutted dirt track between scrub the height of the car. The shack nestled ahead under gums. Built on low stumps it was made of wood and tin, and had the look of a log cabin except that the roof was of shallow pitch and extended out over a simple veranda. Clement pulled up about twenty metres short and climbed out, taking his torch. The cabin was in darkness, which he expected. There was no electricity service out this way. Clement switched on his powerful torch and stepped from the ground straight up onto the veranda. A cable and light globe was slung over the open doorway on a hook, suggestive of a generator somewhere. A well-worn cane swinging chair was hooked to a beam under the veranda roof. Also hanging from the beam was a hodge-podge of old iron implements, dingo traps, farm tools. The mix of jagged teeth and prongs was malevolently artistic. Clement's beam traced the cable leading from the light bulb. It headed inside the shack. There was no door, just a permanent space for entrance and exit, about double the width of a normal door.

Stepping inside, Clement was surprised. Going on the condition of the Pajero he'd expected to find a dump, a mess of empty bottles and wheezing furniture but while it was rough and simply decorated, the place was well-ordered. It might have been one single room but it was a home. Large canvases of aboriginal art lay propped against the walls or hung. Good stuff by the looks, not the quick jobs dashed off to flog to a tourist coach. A gritty rug of what might have been South American design covered about a third of the floor. To the left as you walked in was a kitchen of sorts. A rectangular wood table, some odd kitchen chairs and stools. In the city it may have passed as a chic, inner city café. From the kitchen a window space without a window gave onto the bush. The electric cable continued its route and snaked out of it. Clement walked over and shone the torch. The cable ended at what may have been a converted dog kennel housing the generator. A rainwater tank was outside to the right. It looked relatively new. One tap was fixed near the window above the bench but no sink. An old washing machine, its power cord cut, sat on the floor, its outlet hose hooked over the window sill to deliver water to a small garden. Clement smiled at Schaffer's economy, presumably he hand-washed his clothes in the tub and then used that water on his garden. Beside the washing machine squatted a plastic tub which may have been used as a portable sink. Nailed up on the wall was a framed poster of a soccer team, HSV, 1978–79. It appeared to be from the same season as the t-shirt Schaffer had been wearing when Clement hauled out his body, though this looked older, an original. The players were grinning and holding some trophy. Premiers he guessed. HSV? Clement wasn't a soccer nut but Hamburg rang a faint bell. Had Osterlund mentioned Dieter Schaffer was from Hamburg? Could explain it, local team wins. Fixed to the wall were hand-made wooden shelves which held the basics; a few tins and jars, coffee, biscuits, sugar. No sign of a fridge. On the kitchen table was one of those plastic dish racks sporting a few odd plates, cups and saucers, all clean. A toolbox did for the cutlery drawer, neatly arranged in forks, spoons, knives.

The central part of the room offered an old sofa and coffee table, a standard lamp on sentry duty beside them. It looked a comfortable enough set up. The far end of the room served as the bedroom. A queen size bed covered in mosquito net, practical, as was the open rack beside it on which was hung a few shirts and pants. Lighting was apparently from battery driven lamps. There was one either side of the bed, neither switched on. No sign of a toilet so that was presumably outside. The cabin was wider than it was deep. It only took half a dozen paces to reach the back wall from the front door. A rough wooden bench here held ornaments, old jars, a few novels. There were also two smallish photos in frames. One showed a smiling young woman in a skivvy. She had a pleasant face with dark, wavy hair. It was hard to date but faded, clearly not recent. The other showed a group of five young men and given the moustaches, sideburns and style of leather jackets, was much easier to place as 1970s. Though it was shot close it looked like they were in some kind of office, an old photocopier could be seen behind them. If one of them hadn't been wearing a uniform, Clement would not necessarily have picked them as cops. That uniform made all the difference. Those comradely arms around each other's shoulders, the gleam of triumph in their eyes, the cockiness; he'd been part of a hundred such photos every year. Second from the left, with chubby face and handlebar moustache, was a young Dieter Schaffer. So, he had been a cop after all.

It was as he glanced at the photo that Clement noticed for the first time a small set of wooden drawers to the right. The top drawer was half-open, papers swimming unevenly, while the lower drawers looked like they'd been quickly shoved closed, jamming papers in there. On the floor more papers. It was out of character with the rest of the place. He picked up the documents on the floor, old invoices, nothing exceptional, then began checking the drawers. The top one yielded a bank passbook, ruler, pencils, pens, some official looking certificates in German; one of which, from what he could decipher, was the death certificate of Schaffer's mother, Adele. The second drawer was almost empty. Curious, considering the other drawers were also crammed. One drawer was full of printouts from web pages mostly in

German but some in English. Featuring prominently was HSV, confirming them to be the Hamburg football team, as he'd supposed. Travel tips to South America were also well represented, and cultivation of cannabis. Jammed in between the football printouts were some news items. The first featured what seemed to be a photo of a crime scene at a park with the inset photo of a man about sixty. The next was an article which showed a grainy photo, surveillance style, of a balding man with low forehead reading a newspaper. It had been blown up from a smaller original. Both of these printouts were from web downloads. There was also a real and yellowing newspaper clipping which showed a photo of a young Dieter Schaffer in police uniform.

Clement looked carefully but could see no printer. It was unlikely there would be any internet reception out here but the empty space in that second drawer would fit a laptop perfectly. He'd have to see if anybody knew whether Dieter Schaffer owned one. Maybe somebody had heard about Schaffer's death and come out here to steal what they could. It must have happened since di Rivi and Restoff had come by, they would have noticed this mess, surely. Clement made a note to check just in case. He shone his torch on the doorless portal that led out the back. This space was narrower than the front entrance.

He stepped out onto a back veranda about the same dimensions as the one out front. No sign of any outboard or rifle. A bar fridge was to his left but without the generator running, it was inert. He checked inside: beer, eggs, cheese, bread, part of a lettuce. Presumably Dieter Schaffer would turn on the generator when he was there and turn it off when he was away fishing. Clement stepped off the veranda shone the torch beam outwards and immediately saw thriving marijuana plants laced in with virgin bush. It was no plantation but it was enough to keep Dieter supplied for his own use with plenty left over to trade or sell.

Clement headed towards it for closer examination. A sound made him turn to his right. Something swung through the air and slammed into his skull.

8

Clement blinked open his eyes. His head throbbed. The part of the world that was not dark was blurred. Almost at the same instant he realised he was lying in dirt, he heard the faint but distinct sound of a motorcycle peeling away. He sat on his haunches a long minute, the smell of earth assuring him he was alive. Unsteadily he climbed to his feet and touched the side of his head cautiously. His fingers felt the stickiness of blood. A rivulet was trickling down his temple onto his cheek. His torch, still on, had tumbled a metre away. Beside it was a long handled shovel. He guessed that may have been what hit him. He picked up the torch and staggered back inside, his head throbbing.

In the kitchen beside a brush, shaving cream and a packet of disposable razors, he found a mirror the size of an A4 sheet of paper. It was tricky angling the torch to check his scalp but as far as he could tell the wounds were superficial. He contemplated what he should do next. This wasn't the city with shifts coming on and off. All his people were already knackered or likely in bed, but his head ached and it was a long drive back in the dark. He made his way to the back veranda, pulled a warm beer from the bar fridge, cracked it and gulped. The throb began to ease. He drained the can looking up at the stars; the only sound the fluid in the can and his own breath, and all at once he understood how seductive this life must have been for Dieter Schaffer. When everything was stripped back, what did we really need, but a knife and fork in a tool box, water, a bed, a beer?

He finished the can, walked back inside and over to the bed. He sat down on it and pulled off his shoes dimly aware that his socks had been far too long on his feet. The mattress was soft. Strange that a man who lived so frugally had preferred such a soft mattress. Or maybe he just found one discarded on the street and took it, somebody else's preference automatically becoming his. By now the pulsing throb had become a more chronic, less intense ache. Fatigue had hit him quickly like the shovel. No chance he was driving anywhere now. Clement lay back on the bed and pulled the mosquito net around him. That took him back many, many moons, to open verandas and the sound of the Gloucester Park trots on a radio. His thoughts drifted to Phoebe sleeping in the same bedroom her mother had as a child, on the cliff far above a green ocean.

Then he slept.

...

Daylight and the smell of morning woke him. He was surprised how lucid he was. He remembered everything. Well, he thought he remembered everything, he supposed he might not realise if he didn't. He touched his matted hair. The blood had congealed. He sat upright and his confidence evaporated. His head began to throb again, he felt nauseous. He slowed his breathing and gradually began to feel a bit better. He pulled out his phone and with it the card from Dieter Schaffer's phone. Shit, he should have been onto that already, valuable time had been lost. He popped it back in his pocket, slid off the bed, saw he'd bloodied up the pillow but that was all, and walked towards the kitchen end of the house, thirsty. Halfway across, he stopped and flopped on the sofa. He stared at his phone, saw it was five fifty a.m. This time the man with the hammer was in his own head. He dialled Graeme Earle.

...

Seventy minutes later Earle pulled into the area in front of Dieter Schaffer's shack and parked beside Clement's four-wheel drive. Clement watched him from the swinging cane chair on the veranda. He'd been enjoying the sun's early rays and was feeling much better. Earle spotted him and hustled over. He was clutching a brown paper bag.

Clement said, 'I could get used to this.'

Once he was on the veranda, Earle gave the boss's head the once-over.

'I've had worse falling off a bar stool.'

'Bloody high bar stool.'

Earle handed over the paper bag. Clement dug inside, pleased to find fresh currant buns. He raised an eyebrow to show he was impressed. 'How many for me?'

'How many do you think? One, you greedy bastard.'

Earle was the only one at work who was game enough to talk that way to him. Clement chewed into his bun. His appetite hadn't been affected. Earle grabbed one for himself.

'What'd he hit you with?'

'Long handled shovel I think.'

The men chewed in silence.

'You need to see a doctor?'

'Think I'm okay.'

'That nurse at the hospital will make you feel better.'

Clement suppressed a smile. 'You call Lisa?'

'On her way. She's rapt with you. She'd had about ten minutes sleep she said by the time she got in from Jasper's. You didn't get a look?'

'I heard a motorcycle. In the distance. I'd probably been out a few moments. How was the fishing?'

'Three nice barra. Then I got home and heard about this shit. One or more?'

'Just one I think.'

'You think this is related to Jasper's?'

Clement savoured the fresh bun. 'We need to run Schaffer's phone, see what might turn up.'

The sound of a vehicle arriving swung them back to the driveway. It was Lisa Keeble. Earle took a very big bite. 'She must have had her foot to the floor the whole way.'

She pulled up hard and dust swirled. Earle watched her climb out.

'You two should get together.'

Clement's face was kind of numb which aided his deadpan. 'First the nurse, now Lisa?'

'The nurse is just a bit of divorce therapy.' Earle's eyes tracked Lisa as she approached. 'You'd be good for one another. She needs to dump that no-hoper muso bloke.'

Clement didn't mind Lisa's boyfriend. Everybody called him Osama because of the dark beard he wore. He was a bit alternative but he had a tuneful voice. Neither man spoke as Lisa joined them. She was detachment itself as she studied him up close.

'You should get to hospital.'

'I'll be fine. I want you to dust for prints inside, especially a set of drawers. There's a long-handled shovel, DNA it, print it. The can of beer on the back veranda was me. Same for the blood on the pillow, don't get excited, it's mine. ' He looked at Earle. 'Mate, go through the place, see if there's anything I missed.

Bag all the documents in the drawers, bring them back to the station, I'm going home to change. Stay in touch.'

He turned back to Keeble. 'Sorry to dump you in it again.'

'It's my job. You didn't see your attacker?'

'Just a blur. '

'He heard a motorcycle leaving.'

Earle offered her the last of the buns. Lisa shook her head, Clement shook his. Earle took another large bite. Clement asked if Lisa had found anything interesting at the creek since they'd spoken.

'Yeah, a shirt underneath the overturned dinghy. And guess what? At a rough estimate, the marks on it matched the bruising on Dieter's body.'

'He was wearing that when he was beaten?'

'He was wearing that when somebody took an axe to his head. A lot of blood had washed into the creek but you could see the stains.'

Clement pondered. 'How could he change shirts if his head was caved in?'

'Maybe he didn't.'

Earle spoke through masticated bun. 'Somebody else put a different shirt on him?'

'I think so.'

'And then dumped him?' He looked over at Clement. 'Did they feel guilty? Somebody who knows him?'

Clement, thinking along the same lines, gave a thoughtful nod. 'What else?'

'Lots of litter, might be useful but who knows. Right out at the edge of the search area I found a space that looked like it had a car recently, empty beer cans.'

'How recent?'

'There was still a tiny bit of beer in the can. I'm guessing forty-eight hours. No useful tyre tracks.'

Clement asked if she had printed the cans. Naturally she had. She also thought they might be good for DNA.

'That's not the area I found?'

'No. There was nothing there except the depression in the ground that indicated some sort of vehicle.'

Two cars, he thought, but no way of telling when exactly they were there. Clement asked her opinion on what might have happened, now she'd had time to sleep on it.

'Sleep?' she joked. Then more seriously, 'I think he was killed with an axe or machete while he was standing near the tent. He was there for some time, bleeding into the ground. He was beaten while he was dying. When he was dead somebody changed his shirt and dragged him to the water in a tarp or something, pulled it up into the boat, drove to the middle and dumped him.'

'You don't think he might have changed himself like you said before?'

'With the beating he took I doubt he could have got it off, and it would have been almost impossible to get that t-shirt on by himself. And there's very little sign of blood on that t-shirt so the axe blow must have come first.'

'So the killer or somebody else re-dressed Schaffer?' Clement was trying to bend the scenario to make sense.

'It fits.'

Clement was now thinking through the rest of the action, how the body came to be in the creek. 'The tourists didn't mention hearing an outboard.'

Earle said. 'They could have been asleep.'

'Or there was no outboard in the first place,' suggested Keeble.

Earle didn't buy that. 'An experienced fisherman wouldn't come to croc territory without one.'

Clement said, 'Well it's not here. So I think either it's in the creek or somebody took it.' He asked Keeble, 'One or more perps?'

'No idea. One person could have got him into the dinghy.'

Clement's brain was fuzz. 'Was Shep a problem?'

'I told you, I can handle Shep. And Briony, one of the techs from Perth, is blonde and kind of cute so that got me off the hook.'

'Where is The Walking Complaint?' asked Earle.

Clement wished he'd taken him up on the last bun.

'Out at the creek. I called him right after I called you. The Fisheries blokes are there too, searching the creek.'

'Rather them than me.' Lisa Keeble gave a little shudder at the thought.

'Oh well, you better get on with it.' Clement headed to his car. 'Call if you find anything important.'

It was the sight of the chopping block and axe that stopped Clement in his tracks and had him cursing his own stupidity. It was located at the right-hand end of the veranda, with a small wood stack beneath the veranda for cover, a blue plastic tarp draped over the top as insurance against rain. Clement had missed it last night and the angle had been wrong to spy it from the veranda this morning. He advanced and checked it over. Nothing to indicate this was the murder weapon but he wasn't thinking about this particular axe. The day before yesterday Mal Gross had been taking notes with that couple who claimed an axe had been stolen from their property. Of course it could be a coincidence but even so, Clement knew he should have thought of it way back at the creek. What the hell was happening to him?

9

It took Clement a bit over an hour to drive to his flat down at the wharf. On the way he called Mal Gross, told him what had happened and took the details of the Kellys, the couple who'd had their axe stolen. He also fed him the details on the witnesses and asked Gross to check with Victoria if they'd been in any trouble before. Any hope he would enjoy a weekend with Phoebe was fading fast. The case was too ugly and there was no clear suspect yet. As he turned his car towards the wharf, Clement called Shepherd again even though he assumed he would have phoned if there were anything to report. Shepherd told him the croc guys and techs had dragged the bottom of the creek and got nothing but crap. They had assured them there was no croc around. A couple of the guys were suiting up ready to dive. He'd call if there was anything good. He also mentioned that he thought one of the techs fancied him.

'Briony?'

'How did you know?'

'Wild guess.'

'Did Lisa say something?'

'Stop thinking with your prick, goodbye.'

A ute was in the space where Clement normally parked alongside the chandler's four-wheel drive.

There were no other vacant spaces so he parked in behind both cars, scrawled a note saying he would be back down in ten but was upstairs if it was urgent. He left the note on the windscreen.

Usually he bounced up the steps two at a time but not today. He showered quickly and checked the scalp laceration in the mirror as best he could. He didn't think he needed stitches. He grabbed a clean shirt, changed jocks, climbed into his alternate suit, found a tie from the back of his chair and dashed back out to find the ute owner, a tattooed bloke with a thick neck, scowling.

'Sorry,' said Clement, though he wasn't sorry at all. He'd left a note. If the bloke wanted to get out he could have climbed the stairs and asked. For an instant it looked like the bloke might make an issue of it but he held his tongue. At least I must still look like a cop, thought Clement, still pissed off at taking so long to follow up on the Kellys.

...

It was only a ten-minute drive to their house, an old-style fibro with tin roof surrounded by overgrown straggly garden that could almost be described as bush. Nobody was about, not only here but in the whole street. Clement made his way up the little track between almost dead grass and the more adventurous stretches of bush. He heard a radio on inside the house and knocked on a door that could have done with a lick of paint. The door swung open pretty quickly. Mrs Kelly was in a dress but wore no makeup and her hair was straggly with grey streaks, the real kind, not the whimsy of a hairdresser.

'Mrs Kelly, I'm Detective Clement. I was at the station the other day. I believe you reported an axe stolen?'

'Finally.' Her hands formed a circle then dropped by her side. She called off to her left to somebody out of Clement's line of sight. 'The coppers have finally come about the axe.'

Her husband shuffled into view, probably not as tall as her, it was hard to tell because he was bent as if it took an hour or two in the morning before his spine warmed and unwound. He had a large forehead and was bare-chested, wearing short pyjama bottoms and slippers.

'You find it?'

'Not yet.'

They edged back allowing him to enter.

'You run into a door, mate?' asked Mr Kelly with an impish smile.

Clement didn't bite. He scanned the small room, neat, modest, and followed the Kellys down a narrow passageway to the kitchen where the radio played. Mrs Kelly made no move to turn it down. The floor was chipped lino and it sloped.

'Wanna cuppa?' Mr Kelly offered. Mrs Kelly shot her husband a look that suggested he'd be making it.

'No thanks. I wonder if you could just take me through again exactly what happened. And show me where the axe was taken from?'

'Out the back here.' Kelly played guide. The back door opened onto some sunken paving bordered on all sides by a jungle of a garden. Mrs Kelly took up the tale. She'd heard, or thought she heard something Sunday night along the side of the house. A sound, that was all, like somebody brushing past and the bush slapping the pipe or something. They were in bed, her husband fast asleep, but she'd woken up.

'He's too deaf anyway'.

'I'm not deaf. I heard that.'

She'd sat up and listened but heard nothing more

and eventually went back to sleep. She wasn't sure of the time except that it was after midnight, which meant technically they were talking early Monday morning. It was Wednesday before they realised the axe was missing.

A small woodpile directly in front about five metres from the back door indicated where the axe had been taken from. Clement looked it over carefully trying to keep his distance.

'Has anybody been up around here since?'

Mrs Kelly shrugged. 'Not really. But we need the axe for the hot-water heater.'

There were marks in the dirt, no proper images of shoes or anything but Keeble might find something useful. The thief could simply have walked up the side of the house or come through the back way. Clement decided to have a look up there.

He made his way through thick undergrowth expecting to find a back fence but there was none. The boundary to the property behind was marked by a couple of small brick pillars at the extremities, beyond which the jungle-like garden stopped abruptly. The property at the back had stubble for a rear lawn and then a tumbledown fibro cottage facing the opposite direction. He fought his way back and asked the Kellys who lived there.

'An old lady. She wouldn't take the axe, she's not strong enough to swing it,' said Kelly.

'It was normal size?'

The Kellys confirmed it was. They couldn't recall the make or where they'd got it from but decided they'd had it longer than five years and less than ten.

'Who would know it was here?'

'Anybody who's been here,' offered Mrs Kelly.

'Don't have to have been here. You can hear me chopping the wood out front.'

Kelly was right, thought Clement, feeling a step behind. 'Anybody you think might have taken it?'

Kelly put forward his wife's cousin as a logical suspect. She thought his cousin much more likely. Clement took down their names just in case. He asked the Kellys to stay away from the back yard for now, explaining he needed to send somebody down to test for things.

'What about our axe?' asked Mrs Kelly.

Clement could understand her exasperation, he felt it too. 'We'll do our best to locate it, believe me.

...

Clement made it into the office to find Meg, the civilian secretary, making herself tea. She didn't notice his battered face. Maybe she didn't even notice him. There was no sign of any uniforms. He walked straight to Risely's door and knocked.

'Yeah,' came from inside.

Clement turned the knob. Risely, close-cropped hair, still more or less brown, a bull of a man who looked your archetypal tough cop, was sitting back reading reports. So far Clement had found him calm, measured, the kind of bloke who'd long ago learned it was preferable to go around doors than kick them in.

'Christ, what happened to you?'

Clement told him as succinctly as possible.

'I'm the last to know, eh?'

'It was late. I didn't see much point.' He explained where he'd just been and the potential lead on the axe.

'You call Keeble?'

'Yes, she's getting somebody onto it. Of course it could be a coincidence.'

'Tomlinson got wind of Jasper's Creek and rang me last night. A possible murder is a huge story for him. I told him we weren't sure what we were dealing with yet. He couldn't get it in this morning's edition. I said he could send in a photographer as soon as the area was cleared, and promised him up-to-date reports. Don't worry, I'll handle that. So where are we at?'

Clement listed Schaffer's injuries. He mentioned the likelihood Schaffer had been re-dressed.

'No sign of a wallet, a rifle or an outboard motor. Confirmation he had an outboard but they haven't found it in the creek so far and it's not at his house. I'd like to try and find out where he was from the time he left the Cleopatra Tuesday night till Wednesday night at Jasper's Creek.'

'I'll get onto all roadhouses. He might have got petrol and they have CCTV.'

It was a good idea.

'You're thinking robbery?' asked Risely.

'Not sure. I don't get why you shove a clean t-shirt on him and then put him in the creek.'

Risely raised his eyebrows like he couldn't explain that either. 'He had dope plants there?'

'Yeah.'

'A plantation or what?'

'No. Not a plantation, not that big but more than what he needed for himself. It could be a drug thing.'

'You need to get stitches?'

'I'm okay.'

'You've got full resource, whoever you want. You think it's related? Dope dealer is murdered; you get attacked.'

'Somebody could have found out Schaffer was dead and gone to get themselves free pot. We can't assume it was the killer.'

'Can't assume it wasn't.' Risely pushed back in his chair, considered. 'Do we need help on this case?'

'Not yet. Lisa and the Perth techs are processing the

site. We might get lucky at the Kelly's, pick up a print or something.'

Risely's mobile buzzed. The ID read 'Tomlinson'.

'You going to mention this?' Clement pointed at his wound.

'Any reason I should?'

Clement shook his head. The last thing he needed was to become part of the story himself.

The phone finally stopped ringing. Risely said, 'I'll tell him we're treating it as a homicide.' His desk phone rang. It would be Tomlinson. 'This is your chance, Dan.'

'What do you mean?'

'I know you only came here for personal reasons. I know you've probably been bored out of your skull and think the guys here don't quite cut it but they're good guys, they just need a leader. This is a great opportunity for all of you. Get on with it.'

Clement closed the door and cast around. The IT guy, Manners, was at his computer. He was an unusual confluence of physical attributes: a solid build with broad shoulders but a weak chin and a mouth that turned down as if he were always on edge with how the world judged him. Clement handed him the phone card.

'This is from the phone of the Jasper Creek victim. Download everything you can, contacts, text messages, the works. And it's probably very unlikely, but see if Dieter Schaffer had a Facebook page, Twitter, any of that crap.'

Jo di Rivi and Nat Restoff were just entering via the back door with coffee cups. Once again Clement had to go through the ritual of why he looked the way he did. He deflected more questions and got on with it.

'I want you to see if anybody is trying to flog an outboard motor for a dinghy, or a rifle, Ruger twenty-two,' he said. 'You never know, we might get lucky. Check online, at the wharf, and ring around all the other stations and ask them to keep an ear out. Then I want you up and around McDougall Street. See if anybody saw or heard anything unusual from midnight Sunday to early hours Monday.' He explained about the Kellys and the missing axe.

They started off, buzzed to be part of a murder inquiry. Clement couldn't help himself.

'I guess they put the dog down?'

The last he'd seen of it they were taking the wretch to the pound. Jo di Rivi looked guilty. Clement figured the poor thing had died in transit and they were trying to spare his feelings. Restoff smiled and jerked a thumb at his female colleague. 'She adopted her.'

'She was for the needle otherwise,' di Rivi said defensively.

'Didn't she need surgery?' Clement was still grappling with the idea the dog was alive.

'Angela, the vet, is a friend. She did it for free. I needed a dog. They'll keep her at the surgery for a while.'

'You got a name?' Same dumb question everybody asks.

'No. I'm going to wait till I get her home. See what evolves.'

Clement couldn't think of anything to say so he made do with, 'Find me the gun.'

He hadn't quite made it into his office when his phone rang. It was Lisa Keeble. He asked her to wait, entered the office and shut the door. Its starkness condemned him; only Phoebe's drawings gave it life. They showed the same subject three times over, two stick people of almost equal size holding hands on enormously long arms. Phoebe had designated herself by long hair. He liked to think he was the other figure. They'd been done years ago. He apologised for keeping Lisa waiting. She was unfussed.

'I've got Briony heading over to Macdougall Street to take a look at that scene.'

'Don't get too excited. I think our chances of a print anywhere are unlikely.'

'They climb over a fence?'

'No fence. But maybe you might find some soil or vegetation samples you can compare with Jasper's Creek.'

They both knew that would be a long shot. If anything was to come of the scene, it would more likely be from a doorknock.

'How you doing out there?'

'I found fingerprints on the drawers and in other places inside the shack. Besides yours, one set, Schaffer's.'

'You know that already?'

'Printed his corpse, dabbed his vehicle yesterday, I recognise them.'

'DNA?'

'Found some skin in the shovel handle that could still be viable for DNA. If we'd have got it last night ...'

'I had a slight headache.'

'If Rhino can pull DNA we eliminate Schaffer's, see if it's somebody else's.'

'No outboard, no computer?'

'No.'

And yet there were printouts, so either he had a computer, or a friend who had one, or he used internet cafés.

'Is there an internet café here?'

'Yes. At least two I know of, one next to the real estate agent, the other opposite The Dolphin. The Honky Nut.'

Clement now recalled the one next to the estate agent. It was little more than an office with computers. He was aware of the café opposite The Dolphin restaurant but had never been inside. He thanked Lisa, told her she could wind up and get back to the creek when she felt ready. As he ended the call, the image of a computer and printer leapt into his head. He had seen them recently in relation to the case. Where? It took him a moment to locate the objects in the right space, Osterlund's kitchen. He tried to remember what he'd done with the card Osterlund had handed him and eventually found it in his wallet. He debated whether to call the mobile or the house and settled on the house. The phone rang for some time. He was about to hang up when Osterlund answered in his clipped German style.

'Yes?'

'It's Detective Daniel Clement, Mr Osterlund.'

'You've made an arrest?'

'Not yet. I wanted to ask you something.'

'How can I help, Detective?'

His head had started throbbing again. 'Did Dieter Schaffer own a computer?'

'No idea. Sorry. I never saw him with one.'

'Did he ever use yours or talk about using one?'

'Not that I remember. He didn't seem the computer type. I'm sure I would have recalled if he talked about it.'

Which, Osterlund, being an IT type, had nudged Clement to call him first. He thanked Osterlund and was about to hang up.

'Do you have any leads you can talk about?' Osterlund was trying to sound casual.

'Nothing concrete. Thanks, Mr Osterlund.'

He hadn't checked Osterlund's alibi with the neighbours and made a note to do so. He clicked on his computer and stared at Phoebe's drawing while it loaded, trying to convince himself that this made him a great dad. Once the computer was ready for action he went to his search engine and typed in the address for the OIC website. It conveniently asked which language he wished to use. Clement chose English but may as well have picked Mandarin. OIC offered services for IT solutions, streaming and 'The Cloud'. It seemed to be involved in advising firms with expensive abstract artworks on the walls of their foyers. At least that was the image Clement conjured. It offered a full range of Net publishing and marketing services too. Like a man who finds himself in the women's toilet by mistake, Clement exited quickly. Next he did a search for Broome Anglers, found the club phone number, and typed that in to a casebook master sheet while he dialled. Jill answered in her effervescent manner.

'Anglers, Jill speaking.'

'Hi Jill, it's Detective Daniel Clement.'

'Oh hi, Dan.'

Years of being a confidante to bar flies meant Jill immediately adopted first name familiarity.

'Jill, do you know if Dieter Schaffer had a computer?'

'A laptop. Don't know what make, looked pretty old. He asked me once if he could print off some pages using our printer. I said I was sorry but I couldn't let him. We're only a small club.'

She seemed worried Clement would think her a tightwad. Clement thought Schaffer had a cheek asking. 'When was this?'

'Few months ago. Said he wanted to print out some soccer stuff. Any idea what happened yet?'

'Working on it.'

'Pop in for a drink any time. First one's on the house.'

He thanked her for the offer. He'd established that Dieter Schaffer had a computer. Whether he had one forty-eight hours ago was a different matter. He could have sold it, it could have stopped working. Clement needed a coffee and he could walk to either of the internet cafés Lisa had mentioned in under ten minutes.

He left via the back door.

Getting his legs moving somehow lessened the pain in his head. He tried to run through where he was on things and felt discouraged. He still knew very little about Dieter Schaffer. Perhaps he should have tried to track down the sister first thing? He'd get Earle onto that. Then again, if Dieter had been a cop in Hamburg, the police there might be a good way to locate his origins. So far Clement had no motive or suspect. The one odd thing that he'd turned up was somebody had put a clean t-shirt on the body; why? Surely that indicated a close relationship.

A technique Clement fell into almost naturally on these more elusive cases was to imagine himself conversing with the dead man. It brought the victim home, made him real, made the way he thought of the case more diverse and complete. Clement projected Dieter beside him right now, hunched over a can of beer, smoke from a reefer curling between them. Everybody said you were a loner, so there was some secret life to you, Dieter, wasn't there? All of us have those dark, trembling secrets too frightened to emerge into the light, so you were hiding something, even if that's not what got you killed.

Sometimes he almost expected the victim to answer and furnish him with details of the murder. Today was not that day.

Clement decided he'd try the Honky Nut café first. From the little he had learned of Dieter Schaffer it seemed this would be more his style than the antiseptic office tone of the café up the road. The Honky Nut took its name from the large external seeds that adorned gum trees. Hard and heavy as small rocks, they dropped and littered the ground. As kids you could collect them and pelt them at enemies or throw them on an open fire generating surprising heat. Florists sprayed them gold or silver and used them decoratively but there was no gold or silver in the café which was themed by cheap odd lots of furniture, not unlike Schaffer's own kitchen. A couple of surfer, dope-smoking types sat out front on a narrow wooden veranda sipping milkshakes under vines. Clement stepped into a room that boasted laminex tables and an old sofa up front, and half a dozen work-station cubicles beyond with computers. Two backpacker girls were hunched over one of the computers. Clement guessed they shared the cost. For a while he'd forgotten those days when every cent counted but lately, with the split, they had returned. A large blackboard directly over the counter displayed a menu creatively drawn in coloured chalk. An attractive, dusky young woman with perfect skin and a head full of beautiful dark curls stood relaxed behind the counter reading a magazine. She turned a pleasant smile on him. He felt guilty depriving her of an expected sale, and got the bad news over with, explaining who he was.

'I'm investigating the death of a man named Dieter Schaffer. I think he may have been a customer.'

The young woman looked puzzled and a little afraid. Clement realised he hadn't brought the snap of Schaffer and cursed inwardly. Now all he had was a photo of the dead man he'd taken with his phone. He tried to reassure her.

'Don't worry, I'm just trying to confirm if he used his computer recently. Do people do that? Bring their laptops in here and connect to the Net.'

'Yes they do.' There was a hint of an accent which he couldn't identify. 'What was his name again?'

'Dieter Schaffer.' It clearly meant nothing to her. 'He was German.'

At first nothing, and then a light in her eyes. 'Around sixty? He checks soccer results.'

'That's him.' Small mercy. He wouldn't have to show

her the photo after all.

She was nodding now. 'He'd go on the Net and print out some pages. He's dead?'

'Unfortunately, yes he is. When was the last time he was in?'

'Last week sometime, I think. He liked his coffee black, strong.'

'Did you ever see him with anyone? Did he ever meet anybody here?'

'Not that I remember. He used to come in, have a coffee and use our Net for a while. What happened to him?'

'We're trying to establish that. How did he pay you?'

She frowned as she thought. 'Cash I think. It was never very much.'

'If you recall anything else at all about him please let me know. Clement.'

He pointed in the direction of the station, thanked her for her time and left.

The sun was heating up. He had planned to buy a coffee from The Dolphin after he left here but now that seemed a betrayal to the Honky Nut. He started back towards the station picking up on what he had been mulling over before. Somebody had rifled through those drawers at Schaffer's and probably taken the computer. Maybe it was whoever killed Schaffer, either looking to steal or attempting to remove something incriminating. But he could not rule out that it was simply somebody who'd learned Dieter Schaffer was dead. People figured the dead had no need of their possessions, or at least told themselves that to justify their actions. His phone rang. It was Jo di Rivi. She was clearly excited, speaking faster and in a higher pitch than usual.

'We might have got lucky.'

She quickly ran through the story. As requested, she'd called the other Kimberley stations and mentioned the missing outboard and gun. A young uniform in Derby, Luke Byrd, had got a call from a mate who'd been approached by a young aboriginal man about buying an outboard motor 'for cheap'. His mate reckoned the young bloke could have been a glue-sniffer. He was driving an old Ford station wagon and there was a girl with him who looked nervous. The whole thing seemed suss so he called Luke. Luke had a fair idea who the young fellow was.

'I told Byrd to wait until I called you,' said di Rivi.

Clement was already jogging to the station.

'On my way.' He called Graham Earle and Shepherd as he ran and told them to meet him at the Derby police station.

'Vests, weapons. If you're there before me, wait.'

10

It was around two and half hours before they assembled at the Derby police station. Cutting straight across from Dieter Schaffer's shack, a mixture of dirt roads and open scrub, Earle had managed to arrive ten minutes ahead of Shepherd. Even though starting at Jasper's Creek made him geographically the closest, he had faced the worst terrain. Clement had simply hammered full-bore down the highway. Constable Luke Byrd might have only been fractionally taller than Shepherd but his mass was far greater, and it was all oak. Policing outback Western Australia, size mattered. Byrd ran them through what he knew as the detectives strapped on protective vests.

'Your suspect is Sebastian Kilmorley, seventeen. He's from Fitzroy Crossing. I did a stint there last year and picked him up a couple of times; usual shit, sniffing petrol, bit of break and enter, stole a car. Nothing big-time though, I wouldn't have thought he was hardcore. His girlfriend is Diana. I don't know her second name. Everybody called her "Princess". I think she was from one of the settlements north.'

'How sure are you this is the guy?' Earle was struggling to get the vest to sit over his expanding gut.

'Sebastian drove an old yellow Ford station wagon, exactly like the one the kid with the outboard had, at least as my mate described it.'

'He could have sold it.' Shepherd establishing a bit of pissing room. Clement almost groaned.

'Yeah but the girl sounds just like Diana.'

Clement checked his pistol. 'There's no chance Sebastian could legitimately have an outboard?'

'Some mate might have given it to him to flog but none of Sebastian's mates would have it legitimately either.' Luke Byrd put his hands on his hips, almost defying them to disagree.

Clement had no inclination to. 'So where do we look for him?'

'Fifteen k that way.' The answer came not from Byrd but his sergeant, a dark haired stocky man who introduced himself as Dave Drummond.

'Sarge has eyes and ears all over,' said Byrd.

'Costs me a slab twice a year, best investment ever. Soon as Luke told me, I leaned on a couple of contacts. They said the boy and girl are camping at a place they call Smooth Rock.' There was a large map of the region on the wall. Drummond stabbed a location to the east. Like a body surfer in a wave's aspic, Clement allowed the momentum to carry him; he felt his speech quicken.

'We'll take two cars. Constable, you ride with me. Shep, you're in with Sergeant Drummond.'

Earle drove, Byrd in the back. It was five degrees hotter here than Broome, sparse, primitive. We're like an old-time posse heading after the outlaw, Clement thought as he stared through the bug-smeared windscreen. He had been in this kind of situation before. Confronting a young psycho with a weapon was never routine. Logic might tell them to put down the weapon but logic did not camp in the minds of young stoners. An image of Phoebe mourning her dead father barged its way into his brain. He dismissed it but not before reminding himself he was supposed to get her this evening, which would not be possible now, whatever happened. He dialled.

'Yes, Dan.'

Did Marilyn save the world-weary tone especially for him or was Brian subject to it too?

'I'm in the middle of this thing. I can't get Phoebe today.'

'Don't worry about it. She was invited to go on Ashleigh's boat anyway, but didn't want to hurt your feelings.'

He knew she was waiting for him to ask who Ashleigh was thereby confirming he wasn't really part of the family unit only an interested onlooker.

'This might be done by tomorrow sometime.'

'That's not going to work. I just told you, they're sailing.'

She hadn't explained it was for the whole weekend but what did that matter? She had the high moral ground.

'I'll call her when this is wrapped up.'

'Okay. Good luck.'

His relationship with Marilyn had devolved into a series of skirmishes that were never decided in his favour. And yet he sometimes felt she could have been a more ruthless foe if she really desired. Clement was aware the other men were staying studiously deaf.

'Up here,' said Byrd, pointing at a turn-off.

Earle turned down the narrow, rutted dirt track. The usual savannah-style topography gave way to something dense. Clement checked the rear-vision and saw Drummond and Shepherd follow. A couple of minutes in, Drummond flashed his lights. Earle read the signal and pulled over.

The men clambered out of the vehicles and were instantly desiccated. There was no breeze and the smell of bush grasses was strong. Drummond pointed at a grove of trees.

'Likely just down through there.'

The words were no sooner out of his mouth than two shots rang out, blended with a volley of screams.

'Shit.'

Clement couldn't even be sure which of them had said it. He was already running through the bush, changing direction to home in on shrill shouts. The others were either side and behind him. They emerged into a small clearing. A yellow station wagon was parked under a gum tree. A bare-chested young man, really only a boy, was pointing a rifle at a girl. He turned, confused and half-dazed at the commotion.

'Sebastian, put the gun down.' Byrd put his hand out in a calming manner. Earle and Drummond already had pistols drawn. The girl let loose a stream of invective at the boy.

'You dumb shit. I told you. You're fucking dumb.'

The boy's eyes were white bubbles. They darted between her and them. Clement could see it was a Ruger 22 he was holding.

'Put the gun down, Sebastian.'

'I'll shoot her.'

'Fucking try it.' She leapt towards him, blocking their lines of fire and tried to beat him with her fists. He shoved her backwards towards them and was gone into the trees in a flash.

Clement hollered, 'Shep, stay with her!'

With the girl's expletives ringing in their ears, Clement and the others broke into the bush which was surprisingly thick. Clement pointed right.

'You guys that way; don't fire unless you have to.'

He and Earle started left but quickly slowed. There was no sign of the boy in the surrounding bush which varied from sparse tall grass to squat thick clumps.

Clement called hopelessly, 'Sebastian this is pointless. We just need to talk to you. Nobody's going to hurt you. Put the gun down and come out.'

Nothing.

It was hot and uncomfortable in the vest under the baking sky. This was the boy's territory but Clement had to pursue. He and Earle edged carefully forward listening. Not even a rustle of leaves. If Sebastian had been running, Dan figured there would have been some sound so he reasoned if the boy came this way he was lying somewhere, motionless. Catching Earle's eye, he signalled they split again and circle in opposite directions. Crouching low, he pushed along the rough, hot ground through tall grass, wary of the weapon in his hand. He had never fired at anybody. The last thing he wanted was to accidentally shoot a fellow cop. He fixed on a clump of trees fifteen metres ahead as a likely hiding spot. Slowly he began to flank it. Whenever he paused longer than a few seconds ants crawled all over him. He flashed back: schooldays, Bill Seratono, him, a couple of others playing sniper, honky nuts as ammunition ...

There, from the thicket, a sound like somebody edging backwards. He stood and advanced.

'Sebastian, we need to talk. I'm not holding a weapon.'

Too late he heard the sound behind him and swung round. Sebastian pointed the rifle, a smile spreading over his crusted upper lip.

11

This was Clement's nightmare made real: a desperate young man probably off his face, a deadly weapon in hands. And that weapon pointed right at him. It was impossible to tell if Sebastian was sneering or amused.

'Gotcha a good one.'

'Yeah, you did. Now Sebastian, please.'

'I'm not going to jail. They'll take her back.'

'Who?'

'Princess's family.'

'We can talk about that, just put down the gun.'

Sebastian's aim shifted from Clement's chest to his head.

'That jacket not gonna stop a bullet in your head.'

Behind Sebastian, Earle appeared, his Glock 9 pointing, ready. Clement tried not to make eye contact. He spoke more firmly.

'Sebastian, put the gun down.'

The boy's focus phased in and out. Then he sighed and let the weapon drop. Earle launched at him from behind, drove him down into the ground and pinned him as he wriggled and swore.

...

'So Princess, how did you get that outboard motor?'

The girl looked sullenly over at Clement. They were

seated in the small interview room at the Derby station. Clement had decided to start with her first. Sebastian was still high on something.

'Princess, you answer him.'

Earle stood behind Princess, playing bad cop. When they had checked the back of the station wagon, there was the outboard motor.

'You want some more Pepsi?' Clement offered the squat fat bottle.

Princess nodded. Clement poured it slowly into a plastic cup so it plopped and fizzed and was impossible to refuse. He held up the cup, tempting.

Princess snatched it and gulped. 'Found it.'

'You found the outboard motor?'

'That's right.'

Another gulp and the Pepsi was gone. The claustrophobic bare brick room smelled of disinfectant. Clement had the air-con on as low as he could stand it.

'At Jasper's Creek?'

'Yeah. That one ...' she pointed at the wall to indicate her beau whom she assumed was beyond it somewhere, '... he's an idiot. I told him leave the fucking thing. We got no need of that. We can't sell it. He don't listen.'

She shoved the cup out and Clement obliged with more Pepsi.

'You took a rifle too,' said Earle. She answered without turning to him.

'Well that's useful, you can shoot some parrots or roos to eat, except he wastes all the bullets firing at nothing.'

'And a wallet too, right, you took that?' Clement, smooth, casual.

'Nope. No wallet.'

Her eyes dove down. She was lying about that. He moved on though.

'So, what did you find exactly at the creek?'

'We were parked, right? We were going to camp.'

According to Princess they heard music nearby and snuck a look. They eased towards the sound and came upon the clearing. The car door was open, the headlights on, nobody around. They figured somebody might have got drunk and gone to sleep in the tent, so they called out and when nobody answered they checked. The tent was empty except for some chicken. Flies were already helping themselves. Around then, the car battery must have died because the music stopped and the light went out. They were trying to work out what to do when Sebastian saw the empty boat floating just off the bank. The motor smelled like it had been used. He remembered there was supposed to be a croc in that creek.

'We figure the croc got him.'

'Him?'

'Don't know any women go camping out there.'

'So you figured whoever this car belongs to, he's dead, we might as well take his wallet, gun and outboard.'

'That wasn't my stupid idea.'

Clement pretty much had confirmation on the wallet now but chose not to go there yet.

'What time did you get there?'

She cast for the memory, lost focus.

'Eight? Nine? Midnight?'

'I dunno. After nine.'

'You saying you didn't see anybody at the camp.'

'That's right. Hey, if a croc got him we're not going in there to look.'

Earle looked over at him, wondering what he thought about this.

'So how did you get the boat?'

'It was close. Dickhead got a branch and kind of pulled it in.'

'What about the blood?'

'What blood? I didn't see no blood.'

'It was all over the tent.'

'I didn't see it. It was dark.'

'You said you checked the tent then the car lights went out.'

She shrugged. 'I didn't see any blood.' Then she understood. 'Hey, you saying we hurt somebody?'

'Does Sebastian own an axe or machete?' Earle walked around so he was in front of her, a looming threatening presence.

'We didn't do anything. We found that stuff.' She was growing strident.

Clement pulled her attention back to him. 'You didn't find any clothes, say?'

'I told you. Seb took the motor off the boat and we left.'

'And the gun?'

'The gun was under the car seat.'

'Did a man find you stealing his things come back and fire at you?'

'No. We didn't see no bloke. I told you. We found the gun, we got the boat and the motor then Sebastian fired the gun for a while and then we drove off.'

'What did he fire at?'

'Nothing. The moon. He's fucking stupid, I told you.'

...

Later, as sun reflecting off the paving smacked his face, Clement stood in the rear courtyard with Earle and Shepherd, sipping tea too weak for his taste. Shepherd had made it and he didn't want to criticise. Earle enjoyed a cigarette. They still hadn't interviewed Sebastian. Shepherd stretched and batted away Earle's smoke.

'So what do you guys reckon?'

The sergeant deferred to his senior to answer.

'I'm more inclined to believe her than not.'

Earle finished his smoke and ground it into the paving. 'Why?'

'Her story is consistent with what we found. Somebody kills Schaffer, dumps him in the creek and leaves everything just as it was. If the tourists had found that scene and not Princess and Sebastian, what would they have thought?'

Shepherd practised a torpedo punt with an invisible ball. 'Crocodile.'

'That's right. Same as she claims.'

'Or that was what they tried to make it look like. Lot of blood.' Earle squinted at the harsh sun.

But Clement reckoned she was telling the truth and she just hadn't seen it in the dark. He'd interviewed enough callous teens who didn't care about taking a human life. Princess didn't strike him that way; she was cocky, sure, but from ignorance.

'Most likely she doesn't want to tell us she saw it because she thinks we'll fit them up. If they killed him why not take the phone too? And changing the shirt, I just don't get it. That feels odd, doesn't it?'

Clement flipped through the time line. 'Tourists arrive around sunset. They hear music, so maybe Schaffer has the car CD running. They go to bed. Somebody cleaves in Schaffer's head then kicks the shit out of him. They rip off his shirt and replace it, put him in the boat, head to the middle of the creek, dump him, come back, leave the boat like he's maybe fallen in, and go. Princess and Sebastian rock up around one a.m., hear music, investigate, battery dies, they make their score. Sebastian fires off some shots and wakes the tourists. They leave.'

'Or they rock up and kill him and dump the body.'

Clement was beginning to understand Earle was one for simple explanations.

He persisted. 'I just get a gut feeling the kid is a

dumb Romeo. I could see him accidentally pulling the trigger but an axe? And where is it?'

'Let's ask him,' said Earle who was about to start another cigarette but then tucked it back in its pack. Before they could head inside Clement's phone rang. It was Risely.

'I called Tomlinson and told him we had located persons of interest.'

This irritated Clement. 'That's premature. I'm not sure they did it. The girl says they found the camp deserted.'

'You believe her?'

'More than not. We're going to talk to the boy now.'

Risely was pragmatic. 'They're still persons of interest, so no drama. The city TV stations are onto it.'

The shorthand being he could expect a call from Police HQ and wanted to be able to tell them something satisfying.

'We're pushing about as fast as we can.'

'Understand, Dan, just don't want them all in Perth to think we're hicks.'

...

Sebastian Kilmorley's eyes were a lot brighter than an hour or so before. Perspiration beaded his forehead.

'Where's Princess?'

Clement felt an affinity with the boy. There'd been a time, if situations were reversed, he'd be asking 'Where's Marilyn?' and she'd most likely be slagging him off too. But when you love somebody, what can you do about that except banish love to a very distant room.

'She's fine, don't worry. She's not pleased with you though.'

The boy's eyes moved uneasily.

'She blames you, says she told you not to steal that outboard.'

He was watching them carefully, trying not to implicate himself. Earle leaned back against the wall. 'Things could be a lot easier if you told us where you left the axe.'

Sebastian looked from one to the other, a tennis fan. 'I didn't take no axe.'

Clement liked his partner's move and went with it. 'Machete, whatever.'

'I didn't take anything like that. The motor, the rifle ...'

'The wallet ...' Clement as if it were a given. Sebastian shrank into himself, guilty. His silence condemned him.

'How much money was in it?'

Sebastian shrugged.

'We can find out. Easier if you tell us. A hundred dollars?'

'About that.' Sebastian stretched his legs nervously.

'Where is it now?'

He repeated his trademark shrug. 'Tossed it out in the bush somewhere.'

'Where?'

'I dunno, okay?'

'What time did you get to the creek?'

He couldn't tell them for sure but working through his movements he came up with around eleven. Clement asked what happened then. Sebastian recounted pretty much the same as Princess. They heard music. They went to take a look. They couldn't see anybody. The dinghy was just out of the water close to the shore. They called out. Right away Sebastian was thinking crocodile. Then the car lights and music stopped. Then Princess saw the tent. Graham and Clement made eye contact. It could explain how they missed the blood.

'You checked the tent?'

He poked his head in, nobody in there. Just some cooked chicken but he wasn't touching that, might have been in there for hours with flies and ants.

'So then you took what you could find?'

'You got the outboard and the gun back. It's only a hundred bucks. Come on, please. Her old man's a prick. He'll kill me.'

...

'You're sure?' Risely leaned elbows on his desk and rubbed his face. A smell of cologne emanated from him, which seemed at odds with his tough look. A Christmas present from the missus, thought Clement, remembering those days.

'They didn't do it. Derby charged them with theft.'

As soon as they'd finished interviewing the boy Clement had warned his boss. Then he'd driven back here fast, which was still around two hours' worth of hot rubber on hot bitumen.

'So what do we have?'

'Not much. The stuff from the sites is being processed. Shep is doorknocking to see if anybody saw anything the night the axe was stolen from the Kellys. The witnesses are cleanskins, Vic police have nothing on them. Earle is trying to locate Schaffer's sister via Immigration and sorting all the documents from the shack. We can rule out robbery, I think. Whoever killed Schaffer took nothing obviously valuable from the scene, not even the wallet.'

'Why go to the trouble of dumping him in the creek?'

'Maybe to destroy DNA. Maybe the perp hated him so much they wanted him eaten by a croc.'

'He was an ex-cop. You think it's possible he came across somebody he banged up?'

Clement had asked himself the same question. 'It seems remote. I mean he's mid-sixties.'

Before letting him go, Risely warned him he'd need to front the press sometime before the day was out.

Clement made himself a coffee and was on his way to his office when Manners the IT guy appeared. 'I've got the contacts from the phone and the text messages; also, a list of all the calls to and from the phone in the last fortnight. I've printed them out. And I've put the photos and movies onto a DVD and thumb-drive for you. There's hardly anything. No sign of him on Facebook.'

Clement returned to his office with a bounce in his step. He put on the DVD and called in Earle who was at his desk sifting computer printouts found at Schaffer's house. Manners was not exaggerating. Dieter Schaffer clearly did not see himself as a photographer. There were thirty-six photos going back six months. More than half came from some fishing trip with members of the Anglers Club. The last photo was dated the night before he died and was in the Cleopatra Tavern. It looked like Schaffer had snapped it himself at arm's length and showed him smiling between the two young women from the Mimosa. They looked a little out of it, a typical pub photo.

There were only six videos. Three of them were under one minute's duration and comprised a dog in the main street rifling a bin, a sunset shot of birds leaving a lake, and a barbecue with a few of the Anglers people including Bill Seratono and his mate Mitch. Cinéma-vérité style, the photographer, one assumed Schaffer, wandered through the gathering with the camera. As it reached them, the happy anglers raised cold stubbies, shot the finger or pulled a stupid face. The other three videos were of struggling fish being hauled out of the water. Clement and Earle sifted through text messages. There weren't many and nothing stood out. They progressed to the 'contacts' list. Everybody was listed by their first name only. Hadn't Manners noticed this?

He walked out and found Manners hunched over his computer.

'The contacts are all just Christian names.'

Manners stared at him blankly.

Clement explained, 'We need full names. In case any of these people have a record for example.'

Obviously the idea simply hadn't occurred to Manners.

'You want to me to ID the people from the numbers?'

Clement fought the urge to de-scrote Manners in a painful and public manner. 'That would be good. How long will that take?'

'There's not many. Not long.'

It was four-thirty now. Graeme Earle had moseyed on out of Clement's office. Clement's head began to ache again, just a little. Clement looked at Earle.

'Can you get everybody together for a meeting in half an hour? We need to run through what we have.'

'Lisa too?'

'Yeah, everybody.'

Clement retreated to his office and sat back down to think. Somebody viciously chopped through Schaffer's skull, then dumped his body in the creek. Then last night somebody had bashed Clement at Schaffer's with a shovel before fleeing. Were the two incidents related? Was it the same person? Dieter Schaffer grew marijuana. Maybe he was dealing. It had been a violent killing. It seemed the killer had not been satisfied to put an axe into his skull but had proceeded to beat him as he lay dying. Leaving aside the possibility that Schaffer just happened across a homicidal psychopath in the middle of nowhere, a possibility that actually had more credence up here than people might think, what other clues were there in the personality of Dieter Schaffer to explain the brutality of his murder? He had no de facto that they knew of. Nor had they found any sign of any such person in his shack. Could he be gay? A paedophile even? Somebody living alone like that had privacy. Clement suspected his old case of the music teacher was playing on his mind but the mood of that murder was a fit. A spurned lover or a victim could have killed him with that ferocity, Clement believed. Bill Seratano and his mate Mitch had said Dieter Schaffer was a bad gambler. Maybe that was the genesis of this, a bad debt? If you owed money to the wrong people for too long they could become impatient. But would they go so far as to kill someone? Clement trawled through his experience in Homicide. He could recall only one instance where this had happened. A businessman had been stiffed by his ex-business partner. There had been months of discussions and promises about repayment. The debtor kept finding a way not to pay and eventually the businessman snapped and shoved a bread knife through his partner's ribs. On the other hand, Clement could think of a number of murders which had been brought about because the killer did not want to pay the victim back. Mostly it was over drug dealing but sometimes it was just a money loan. Clement had dealt with sons who blew parents' money on coke and wild business schemes and then killed the parents to avoid the repayment. Could Schaffer have actually been owed money by somebody? That was possible. It could have been a drug debt, or a bet. Experience had taught Clement that the amount was immaterial. People could kill for ten dollars or ten thousand.

Still, he was left with an overhanging question. Somebody had sliced Dieter Schaffer's head open like a melon, then kicked and beaten him before changing his bloodied shirt for a clean one. Who would do that and why?

12

The peppery smell of eucalypts hovered over him as he drifted into a zone that verged on sleep yet was not, for he was aware of hot dirt beneath his back, and above, blue sky through whispering gum leaves. His senses were on high alert and yet there was an overwhelming inertia about him. He had read of curare, the poison certain natives used to immobilise their prey, and supposed it could induce a sensation close to this. The police investigation neither deterred nor stimulated him. He was curious yes, but it ran in parallel to him and could not stop him. Nothing could. The axe he'd leave here until needed again. If it were found, unlikely but not impossible, the police would stake out the place. As a precaution he had left a number of safeguards starting with the broken branch in the shrub that blocked the narrow track into here. If anybody pushed through, the branch would fall to the ground.

He was, he admitted, disappointed a croc had not eaten Schaffer. That would have made his day. Still, there was a lot to enjoy: Schaffer's skull cracking, the feel of his boot in his chest. Any fool who watched TV these days knew how much 'trace' boots carried in their grooves so they had been the first things discarded, a long way from here.

He felt a burning pinch in his hand and sat up.

Something had nipped him. He searched, found an ant, red. He crushed it between his fingers.

Things were in hand. Protected by higher powers, he had been led, had he not, or more correctly carried like Moses in that basket, downstream by a flowing source that existed outside of him, to his destiny. The task had seemed impossible at the outset but everything had fallen into place. If he wanted he could act right now but he would rather wait. For so long he had lived as if he were made of cardboard. There had been momentary glimpses of a much better existence but now every new second his heart pumped life. Yet this was how it could have been all along. This was how it should have been, how it would be from here on.

His preparations had been extensive. Had he missed anything? Was there anything to give him up before he was ready?

He picked through his precautions and could find nothing lacking. He stood and brushed off the dirt. It was as if he had been immersed in the land, part of the landscape. That was a joyous sensation, this feeling of wholeness, permanence.

In the beginning, what would happen to him after had not been a consideration. If he were caught, so be it. If not, he had accomplished his task. Care for his own safety had seemed mean-spirited and self-serving but now he was beginning to feel a shift within, as if this new state, this aliveness, could be permanent. Wouldn't that be apt: in the blood of his enemies, he would actually be reborn?

He kept the thought at bay. It was dangerous to get ahead of himself. He had sworn to do this without contemplation of his own future. He mustn't complicate things. The stones must fall wherever.

And yet...

He remembered the ceremony he had witnessed in

the flicker of campfire. The men painted like ghosts, the drone of the didgeridoo, the clap and stomp of flesh, so like a more familiar theology, the spirit was both God and man. He had committed to memory the dance. He found his limbs moving now as if of their own accord, given life by a force outside of him. The words didn't matter. The drone of the didgeridoos lived in his memory. He swung right foot down, left foot down, shifted weight, turned, scooped dirt and threw it into the air, and as he did so felt even more power, like he was drawing it from the very heart of this great earth.

13

At five o'clock Clement's team, including Lisa Keeble, was assembled in the main area of the Major Crime unit. Risely slipped out of his office and propped himself against the wall. Clement had wheeled in a whiteboard and written up the most important points. Manners poked his head in to inform Clement he was printing off the contact list from the phone. Clement studied the group which sat facing him over chairs and desks. It was now around thirty hours since he'd found the body and though he felt time slipping by, he refused to let that hurry him.

'Okay, anything new, before we begin?'

Lisa Keeble stuck a finger in the air and spoke at the same time.

'Perth Coroner has checked the body over and confirmed death was caused by blood loss and the blow to the head. The other trauma was inflicted while the victim was still alive, definitely some after the head trauma but we can't be certain there wasn't also a beating beforehand. Also spoke to Rhino who checked fingerprints from the drawers. Two sets: yours and Schaffer's.'

She made nothing of having already identified Schaffer's prints herself. Clement supplied the conclusion.

'So either Schaffer removed the computer himself or somebody was careful and probably wore gloves.'

'Rhino also believes the murder weapon is an axe not a machete.'

Clement wrote AXE on the board, alongside time of death which he had written as BETWEEN 9PM WEDNESDAY AND 1AM THURSDAY.

'How about the Kelly yard, anything?'

'Briony has processed it but we have no analysis yet as to whether any trace matches the Jasper Creek crime scene; ditto where you were attacked. But I did find a few traces of gravel near where you were hit and also where I think the bike was parked, that didn't seem to be anywhere else on Schaffer's property.'

'You think the attacker may have transferred it?' Clement said.

'It's possible. I didn't find it on your shoes for example and it would make sense that if it came from boots it might be where the bike was parked.'

'But none in the house?'

'No.'

Nat Restoff looked around to his colleagues. 'You being attacked has to be related, doesn't it?'

Clement could have given him a lecture on jumping to conclusions but he restrained himself.

'We need to let the facts tell us what is and isn't related.' He looked over at Shepherd to prompt his report.

'I've done all around McDougall. Nobody saw anything or heard anything unusual except Mrs Kelly. At the creek there's no sign of the weapon, in the creek or the bush.'

'So our murderer may have taken it with him. Mal? Any gambling history with Schaffer?'

Gross shook his head. 'None of the bookies I know had dealings with him. But these days there's so much online gambling ...'

He threw his hands up to emphasise the vastness of possibility.

'We need that computer.'

Clement wrote COMPUTER on the board and underscored it.

It was Graeme Earle's turn. He had checked with Schaffer's neighbours. They were a kilometre away from him on either side so they rarely had much to do with Schaffer except to borrow or return a tool, or pass each other on the highway. No alarm bells rang for him when interviewing them. Neither of the neighbours recalled seeing regular visitors to Dieter Schaffer's. They described him as a bit of a hermit. None of them saw motorcycles around. None of them rode motorcycles.

'Schaffer owned his place outright, two hectares, paid cash three years ago. Three years ago he opened his savings account with a transfer of around twelve thousand dollars from a German bank and for the last year his balance has remained steady around eight thousand. He pulls a few hundred out now and again and deposits a few hundred, always cash. I've gone through all the documents we found and sorted them into receipts and so forth. There is only one letter, in German. I've got a friend who is German, Ellie. She is translating it as we speak.'

'You can use the computer to translate.' Having scattered this wisdom, Shepherd sat back, superior.

'Really?' Mal Gross was as surprised as Earle.

'Yeah, most languages.'

Gross was working his way through it. 'But you'd have to scan it or type it first.'

'Anyway ...' Clement urged the story on.

Earle continued. The letter writer was a 'Mathias', no surname, dated three months ago. The other stuff was various computer printouts from Google pages, a lot of them to do with Hamburg, especially the football club.

'Maybe he was homesick?' offered Gross.

'There were these from German newspaper websites.' Earle held up the pages Clement had spied among the football stuff. 'Ellie's having a go at them for me too.'

'Looks like a crime scene.' Lisa Keeble was craning forward to check out the page Clement had noted.

'He was an ex-cop,' offered Gross. He didn't extrapolate but they got the point, Schaffer's interest might be natural.

Earle held up the old newspaper clipping showing a young Dieter Schaffer in uniform.

'Back in seventy-three he got a citation for bravery. Knife-wielding loony was holding a mother and kid hostage, Schaffer got called in off the street, and tackled the guy unarmed, alone.'

And now on the other side of the world he gets an axe buried in his head, thought Clement.

'Anything on the sister?'

'I've asked Immigration to get back to us with next of kin address but haven't had a chance to follow it up.'

Manners pushed into the room and, over the heads of those seated, handed a printout to Clement. 'Three of them have records, two for possession of cannabis, one for assault.'

Clement addressed his team as he digested this and scanned the page.

'Phone contacts off Schaffer's mobile. Gerd Osterlund, a businessman, I've interviewed him. A Mitchell Karskine. Looks like he had some form years ago, petty stuff, pissing in public, and an assault that had him placed on a good behaviour bond.'

Clement suspected this would be the Mitch he'd

met at The Anglers. The assault meant he had to be considered somebody of interest.

'Jenny Messiano, Rory Clipsall, possession of cannabis. Then Trent Jaffner, Sally Nightcliff and Romano Grigio.'

The uniforms were smirking from local knowledge.

'Potheads,' explained Jo di Rivi.

Clement turned and wrote MOTIVE on the board and, under that, POT. 'So the people in his contacts are most likely his clients. We can't rule out that one of them was into him and wouldn't or couldn't pay, so took him out; or was just greedy for that matter. How big was his crop?'

'About as big as a one-man operation would allow,' said Graham Earle.

'We have to ask what Nat mentioned before: is the break-in at Schaffer's house related to his killing or not? Was the assault on me related? If related, is this about the pot or the missing computer or both? Was the same person responsible or different people? We need to look for facts, people, that will tell us what the right direction is.'

Shepherd stuck a hand up.

'Yes, Shep.'

'It could have been a crime of opportunity at the creek. But then the kids show up and the killer has to take off before he can take anything. But he knows where Schaffer lives so he goes back to score what he can there.'

The kids hadn't mentioned hearing anything but, in their state, who knew?

'True.' It was a sound point.

Shepherd sat back, chuffed.

'Are we sure it's not the kids?' Angus Parker was a large constable, early thirties, used to being on the front line. Clement glanced at Risely, whose look suggested he was asking the same question.

'It's not them kids.' Jared Taylor twisted around in his chair to address Parker. 'They're not going to go out in the middle of a creek when they think there's a croc around. They'd just leave him. Maybe drag him to the edge.'

Clement spoke in support. 'I'm confident they're telling the truth. There was an area about fifty metres back where a vehicle had recently been parked. That could have been the killer.'

'Any decent forensic evidence from there?' Risely asked from the back.

Keeble explained she had paid particular attention to the area but there was no litter, no blood. 'There was part impression of a boot in the sand. I made a cast.'

Shepherd tried his hand again. 'So it could have been anybody parked there, not necessarily anything to do with this case.'

'It could have,' said Lisa, 'but virtually every car that parks in the bush here leaves some kind of litter. Beer cans, cigarette stubs, chip packets, tissues. They're all slobs. This one left nothing, like somebody was being careful.'

Clement had been thinking about Schaffer's drug operation.

'The way Schaffer lived was extremely frugal. Even with only a dozen regular clients he would have made surplus cash which he probably wouldn't put in a bank. People involved in drugs sniff that kind of thing out.'

'So maybe somebody figured he had a stash and killed him for it?' Lisa Keeble was following the reasoning.

Earle had a habit of chewing his pen. He pulled one from his mouth to point out that the shack had been thoroughly searched and nothing had turned up.

'Two hectares, that's a lot of land to dig a hole,' said Mal Gross.

Clement cautioned he was just floating theories but laid out some scenarios. 'The reason the killer didn't take the wallet might have been he didn't need it. He could have stolen Schaffer's stash then killed him; or beaten him, found where he'd hidden it, killed him, then stolen the cash.'

Risely eased himself off the wall, liking this train of thought. 'Schaffer could even have carried it on him, or in his car. I've seen it before.'

Everybody was nodding like this could make sense. The change of shirt still nagged at Clement but he wrote STASH? on the board anyway.

'Has anybody had any bright ideas on why the killer would change Schaffer's shirt?'

Shepherd had a stab. 'DNA? Trying to degrade it.'

Keeble couldn't see it. 'Why leave the bloodied original shirt?'

Clement sensed they were running out of steam. 'Okay, there are promising lines of enquiry here. Also we can't ignore the fact Schaffer was a policeman. However unlikely, we need to consider some criminal may have caught up with him. I'll ring Hamburg and see if they can tell me anything of interest. In the meantime, Graeme, you and I will go through his phone list and interview each of the people on it. Shep, you, Angus and Jared search every inch of that property for a stash. The rest of you, I want you looking for the computer and any whisper Dieter Schaffer had a stash. Even if he didn't, somebody may have thought he did.'

He warned them all they would be working through the weekend but there was no need to start a search of the property until light tomorrow.

'And the car, can we make sure there's no stash hidden anywhere in it?'

Keeble announced it was in the compound out the back of the station and she would get onto it right away.

Risely stayed behind after the rest had shuffled out. 'There could be something in this business of a stash. The killer could have gone back to take the plants too but you got in the way. I'll tell the media we are pursuing several lines of enquiry. Perth is all over it now so it's going to get hectic.'

'Well, let them get their pictures at the creek and we'll follow the leads up.'

Risely disappeared into his office. Clement looked up the time in Hamburg on his computer and saw it was morning, a suitable time to call. It was only as he checked for a telephone number it occurred to him he might need to speak German. It wasn't like he hadn't pursued overseas lines of inquiry before, but it had been a while, and he'd gotten rusty. Things that had been second nature were leaving him. His work was the one compartment of his life he had been able to take as a given—if that went, what was he? Could he really afford to stay so far away from the action in this backwater? And what was the point? Either there was no work or a case presented that drew him away from the only reason he was there in the first place. Clement tried the number indicated. He wasn't even sure he had the country code correct and was half-surprised that he'd got it right. He was answered in German and did his best to communicate his needs. Eventually he was passed onto some English-speaking young woman and tried again. The young woman explained she understood he was a 'police' in Australia but he should put his request in writing.

Of course this was what he should have done in the first place. In Perth he would have had translators or other support staff to get this in train.

He hung up having achieved nothing except an email

address. He wrote a short letter requesting to speak to any current or former police about Dieter Schaffer, and asking if somebody from Hamburg police might visit 'Mathias' and get him to contact him direct. He ran it through the translator and sent it off.

Earle was checking his computer screen and looked up as Clement emerged.

'Why don't you go home and have dinner?' said Clement. 'I'll pick you up at nine and we'll pay a few visits.'

'I can work through.'

'No need. Get a break, get fresh, we've got a bit to knock over.'

By now it was a little after six. A thought occurred. Clement rang Marilyn's house and his stomach tightened at the thought of her mother answering. He was in luck though. It was Phoebe. He apologised right off.

'I'm really sorry about the weekend.'

'That's okay.'

'You're going away on your friend's boat.'

'Mmm. It should be fun.'

'Have you had dinner?'

'Not yet.'

'Would you like to have dinner with me?'

The slightest hesitation. 'Okay.'

He was not going to offer her the chance to reconsider. 'I'm on my way. Tell Mum I'll have you back by eight.'

He hung up and grabbed his keys before Marilyn could intervene. On the way out he passed Mal Gross hunched over his desk demolishing a hamburger. Gross waved as Clement took the back door through to the yard where Keeble was getting started on the car with Jared Taylor and a mechanic. He felt guilty he was deserting them but did not consider hanging around.

'I'll be on my mobile if you need me.' He threw the comment like a chip to a seagull and hurried to his car.

...

The drive to Marilyn's house took around thirty minutes, a lot less than it legally should have. He turned up the familiar driveway that snaked over a magnificent bluff. The sun was red pink in its last throes of the day, the ocean a mirror. Old Nick had been at the game a long time. In the glory days of Broome, before the cultured pearl farm operations, the oysters of the region had yielded many pearls and Nick had claimed his share. During the 80s the Japanese had moved in, paying full-tote odds for existing businesses and generous incentives to keep the former proprietors involved. That was one reason the driveway was smoother than any you'd likely find in town. The residence came into view. Clement could query how Geraldine raised her daughter but not her garden. It was lush and bright with pinks and violets. This time of night it glowed. Tall palms gave it majesty. At least one gardener was employed full time but it looked like he had headed home, for the only cars visible in the carport near the house were those of Geraldine and Marilyn. Brian lived in Perth and used Marilyn's car when here so this didn't mean he wasn't in situ. The driveway culminated in a loop where you could park within easy walking distance of a typical big homestead-style house circa 1920 that would not have been out of place on a horse-breeding property. Crimson bougainvilleas and frangipanis followed the line of the veranda. Vines offering small pink and yellow flowers twirled around the poles which, like the rest of the house, were white and seemingly always freshly painted. Nick had done extensions back in the 80s but retained the single level. People who made their living from the sea didn't need a bedroom view of the ocean. Nick figured he could smell and hear it from his porch. If he wanted the view he could walk five hundred metres and enjoy a beer looking out over the ocean that stretched as far as the eye could see. Paths led to a small gazebo and old stables dating from the 30s. Clement remembered kissing Marilyn in that gazebo, reaching up under her skirt. He tossed the memory. It wasn't helpful. He climbed the steps and was about to rattle the oval-shaped flywire door when it sprang open on Phoebe, with a smile bright as the kind of globes that burned in ceilings before environmental prefects hushed them.

'I'm ready.'

Clement tried to see any of himself in her but as usual failed. Mind you there wasn't much of Marilyn either except the shape of her eyes. Unfortunately that characteristic was shared by Geraldine, who loomed out of the grey interior. She was a traditionalist so he guessed the glass in her hand contained gin and soda.

'Eight at the latest.'

'Marilyn and Brian here?'

'Brian's overseas on business. Marilyn is having a bath.'

Dismissing him as a maid might.

'Thanks, Geraldine. I'll see you later.'

...

He enjoyed opening the door for Phoebe and watching her wriggle into the passenger seat, a big girl now, the baby seat probably expunged from her memory. As a special treat, he told her, he was taking her to the Mimosa.

'I love the Mimosa. The lasagne is so yum. We go there every Tuesday.'

Not so special then, he guessed, but it didn't matter. This was enough, having her beside him, her pretty shoes not quite touching the floor.

'So tell me about the boat.'

Phoebe couldn't tell him much at all. Only that it

was big with sails but an engine too in case there was a problem: Mummy had checked. Of course she had, Marilyn missed her vocation by fifty years, she should have been of those wartime code-breakers; nothing would have escaped her. He tried to elicit something about Phoebe's friend Ashleigh.

'She has problems with her teeth.'

That was about all he learned by the time they reached the resort. A feature of resorts here was the outdoor dining setting, Tahitian lamps, cobbled walkways, tables that sat square on the ground. The dining area was a quarter full. They had beaten the rush but only just.

'You want a Coke?'

'Mango and orange please.'

Everything made him aware of the growing distance between them, despite his efforts. The same Irishman took their orders. Clement followed his daughter's lead and asked for two juices. He ordered the lasagne for her and a chicken salad for himself.

'Not the barista tonight?'

From the waiter's face, Clement realised he hadn't been recognised. The waiter did a good job of covering.

'Oh no, only till five.'

Clement and Phoebe sat in silence waiting for their drinks. It reminded Clement of so many evenings like this with her mother. Phoebe stared out into the growing gloom. That look like she was off thinking her own undisturbed thoughts, maybe that was how he'd seemed to Marilyn, impenetrable. Much as he was curious about Brian and Marilyn, he avoided that subject.

'And are you going diving?'

'I don't know. I think Ashleigh has a wetsuit.'

He had taught Phoebe to swim and an image hit him: water wings inflated with his breath encircling her tiny arms, goggles making her face laugh-out-loud cute.

'Ashleigh's dad fishes but I don't want to kill any fish.'

He lit upon an attractive young woman just arriving with a similarly good-looking young man. It was only when her eyes widened too in recognition that he clicked it was the young woman from the Honky Nut, dressed up for the night. She said something to her partner and started towards him. Twenty-four hours earlier Marilyn had advanced on him almost in this exact spot. Hoping for a better reception he rose from his chair.

'It's incredible,' she said with a kind of wonder in her voice that he associated with yoga and activities alien to him. 'I was only just thinking I have to contact you.'

She smiled at Phoebe. 'Hi, I'm Selina.'

He hadn't even taken her name before, more proof he was on the way out.

'My daughter,' Clement threw a hand out in her direction. 'Phoebe.'

'Nice to meet you, Phoebe. What are you having?'

'Lasagne.'

Selina made her finger into a gun. 'Good choice.' She turned to Clement. 'I remembered something ... about that man.'

14

It took Clement a moment to orient himself and realise she was talking about Schaffer, trying to avoid mentioning murder victims in front of Phoebe.

'Oh, right. Excuse us for a minute, sweetie. You okay?'

'Yes.'

He envied her easy assurance, mother's girl there. Clement indicated Selina should move to the terrace cocktail bar which was about twenty metres away.

'It was only on the way in with my boyfriend. A motorcycle passed us going the other way and I suddenly remembered about that man, the German.'

Clement's curiosity was whetted. He threw a glance at Phoebe who seemed unperturbed, balancing a fork over the stem of her spoon.

Selina continued, 'It could be nothing, but around the last time I saw him, it might have even been the last time, I was putting the bins out at the back of the café, there's a carpark there, you know it?'

Clement was aware of it, a flat area of bitumen. Businesses from parallel streets backed onto it so customers could park and enter via back entrances.

'I heard some kind of argument, not exact words but you know, like ... an argument, and when I looked up I saw the German man arguing with a biker.'

'You mean a man on a motorcycle?'

'Yes. Like a bikie, you know, big muscles and tatts but I didn't see any colours. I'm so stupid I forgot all about it.'

'It's not stupid. You didn't recognise the biker?'

'No. We get them in the café sometimes. The Dingos, I think they are called? But I don't know if he was one of them. He wasn't wearing colours and I hadn't seen him before. He was Maori, I'm pretty sure.'

'Could he have been aboriginal?'

'I don't think so. I'm part Islander. I think he was Maori.'

'Maybe you heard him speak?'

'Maybe but I can't remember any words, not exact ones, just he seemed angry.'

'He seemed angry or Dieter Schaffer seemed angry?'

She cast her mind back.

'The German man, actually. The biker guy he was just sitting on his bike kind of calm, with the attitude, you know? I thought, I don't know what I thought, maybe the biker had nearly caused an accident or something. I didn't stay. I went back inside. They weren't throwing punches or anything. I'm so sorry I didn't think of this before.'

'No, that's fine. That's great you remembered.'

The waiter had materialised with the juices. 'You want these here?'

'No take them to the table, please.'

'Food won't be long.'

Clement turned back to Selina. 'Can you think hard when this was? It's important.'

'It was a Monday. I'm pretty sure of that. Our bins are always full after the weekend. But I can't remember if it was last Monday or the one before. Last Monday I think. Yes, last Monday.'

'What time?'

'Morning. I usually do it just after the early rush, I'm guessing about nine.'

'Can you tell me anything about the bike? Colour, size, anything?'

'It was big, you know. I think it was black but I don't remember. I wasn't looking at the bike.'

'Was there anybody else around?'

'I didn't notice.' She closed her eyes to remember. 'There were a few cars, not many, somebody may have been in them.'

'Do you know if there are any CCTV cameras in that carpark?'

'There might be one at the back of the bottle shop on the opposite side.'

It was something he could look into.

'Could I ask you to do something for me after your dinner?'

'Sure.'

'Would you mind dropping into the station and seeing if you can identify the man you saw? We have photos there.'

'Um, okay.'

'Thanks, that would be a great help. I'll call the desk sergeant, his name is Mal. He'll take care of you.'

'Alright.'

'Thanks again, Selina.'

She moved off. He looked over to see Phoebe's juice almost drained, she was kicking her legs happily. He quickly dialled the station and told Mal Gross he was sending an attractive woman his way.

'We may have a lead.'

He explained the nature of Selina's information and Gross said he would make sure the biker file was ready. Part of Clement wanted to be there when she went through the books but the argument she witnessed might prove to have been nothing after all. Running down the contacts in Schaffer's phone was the priority. He asked Gross to see if there were any CCTV cameras in the carpark and mentioned the bottle shop.

'If you can get the footage, we're looking at the Monday before the murder, the morning, specifically around nine.'

Gross said he would get onto it.

Clement returned to the table, buoyed. At Schaffer's, right after he had been hit, he'd heard a motorcycle leaving; Dieter Schaffer had been in an argument with a biker forty-eight hours before his death. Things were lining up.

'Is she your girlfriend?' Phoebe asked as he sat down. There was no judgment, no guile, just a straight out question of fact.

'No.'

He pulled a disapproving face. The days when a young woman like Selina might be his girlfriend had long gone. He'd had many chances working cases. Unlike most of his colleagues, he never took them.

'But Mummy has a boyfriend?'

'Yes. Doesn't mean I have to have a girlfriend though.'

Their meals arrived and Phoebe instantly started on her lasagne.

'Are you the head detective at your work?'

'We're a team. We all have our jobs to do.'

She wasn't convinced. 'There's always a boss.'

They ate their meal quickly. Phoebe knew she was on a time limit but wanted a banana split with chocolate topping. He watched her demolish it while he played with scenarios about the biker. Had he killed Schaffer, then gone to Schaffer's place, perhaps to steal the dope plants? Were they involved in distributing dope?

As soon as the last mouthful of ice-cream was downed, he motioned Phoebe to join him. There was no way he would have her back home by eight.

It was around eight-twenty by the time he dropped Phoebe back. She hugged his neck before she ran inside. He saw the porch light come on and a shadow at the door and then she was gone, and in this he saw what he feared might be the inevitable destiny of their relationship: shadows and absence. He spun the wheel and left fast and arrived at Earle's ten after nine. Earle was waiting in the driveway of his modest brick home enjoying a smoke. His fibreglass runabout, his pride and joy, slept on its cradle beside him. He stamped out the cigarette and hauled his big body into the passenger seat.

'Who's first?'

Clement thought they should leave Mitch till last but other than that it was a matter of proximity. On the way to the first of Schaffer's contacts, Sally Nightcliff, he filled Earle in about the confrontation between a biker and Dieter Schaffer.

'Think it might be the bloke who conked you?'

'Could be. The witness is going to the station after her dinner.'

...

In the end it didn't take them anywhere near as long as Clement had estimated to locate most of those in Schaffer's phone contact list. Sally Nightcliff was not at home but her housemate pointed them in the direction of the Roebuck Bay Hotel. They found her and another of those on the list, Romano Grigio, drinking in different parts of the pub. Both had the demeanour of chronic potheads, were close to sixty, wearing worn shirts soaked in their BO. They had alibis. Grigio was playing cards with mates and gave details. Sally Nightcliff was in bed with her on–off boyfriend after a night of karaoke. Clement's bullshit detector did not trigger and a glance at Earle suggested it was the same for him.

Jenny Messiano was located at home with her de facto watching TV, telltale dope seeds on the coffee table. There was a feeling of desperation in that house, coiled animosity, mainly towards each other, an atmosphere not foreign to Clement. He didn't rule them out as the kind who might kill somebody for a supposed stash. Jenny Messiano had a shift job packing meat at the abattoir, so on the face of it she was alibied. The de facto worked the same shift. Earle would check up on them. Trent Jaffner was a strikeout. According to his mother he'd driven to Port Hedland a week ago for a job. Something more to be followed up. Rory Clipsall was a young dude with a very old panel van who dossed wherever he could, often in his van. They found him at a mate's place with rap on the speakers. Clement's prejudice against rap was not enough to convince him this stoner would be up to killing anybody, at least not without leaving a trace the size of an elephant print. Clipsall had no idea Dieter was dead. Clement didn't think the kid was putting it on, he looked like he was out of it 24/7 and the fact he couldn't remember where he was the night Dieter was killed rang true.

Essentially every one of the people they interviewed reacted in the same way. First, blank denial about buying cannabis off Dieter Schaffer. When assured they wouldn't be charged with dope offences if they levelled, they became wary but hopeful. What surprised Clement though was how much, or more correctly how little, Dieter Schaffer had been charging for his dope. If they were to be believed, and again Clement found he had no reason not to, old Dieter was doing 'mate's rates', pulling in about half of what Clement had originally estimated. When Clement suggested Dieter Schaffer was their dope dealer, Sally Nightcliff's response was typical. She wrinkled her greyish skin and said, 'Dieter wasn't no dealer. He was just a mate who grew dope and sold a bit around the traps for beer money. He gave it away sometimes.'

Clement and Earle asked judicious questions about whether Dieter ever flaunted cash. His clients claimed he never seemed to have that much money. Romano Grigio confirmed Dieter liked to punt.

'He played poker with us a few times but he wasn't very good. I had to slip him some cash and he gave me some heads in return. I told him to stick to the ponies but I never saw him bet big or win big. Fifty bucks here or there, that's all.'

...

After they left Clipsall, the last one in the run, Clement and Earle stood by the car. The night was soft now.

'I'm not convinced there is a stash.' Even if it did niggle, Clement had long ago learned not to get too attached to theories the facts didn't support.

Earle shrugged. 'He could have other customers he didn't put in his phone. I mean, if he was supplying bikies he could afford to give the stuff away to his mates.'

'They all say the same thing though. He was just selling a bit to get by.'

'If he was smart that's what he'd let them think. And even if he had no big money somebody might have thought he did. You know what it's like with these types. They love a rumour.'

The suggestion could not be ignored. Clement recalled an old Croatian pensioner in Perth who had been bashed to death in a home invasion because the whisper was he kept cash in the house. The reality was he was on the bones of his arse. Meanwhile, they still had Mitch Karskine to interview.

Clement checked his phone and realised that forty minutes earlier he had received a text from Mal Gross to call him. He did so now. Gross had only been home a half-hour and was sitting down with a quiet beer.

'The girl came in but we drew a blank. I showed her photos of all the Dingos we've got on file. She said it wasn't any of them. I even pulled out a couple of likely types from the general files but she said it wasn't them either. I also checked up on the CCTV. You were right, there's a camera at the back of the bottle shop and they say it's working. I sent Manners to pick up the hard drive and find what we need.'

Clement left Gross to his beer and passed the news on to Earle as they drove to the address they had for Karskine, a duplex circa 1980, one level, salmon brick, dark grey concrete driveway. Various fish traps were lying around the small front yard. Apart from a porch light over the door, there were no lights in either this or the neighbour's. There was also no car in the carport.

'What time does the Cleopatra close?'

The words were barely out of Clement's mouth when an early-model Toyota Hilux cruised in and parked. The headlights extinguished. Karskine climbed out and looked them up and down. He was wearing an AC/DC t-shirt, shorts and thongs.

'This about Schultz?'

'Yeah. You want to go inside?'

'Nicer out here, believe me.'

Clement had to assume Karskine had been drinking but he didn't seem drunk. Mitch Karskine leaned back against his truck like they were old pals. Earle jerked a thumb to the adjoining unit as if they might be disturbing them.

'What about them?'

'Fuck 'em. What do you want to know?'

He looked directly at Clement as he spoke, pulled out a cigarette pack and offered it. They declined. He stuck a cigarette between his lips and lit it with a disposable lighter.

'You bought pot off Dieter Schaffer.'

'Is there a law against that?' Karskine smirked and flicked his ash. 'Yeah, okay. He'd fix me up with a little pot here or there. Ex-cop and all.'

'You didn't tell me this before.'

'I'm not stupid. I've been in the slammer. You probably know that. That's why you're here. I'm an ex-con, I bought pot off Schultz, gee I must have killed him.'

'Where were you the night he was murdered?' said Earle.

Mitch Karskine pointed his cigarette at his unit. 'Asleep. I had work next day.'

'No witness?'

'Not that night.'

Clement stepped out of the slipstream of the cigarette smoke.

'We've spoken to his other clients. They say Schaffer wasn't into it for the money.'

'That's right. It was the cheapest stuff around. Dieter wanted a few friends that's all.'

Earle changed tack. 'You ever been to his place?'

The moment's hesitation gave him away and he knew it.

'Once. He asked me to help connect his water tank. I used to be a plumber. Sort of.'

'So you knew where his dope crop was?'

'I wasn't the only one. Shit, anybody who went there could have seen it.'

Karskine was the first person Clement had spoken to who admitted having been in the shack.

'You remember if he had a computer?'

Karskine cast through his memory, shook his head. 'Might have. I don't remember that much about the place except this big fucking framed poster of his soccer team. Frankfurt?'

'Hamburg.'

'Some paintings, abo stuff.'

'You mind if we have a look around the house?'

'Yes I do mind. Nothing personal but you might plant something. It's been known to happen.'

'We can get a warrant,' said Earle evenly.

'Go for it.'

By the time they got warrants he'd have time to dispose of any evidence. Clement tried again.

'Are you sure there's nobody can alibi you? We don't want to waste our time or yours.'

Karskine thought back. It seemed an effort. 'Wednesday night.' He was in a galaxy far far away. Then back on earth. 'Bill called. About ten. A bit before maybe.'

'Bill Seratono?'

'Yeah.'

Even if that were true it didn't rule out Karskine although it meant the window to kill Dieter Schaffer was narrow. Clement figured it might be best to keep that to themselves.

'That's good. We'll confirm it with him.'

'You own a motorcycle, Mitch?' Earle rested against the ute, mates.

'Wish I did. Why?'

'Just thought you might. Lots of guys with boats own bikes. I got a boat. Fibreglass runabout. Bung the trail bike in sometimes.'

'Not me. I'm a bit tired. I like to get my beauty sleep.'

Earle looked to Clement for direction. Clement nodded slowly to Karskine.

'Thanks for your time.'

As they walked to the car Earle remarked that the phone call didn't get Karskine off the hook.

'It would have been a squeeze but he could have done it.'

'Yeah, but if there's any evidence I don't want him destroying it before we turn up with a warrant.'

'We'll be lucky to get one before tomorrow midday.'

'Think he's the sort who could kill somebody with an axe?'

Earle yawned. 'Can't rule him out. I'll speak to the neighbours, see if they remember if his car was in. You know this Bill?'

'Seratono, old schoolmate, it might be best if you call him.'

Clement hadn't got that hunter's instinct that Karskine was his man. Yet maybe he'd left that behind with the rest of his life. He felt he was running in beach sand here. He phoned Risely, caught him at his house and filled him in on what they'd learned so far. Karskine pricked Risely's interest, so did the talk of bikers.

'You got the CCTV footage?'

'Going back to check it out now.'

'I'll see you here.'

...

'The quality is really poor and it's shot from a distance on the other side of the carpark so it's not sharp.'

Manners was hunched over his desk in the room they used for audiovisual matters. Screens, players, mixing desks were banked all around making it claustrophobic. Clement sat beside Manners in an adjustable chair; Earle and Risely stood, all eyes glued to a forty-two inch flat-screen monitor. The video was typical grainy, grey CCTV footage. The time code showed Mon 13-01-14, 09.12. The camera was situated high and captured the area about ten metres either side of the bottle shop where it was mounted, across the width of the carpark so that any cars parked on the other side might have their rear-number plate visible but nothing much more of the car. From this angle the rear of the Honky Nut was down at the right-hand corner but was not captured by the camera so Clement had to estimate where Selina's position would have been. Manners tapped the screen in that region to show him.

'Here.'

The carpark was lightly populated for vehicles, only five in sight including the rear of Dieter Schaffer's Pajero which had been parked facing where the back of the Honky Nut would be. Dieter Schaffer, identifiable by shape only, advanced alongside his car gesticulating with a biker. No colours, no numberplate identifiable, not wearing a helmet, facial features a blur.

'Kawasaki, eight hundred, something like that,' offered Mal Gross.

'Any Dingos with a bike like that?'

'One. But he's a lot fatter than this bloke.'

A bit more of Schaffer waving his hands.

'It finishes about now,' said Manners.

And it did with Schaffer offering a dismissive gesture as if shooing a fly. The bike lingered a moment then turned, disappearing quietly off-screen the way it had come. Schaffer lingered before also leaving the screen, presumably into his car because a moment later it reversed and cruised slowly from the carpark. Clement asked for it to be cued again. The sequence was: inactive carpark, Schaffer emerges from top right of screen as if he may have been heading to his car when he saw the biker who at that stage was off-screen. He advances and waits for a second as the bike cruises in and stops. The argument lasts for around forty seconds then the biker rides off. Schaffer leaves in his car, without haste.

'Can they enhance that at HQ?'

Risely wanted to hear the tech man say, 'Yes we can turn any shitty evidence into something pristine.' Clement would have liked that too but Manners offered no consolation.

'Not enough to get a numberplate or a look at his face.'

Clement was wondering if any witness might have been able to hear the conversation.

'Let's try and identify these vehicles, just in case the owners heard something. And I want you to go through the tapes for up to three days before this, and then from this up till last night, see if this bike is there some other time. I'd also like us to get all CCTV footage for the same period we can around Broome, try and identify this biker better and see if we can spot Schaffer's Pajero anytime.'

'That's a big job.' Manners was already sweating in anticipation.

Risely said he could get Perth to assist.

'Good. Let's leave the big picture to them.' Clement rested a hand on Manners' shoulder. 'You just stay with this camera. The biker might have been waiting for Schaffer. He must have had some idea of his movements so maybe he came in before or after. And when you get a chance, I need Mitch Karskine's phone records.'

It would be a grind but they had a number of avenues of inquiry.

Risely announced he was going to bed. 'I'll get onto HQ about some tech support first thing tomorrow. And I'll organise the Karskine warrant. See you in a few hours.'

Earle yawned again. Clement checked his watch. It was two-thirty.

'I'll drop you home.'

Manners looked at him hopefully. Clement could see he wasn't used to the long shifts such a case demanded.

'Get the numbers and details on any of the cars you can, you can come in an hour later tomorrow. I'll be back after I drop Graeme.'

Clement and Earle weaved their way through the

few deserted streets that made up the town centre. Here and there an old poinciana drooped as if gathering all its strength to fight the sun again in a few hours but there was no life; not even a stray dog peeing against a trunk. Clement had the window down and this generated some breeze to fight the humidity. Finally Earle said, 'Pity about the vision.'

Clement was phlegmatic. 'It's more than we had yesterday.'

He pulled up outside Earle's house. It dark and quiet, a front light had been left on.

'See you soon,' said Earle leaving with a wave.

Clement drove back pondering. Dieter Schaffer was proving as elusive as his killer. There was something odd about the man. He was an ex-cop who sold dope; well, he wouldn't be the first but still, he sold it at cut-rates to a small circle of 'friends' and gave it away to strangers. That suggested a low-level distributor. But he was talking of his ship coming in or words to that effect. Bikers meant drugs. Had there been something in the encounter between Schaffer and the biker? Had Schaffer encroached on somebody's territory? But why kill him in such a brutal way and then re-dress him? There was an intimacy in that.

Clement parked in the bay reserved for detectives. Night shift had taken over now. Clement passed a couple of uniforms heading to their vehicle, their voices bells in the still night. The Major Crime section was deserted. Clement sat down at one of the desks thinking about loose ends. Schaffer's client Trent Jaffner was supposedly hours south in Port Hedland. They would have to investigate if this were true or not, along with the other alibies. They had yet to speak to anybody in Hamburg who knew Schaffer. Immigration would have to be chased up about the sister's details. At least the CCTV footage was in train. This was the hard grunt of casework, slow and steady elimination of possibilites. On cue, an exhausted Manners emerged from the audiovisual room.

'I only got the rego on four of the vehicles. Owners' details.'

He handed over a piece of paper with details neatly written.

'Good work. See you tomorrow.'

Clement glanced at the names. None of them meant anything to him. In all likelihood they were staff from the shops. Something Shepherd could follow up in the morning.

...

Clement stood in his jocks in the little apartment above the chandler's staring out over the mute wharf for a long moment. The moon was a fingernail, the air like the hug of an old aunty who after too many sherries refused to let go. Everything was in stasis: Clement, the moment, the whole ocean. He broke that by lying back on his bed underneath the ceiling fan, the thunk of its blades almost calming. How had his life tumbled so effortlessly from where it had been to here? The night he'd met Marilyn, met her properly, had been a night like this, still and muggy, a sprawling backyard party in Mount Lawley, coloured lights slung along the scalloped wall of one of those wide concrete porches. He was a young detective on the rise, on the news sometimes. He'd never had a lot of confidence in himself, not until he'd begun work as a detective. Up till then he saw himself as a kid from the sticks with a very unnoteworthy family. At high school he'd generally been close to the top of his class but it wasn't Harvard. And then mid-twenties he'd slowly hit his stride. He was good at his job, he knew it and so did everybody around him. He even displayed some leadership qualities. It was foreign to him but exciting.

He'd always been the follower, the kid who sat in one of the back seats of a mate's car, never the privileged front, the half-back flanker who wasn't the last picked but never the first. Then he just blossomed and around the time he met Marilyn he was at his peak socially. He had confidence. He felt good about himself, dated women, slept with them usually, and when he looked in the mirror no longer saw the shy kid from the outback with a dumb fringe but a well-dressed man at the top of his game. But even he'd been aware that this braggadocio was surface, non-permanent, fragile, and one glance at Marilyn told him she was from a different tribe and any such approach was doomed. Kylie Minogue was playing on the stereo, no iPods yet, not that he recalled anyway: 'Can't Get You Out Of My Head'. Normally he wasn't big on Kylie but he liked that song, even more when it coincided with the sight of the unknown young woman standing by herself clasping a plastic cup with an elegance that suggested Kenya, white gloves, military men in dress suits and billiards clicking quietly under a ceiling fan. He moved to her, confident he could win her but only if he kept the real Daniel Clement buried in a bottle.

Her dress was watermelon pink. They talked easily. She was a primary school teacher, friend of... memory had long worn down the name of the party's hostess whom he'd never actually met. One of the Fraud guys had a sister who was a teacher—that's how they came to know about the party. After small nonsense talk he played the detective card and Marilyn was impressed.

So are you from around here? And she mentions Broome and he goes you're kidding and then realises she's the daughter of Nick Menop, one of the big pearl guys, and his confidence is cracked and he's worried the old Dan Clement, the real Dan Clement might burst out of the bottle, shattering it. But he's not going to lie, the lie he's propagating isn't about who he was but how he feels about who he was, and when he mentions the caravan park she's not even aware of it, she was down here at boarding school, and it's as if she's the one who is slightly embarrassed. Like girls at parties do, some girl keeps cueing the same Kylie track over and over and normally he hates this but it's so appropriate because he can't get her out of his head. Not on the way back to his flat after he'd left her with a lingering kiss, not the next day when he called her, fighting himself to make it stretch till four in the afternoon because the new Daniel Clement realised there was science to the art of courting just like there was to boxing.

And here he was reliving that moment, that song. He couldn't get her out of his head even now in this pokey 'apartment' but he could mask her for a while. Superimposed over Marilyn and the pink dress came an image of Phoebe climbing out of bed just a few hours from now, ready to head off on her adventure. He soaked himself in regret for just a few more moments, scolded himself for his lies and thanked them for what they had delivered, despite the impermanence of its beauty, and the pain of its loss.

And then he slept.

15

HAMBURG 1979

The car was an icebox. Chill bit through his scarred leather jacket and gnawed on his bones. Eleven minutes had passed since Wallen skulked down the laneway, knocked on the rear door and entered the tacky sex shop which covered for a heroin distribution hub, right here in the heart of the Reeperbahn. Talk about hiding in plain sight. It was so obvious, the drug squad hadn't given it a second thought. And it was extremely convenient for the dealers who could load up with supplies and slip straight out to their ever-eager customers, the hookers of Hamburg. Tempting as the thought of being indoors was, he decided to wait. After sixteen long months, nearly an entire year of that in deep cover, a few more minutes wouldn't hurt.

He had passed on his intelligence to his controller. This would be his next to last buy. He just needed to act as he always did, not give them any grounds for suspicion.

He sat back enveloped in tobacco smoke and let the moody sounds of Elvis Costello dance around him. 'Watching The Detectives'. Ironic. One of the few side-benefits of this job had been his introduction to this British New Wave music, The Stranglers, Elvis Costello, Ian Dury. His colleagues hadn't a clue about this kind of music. The Stones were as adventurous as they got but he'd found himself dealing with a different class of person in his role.

He'd always thought he had pretty good English but maybe there was something he was missing in this weird song. A girl files her nails as she watches the detectives dragging a lake. So has somebody been murdered? Was she part of it? Or is she just an observer, maybe even watching TV? There was a sense of unease in the song, of a truth obscured to the listener. For the briefest instant he allowed his mind to drift forward to what life might be like in a week when the operation was complete. He would lie on the bed that was far too big for the little boy and read stories about lost bears and princes and woodcutters, and his son would have no idea that his father was a modern-day woodcutter out in the forest slaying wolves. Since going under deep cover he'd barely seen his wife or boy. Two days per month, that was all that could be allowed.

The song finished. He ejected the cassette. He preferred vinyl but you couldn't fight technology. He climbed out. The Elbe's breath lashed him. He huddled into his jacket, walked briskly down the lane past rotting garbage to the door and knocked. It swung open on an iron security grill. A huge man looked him up and down, checked he was alone and opened it without a word. There was no heating in here either but it was preferable to the car.

As he headed down the narrow uneven passageway the tall, skinny Wallen was coming the other way, no doubt loaded up with his week's supply. When he started this assignment he had despised Wallen and those like him. They had waited together for their 'stuff' barely exchanging a word, mutually mistrustful. Then one night some skinheads had jumped him near the Hauptbahnhof. He was taking a hammering until

Wallen had appeared. The two of them had quickly turned the tide. Most of his assailants fled but they caught one, and punched and kicked the skinhead into a bleeding pulp. Afterwards they had beer and sausage and Wallen talked about his two small children with a father's pride before heading to the lavatory to shoot up. From then on, he could only pity Wallen. They became friends despite everything, for no longer could he deny the man's humanity.

He stopped by a tall pile of videos, the cover showing a blonde with enhanced breasts spilling from a nurse's uniform, her mouth wrapped around a thick black penis. He asked Wallen how he was doing.

'Rolf has bronchitis and his mother is working tonight. I have to do my rounds and get back to him as soon as I can.'

The dealer couldn't complete his rounds till the early hours of the morning and the guilt played over Wallen's face as clear as a slide show on a white wall.

'You should go on a holiday for a week or two, somewhere sunny, sooner the better.'

He hoped Wallen might take his advice though he knew it was unlikely. He was a user, how would he prise himself away from his supply? But he hoped he did. He didn't want Wallen banged up and his kids suffering. He'd left Wallen's name out of his reports but if he was caught in the raid there would be nothing he could do for him. Wallen gave him a thoughtful look.

'I might do that. We should have a beer later.'

'Sure.'

Then he was gone. Gruen advanced to what they called the vault. Behind that door would be the Emperor, whose real name even now remained unknown. Tonight it was the crew-cut one, Klaus, on sentry duty. Gruen raised his arms for the search as a matter of course. Nobody got into the vault with a weapon.

'You're eating too much strudel,' joked Klaus patting him down. Wallen had told him Klaus had been a mercenary in Africa in the 60s. Klaus had proudly talked about burying enemies alive up to their necks and then driving armoured carriers over them one by one until a prisoner talked and gave them the intelligence they needed. Just as Klaus was down at his ankles, Gruen looked up and saw resting on a high box, momentarily forgotten, the Emperor's cigarette lighter. On impulse Gruen snatched the lighter. Satisfied he was clean, Klaus pressed a buzzer. There was a click as the inside lock was released and the thick steel door swung open.

It didn't matter how many times he'd done it, his sphincter tightened every time, but especially now. He was already cursing his impetuosity. This time next week the Emperor would be in custody, they would know his identity, getting his fingerprints off the lighter would be a waste of time. And he may not even have a record. There was no choice now though, he buried his fear, strode in and the door shut behind him, courtesy of the two interior guards. One bright electric bulb burned over his head. The heroin was packed in bags on a trestle table, already cut to the specific percentage the operation had gauged as optimum. It could have been icing sugar at the supermarkt. The Emperor sat behind it as always and handed him his weekly stock.

'Sometimes dealers think they'll make a little extra, cut the product down a little further. That ever occur to you, Pieter?'

He'd heard the stories of such dealers being sliced apart live by a chainsaw wielded by the seemingly mild man currently sitting in front of him.

'No.'

'You're one of my only distributors who is not a hopeless junkie. Never tempted?'

'Never. I want to make my money and get out.'

'You have ambition?'

'Yes. I suppose so.'

The Emperor sighed. 'In most occupations, ambition is good. But I always get a little worried about ambitious men working below me.' The warning was clear. Don't ever think about crossing me. The Emperor stuck a thin cigar between his lips and looked for his lighter. 'Go. Make us a good profit.'

Gruen headed for the door.

'Wait.'

The blood in Wallen's veins froze solid. He turned and forced himself to look into the Emperor's eyes.

'You've been doing a good job. You keep this up, I can expand your territory.'

He did not answer, probably his tongue would not have worked, instead he inclined his head respectfully and got out.

...

He always felt relieved when he stepped back out into the bitter cold but never so much as tonight. The slicing freeze over your cheeks confirmed you were still alive. The job he was doing was grubby, feeding addicts the drugs that would destroy their lives; but he never had second thoughts. If he wasn't giving them smack someone else would be. Sure he could arrest them instead, some might even be rehabilitated but wasn't it much better to cut off the snake's head and save all those as yet untainted bodies? When medical researchers were trying out a potential lifesaving drug, there had to be a control group, the ones who only got a placebo. His clients were the control group, sacrificed for the benefit of others.

In the movie world, undercover cops could just present themselves as big heroin players, buyers with a heap of cash. That happened sometimes but with the

Emperor and his crew, you had to live it. No going to the quartermaster with your smack and having it bought by the government to be destroyed. The Emperor was always checking up. Your clients could be real or traps. You took nothing for granted.

The ignition took several times to catch but eventually it did. He drove off into a quiet street, carefully pulled the lighter from his pocket, sealed it in an evidence bag and placed it in his glove box. Tomorrow morning he would drop it in the locker at the swimming pool, the collection point.

He drove to the back of the train station, found a park in a lane, did a quick run, selling to a few regular customers and walked through the cold air to a basement bar where he knew he'd find Wallen. Freiheit was once a small bar of dark furniture, low light, a man in a suit playing 'Danke Schoen' on a piano, catering to travelling businessmen and sailors. The piano had gone, along with the sailors and businessmen, the furniture was still dark, the light low but now it was a mecca for the New Wave, with their stovepipe trousers, leather jackets, spiked hair. The band tonight veered towards punk, the singer in a red vinyl nappy, the songs little more than shouting. Not surprisingly, the crowd was thinner than usual, some girls in short skirts, vinyl or tartan held together with big safety pins, ripped stockings, razor blade earrings, stood up the front making a lot of noise. Probably the band's girlfriends, guessed Gruen. Wallen was leaning against the bar. He used his finger to order a beer for Gruen and indicated they should move to the furthest reaches away from the stage. They relocated to a small table behind the staircase.

'Not your taste?'

'Too angry,' said Wallen draining his pilsener. 'Smackheads don't get angry, you know that. We mellow out.'

'Except when a new batch hits the streets.'

Wallen was happy to contradict his statement of a moment before.

'It's like a stampede out there. Jesus, I could have sold half my stuff already but I like to look after the regulars. You?'

'Same. There was a big bust, some Turkish outfit so there's no competition: supply and demand.'

'It's all fucking economics. I studied that, you know?'

'Really?'

'Yeah. I did six months at university but I dropped out. It wasn't for me. You know what I really wanted to be?'

'Musician?'

'Can't sing a note. Archaeologist, that's what I wanted to do; pharaohs' tombs surrounded by hot desert, away from this cold fucking place. You?'

'I wanted to be a tennis player.'

'All those good-looking women?'

They laughed. Wallen sipped his beer and regarded him with the same thoughtful look he had earlier at the porn shop.

'I got to ask you something, man. You a pig?'

It was so direct it rattled Gruen. He could have lied. He should have. 'Yes.'

Wallen took a deep breath, pulled a cigarette from his jacket and lit it. He inhaled fast and deep and blew a stream of smoke to the side. His eyes were cobalt-blue beams boring out of him. 'You're really a fucking cop?'

'Yeah.'

Now Wallen looked anxious. 'You didn't have to tell me.'

'I know, but I don't want to lie to you, we're friends.'

Wallen regarded him suspiciously like this might be a ploy to make him say or do something he would later regret. He shook his head. 'We can't be friends. You lied to me.'

'I had to.'

'Then you should have kept lying. You know if they find out...' He shook his head again, stressed.

'Listen, that's why I'm telling you. You have to get out. Everyone is going down. In my reports I gave you an alias. Nobody knows about you, you can go but it's going to happen soon, any day, and whoever gets caught in the sweep is going to jail for a long time.'

'I can't go. Go where?' The veins were bulging from his neck.

'This time next week the Emperor and his operation will be finished. Sell the shit, take your family and leave.'

Wallen looked trapped. He ran his fingers through his hair. 'This is my fucking living.'

'We both know that can't last. You'll never make thirty, you keep this up.'

Wallen stabbed his finger like a cobra. 'What's to stop me from going to them now, hey?'

'Nothing, except I don't think that's who you are.'

'Those things you told me, about your family? About your boy. Were they lies?'

'No. That's why I am telling you this. That's real.'

A battle seemed to be raging inside Wallen. 'I walk out of here, you going to follow me?'

'No. Wallen, one day, years from now, maybe I'll be somewhere with my boy. Manfred might be sixteen, say. Maybe we're in Luxor, looking at the pyramids and I look across and I see you and your kids, laughing. You're showing them all the stuff about people who lived and died thousands of years before us and I know that whatever shitty things I had to do in my life, I did one good thing. You love your kids, I know you do. This is your chance to really show it. Do it, man, change your fucking life.'

Gruen still wasn't sure why he was acting like this, talking like this, breaking all his training, only that he should.

Wallen stood up. He seemed about to say something but just shook his head and turned to leave.

'Goodbye Wallen.'

Wallen offered the hint of a smile. 'Pyramids are in Giza.'

And then he walked up the stairs.

16

For some reason there was no hammer today but Clement still woke at six a.m. Since childhood he had been possessed of the ability to bid himself wake at the appointed time, no alarm clock needed. He showered, the water tap-dancing on his skin as consciousness warmed. Before shaving he forced himself to truly regard his image in the mirror. For a very long time, maybe twenty years, it was as if he had been looking at the same face every day. Nothing changed. Then just before he left Perth, one day, there it was, a different face, older, void of any belief the next day might be better than the last. Like a lump that appears overnight on your body which you hope will work itself out, he morbidly studied that face hoping for a reversion. Most days he glossed over it. Today he felt obliged to take his medicine, to acknowledge the apex of his life had been reached and he was plunging in a billycart down the other side. How long before a different face looks back at me? he wondered. Another twenty years or is it a law of diminishing returns, and maybe it's only ten years next time? He was ruminating on this as he searched the rack for a clean shirt, found one, and dressed. Finally the anonymous worker began clanking. It made Clement feel less of an island and he smiled, wondering why the man had begun late. Slept in? Car didn't start? Gave the girlfriend one? Late start Saturday? Clement had no such luxury.

...

Graeme Earle was at his desk by the time Clement reached the office. He had spoken to Bill Seratono who confirmed he had called Karskine around ten on Wednesday. They had chatted for about ten minutes.

'You think he'd lie to us?'

'I hadn't seen him for years but I doubt it. The phone records will tell us.'

Earle waved printed documents.

'Ellie finished translating the letter from "Mathias". 'It's not very long. Sounds like an old work colleague. The Reeperbahn is the red-light district apparently. She also translated the news printouts and newspaper article.'

Clement entered his office to find that Lisa Keeble with trademark efficiency had left a report on Clement's desk stating they had been over Schaffer's car and found no cash anywhere. It was signed with the time of two forty-five a.m. He did not expect she'd be in before ten. He turned his attention to the letter.

My old pal,

How are you travelling out there in the land of crocodiles? It's a while since I wrote, I know but Greta is being married to a Swiss fellow and it has been chaos. Can you believe it? I can't. It seems like yesterday we were all together. Only the other night I was thinking of that time we had young Pieber nab the transvestite. I'll never forget his face. Heinrich has had some health scares with his heart but I think it's alright now, after a minor operation. And he was always the healthy one. But enough of that. Any young women taking your fancy there? Although I suppose young now is under fifty. I am still working two days a week, not that I really need the money but it keeps me occupied and I like being around my worker pals. Stacking supermarket shelves is a long way from the Reeperbahn. Anyway, please write to me, I enjoyed your last letter and was envious of your description of the hot nights there. It's cold as hell here as usual. My blood and bones are getting thinner.

Mathias.

Not a lot to go on in that. He turned to the first news item which was from the online *Rheinische Post*. The date was September 2012. Ellie had scrawled translations on the headlines and then a summary.

MAN KILLED BY ARROW. It is believed Klaus Edershen, sixty-five, a local of Dortmund, was walking his dog in Westfalen Park, Dortmund when he was shot through the neck and killed by an arrow fired by a person or persons unknown. The body was found by a father walking with his children in the popular park but there were no witnesses to the event. The police were unable to speculate on whether it was murder or a terrible accident but asked anybody with information to come forward. Herr Edershen, a retired soldier, lived alone. His neighbours described him as a quiet man who kept to himself. It was believed Edershen had spent some time in Asia in the nineteen

> *eighties working as a security adviser for European firms.*

Ellie had also placed a yellow post-it on the bottom, *crime unsolved as of November 2013.* The first thing that occurred to Clement was Edershen may have been some former colleague of Schaffer's. Perhaps after Schaffer had left the police they both worked security somewhere. All the same, he would see if the German police could give him any information. A bow and arrow and an axe were primitive weapons but tying them on that basis might be, well, a long bow. The second printout came from some sort of True Crime retrospective. This was number eight and titled THE DRUG CZAR WHO GOT AWAY. The gist of the story was that in the nineteen seventies the man pictured, Kurt Donen, 'the Emperor', ran Hamburg's biggest drug syndicate. This was the only photo ever taken of the shadowy Donen who was responsible for numerous deaths including that of an undercover police officer. Donen had escaped a police dragnet and never been captured.

Schaffer was working the drug squad then and Clement supposed he may have been on the case. Was it possible Schaffer had come across him here in Broome? He looked at the photo again. The man looked forty-five then which would make him around eighty now but it might just have been he was balding with a low forehead, he could have been thirty. Even so, if Schaffer recognised him surely he would tell somebody. He took the printout and found Mal Gross.

'Add thirty-five years. This guy look familiar?'

Clement couldn't believe there would be anybody in the region with whom Gross hadn't had a beer or barbecue. Gross studied it hard, shook his head.

'Speaking of newspapers. The latest *Post*.' He slapped

it into Clement's hand. Front page showed a photo of Jasper's Creek with crime tape and an insert, a grainy blown-up photo of Dieter from goodness knew where. The headline read POLICE ZERO IN ON KILLER.

'Not,' was Clement's immediate reaction.

Gross made himself an instant coffee. 'If it's okay with you I'm going to pay the Dingos a visit. Put it right on the line they had better cooperate if they know this Maori-looking bloke.'

Clement thought it a good idea.

The phone rang, Shepherd. He had again checked Schaffer's house for any possible stash, everywhere, including the roof but had come up empty-handed and was preparing to start on the property. Clement brought him up to speed on what he had learned from the clients: Schaffer seemed small-time, never flashed much money. Shepherd's immediate reaction was predictable.

'Is it worth it then? It's a lot of manpower.'

'Manpower,' Shep talking like a commander now. Clement had a good mind to order him to start digging, even though he had the same misgivings.

'Come back to the station, let the other guys check the property. I have some vehicle owners for you to chase up.'

He left the list Manners had prepared on Shepherd's desk.

Out the corner of his eye he caught Mal Gross heading for the back door.

'Hold up, I'll come with you.'

Earle was finishing up on the phone. Clement waited to hear what he had to say.

'Spoke to the abattoir and they confirm Nightingale and the boyfriend were working there Wednesday night.'

Clement grunted and followed Gross through to the carpark. Mal Gross was the kind of man who kept his government vehicle in immaculate condition. Clement eased himself into a spotless passenger seat. Gross talked as he drove.

'Dean Marchant is the President of the Dingos. We may as well go straight to the top. There's only about twenty of them anyway.'

Clement had heard they were the only outfit in this part of the Kimberley.

'There's no other small gangs?'

'Not here. Hedland there's a couple. The Dingos keep their heads down. They push speed around the place, eccies, a bit of weed but there's usually no trouble.'

Clement was surprised when Gross pulled the car up suddenly on the outskirts of town. There was nothing here. Gross pointed to a manhole on the side of the street surrounded by small metal barriers, the kind to protect men working in a pit.

'He's a telecom tech. I called ahead, found out where he was working.'

They got out of the car and walked over. Two men in orange overalls were standing in a hole in the ground doing something with wires.

'Hello, Dean.'

Mal Gross addressed the worker with a full beard, pepper and salt. He looked about forty, large, the kind of complexion that burns easily.

'I'm busy, mate.'

'Detective Inspector Clement, Major Crime. We need to talk to you a moment.'

Marchant sighed, handed the cable he was working on to his partner and climbed out. He was big, but no bigger than Clement, solid with a bourbon and Coke gut. Gross played herald.

'Inspector Clement is on the homicide out at Jasper's Creek.'

'We're looking for a biker who was seen arguing

with Dieter Schaffer in the days before he died. Maori or Islander type.'

'Mal shoulda told you, mate, we don't go around killing people.'

Clement couldn't read him.

Mal Gross said. 'We just need to talk to whoever it might have been.'

Marchant's grunt suggested he thought that was in the same realm as flying pigs. Clement looked him in the eye.

'You don't want to get on the wrong side of a homicide investigation.'

'It's not one of our guys. What do you want me to say? We got two Islanders, Big Willy and Retro, and I know they're on your books so I'm guessing it wasn't them or you would have asked straight out. As far as bikers riding through here, you guys would know a lot more about that than me. It's a free country, or it's supposed to be. What sort of bike was it?'

He looked at Gross for the answer.

'Kawasaki.'

'Hoon Boy rides a Kawa but he's no Maori. He's whiter than me. Can I get back to work?'

Clement pointedly thanked him for his time and walked back to the car. Gross had a few quiet words with Marchant before joining him.

'I told him it was definitely in his club's interests to cooperate.'

'He's evasive, but that's natural for his type. Selina looked at the guys he mentioned?'

'Yeah. I made her go over them a few times. She said it wasn't them.'

Clement had an idea. He called Manners.

'Could you send the image of that biker to my phone?'

Manners asked when.

'Right now.'

Manners told him to wait a few minutes. They rested their arses against the car. The day was not yet drugged with humidity. He asked Mal Gross how long he'd been in Broome.

'Nineteen ninety-nine. Remember that Prince song? I grew up on the wheatbelt.'

'You must like it here.'

'I think it's beautiful and I love the people. You grew up here but you left.' It was a question.

Clement nodded. 'I thought it was ugly and I didn't like the people.'

'How are we doing?'

Mal Gross was probably twelve years his senior. Clement shifted his weight. 'You're doing well. How am I doing?'

'That's like when the missus asks what's her worst feature.'

They shared a smile. Clement's phone pinged. Manners had sent him the video via some link. He checked it worked, then went back to Marchant. Clement knew the bikie had been watching them on and off.

'One more thing before we go. Something we want you to take a look at.'

'I'm busy.'

'It won't take long.'

Clement crouched down into the pit where the phone screen was visible.

'This is the guy and the bike.'

He watched closely while Marchant looked.

'Not one of ours.'

'You don't know the guy?'

'He's a fucking blur.'

'You really want to rethink the cooperation, Dean.'

'I don't know the guy or the bike, satisfied? Now let me do my job.'

Clement pocketed the phone and they slowly walked back to the car.

'What do you think?' asked Gross.

'I think he's lying.'

17

At the station, Earle had made progress. Immigration had come back with a contact number for Dieter Schaffer's sister but so far she hadn't answered his calls. Clement suggested Earle get his translator friend to help.

'She left for Bali this morning.'

Clement suppressed a groan. Of course she had. 'Give it to me I'll see what I can do.'

Earle handed the numbers to Clement as Shepherd walked in the door.

'I left Jared and Angus out there checking for any earth that looked turned.'

Clement directed him to the list of vehicle owners he had prepared for him. 'Any of those ring a bell?'

Shepherd scanned, pouted, shook his head. 'Not offhand.'

'I'm going to try the shops, see if anybody saw anything more. If you get through it, call me.' Clement turned to go and found Mal Gross waving a printout.

'Email from the Hamburg Police.'

It contained a brief synopsis of Dieter Schaffer's time as a policeman rather than a full service record and was written in German. There was also more information in the email body and a name, Mathias Klendtwort, the Mathias of the letter, no doubt.

'You copy this to me?' asked Clement.

'Yep. You should have it.'

In his office, Clement opened the email and ran it through the translator before printing. Then he sat back to read it. The email noted Hamburg Police had sent officers to the home of Mathias Klendtwort, a former Hamburg police colleague of Schaffer. He was not at home when the officers called but they left a note asking him to contact them about the death of his friend Dieter Schaffer. Clement decided the short CV would occupy him while he got a coffee. He left the station and out of habit started walking to The Dolphin but changed his mind and headed for the Honky Nut instead. A few tourists in shorts and shiny new caps strolled the streets. Most of the locals were probably still sleeping off a big Friday night or picking the form for later in the day. He thought of Phoebe and how excited she might be on the boat. A holiday they had spent at Rottnest Island came back to him. How old had she been then, six? No more like five. It was a pleasant time, the three of them, a real family; the scent of Moreton Bay figs like incense. Fish and chips. He'd cooked a curry and Marilyn and he had made love after too much red wine and had not even fought the next day. They rode bicycles around the small island, Phoebe at first tentative and then after a few days becoming a terror on two wheels.

The Honky Nut was busy, nearly all the tables occupied, a smell of fried eggs and bacon permeated. Fortunately the counter was free. Selina was not present. A young man with a sleek body served him. Clement was pretty sure this was the boyfriend whom he had seen in the distance last night at the Mimosa. He found himself envying the young man. It was an emotion foreign to him and it suggested to him again that coming back to Broome might have been a mistake, like it would magnify his weaknesses. He ordered a flat white.

'You're the detective?'

A slight accent, Clement couldn't pick it but thought it probably European.

'Yes. Dan Clement.'

'Lex. Selina said she didn't see the guy in the photos.'

'No. But the information was important.'

'I hope you get him.'

'Did you know Dieter Schaffer?'

'The German guy? Na. I served him a couple of times. He used to chat with Selina a bit. He liked to chat up the girls, you know.'

'You never saw him with anyone in here?'

Lex handed over Clement's coffee. 'He would talk to people, especially girls, harmless, not a pest, but I don't remember him coming in with a friend. He was one of those older guys ... solo, you know?'

It was a description Clement realised might apply to him in years not too distant. A male customer came up to the counter and Lex left to take his order. The man wore socks and clean sneakers with a polo shirt, white, forty, a successful banker on holiday would be Clement's guess. He saw the man's wife or partner sitting at an outside table taking a quick check of herself in a compact. Maybe she was like Clement a few hours earlier wondering how long that same face would be the one she knew as her. Ridiculously the idea of a stranger's fragility comforted him. We walk on eggshells together, he thought. He grabbed one of the bench stools and dragged it over to the corner of the counter. The coffee was excellent, not that Clement considered himself a connoisseur. It irritated him when people talked about coffee as if it were a wine, and promoted themselves as experts insisting that they could only meet at one particular café with 'the best' coffee. He had felt the same in his youth when his colleagues had waxed lyrical about one beer or another, as if drinking a particular brand imbued you with any other quality beside inebriation. It was a pose. The key to successful detective work was often just zeroing in on that, the false note, the conceit, the façade. Perhaps that was why he was good at this. He knew his own false notes so well, plenty to practise on.

Dean Marchant had lied to them about the biker. Maybe the man they were looking for wasn't a Dingo but Clement sensed Marchant knew something. He wondered if they should try to follow Marchant: did they have the manpower?

Clement let the question hang while he read the synopsis of Dieter Schaffer's service record. Schaffer had joined the Hamburg state police in April 1970 as a Schutzpolizei attached to the Davidwache station in the Reeperbahn: Clement read that as shit-kicker uniform posted to a tough station. Schaffer was commended in 1972 and 1973. One of these commendations clearly related to the newspaper clipping he'd kept. In 1976 he was elevated to Kriminalpolizei and there was mention of Vice investigation. Clement concluded Schaffer was now in a detective post. In 1978 Schaffer was involved in Narcotics investigation. Whether this meant transferring to a different squad or the same squad with a specific operational focus was unclear but Clement was immediately interested in a drug detective who winds up growing pot. In May 1979 Schaffer was working in auto-theft. Five years later he moved to the Water Police. He finished his service with the Wasserschutzpolizei in August 1991. He would have been a little over forty, half his life up till then in the Force, pretty much where Clement found himself right now. What did he do in the intervening years before coming to Australia, wondered Clement. What would he do himself if he suddenly quit? Did he have any other skill?

The answer so far as he could judge was no.

Clement had to speak to somebody in Germany who knew Schaffer, preferably the sister, but for that he would need somebody who could speak German to interpret. Just at the inflection point where his mood was ready to pitch blue he realised he did know somebody who spoke German: Gerd Osterlund.

He dwelt on Osterlund for a moment. Could he have been one of Schaffer's dope clients, a little grass to smoke while relaxing watching the sunset? Call Clement shallow, but IT exec, espadrilles, Bali; it fitted.

He looked about him, Lex flat out making coffees, making money. He recalled speaking to an ex-con who had turned his life around and gone into the café business. There was a much bigger mark up from coffee than booze and a lot less regulation. He doubted he could do that, run a café, wait on people, even if he could afford to set one up. His thought jumped tracks as he wondered whether Brian was one of those who compared the quality of coffee, café to café. He doubted it. Wine would be more his milieu. Clement paid for his coffee, waved to Lex who was busy serving another customer, called Earle and asked him to meet him outside.

The small array of shops contained a pharmacy, bottle shop, lunch bar, podiatrist, laundromat and shoe store. Except for the podiatrist, custom was pretty evenly divided between tourists and locals. Earle was there in under five minutes.

'You want to split up or do it together?' he asked.

'There's not that many, we'll do it together.'

There was no such thing as rush hour in Broome, so a cop asking questions was not an irritant as it may have been in a big city. In fact everybody was curious. They started with the pharmacist, a young guy with thinning hair and glasses. He weaned himself away from flogging disposable nappies to a female French tourist in sarong and bare feet and examined the photos they offered—a Schaffer close up, and a still of the carpark altercation—but didn't recall Schaffer or the biker and couldn't find Schaffer's name on his computer. The girl who worked for him, bubbly with black curls, was also a no go. It wasn't a complete waste of time; Clement forked out for a tube of toothpaste that supposedly was the ants' pants for sensitive teeth. Seeing the pharmacist also gave Clement the idea they should try the various health clinics. He called Shepherd who had so far struck out with the vehicle owners, and told him to ask around at the clinics to see if Schaffer had visited a doctor and if so what he may have confided. For close on an hour they canvassed the shops but the only person they got a hit off was the bottle-shop guy, a dude about twenty with a goatee. He remembered Schaffer as buying the odd bottle of cheap red, and sixpack. But like all the others he never saw the altercation and did not remember the biker.

Clement wanted to call Germany but it would still be too early.

'Let's head back out to Jasper's, take another look,' he suggested.

...

It seemed eerier now. If the media had been out there, they had left. The crime scene was cordoned off by tape, which was always ominous, suggesting something criminal had happened, something that was permanent and couldn't be taken back. This time Clement and Earle had circled the creek and come in from the opposite direction, the direction Dieter Schaffer had taken. Clement stood approximately where the tent had been, looking down towards the mud and gloom of the creek. Some insect was biting him.

'He was gamer than me,' said Earle standing beside him. 'You can almost smell croc in there.'

Clement turned and walked up to the area he'd found the first time here.

'This is where Sebastian parked. Our killer parked way over there.' He'd familiarised himself with Lisa Keeble's crime scene sketch and was pointing about forty metres north-east. 'You have to figure he didn't come with Schaffer or arrange to meet him here. Otherwise he'd have parked closer.'

Earle understood. 'He was planning to ambush him all along.'

'I believe so.' Clement trudged back to Earle, thinking on it. 'He sneaks through the bush. Dieter is listening to his radio, eating chicken, getting his boat ready. Our killer comes out of the brush here ...' Clement raised an imaginary axe, '... and pow!'

'Then he kicks the shit out of Schaffer.'

Clement nodded as he imagined the scene but couldn't work out why the killer replaced Schaffer's shirt. Earle sighed like it had him baffled.

'He must have known Schaffer, felt guilty or angry or something.'

'Unless he made a mistake, meant to take that first shirt with him, lost it in the dark.'

Either way he'd be hoping Rhino could find something off them.

Earle speculated the killer may have transferred his own DNA during the bashing.

Clement said, 'I think they're analysing the clothes but the creek probably degraded any DNA.'

They didn't stay long. They'd travelled to the creek in near silence; on the way back Dr John was playing. Clement drove, thinking about Dieter Schaffer and the loneliness of death.

'So what's the story with your ex?'

Clement looked across at Earle, surprised he'd ventured into that territory.

'You think there's a story?'

'That nurse at Derby is hot for you and she's undeniably fit.'

Clement smirked at Earle's turns of phrase. His offsider continued.

'And I mention Lisa Keeble and you react like I've suggested you suck face with the devil.'

'She's a colleague and she has a boyfriend.'

'You'd be doing her a favour if you got rid of Osama.'

Clement had been turning over Earle's first question. 'I suppose I still want her.'

'The ex?'

'Marilyn, yeah. Not for sex, although there is that.'

'You miss her.'

'No. That's the thing. I don't miss her, I'm always aware of why it's better we're not together. And I don't need her. But I want her, sometimes. There's something there I don't know if it can be repeated. Or if I'd want it repeated.'

'You don't, believe me. Chemistry is bad for relationships. You want total non-reaction. Inert elements or whatever the fuck they are called. That works best in the long run.'

'You speaking from experience?'

'Kind of. I learned my lesson back in high school but I've seen plenty of other guys like you. You don't need the girl but you need what she gives you. Like junkies still chasing that perfect first high.'

'I know what you're saying but I don't know that's me.'

'So why aren't you together?'

He'd thought about that a lot. 'I think when we're

together we make each other realise how far we fall short of what we should be.'

Earle didn't pursue it after that and it elevated him in Clement's estimation. Two guys who weren't bullshitting but there's a limit. It must have been a good twenty minutes before Earle broke the silence.

'Who is this? He's fucking good.'

'Dr John the Night Tripper. You never heard him before?'

'I'm a Led Zeppelin guy but I like this. I don't think I've heard him on the radio.'

'I doubt it.'

'How do you know about him?'

'It's a long story.'

'We've got time.'

So Clement told him about the homicide ten years ago in Bayswater. A man about forty had been bashed to death in his house. No suspect, nothing to go on. The victim had a big old vinyl record collection. Clement had spent weeks in the murder house listening to all the records trying to understand the victim, thinking it might help find the killer.

'Did it?'

'No. We never got him. But I found Dr John.'

18

It was just after two when he dropped Earle at the station. Shepherd had called in en route. He had located Schaffer's doctor but she had only treated him twice and had nothing of import to reveal.

'I'm going up to Osterlund's, see if he can help make me make this call to Germany. People should be awake there now.'

Earle said he'd chase up the warrant for Karskine's.

It took Clement only ten minutes to drive to Osterlund's. Osterlund's wife was on the veranda using a large watering can on a bevy of colourful potted flowers. In a simple shift of bright batik design and wearing a pristine bonnet, she had that elegance Clement associated with Japanese women.

She smiled in recognition. 'Do you have news on Dieter?'

'Not yet. I need help in translating something from German. Is your husband in?'

'He is walking along the beach.'

'I can come back.'

'I might be able to help.' Her accent elongated the vowels.

'No it's okay. Actually I need somebody to call Germany for me and speak in German.'

'He won't be long. Come in. You want a drink?'

'Thanks, I'm fine.'

He followed her into the house. She turned left towards the large kitchen area and indicated he take a seat at a kitchen table big enough for six. It was made of a type of marble stuff that cost more than he could afford. He knew this because years before it was what Marilyn had wanted for their kitchen. Geraldine had insisted her daughter have it and had paid for it herself, so that even over breakfast or a quiet glass of wine she had a presence mocking her son-in-law for his inadequacy.

'Please.'

He sat down.

'So you haven't found the person who killed him?'

'Not yet.'

She pursed her lips and shook her head.

Clement said. 'Did you know him well?'

'He used to telephone my husband, a couple of times a week. We saw him sometimes in town. He was always friendly but ...' her nose wrinkled, 'he smelled of beer, a bit drunk, you know?'

Having seen the Pajero, Clement could well imagine that.

'We believe he grew his own marijuana.'

'Really? Dieter?' She clearly disapproved. 'I did not know that.'

'Did he talk about his friends at all, whether he was worried about anything?'

'Not to me.'

A scuffing of soft shoes in the hallway advised of Osterlund's arrival.

'Good morning, Detective. Any news?'

If he was annoyed at finding Clement cosy with his wife he didn't show it.

'Not really. A few leads we're following.'

'He says Dieter smoked pot.'

'Grew it actually,' Clement said.

Osterlund pulled a face. 'I smelled it on him sometimes.'

'He never offered you any?'

'He may have, early on. I don't take drugs except for cholesterol.'

Clement wasn't sure if he was telling the truth. 'I came to ask a favour. I'm trying to track his sister and I need somebody who can speak German.'

'No problem.'

Osterlund spoke to his wife in German, requesting a coffee, Clement thought. She was off the stool with alacrity.

'Tuthi is making me a coffee. Anything for you?'

'Thanks, I just had one. I have a phone number on his sister.'

He handed across the number Earle had given him. There was a telephone number and the name Christiane Hohlmann. Osterlund pulled reading glasses from his pocket and studied it.

'This is a Munich number. You want me to call for you?'

'If you don't mind.'

'Of course not.'

Clement offered his phone. 'I think this will work.'

Osterlund waved him away. 'I have an all-in-one deal.'

He swung the laptop towards him and dialled the number as the espresso machine roared into life in the background. Osterlund called out for his wife to stop and waited as the phone rang on the other end. Clement was not used to people using computers for phone calling, well, Skype; he'd tried a few times but it looked like Osterlund did this every day. A woman answered. Clement deciphered Osterlund's enquiry in German, was it Christiane Hohlmann to whom he was speaking? He understood the reply 'nein.'

Osterlund followed up in rapid-fire German. Clement lost track then. Osterlund fired off a few more questions, typed something on his computer, thanked whoever it was on the phone and hung up. The espresso machine recommenced its gasping.

'Christiane Hohlmann left that apartment two years ago for a retirement home. She doesn't know the name of it but one of her neighbours might, a woman who was friends with Christiane Hohlmann, a Frau Gerlanger. She gave me her number. Want me to try it?'

'Could you?'

'No problem.'

Astuthi Osterlund arrived on cue with his coffee, black. She slid quietly into a seat. Osterlund sipped as he dialled. The phone rang out the other end.

'I'll try it again. Are you sure you won't have a drink? I have beer if you prefer?'

'No, I'm fine thank you.'

Once again the phone rang out.

'No answer machine even. She must be elderly.'

'I'll try later.'

'You can come here anytime.'

'Thank you. Did Dieter by any chance mention to you he was coming into money?'

Osterlund infused a snort with a sense of comedy. 'But I didn't know him that well. Maybe one of his bets paid off. You think that's why he was killed?'

'We can't discuss cases.'

'Of course.'

Clement noted that Astuthi Osterlund did not attempt to answer questions when her husband was present so he directed his question specifically to her. 'To you? Did he say anything about coming into money?'

'No.'

'Do either of you know what he did after leaving the police?'

A quick calculation told Clement that Dieter Schaffer had been out of the police force for around twenty years before coming to live here. Osterlund spun his coffee cup.

'He talked about working the docks one time. I can't remember the context. It didn't sound like it was for that long.'

'He told me he wanted to go to South America but had never been.'

Osterlund looked at his wife as if this was some revelation. 'See, my wife knows more than me about him.'

She blushed. 'No, he just asked me one day if I had ever been to South America. I haven't. He said all his life he had wanted to and maybe one day soon he would. But he didn't mention money. I just thought it was a dream.'

'Ja, that was Dieter, the dreamer.'

Clement stood and thanked them both again.

The garden was fragrant and made him feel relaxed. Living here would be like permanent holiday. He supposed he should talk to the neighbours to confirm the Osterlunds' alibi but on second thoughts decided that was something that could be delegated. Osterlund did not strike him as the kind of man who would make a stupid alibi in the hope that it would not be checked, and Astuthi Osterlund had a kind of innocence about her that reminded him of the Balinese people he'd met when he'd holidayed there twenty years ago. Everybody was going there these days, especially from up around here. A lot of the fly-in fly-out mine workers were actually living there. Maybe he should take Phoebe for a week or so? It was inexpensive, they could have fun getting rough 'massages' on the beach. Geraldine would be against it of course, 'too dangerous'. That negative image pulled him back down.

For the time being he was grounded on Schaffer's identity, who he was, how he ticked. He was keen to talk to the sister and try to discern a little more of the elusive ex-cop. What he had learned was intriguing but far from solid evidence. There may be a pattern though. Schaffer worked Vice and Narcotics. He comes thousands of miles away, grows his own dope and distributes it, albeit to no obvious profit. But, he is seen arguing with a biker and somebody who rides a bike turns up at Schaffer's the night after his murder and clobbers a cop. It was suggestive at the very least.

...

When Clement re-entered the station and saw the look on Graeme Earle's face he knew something was wrong. His immediate thought was of Phoebe. Some disaster had befallen the boat. He should never ...

'Your mum rang. Your father has had a stroke. He's in Albany Regional.'

19

'Hello, love.' His mother sounded like she was holding it together but just.

'How is he? Can he move? Can he talk?'

'I don't know. They've been running tests. He's in a coma. They said he was fortunate I was there and called the ambulance straight away.'

When Earle had told him the news Clement had first off entered some weird state where objects seemed stagey, props without substance. He half expected the computer to be light as cardboard but it wasn't and he momentarily forgot why he had sat down at it, then remembered he was after the number for Albany Hospital. His fingers felt like somebody else's as he typed on the prop computer, picked up the prop phone and dialled. His mother and father were just shy of eighty and neither used the mobile phone he had bought them. It had taken him two receptionists to locate his mother at the ICU. At least by that time he was returning to something normal. She ran through what had happened. A typical Saturday morning, they both liked to rise early and walk. His father had emerged from the bathroom dressed and ready to go. She'd turned to get her scarf and when she looked back he was on the floor. She called the ambulance straight away. The paramedics came quickly and said his heart was beating strongly which was a relief, for her first fear had been a massive heart attack.

'I've been here since and they've run lots of tests on him. The main doctor said it was a stroke. He is in a coma. He could come out of it soon or never.'

He felt for her, alone, trying to hold it together. 'I'll come down today.' He was wondering if he'd be able to get seats on the various planes required to get from here to there.

'You don't need to.'

Of course he did. His sister Tess lived in New Zealand with her family.

'Does Tess know?'

'Yes, I rang her. I told her to wait until things became clearer but she said she'll make some arrangements.'

'Do you need anything?'

'Jess Granger is being an angel. You don't need to come, really.'

'I'll be there. Take care.'

He went online and searched for a flight to Perth. A flight was leaving in an hour. A connecting flight to Albany was leaving within forty minutes of his arrival in Perth. He booked seats at full-tote odds, mindful that that put an end to any hope of flying somewhere for a holiday with Phoebe. Western Australia was a big state and he'd be covering most of its length but he estimated he could make the hospital by eight thirty p.m.

As for the case, he didn't think there was anything he could do at this point that Graeme Earle couldn't. He called Scott Risely and found him on the golf course. Risely gave him his blessing to go, his one concern being the warrant for Karskine's house and car. He expected to have it within the hour.

'Graeme can handle that. Basically we're looking for an axe, clothes, shoes, blood in the car.'

Risely wished him luck.

Clement filled in Earle. 'The boss will have the warrant ready soon. You can handle that with the techs. I'll call you between flights. If I can organise Rhino, I'll stop off in Perth on the way back to catch up about the case but whatever happens I will be back tomorrow evening ready to go Monday.'

Earle wished him all the best. Clement shrugged hopelessly.

'There's nothing I can do really. Keep trying to find that bikie, get some eyes on Marchant, he knows something. If you find a blood-stained axe at Karskine's, leave a message.'

...

Forty minutes later, the shimmering heat from the tarmac barely registering, Clement trundled behind an eclectic bunch, Asian tourists, a few families, kids bent over electronic handsets, elderly couples, young mining bods. The wealthier tourists wore new akubra hats, the mining rats workboots and singlets. This is fun for you, he thought watching tourists cram bags into overhead lockers. This journey is about all the good things you will discover. He considered how often he'd flown and how many times there must have been somebody on the plane feeling like he was now, apprehensive, alone.

The flight was full and he found himself beside a couple of young miners. They put us single men together where we can only offend each other, he speculated, but wasn't sure if airline staff really were that thorough in their planning.

It was twenty minutes into the flight, after the miners had ordered some can mix of spirits and coke and the various children were immersed in their computer games, before his thoughts bore down and focused on his father. Who ever knew their father? Sure he knew his habits, hobbies. He'd been a pretty fair tennis player in his day and had continued playing competitively well into his sixties. Wimbledon on tele was the highlight of his year. He preferred beer to wine, liked hot English mustard on his steak, cooked medium. So far as Clement was aware his father had always loved his mother. There had been squabbles but no huge domestic where somebody had moved out or run off with the neighbour for a fortnight. But what did he know of his dreams as a young man? Did he play jokes on his friends, was he a wag? Was he a studious, serious kid?

Clement hadn't really seen any of that in him but you changed when you were a father, you lost individuality and you morphed into the status. Clement had, anyway. Once Phoebe came along his life reduced to only two modes, work and family, and this he saw as a continuation of his father's modus operandi. As a kid Clement had not been exposed to many of his parents' friends, who were all left in Perth when they'd come up here to run the caravan park. Very occasionally some old pal would drive up and spend a few days at the park. There'd be laughter, beers, but no stories he could recall. His father was one of five kids and had grown up in the wheatbelt. He should check with Mal Gross, see if they were from around the same neck of the woods. Clement did not remember his grandfather who ran a store and died of a heart attack in his fifties when Clement was two. Clement imagined his father, Alan, driving back to the hometown for the funeral in the old Kingswood, reliving his childhood. Alan Clement had finished high school, not all that common in those days, especially in those parts, and had found a job in the public service somewhere for a few years before joining the Roads department. His parents had met, married, Tess born first, then Dan and then that life had ended for whatever reason, presumably opportunity, and they'd headed north when Dan was six. As a boy in that wheatbelt town, what had been his father's dream? To play in the Davis Cup, sail the high seas, feel the spray, the wind, chasing down the America's Cup, to own his own pub, to fly high over the flat brown earth as Clement was now? Surely it can't have been to run a caravan park in the Never Never. On occasion as a kid, Clement would flip through black and white photos in the family photo album. A handful were of his father's childhood. They were small with serrated edges and Clement could still remember his thrall as he sat on the floor, or the grass under a shady tree, confronted by these strange physical things that represented a mysterious and foreign world. He pictured them now, farm life, his father with his brothers and a sister all standing against a water tank or propped against a farm ute. Clement's uncles he couldn't even name he'd seen them so infrequently but his aunt Meg he knew, being the only girl. She was the only one besides his father still alive. There were only a few photos, maybe a dozen in all. In the 1940s and 50s, cameras and printing a luxury; they didn't own a fridge until his father was fifteen. The frugality had continued after his parents married and very few snaps chronicled the years before Tess and he came along. Most of those that did exist, a youthful Clement had committed to memory, flipping through the creaking album up here on hot oppressive days with no television and a surfeit of boredom. The courting years of his mum and dad featured group shots of people he had never met, holiday snaps, a wedding or christening. There was little of everyday life. In attempting to capture what they thought was extraordinary, all people had done was replicate the same uninspiring scenes of smiling faces looking at a camera. There was no photo of his parents sitting on their chairs gazing into a strand of distant trees, a solitary bottle of beer between them.

One group of photos always caught his attention though. It was well before his sister was born, his mother and father at a tennis club New Year's Eve fancy-dress party. His mum was Little Red Riding Hood, his dad a musketeer. The table was littered with large bottles of Swan Lager, the only beer available then. The snap that particularly intrigued him showed his father lunging with a foil—it looked like real one with a button on the end—at a jolly friar. In his father's eye was a gleam and his youthful body was taut with a theatrical hand caught in a mid-air twirl. The friar was doing a good job affecting wide-eyed surprise at his own 'death'. This was a side of his father Clement could not recall in the flesh. In that split-second there was a man dashing, theatrical, full of life. Was it simply the booze talking? Or was it a moment where his father's spirit broke to the surface and ran?

This same man could be on his deathbed and Clement still had no idea of who he was underneath the shellac of fatherhood. There had been times he'd attempted to get closer, inquiring about his dad's schooldays, his mates, their holidays, the first car he owned, but his father would make a one sentence comment and turn his attention to something practical like unblocking the septic tank or fixing a window. Clement understood the barrier. Parents want to live every aspect of their children's lives but don't want their children to know them. He didn't want Phoebe to know how he felt about himself. Hell, he wasn't even sure how he did feel about himself. You could say there was a sense of failure and a little guilt, like the draft prospect who never delivered big-time, but that wasn't quite right. There were moments he was proud of his work, proud even of the fact that at some point Marilyn had been in love with him, proud to be Phoebe's father, yet that did not mean he wanted Phoebe in on this. Ultimately he assumed the real him would be a disappointment and yet he did not attempt to cultivate a 'fake' him, he simply chose to restrict aspects of his old self, to present what he wanted. He was sure that in this he was following a family tradition.

...

The plane touched down in Perth. Even though the sun clung to the sky only by its fingernails it was still hot, the Doctor thin and wan today as its patients. He had to scoot over to a separate terminal for the flight to Albany. En route he called Earle and listened to his report.

'I'm at Karskine's now. Nothing yet but we've only been here forty-five minutes or so.'

'How was he?'

'Not too bad. Told us we were wasting our time and was not impressed we were impounding the vehicle. Apparently Mathias Klendtwort called the station and left a contact number, sounds like he speaks good English. You want me to follow up?'

'You're busy, I'll do that.'

Earle gave him the phone number and Clement wrote it on his hand.

'Shep have any luck with those vehicles in the CCTV?'

'No. Three of them belonged to people working in the shops. Nobody saw the biker.'

The Albany plane was boarding by the time Clement reached the terminal. It was a smaller craft but most of the twenty-odd seats were claimed. The passenger list this time was more homogeneous, ninety percent locals heading home. He edged down the narrow aisle and squeezed in next to a man with ruddy cheeks and nose, and a full crop of snow-white hair, probably in his sixties. The remnants of skin cancers burned off the man's face suggested outdoor occupation. Odds on he was a farmer. They nodded politely to each other and that was it.

On this leg, Clement dwelt only on whether his father would survive. He had long steeled himself for the death of his parents so he was not shocked to find himself in this situation but he did not want his father to die, not now, not ever. Practical considerations began to pepper him. If his father did survive would he be mobile? Would he have to go to a home? Could his mother cope? No highlights announced themselves, just varying degrees of unpleasant realities that other people were dealing with every day and once more he felt vaguely guilty. Had he earned more money maybe he would have been able to afford nurses and private facilities. He had settled for an acceptable existence, not a good one.

The female flight attendants barely had time to scoop up the tea and coffee cups before informing them they would soon be landing. Clement had taken a sip of his tea, felt his tooth twinge and decided not to tempt fate further. He pressed his face to the porthole and through gloom saw thick forests below. The contrast between where he had come from and here could only have been more powerful with snow on the ground. They landed and de-planed, as the Americans like to say. It was dark and much cooler than Perth, but mild not cold. Whereas the north air was full of desert dust, down here it was clean and invigorating, something to do with negative ions from the Great Southern Ocean, Clement had heard, though he could not remember where. Albany had been a whaling port into the 1970s but a century earlier had been more internationally famous than Perth, for besides the whaling it acted as a gateway to the Kalgoorlie goldfields.

The taxi driver was overweight, with a form guide folded on the dash, simple pleasures. Clement thought of cautioning him on the dangers of stroke but held his tongue. Before entering the hospital he called Earle again. They had finished up at Karskine's. No axe, surprise, surprise. Mal Gross had been overseeing the biker lead, getting the uniforms to do the legwork. Nothing had turned up yet and they were sending patrols by regularly to keep an eye on Marchant.

...

Hospitals might offer a small degree of variance on the outside but Clement found once inside they were of a type, almost interchangeable, the same cool air with the faint smell of heated meals, the same church hush. His father had been shifted to a private room. Clement found him on his back, seemingly asleep among a tangle of monitoring devices. His mother sat in the chair beside the bed gazing into space. It took her an instant to come back. She stood up and hugged her son. Clement dragged over the remaining chair in the room.

'They say he's serious but stable. His body is functioning normally but they don't know what damage there might have been.'

'You want something to eat?'

'I'm alright. They brought me a roll, they're angels. What about you? You must be starving?'

Actually he was. He asked again about what had happened and listened to the same details in more or less the same order. Since they'd last spoken there had been more doctor visits but his mother knew nothing substantial although they had said he was stabilised. Clement excused himself, found a dispenser machine up the corridor fumbled in his pockets for coins as he read instructions without taking them in and selected

Mexican-flavoured corn chips. His fingers felt stiff and awkward as he fed coins. He managed to work it all somehow, came back and resumed his seat.

'Tess called. She's booked to fly in Wednesday.'

'That's good.'

He said it even though he was neutral on whether Tess would be much help. Had it been his father having to cope she could have done the basic—cook a meal, clean, wash—but his mum was capable of fending for herself in that regard. Decoding the medical half-truths was where she needed assistance and he doubted his sister would be much use. Tess had never been able to pick up an inference, she had to be hit over the head with directness and her manner could seem brusque for the same reason. Still, he supposed it would be company for his mum, and if his dad was not showing signs of recovery by Wednesday she might need a lot of support.

'How's he been?'

'Fine. Really good. He's been on blood pressure tablets for a few years now but he's usually good.'

'Not stressed about anything?'

The slightest hesitation. 'No.'

Clement realised the stress was probably to do with him. He was a forty-two year old man whose life had at best stalled, at worst fallen apart.

'You're on a murder case?'

'Yes. I'll have to head back tomorrow.'

His mother understood. She still had vivacity in her eyes but the price for those days in the deck chair was written over her skin. Like a sheet washed and left to dry too many times it was thin and fragile. She wore cream slacks and a light-knit long-sleeved top.

He'd already reached the end of the corn chips and licked his fingers as he asked, 'How have you been?'

'Good. Your father and I have both been really very

good. The garden looks beautiful.'

She glanced over at her husband. A smile played on her lips. 'Like he's sleeping. How's Phoebe?'

'She's off sailing with a friend of hers.'

'He would have loved that.'

'He likes sailing?'

'Oh yes. Well, he likes the idea of it.'

'And yet he went to Broome. Did he fancy himself as a lugger captain or pearl diver?'

It was never too late to try and learn more about him.

'No. He did what he had to for the family. He couldn't see much of a future at Roads. Those days you had to wait for somebody above you to retire or die. And somebody did retire but then one of the other blokes got the job and he thought, "that's that". He could see himself waiting another twenty years for his next chance so he said we're going north, that's where the future is. '

'I bumped into Bill Seratono. He's still up there. You remember him?'

Her small eyes narrowed as she tried to fish his name out of a deep memory.

'Small, dark hair?'

'Tall, dark hair.'

The conversation petered out. Neither of them wanted to go to unpleasant places but he had not travelled this far for nothing, things had to be said.

'Have you thought what you might do if he doesn't come back ...' he tried to find a good way to say it, '... how he was?'

'There's a good chance he's going to be fine.'

'But if he's not. We have to ... I'll help. I'll get time off.'

'I can manage. We have a good circle of friends here.'

'You're not as young as you were, Mum. Neither are

your friends, right? Tess won't be able to stay for long. I'll be there to help.'

She reached across and held his hand and they sat there like that for some time. Eventually they began to talk about small things, her friends and their various health ailments, Broome and what had changed and what had not. And Phoebe. Her disappointment her only grandchild was more an idea now than a reality manifested itself in every mannerism she adopted to disguise it. Clement realised he would have to tell Phoebe about her grandfather; Marilyn too. One advantage in Phoebe being away on the boat was he could postpone that. His mother was too polite to enquire about Marilyn and probably had no need because they remained in touch. He wondered if she knew about Brian, reasoned she most likely did but was not keen to go there with his mother.

'I'll bring Phoebe down in the holidays,' he said, knowing it would be a promise difficult to keep.

'We'd love that.'

We, his mother was not affecting the royal plural, she was including his father, refusing to concede an inch on his prospects. By now Clement had adjusted to the air-conditioning and found it almost too cool. A nurse entered and checked the monitors. She was mid-twenties and considerate. She said if they were hungry they were welcome to make some toast in the nurses' kitchen. There was coffee and tea also.

Around eleven o'clock, after two or three nurses' visits, he suggested his mother go home, have something to eat and a decent sleep.

'I'm here. I'll call you if anything important happens.'

It took a little while but eventually he convinced her that she would be a lot better off continuing her vigil in the morning as he would have to return to Broome. She was worried about him not eating but he said he would check out the nurses' kitchen. He organised the cab and waited with her until, with the vulnerability of the elderly in a foreign land, she stepped into the taxi. It may well have been the very one that had delivered him. Before returning to the room he wandered along the hushed corridor to the toilet and peed, thinking of his father showing him how to piss standing up. He guessed he must have been four. On the way back he passed the small kitchen and after a momentary debate, diverted to it. Initially he was going to just make himself an instant coffee, as if to eat would have been disrespectful of his father's condition but hunger won out and he wound up consuming two slices of toast and vegemite. It was then he saw the number written on his arm and on the spur of the moment called Mathias Klendtwort in Hamburg. The phone rang for some time and he was about to hang up when a man answered.

'Ja?'

'Mr Klendtwort? This is Detective Daniel Clement in Western Australia.'

'Oh yes, you got my message. The Hamburg police gave me the number to call.' His English was better than good. 'Poor Dieter. He's dead eh?'

'Yes, I'm sorry. You were a friend of his?'

'We worked together, quite a long time ago. How did he die?'

'He was murdered. At a remote fishing area.'

Klendtwort uttered a curse in German. Clement thought he heard a soft sigh. He imagined the German gathering himself. 'Sorry. He seemed so happy there. Finally. Shit. You have the person?'

'No, we don't, no clear suspect and we really don't know very much about Dieter. Did you speak to him often?'

'We wrote, usually longhand. I tried emails but they have no personality. I'm sixty-three, I like the old ways.

And if you're going to ask me if he told me of anybody he was worried about, the answer is no. He seemed to enjoy his life there. He loved the heat, being in the open. He had become a hermit I think.'

'He had no lover?'

'Not that I know of.'

'He wasn't gay?'

'Dieter? No. He was married before. When that fell apart he was really cut up.'

'How long ago was that?'

'Twenty, thirty years.'

'Is there any possibility, however remote, some criminal from his past might have held a grudge and killed him?'

'It's a long way to go for that.'

He thought he heard a match striking.

'I need a cigarette. My ex used to nag at me but now I'm on my own I can smoke indoors. Pardon, I don't mean ... it's a bit of a shock.'

'That's okay, take your time.'

All the time Clement was acutely aware of his own father battling for survival in a room down the corridor. The German came back on.

'We had some hard customers, mind, but none who were that angry. And it's so long ago.'

'You did Narcotics with him?'

'We started around the same time with another guy, Heinrich, working out of the station at the Reeperbahn, mainly what you call Vice then. But heroin became a huge problem real quick in the late seventies and they formed us into a narcotics unit around seventy-seven, I think.'

'We know that Dieter was growing cannabis plants here but so far it seems just for himself and a few mates.'

'It doesn't surprise me. We smoked a little reefer back then. Who didn't? No hard drugs though. Anybody dealt hard drugs, we fucked them over. Dieter was a good cop. He drank too much and he gambled too much but it goes with the territory, right?'

'Did anybody hold a grudge against him?'

'From those days? No, it's too long ago. I mean we made enemies but no, I can't see somebody travelling halfway around the world to kill an old cop.'

'Did he have any problems with his gambling?'

'He gambled a lot but only small stakes.'

'Do you know where his ex is?'

'No, I lost track of her years ago. She remarried.'

'I found a download of German news. There was an article about a man, Klaus Edershen, who was killed, shot through the neck by an arrow. Do you know why he would have that?'

'Edershen?'

Clement could feel the German trawling.

'The name does not seem familiar but, shit, it's so much harder nowadays, the brain just leaks. Killed by an arrow?'

'In a park in Dortmund, I think the case is still unsolved.'

'When was this?'

'September two thousand and twelve.'

'I was away with my younger daughter in Spain from August to October then. I must have missed it.'

'How about a seventies drug czar who got away?'

'The Emperor.' There was bitterness in Klendtwort's inflection. 'We worked that together. We lost a colleague. None of us forget that.'

That would explain why Schaffer had downloaded that. Clement carefully gave Klendtwort his details. 'I might need to speak to you again.'

'Feel free. I hope you get your guy.'

Before he ended the call Clement had the urge for one more question. 'Do you miss it?'

'It screwed my life up but then maybe it would have screwed up anyway. I've got a girlfriend, my kids and I are fine. You bet your arse I miss it. Enjoy it while you can.'

Clement had long finished the toast and his coffee grown cold. He dwelled on what he had learned of Dieter Schaffer and once again had the uncomfortable feeling that Schaffer might be an early prototype of where he himself was headed. Maybe Klendtwort was a closer fit but even that didn't inspire him with confidence.

Back in the room he sat in the armchair in the dim light and studied his father's features. Truth be told he didn't see that much physical similarity but he knew there were mannerisms they shared, a way of phrasing sentences, something he did with his neck.

More memories came back now they were alone, his father teaching him how to shave, and drive. 'You have to learn in a manual,' his father had insisted, 'you may not have the money for an automatic and I won't be buying you one.' True to his word he hadn't. But he had lasted through the kangaroo hops and the clutch grinding. He tried to impart tennis to his son but with little success. Clement never really had the balance. He was better at cricket where he could club the ball artlessly or charge in and bowl fast.

Out of the blue another memory, before Clement's wedding reception, his father worried about the speech he would have to perform. Clement had caught a peek of him at the reception centre practising in the mirror. He had never let on, a small detail in such a momentous day. He remembered it now, that vulnerability sons rarely associate with fathers. He felt a pang of empathy that he'd ignored at the time when it had been no more than a curiosity. His dad had done a fine job, spoken of him as a determined young man who would strive to do his best for Marilyn.

He'd let him down, hadn't he?

He recalled his father and mother dancing. His dad was an excellent dancer and enjoyed owning the floor, spinning his mother expertly. Light on his feet, was the old expression. Clement gazed over again and could see the slight rise and fall of his father's chest. He tried to contemplate what it would mean if his father died. He supposed it made him responsible for his mother. This was more proof to Clement of his retroactive life, lose a wife and daughter, gain a mother.

...

At some point he must have dozed off. He woke feeling chilly. The hospital was deathly silent and he was gripped with a fear that his father had passed while he slept. Edging over to the bed, he looked down and froze in horror. Dieter Schaffer lay there chopped and bashed, blood congealed over his wounds. Terrifyingly his face turned towards Clement, his dark eyes fixing on him as he tried to speak. His hand reached out to pull him closer for the whisper of dead breath.

Clement recoiled and then blinked awake, woken by the actual jolt of his body. It was three fifty a.m. His father was as before, still breathing regularly. Clement's heart rate slowly returned to normal though he was aware of the irony that his reality was a bigger nightmare than the nightmare. His father may never regain consciousness. He might join Dieter Schaffer in the land beyond where they could both talk about his failings. The dream made its point. He owed Schaffer. Somebody had murdered the man in the most brutal fashion. Watching over his father, Clement assembled in his head everything he knew about the case thus far, everything he knew about Dieter Schaffer.

It was like holding sand.

20

The biker took a long slug of semi-warm beer. They were looking for him. Let them look. The Dingos were solid. He had no doubt about that. He could have run but that was piss-weak. It was only another couple of days before the shipment from Adelaide came. He would finish off the business and get out of there. Even if they learned his name he'd be a ghost, they'd never track him down. He drained the beer and crushed the aluminium can. There had been a time the heat up here had sucked every sip of life out of him. Coming from where he grew up, where you woke up to frost on the ground, what could you expect? But eventually his body and the heat had equalised. Like a siege back in days of swords and armour, neither side gaining ground, neither relenting. A truce had been settled. Now the heat just bored him. He wouldn't mind getting overseas, the States. These shit places got to you eventually. He looked around the shithole where he found himself, sagging furniture, asbestos sheet walls, a tiny box of a kitchen. He wanted to go into town, find a woman, but that would have to wait.

Forty more hours. It hadn't been so bad with the Dingos boys hanging here too. The pool table was scarred and tilted but you could still knock out a game. But with the cops asking questions they'd had to piss off.

All because of that stupid, fucking Kraut.

The only plus was the garage. He could keep his bike out of sight and store the gear when it arrived before shipping it on. This used to be a mechanic's place. He imagined living here, working in the garage fixing trucks. Not much of a life, too fucking hot and boring. He pulled his big frame out of the chair and stretched. No TV, nothing except his iPod. The air-conditioner was one of those ones you wheeled. It was old but it worked, sort of. The front windows were boarded up so there was nothing to look at, but in the back where the pool table was there were louvered windows. They let in a breeze and cooled the place down but of course then insects came in too. There was no way to pass time except to drink and walk around outside looking at the stars. That was risky during the day but it would be safe now, it was mostly hidden from the passing traffic and too late for the kids who walked about or rode bikes during the day. He picked up his iPod, opened the door and strode out.

It wasn't too bad tonight. The edge was off the heat and it smelled clean, unlike the house. The nearest houses were about half a k away, no street lights, so even if he passed somebody, they couldn't get a good look at him, and they were most likely high on glue or petrol so what would they see? He jammed the headphones in and started walking east. Slayer belted into his brain. He'd gone maybe a hundred metres towards the road when a small green flash caught his eye about fifty metres to his left. He stood quietly and stared. There it was again. Something on the ground was flashing on and off. For an instant he thought about heading straight back to the house but curiosity got the better of him. He scanned around him. No vehicles that he could see. It was nearly pitch dark out here with a thimble of moonlight only. Cautiously he headed over, confident of the knife he kept in his boot and his ability to use it. It occurred to him that it could be a message from the Dingos, perhaps worried to come to the house. He pulled the headphones out and listened to the air around him, the faintest drunken voices from the closest houses, nothing else.

Whatever it was flashing over there, it was small. He advanced towards the tiny light which continued to flash regularly. Finally when he was right on top of it, he was able to see it was a small digital clock in the shape of a turtle. A kid's toy, the sort you buy from a servo to get the discount on a tank of petrol.

As he bent to pick it up, some black shape raised itself from the earth. It made his heart jolt, this black demon sweeping up like smoke, and he reached for his knife; ghost or not, he would fucking gut it. His hand closed on the handle of the hunting knife and whipped it out. His head exploded. Then he was on his back looking up at a vault of stars only to have them blotted out by the black demon and its green eyes looking down. Slayer played his requiem through the headphones and the green turtle flicked on and off, on and off. On.

And off.

21

Rhino was partial to a colourful shirt and Clement had to admit a colourful shirt liked Rhino. Some men couldn't carry it off. They would forever be accountants wearing a souvenir. Rhino on the other hand looked like he'd come back from killing Japs at Guadalcanal with a new lust for life and become a trader on the Fly River. He was tearing into sausage and egg and swiping at flies. He had been happy to catch up with Clement to talk about the case but had resisted suggestions they meet at the lab.

'I spend too many hours there as it is. Come after my swim, I'll see you at Swanbourne.'

Rhino had swum his way from Swanbourne to Cottesloe and back, a good four k, and they were dining now on a rickety garden table out the front of a newsagent-cum-café in the Cottesloe backstreets. The sun was still only a hot needle, by midday it would be a branding iron. A tad under one hundred and eighty centimetres, Rhino was shorter than Clement but he was broad, the physique Disney used for those guarding dungeons, a ball of muscle, and he weighed something in the mid-90s. He normally wore his hair in an absurd 1960s left-hand part, fringe sweep like Troy Donahue, but he'd mutilated it after a Pernod binge, being too cheap to pay a barber. Post-swim it had fallen like Moe of the Three Stooges. The man looked more like he worked an odd-job at the races, sweeping butts or shoving horses into barriers, than a professor.

There had been no change in Alan Clement's condition by the time Clement had to leave Albany. He'd had no chance to shower the funk of the cramped night from his person but the air-conditioning had managed to contain the unpleasantness. Clement had changed into a new shirt and jocks and breakfasted on a museli bar before farewelling his mum who had arrived just after five a.m.

'I'll call you. I'm sorry I can't stay.'

'Your father wouldn't expect it.'

'You still have the mobile phone I bought you?'

She flushed ever so slightly, guilty. 'Yes.'

'It would be a lot easier if you brought it with you.'

'I will, love.'

'You know how to charge it?'

'I'll bring it in. The nurses will help.'

He spared her the lecture on how busy they might be.

'Charge it and keep it on you, that's all you have to do. I can ring you anytime. It's much easier.'

At the airport waiting for his plane he'd rung Earle but there was no more news. There were no definitive sightings of the biker, though a couple of maybes. Marchant was staying put. Lisa and the techs had been going through Karskine's clothing and vehicle. Their initial tests showed the tray of the truck had traces of blood, to be expected given his fishing expeditions. So far nothing human had revealed itself.

Clement had finished his serve of bacon and eggs in record time. A light breeze spun the scent of pine around the little table. He sat back as Rhino confirmed things he already knew.

'He was killed between ten p.m. and one a.m. by an

axe. He was probably struck and incapacitated, then kicked and beaten, but he might have been beaten then killed and more trauma inflicted post-mortem. One thing that's curious: there wasn't much blood on the t-shirt.'

'That's what Keeble said: it was put on after he was beaten and hit with the axe.'

'Not only that but whoever dressed him tried to keep the blood off it. I mean Schaffer would have been soaking in blood. He would have to have been wiped down. Maybe your killer used Schaffer's old shirt.'

'Any idea why?'

'Isn't it because they have some respect for the victim? That's what the crime shows say but I'm not a cop, you tell me.'

'How about the killer's blood?'

'Nothing we could find.' Rhino shoved a large piece of toast in his mouth and gulped black coffee. 'Something else, the t-shirt was printed in nineteen seventy-nine for Hamburg's championship. The one he was in was an original.'

'From nineteen seventy-nine?'

Rhino nodded as he ate, managed room for words. 'I had a German mate send through an analysis of the original batch of tees. This one matched. It had no signs of ever having been worn before.'

'A collector's item?'

'I guess so. It was tight on Schaffer. I'm guessing he added a few kilos in the last thirty-five years.'

Why had somebody re-dressed Schaffer? Why in that t-shirt? Were they mocking him? Had he owed somebody money and they'd thought he'd wasted it on football ephemera and he should be made to suffer that final humility? But then why go to the trouble of wiping blood off Schaffer? Rhino's gaze had drifted to a brace of bronze women walking past. Rhino had a passion for women with strong, muscular thighs and these two made his cut.

'Choice. Is that the sort of thing he'd carry around in his car?'

Clement took a moment to get he was back talking about the t-shirt.

'Can't see why. Most people keep those things at home.'

He wondered if the shirt could have been in the drawer with the computer. But that would mean the computer was stolen before Schaffer was killed.

'He could have been trying to impress some babe,' offered Rhino.

Clement supposed that fitted with Schaffer trying to chat up young women by the offer of free dope. Even so, it was odd, but Schaffer was odd too. Rhino had an alternative.

'Or maybe he was going to sell it?'

'Hardly the kind of thing you'd take with you fishing.'

'Unless you were selling it to your fishing companion.'

'But then why park so far away? If they were mates, you think they'd park together. You didn't find any sign of another person in the car?'

'Just the kid you picked up and cleared.'

'And the DNA from the skin attached to the shovel?'

'Onto it as we speak. It's viable.'

That was some good news.

'You were holding out on me.'

'Waiting to see if you were going to shout my brekky. How's Phoebe?'

'Out on the ocean.'

'Best place to be. She know about your old man?'

'Not yet.'

'They close?'

'They don't see much of one another.'

There wasn't time for much more chat. Clement

had to get back to the airport for the Broome flight. He called a cab. Rhino, despite his previous quip, shouted him the meal and waited till he was on his way.

...

While his father's fate hovered in the background like a good soundtrack, present not intrusive, on the flight back Clement crammed all the things they knew about Schaffer's killing in a blender and hit go. The killing had been brutal but careful. There was none of the detritus that a mad impulse killer might have left. No, it had been planned. If the killer had chosen Schaffer for a reason, they had more chance of snaring him but for now the reason was obscure. Why change the shirt? Had the killer felt a sudden pang of guilt and grabbed the first thing available? What of Rhino's idea that Dieter Schaffer took the shirt to impress a woman? Well, she'd probably have to be German or a soccer nut. Could there be a woman in league with somebody else? Maybe they were trying a shakedown of some sort on Schaffer? The young woman at the café, Selina, popped into Clement's head. Selina and her boyfriend working as a team? Clement hated this part of himself. Trust nobody, turn over the rock of people's lives and see what crawled beneath.

It was a little after midday, Sunday, when he stepped off the plane. The air was so much thicker here, rain imminent. Scott Risely was waiting, fresh from a game of golf. Clement's immediate reaction was that something in the case had broken but it was simply Risely checking in face to face. They sat in Risely's car and, after he'd answered the usual polite inquiry about his father, got down to the case. Risely had one piece of new information.

'We got a call from a truck driver heading to Derby last Wednesday. Says he saw Dieter Schaffer's vehicle around two thirty p.m. heading towards Derby, one person in the cabin as far as he could tell or remember. The car overtook him and he thought it was dangerous, so he filed it away.'

'If he's right then it wasn't somebody along with Dieter who did him in.'

'If he's right.' Risely emphasised the conditional 'if'. 'He wasn't certain. Of course Schaffer could have arranged to meet somebody there.'

'True but then there was no need to park so far away. What about Perth with the CCTV footage, did they spy the biker anywhere?'

'No. They're looking again just in case. They did pick up Schaffer's Pajero once, Sunday before he was murdered, just driving down the main street but there was no sign of the bike.'

Running through what he'd learned from Rhino, Clement saw Risely become gloomier by the second. The window to apprehend the criminal was shrinking fast.

Clement tried to sound more hopeful than he felt. 'Maybe the DNA from the shovel will turn up somebody.'

...

Clement drove straight to the station, fielding a call from Shepherd who had just interviewed the neighbours of the Osterlunds. They had confirmed their story about the dinner party.

At the back of the station he found Lisa Keeble and her team still working on Karskine's car. She anticipated his questions.

'The car wasn't cleaned, so either he's innocent, or cocky or stupid. No blood on his seat or around the pedals, wheel or window buttons which is where you might expect transfer. I did get up under the mudguards and scraped out the soil, twigs and stuff. There's a few interesting anomalies at Jasper's Creek so there might be a chance for a match.'

Inside the station he found Graeme Earle feasting on a tomato sandwich.

'No cheese, Barb's put me on a diet. How was it?'

Clement never got a chance to answer because Mal Gross swept in waving a piece of paper.

'I had triple 0 on the phone. They've got a report of a body near the old servo at Blue Haze. The caller is a Mr Orese. He's been told to wait there. Paramedics are on their way.'

Clement's assumption was the body would turn out to be a derelict, natural causes, but he couldn't rule out a hit and run. The uniforms wouldn't be any quicker getting there than them. He looked at Earle.

'Let's go.'

Gross walked with them. 'I had an idea about finding that bikie. He could be from an interstate gang, Darwin or Adelaide most likely. I've spoken to the biker squads and they are having a look for me.'

Clement managed a wry grin. 'Not bad for an old bloke.'

Gross said, 'You're doing alright too.'

...

Clement remembered the servo from its halcyon days of the late 70s when he'd ride his bike hour after hour across Broome, looking for something, anything to break the monotony. Sometimes Bill Seratono would ride with him, he remembered that now. Bill was always one to adorn his bike with a flashy chain or streamer. Hot sun baking low, thin scrub hour after hour, the asphalt shimmering; they would tour all over the place. The servo had been Valhalla to the young Clement. It had air-conditioning and sold soft-drink, chocolates, and ice-creams; his personal favourites the weirdly named Golden Gaytime or Paddle Pop. In those days it had been the only building around for several ks but more recently cheap housing had been built close by. As if tuned into his head, the radio played ELO, 'Telephone Line', one of the definitive songs of his youth. *I'm living in twilight*, the lyric went. Back then he'd thought it was true but he saw it was even more apt now.

'I spoke to Trent Jaffner,' said Earle, the gleaming road stretching ahead. 'He gave the same story about Schaffer as all the others. The man virtually gave away his pot. If it was up to this lot he'd be canonised.'

It took them a little over ten minutes to reach the place which sat just off the highway behind a wide gravel space so flat it could have been a military parade ground. From the highway Clement couldn't see anything except the boarded up old servo and its adjoining garage. Only when he turned off onto the gravel did he see what had been hidden from the road by a grove of trees and scrub: a white delivery van parked on the southern flank, about fifty metres to the right of the garage. An ambulance was beside it. Two male paramedics were attending, one on his phone. A short, dark curly haired man in a tight polo shirt and shorts was sitting on a flat rock near the delivery van. Clement pulled up behind the other vehicles. They got out and approached the paramedics. He hadn't been back here long enough to know people from the other services by name. The one who was not on the phone, a chunky, prematurely balding fellow, came towards him.

'He's dead. We didn't move the body. I don't think you're looking at natural causes.'

Now Clement saw the crumpled figure lying on the edge of where the gravel met bush. Flies had already zeroed in. He glanced over at the man sitting on the rock.

The paramedic said, 'He's the one who called it in.'

Clement and Earle retrieved plastic gloves and shoe covers from the car and each slipped one set on, cramming more into their pockets. A man's body, bent awkwardly, wearing jeans and a denim jacket, was lying in the dirt on its left side. Blood had pooled around his staved-in head like a halo then flowed down around his torso but his Maori features were visible and he was wearing thick boots.

Earle spoke for both of them. 'Looks like we found our biker.'

22

A hunting knife was close to the body but had escaped the river of gore. Its blade seemed clean.

Earle clocked him. 'His?'

Clement shrugged, checked the body now, stiff.

'A good few hours.' He felt in the pockets of jackets and jeans, found a wallet with a hundred and forty dollars but no ID. There was no phone but there were two keys, one household style, the other shiny silver with black plastic tabs, probably for a cycle. Up close the wound looked like Schaffer's, the skull had been sliced, tissue exposed.

'Get some photos.'

As Earle moved around the body clicking his phone-camera, Clement peeled his gloves and shoe covers and headed to the man sitting on the rock.

'Mr Orese?'

Close up, Clement saw he was green around the gills. He introduced himself then started in.

'When did you find the body?'

'Just before I called triple 0. I do the pies, for Wilson's.'

Wilson's was the local bakery. It had been around since Clement was a boy.

'I pulled over here for a cup of tea. I keep a thermos. As I pull in, I seen this shape on the ground and first I think it's a roo or something then I see it's a person and I think it's some drunk and I'm going to leave him be but he didn't move at all so I got out to see.'

He offered a stricken face at what that had been like. Just telling the story had him sweating up again.

'Okay, thanks, look we'll need to keep everything in place until our techs can get here and check it out.'

'What about the pies in the van?'

'I'm sorry. You can't move anything just yet. Did you touch the body?'

'No way, it was gross.'

'Did you see anybody around? Pass any vehicles?'

'Didn't see anybody, guess I passed cars but you know ...'

The chance of the killer still being around when Orese was doing his pie run was remote. Clement thanked him but cautioned he would have to stay till the techs checked him and his vehicle. A patrol car pulled in and di Rivi and Restoff climbed out. Clement told them to establish a crime scene and returned to Earle who looked up from his phone-camera.

'Looks like the same guy killed Schaffer did him.'

Clement was cautious. 'Maybe. We'll need the techs.'

Earle nodded towards Orese. 'He useful?'

'Doubt it.'

'What was he doing out here you reckon?'

Earle meant the dead biker. It was a good question. There was no sign of a bike or any other vehicle. He may have been dumped there. The gravel was not conducive to tracks and Orese's van would have wiped them anyway. Clement's eyes swung across to the boarded-up servo shop and garage. Whatever door there once may have been on the shop was invisible behind nailed board but the adjoining old brick workshop offered a rusted metal roll-a-door. He walked towards it, shoes crunching over the gravel. He remembered what Lisa

Keeble had said in the briefing about gravel being found at the back of Schaffer's house and wondered if it had come from here. The afternoon sun was ripening, setting off images in his head of defrosting pies and flies. From around ten metres he could see the roll-a-door was secured by padlock, a new padlock at that. He bent down and tried the key he had taken from the biker's pocket. The lock sprang. He unhooked it and lifted up the metal door which moved far too easily for something supposedly abandoned for years.

The space inside was the original garage, a rectangle of brick walls and concrete slab floor. A mechanic's pit was dead centre but the hoist and everything else had long gone except for a Kawasaki Z750, black and gleaming chrome, just inside the door. It bore no licence plate. Dan put on a new set of plastic gloves and felt it. Cold. He pulled the door back down but did not bother to secure it with the lock.

He started west towards what had been the servo shop. How grand it had seemed to him as a ten year old. Now it was revealed as a shell, wood frames and glass windows stuck on a low brick base, although the glass had long been replaced by sheets of ply which were covered in graffiti of not the slightest artistic merit. As Clement reached the end of the structure and began to walk down the western flank of the building which was licked by low bush and scrub he realised the shop area of the servo was a façade built onto modest fibro living quarters. He reached the back of the building and what in his youth had been called a sleep-out, an enclosed veranda. He noted its glass louvre windows, a few still intact. Three old, rough wooden steps gave onto a back door of warped wood, the sort you locked with a long key with three teeth at the end, like in a cartoon. The small brass knob was loose as they always were. It spun when he tried it but finally caught and opened. The key was in the lock on the reverse side, exactly the sort he had imagined, long, rusty, God knew how old. With the bike in the garage it seemed probable this was where the biker had been staying. They'd have to do a property search, find out who owned the place. On the top step he called out.

'Hello?'

Nobody answered. He stepped into the room which sloped towards him so walking up the warped floorboards was almost a climb. An old pool table dominated the space. Empty beer cans with cigarette butts stabbed into them decorated the room. The smell lingered, recent occupation. He stepped through the doorway into a narrow hall. On his right, what had once been an old bathroom. Only the toilet remained. It was ancient and filthy. He pushed down a wonky button and was surprised it flushed. On the left of the hall was what had been a bedroom, now barren, a hole smashed in the outer fibro wall so that it was exposed to the elements. At this point the floor levelled again. He continued up the hallway into the lounge room, the front room that sat immediately behind the old shop. Somebody had recently been living here. A grubby mattress lay on the floor, a sleeping bag thrown on top. Two old armchairs comprised the furniture. More empty beer cans and cigarette stubs. No phone, fixed or otherwise, that he could see. It beggared belief the biker had been here without one. He turned on his heel quickly, went back outside and phoned Risely.

'Christ,' said Risely after Clement's precis. There was a pause— Clement imagined a moment of bitter reflection—then, 'Perth is going to want in. The media is going to be all over this. Fucking serial killer shit.'

'We can't be sure it's the same killer. Could be somebody trying to make it look like it is, or just coincidence.'

Risely didn't care what the truth was, he knew how they'd all react and Clement didn't fault his logic.

'Have we got enough to paint this as a biker killing?'

Clement didn't think so but the Dingos were his first priority. He saw Keeble arrive with her tech team. If she were tired she didn't show it, moving with a spring in her step. They waved to each other.

'We need something soon. This is a tourist town and it could get out of hand quickly.'

Clement understood Risely was being pragmatic but still felt like he was being pressured. The uniforms had already established a crime scene perimeter. Orese was still sitting by himself, waiting patiently. The paramedics were leaving, their services not required here. Risely asked if he should come out.

'Probably not much point. I'd like to know who owns this place.'

Risely said he'd find out and they agreed to meet in the office as soon as Clement was through there. Clement advanced to where Keeble was camped over the body. Earle stood back, giving her space. Close up Clement could see the fatigue in her eyes.

'It's very probable he was killed right there sometime last night,' Keeble said. 'Single blow to the head, probably the same weapon as the other one.'

'No defence wounds?'

'Nope. Like he was just standing there – and whack.'

And yet he had possibly pulled a knife. Somebody had surprised him and at the last second he had tried to defend himself. Clement couldn't ignore the idea the dead man knew his killer, had come to meet him out here and then realised it was a set-up. Clement thought about the body some more.

'He doesn't seem as badly beaten up as Schaffer.'

'You're right. He was pole-axed and left to die.'

Like it was less personal, more business, he thought.

She showed him the kid's watch which was in an evidence bag.

'This was just a couple of metres from the body.'

Clement examined it. He wondered if the killer or victim might have dropped it. It should print up well.

'I found gravel in the groove of his boot, which you'd expect, of course, but it is consistent with what we found at Schaffer's where you were attacked.'

'There's a motorcycle in the garage. You want to do that here or the station?'

'Here will be fine. Shall I do that first?'

'No, van first for this poor bastard.' Clement nodded at Orese.

'I'll print and swab him too.'

Finding a murder victim could be a damn inconvenience, thought Clement. Shepherd arrived, spraying gravel.

'This is going to be big,' he said heading from the car. Jared Taylor followed quietly behind him. Clement told them he wanted them to head up to the nearest houses and canvas everybody about what they had seen last night, and over the last few days.

'Boys notice motorcycles. See if anybody saw our victim with anybody else or any people or vehicles here.'

His phone buzzed. Mal Gross thought he might have an ID on the victim.

...

'Arturo "Arthur" Lee.' Mal highlighted the photo on his computer. 'They had a few on their books fitted the description but he was only one rides a Kawasaki.'

Risely craned in to get a good look. Clement had no doubt it was the same man he'd left back at Blue Haze with his head caved in.

'That's our victim. From Adelaide?'

'Darwin, though I've got news from Adelaide too. Lee's gang call themselves CZG, they were originally based in New Zealand but they've got Darwin and Cairns chapters. I spoke to Adelaide first and while we didn't hit on Lee, soon as I mentioned that the Dingos had been talking of some kind of money rolling in, the Adelaide boys got interested. CZG has been sourcing methamphetamine chemicals from somebody in Adelaide who the biker squad has had under surveillance.'

Risely put it together. 'CZG get the gear from Adelaide to distribute through the north. They've got Darwin and they are spreading south. The garage out at Blue Haze is owned by one of the Dingos, a Stefan Marinovic.'

Mal Gross knew him. He speculated the Dingos might be getting a cut from hooking up distribution. 'The mining camps would be a big market, young blokes with money and not much to do. The Dingos could facilitate that.'

Risely stretched himself back to his full height. 'I have warrants for the Dingo clubhouse and Marchant's house on the way. How does Schaffer fit in?'

He looked at Clement for the answer.

'Maybe Schaffer was a lot bigger than he seemed? Maybe this was the windfall he was talking about? He could have been in with Lee and CZG and somebody else has taken them out?'

'The Dingos wouldn't be up for this would they?'

Gross grunted. 'Na. I wouldn't think so. This is way out of their league.'

Risely said, 'So let's ask them what's going on. And not too politely.'

...

A little after six p.m., Clement, Gross and Earle sat in

Mal Gross's immaculate work car outside Marchant's house. His bike and car were in the driveway. Clement had decided to try the house before the clubhouse. If Marchant were with his family it would be a lot simpler. It looked like they were in luck.

'Let's go.'

They walked up the short, dark concrete driveway. The house was modest, circa 1980, brick, hacienda style with lawn. Cooking smells wafted out. Clement knocked. There was a delay and then the door opened on a squat woman around forty in shorts and tank top. Her over-tanned shoulder showed off a tattoo of a dingo. She looked them up and down with contempt. Clement identified the smell coming from inside as roast lamb or beef. Her eyes narrowed on Gross.

'What do youse want?'

'We need to speak to Dean,' Clement said.

'It's Sunday dinner for Chrissake.'

Through the open door Clement could see a dining table and at least two children. The air inside the house was hot. He didn't know how they could stand it. The hair of Marchant's missus had wilted into tangled strands.

'What's the problem?' Dean Marchant had appeared behind his wife.

'Problem is, Dean, we don't think you were honest with us. Now we'd like you to come to the station.'

'He's in the middle of dinner, arseholes.'

Marchant calmed his wife with a touch. 'Go to the kids.'

She left, glaring.

'Can't this wait?'

'You had your chance, Dean,' said Mal. 'You stuffed us around. You're coming with us. Now.'

Marchant seemed on the verge of objecting. He could point out that if they weren't arresting him he had no desire to come with them but he seemed to think better of it.

...

Clement and Earle sat opposite Marchant in the interview room, Mal Gross on a plastic chair inclined against the wall, arms folded. Clement had decided not to switch on the camera and make this a formal interview. Not yet anyway. He wanted to offer Marchant the chance to talk without feeling he'd be identified as an informant. Clement took the lead.

'Arturo Lee was found murdered this morning. He had been staying in a property which we now know is owned by Stefan Marinovic, a member of your gang. Lee was seen arguing with Dieter Schaffer in the week before he was murdered. You and your gang are right in the middle of this.'

Marchant was trying to look tough but Clement sensed it was a front.

'If you're keeping quiet because you think there's going to be a big payday, forget it. The Adelaide bikie-squad is busting your meth suppliers right now. In about two minutes I'm going to turn on that camera and this will become official. Once that happens you and your gang will be wiped off the face of the earth. Forget about seeing your kids grow up. Or you can tell us everything you know about the murders. That's what we're investigating. You cooperate, it's going to help you.'

Marchant folded his arms but it was a retreat, not a stonewall. 'None of us had anything to do with murdering anybody.'

'Who did?'

'How the fuck do I know?'

'You were importing chemicals with Lee to manufacture ice.'

'No we weren't. CZG contacted us and offered us money to put up one of their blokes and rent a space for a delivery.'

Gross laughed. 'You're not that stupid, Dean. You knew what they were up to.'

Clement bore in. 'Don't fuck us around. We've got multiple homicides pointing at you. Tell us what we want to know or we'll find something to put you away for a very long time.'

'That's intimidation. I want a lawyer.'

'You get a lawyer, this gets very official and those Darwin boys will not be happy. Work with us, Dean. If you didn't kill Lee then we are all looking for who did. We're on the same side.'

'The operation was theirs,' Marchant said mulishly. 'But if we gave them some contacts for the north-west they'd be grateful.'

Clement read into it that the Dingos would be given cash or drugs to distribute through the Kimberley but he didn't push, he wanted Marchant cooperating.

'What was the connection between Lee and Schaffer?'

'There was no connection. Not really. Look, while Lee was here somebody gave him a puff on some weed. He wanted more and someone pointed him to the Kraut. This is what he told me, right? Lee offered him a chance to join his distribution in return for some weed. Kraut tells him to go fuck himself. That was the fight. That was all it was.'

'Not all,' said Clement weightily. 'Somebody bashed me with a shovel when I was at Schaffer's. You?'

'What? No! Lee went there to rip off the Kraut's pot, teach him a lesson. He thought you were Schaffer.'

'Schaffer was dead,' pointed out Clement evenly.

'He didn't know that, 'cause he didn't kill him. Lee was really pissed off because you lot was looking for him and he has to go underground till the stuff arrives. That's the truth. Nothing to do with murder, and we ain't sold any drugs so we've done nothing wrong.'

Earle said, 'You hindered our investigation. You lied to us.'

Marchant stayed silent.

'Why did Lee take Schaffer's computer? What did he do with it?'

'What computer? What would Lee want with a computer?'

Clement didn't detect a lie.

'Lee and Schaffer are both dead,' said Clement. 'Both were distributing drugs. Maybe you guys thought you'd grab it all for yourselves?'

'That's crap. The night the Kraut was murdered Lee was at our clubhouse till about two in the morning.'

'So who else distributes drugs up here?' Clement said. 'Who else might have got pissed off there was about to be competition?'

'Nobody. That's why CZG came to us.'

Gross spoke from the sidelines. 'No other gang who wants the action for themselves?'

'If there was another gang don't you reckon I'd tell you, get them off our patch? I got no idea who killed them or why.'

23

Later Clement had his main team assembled in his office: Gross, Lisa Keeble, Manners, Earle, Shepherd and Jared Taylor. Shepherd was the last in and Clement checked with him first.

'You get anything from Blue Haze?'

'Couple of young blokes said they saw motorcycles there three nights ago. But nobody saw anything last night.'

So far this agreed with what Marchant had told them. The cycles were in all probability the Dingos who had been hanging out with Lee until the police got interested. Then they'd gone to ground until the delivery. Gross's phone rang. He checked the ID and took himself outside to talk. Clement looked up at his whiteboard.

'Schaffer was talking about money coming in. Schaffer's computer is missing. It's possible Arturo Lee took it and then sconed me.'

Lisa Keeble spoke. 'Rhino will know if we have a DNA match from the shovel by morning.' Lee's body had been flown to Perth via Derby. Rhino was working fast.

Clement said, 'Marchant's story of Lee going to rip off Schaffer's pot could be true.'

'Big coincidence,' said Shepherd.

'Coincidences do happen, Shep. It could also be true Lee didn't tell Marchant the whole truth about any relationship with Schaffer. For a start he wouldn't want his mob cut out by the Dingos. So, Marchant might be telling us what he thinks is the truth.'

'There was no sign of any computer at the garage,' said Keeble.

Clement tapped the board.

'We need to find that computer. Also, Lee's phone is gone. It seems whoever did this didn't want us seeing those contacts. They left money but took the phone.'

'I've already asked for the phone records from Optus.' Earle was thorough.

One of the things they had done while questioning Marchant was to obtain Lee's phone number.

Clement said, 'Maybe we'll get lucky and there will be some common contact between Schaffer and Lee but we can't rely on that. Did you find anything on CCTV?'

It was Manners' turn. 'Not so far. I'm back four days, checking the parking lot behind the Honky Nut. Perth have been looking at every other camera that might have something on it. All they've found is that one shot of Schaffer's Pajero driving down the street.'

'I want you guys to check and double check if anybody in town saw Lee and Schaffer together at any time. We know that Schaffer likes to socialise in pubs. Marchant says Lee had a taste of some weed Schaffer supplied so let's recheck Schaffer's regular customers, they're the most likely to have supplied Lee.'

Gross came back in. 'Sorry. That was Adelaide. They busted the meth chemical supplier and he folded right away. There was a van full of chemicals that was coming here to be met by Lee.'

Shepherd peeled a gum for himself. 'The boss will be pleased.'

It was true. Risely would at least be able to point to

one positive that had come from the investigation, a good size drug-prevention bust.

'What did you think from the wounds?'

Keeble didn't bother with notes. 'The head wounds looked very similar but I can't say for sure if it was the same weapon. Rhino should be able to make that call quickly. There was none of the additional bruising we saw with Schaffer. I'm no profiler but Schaffer's killing seemed more violent, prolonged. I can tell you that I printed Arturo Lee, and his were the only fingerprints on the knife found at the scene. I also found Lee's prints on this.'

She held up the kid's watch in an evidence bag.

'Maybe he was holding it when he was struck because it was not covered in blood. It was found close to the body, so he could have just dropped it.'

Clement looked around at his team. 'Any ideas what he was doing with a kid's watch?'

'Could have been checking the time for a meeting.' Earle flicked it out, a possibility.

'But why a kid's watch?'

Shepherd shrugged. 'It's cheap.'

Nobody could think of anything else.

Clement turned to Earle. 'We need to see whether there is any chance Karskine and Lee were connected. See whether they were in prison together or with buddies of the other.'

By now it was closing in on midnight.

'Grab some sleep everybody, this is going to get uglier by the minute.'

As they broke away, Shepherd lingered to quiz Lisa Keeble on Briony the female tech. 'Has she got a boyfriend?'

'Pretty sure she has.'

'How solid?'

'I don't know, I haven't asked.'

'Be good if you could. "Know your enemy" that's what our cricket coach always says. It's from some Chinese general.'

'So Briony is your enemy? Why would you want to date her?'

'Figure of speech, Lisa.'

Clement put an end to it. 'Shep, things to do. Go back to all of Schaffer's contacts and see if anybody supplied Lee with pot.'

'Now?'

'You could try the pubs on the way home. You might get lucky with one or two there. Anybody you don't find, first thing tomorrow.'

Shep moved off, glum.

Lisa Keeble managed a tired smile. 'Thanks.'

'You need some rest.'

'Not as much as you do.'

Clement's phone buzzed. Keeble left him to it. The ID said 'Mum'. Clement braced himself.

'Yes, Mum?'

'He's back.' She was relieved, bubbling. 'A little while ago his eyes opened and he talked. The words were a bit of a jumble but he was able to talk and he can move his arms and legs.'

Clement felt a wave of relief tempered by the reality that it was early days. He spent a little time reassuring his mother and said he would call her again. He advised her to try and take it easy herself. Only Graeme Earle was left. He signalled.

'Karskine did his time at Geraldton. I've put in a request to Corrections for information on who else was there at the time.'

Clement knew it was a very, very long shot. He just didn't see Karskine as a double murderer. But what else did he have?

Earle guessed his thoughts. 'It'll be better tomorrow when we hear from Rhino.'

...

It had been a long time since Clement had enjoyed a shower as much. The fug of the day sat around his skin like grime in an underground railway. Once he stepped out of the cool water though he was back to unpleasant reality. It was sticky inside his brain and out: two murders and nothing to show. He called up Rhino's contact number and pressed enter.

'Can't sleep, eh?'

'It's cyclone season.'

'How's your dad?'

'Conscious. You with the coroner?'

'Just got out. And I'm glad I'm nowhere near Broome. That was a big guy on the slab; whoever did him is big, psycho or both.'

'Weapon?'

'Same killed your biker and the German.'

'You're sure? No, of course you're sure.'

'You'd reckon the guy must have known his killer. The blow was front on while standing, swung from slightly below him. Not like Schaffer, I'd say Schaffer was crouching when he was hit.'

'Can you say how tall the killer was?'

'The angle of the axe this time suggests somebody shorter swinging up.'

Arturo Lee was a big man and yet somebody, possibly shorter, had hit him in the front of the head with an axe. It must have been somebody he knew, surely?

'Thanks mate. I'll let you go.'

'You've had your way with me, now you're tossing me off like a used condom.'

'No wonder you got a D for English.'

'A for anatomy, but. 'Night.'

Clement sank into his single mattress. The room was basting even though the windows were open. He dialled before he'd thought about it. The phone rang long, longer. He was about to end it when she answered.

'You obviously know what time it is?'

'Of course. Did I wake you?'

A moment's hesitation. 'I was reading.'

'Can't sleep either, eh?'

It was one sentence too many. Marilyn snapped. 'You call me at one o'clock in the morning for banter?'

'I was wondering how Phoebe got on. Is she back yet?'

Marilyn was steaming now, her words like stiff jabs. 'Yes. She's fine. She had a great time.'

'Dad had a stroke.'

'What?'

He explained what had happened.

'So is he going to be alright?'

'I hope so, but I only got the call a little while ago that he was conscious.'

'Your poor mum. I'll call her first thing.'

'Let her speak to Phoebe some time will you? She'd like that.'

'Of course. I'll call in the morning.'

The call ended, snap like that, like the way somebody brought an axe down on Arturo Lee's head. The only difference was, Clement was still there to dwell on it.

24

The sand here was like wheat and kept pouring back down the hole. Eventually he had struck a level firm enough beneath the grey soft sand to allow some depth to be attained. It was hard work and he was not used to it but at least on the lower stratum where the earth became black it was cool. Sweat was pouring off him. He stopped digging and took a deep slug of tepid water from the large bottle he had brought with him. The idea had germinated almost at the instant he decided, fortuitously as it turned out, to change course on his original plan. It would of course increase the risk of being discovered here and it made the execution—he liked that word—of his altered plan more difficult than the original. But there were two big bonuses. One, he would give himself a much greater chance of escape and, more importantly, his pleasure would be greatly heightened by the drawn out suffering of his vanquished foe. Really, a good clean axe through the skull was more than was deserved.

Foe; he dwelt on the word and its medieval connotations. How apt. Those were the days men tortured bears for sport and conjured new ways to inflict pain on their enemies: racks, presses, dungeons. That was the world into which he had followed his quarry, a primitive world of life and death, good and evil, no grey areas, no soft academic two-sided debate with prevarication and polite concession, no namby-pamby civilising—but brutal, all or nothing decisiveness.

The sun was at its apex, beating and blistering like the devil's trident. It would be a perfect hell. He began digging again. Timing was the tricky thing. Rather than just appear as he had to Schaffer, he wanted to deliver horror and panic, to tease and fill the victim with dread of impending doom. But as much as he wanted to move on with things he must bide his time a little longer, ensure all was in place. He bent his back to it again. An image of his father loomed. It was perhaps three years before he died. He rarely wore boots but this day was an exception. He dug in the garden, robotically, his face seemingly void of emotion. His father was weak, physically, emotionally, a man who existed on tracing paper, removed from what he might have been. But it was not all his fault and now as he recalled how hard his father had dug, wheezing through his sunken skinny chest, yet determined to bury the dog, he found himself overcome by emotion. His body began to tighten like a snare being tuned, feedback he recognised only too well as a precursor to tears, the physical state that defined most of his youth. He made himself relax. He needed to keep things under control. His father had meant well, fatally flawed though he was. The dog had been a gift from his father, one of the few he ever gave him. Even at that early age he recognised dimly it was somehow important to his father to do this; more important even than to him as receiver; as if this living creature, an expression of his paternal love, could make up for everything else. It was a brown female labrador called, for reasons unknown, Sophie. He had loved that dog but his father had loved her more, cherished her. When Sophie died, nobody being quite sure why—it was around nine years old so maybe just natural causes—his father caved in. Without Sophie he no longer had any physical measure or validation that he had ever loved his son. It was as if he had learned to mistrust what his own soul might be telling him, as if only this physical representation of his love had currency. He had pitied his father then, but all would be put right.

He rested on his shovel, enjoying the sight of his sweat dripping into the dry earth. The pit was deep enough now for reinforcement. Tossing the shovel, he picked up the wooden batons he'd scavenged and then cut and began fitting them into the pit wall for support. The police would now be combing the garage area for clues but he had been careful about leaving anything that might point to him. Of course he could not become complacent. Broome had after all a limited population. Had the croc taken Schaffer's body perhaps the question of homicide may never have arisen but it was too late now; what was done was done. The biker's murder was necessary but there would be media interest, task forces, vehicle searches. It made things more difficult, yet also more exciting. His mettle would be tested. He must hold his nerve. Every day he was heightening his senses, bonding with the land, like an indigenous warrior, or even more than that, like he was a spirit, able to detect a predator's scent on the wind, invisible when he hunted, part of the land itself, without ego. He had gone from man to warrior and from warrior to superman. He was a tribe of one or one million because moment by moment the very pores of his body were transforming into grains of earth, its heat was his blood, the lightest breeze his whispered words.

The biker was a godsend, literally. Not for a minute did he think it some accident he had been placed at a point to intersect him, no, the Unseen Power had manipulated it. A present was offered but with it the challenge.

Are you worthy? It asked him. Yes, he believed he was.

Look at the long sequence of events that had brought him here. He felt he could shout to the sky that he had not faltered.

He reclaimed the shovel and dug for another hour, timing his exertions to finish at the moment his water bottle ran dry. He buried the head of the shovel into the dirt and climbed out of the pit using the handle. The sheet of corrugated tin had been lying in the sun for hours and when he went to drag it over, it burned through the gloves he wore and seared his fingertips. He was forced to take off his shirt and use it as an oven mitt. He dragged the tin over the pit. It fitted snugly just a half a metre over the edge. He picked the shovel up again and dutifully covered the tin with sand. Then he smoothed down the sand so it was indistinguishable from the dirt around.

The air pressed on his lungs. A cyclone was building, pushing to split its constraining skin, and when it unleashed, what could it be but the final expression of his transmutation into something beyond humanity, into the very breath of nature itself?

25

'Are we now looking at two linked homicides, the Jasper's Creek killing and the death of a biker at Blue Haze?'

Tomlinson's clothes exuded the aroma of stale tobacco and sweat, exactly what one might expect of a journalist in these parts. So far as Clement was aware, Tomlinson was single, and Clement could understand why. As soon as he made that observation though, Clement cringed. He was the last person who ought to be judging his fellow man. Ten minutes earlier Rhino had called to confirm the DNA on the shovel matched Lee. One more piece of information, but not enough to make the big picture any clearer.

'The murder weapon would appear to be the same in both cases,' he answered. Clement had been confronted by Risely and *The Post* editor/reporter as soon as he'd arrived at the station.

'I promised *The Post* you'd have a chat.'

Risely angled his eyes in a way that pleaded Clement be cooperative. Clement had agreed to a 'quick one' and tried to keep the grumble out of his voice. They were in Risely's office which was actually smaller than Clement's but, without the meeting desk, roomier. Some charity golf trophy occupied pride of place on newish shelves bare other than for a few folders. Clement found his attention drawn to the detailed maps of the area covering the wall. Somebody had actually gone out into the baking desert and measured this, he thought absently, and then somebody else drew and coloured and printed this work of art. A seemingly fathomless space, hot, hostile, indistinguishable from the cubits of surrounding sand had been measured, comprehended and ultimately turned into informational two-dimensional art. That's what police work needed to achieve, he thought. To take the psychology of individuals, the motion and action of inanimate objects, the decaying matter of human bones, skin, tissue and reduce it to something comprehensible and laudable, almost beautiful.

Of course he did not say any of this to Tomlinson, he just answered politely and waited for question two.

'Do you have any suspects?'

'There are various persons of interest and we are actively pursuing leads.'

'Are the killings bikie-related?'

'It is too early to say.'

'But the second victim was a biker? Is that correct?'

'He had links with an interstate motorcycle gang and we are investigating whether this may be relevant.'

'If it isn't, does that mean we have some axe-wielding psycho out there?'

This is what Clement hated: damned if you do, damned if you don't.

Appreciating his dilemma, Risely interceded. 'At this stage there is no reason for the general public to be alarmed but they should remain vigilant until we have progressed the investigation, and identified a suspect or have somebody in custody.'

Tomlinson scrawled notes. 'Your forensic people searched a house in Atwell Parade and removed clothes and a vehicle. Do we take it the resident is a person of interest in your investigation?'

Clement's turn. 'Yes, but as I said we have a number of such people on our radar.'

'Did you find anything?'

'We're not at liberty to say.'

'Is there any indication the two victims were known to one another?'

Clement thought on how to answer this. 'We have some evidence that the two crossed paths but we do not know the nature or extent of the relationship yet. In a small place like Broome it is quite likely that there would be some interaction and this can't necessarily be construed as a relationship.'

Tomlinson wrote this new information with undisguised relish. 'Are the killings drug-related?'

'It's too early to say.'

'Do you believe the killer or killers are still in the area?'

'We are pursuing the investigation. That's all we can say at this stage.'

Risely jumped in. 'Kev, Inspector Clement needs to get back to work but I can answer questions of a general nature.'

Tomlinson clearly wanted to continue with Clement but he knew he was on a good thing with his exclusive one-on-one and did not want to push it. 'Is there any appeal you want to make to the public at this stage?'

'Obviously if anybody has any information they think relevant they should contact us.'

Risely inserted that a tip-line was being set up as they spoke. Clement gave the dates and times they were most interested in, including the theft of the axe from the Kelly house which up until now had been embargoed. Tomlinson wanted more information but Clement stood to indicate that was that.

'I'm sorry but I do have to get back to it. Your help is appreciated.'

Clement made his getaway. Outside the office Clement headed straight for Earle who began talking as he approached. 'We have the texts and numbers Lee called on his phone. Marchant is the only person he called here. The other calls are to his girlfriend and gang in Darwin, and an Adelaide go-between.'

'Try the girlfriend. See what she has to say.'

'And Manners has checked Karskine's records. Seratono did call the house at six past ten on the night of Schaffer's murder. The call concluded at ten eighteen.'

Which almost ruled him out. But not quite.

...

The haulage business where Bill Seratono worked was comprised of large hangar-like sheds on broken asphalt. In one of them a large semi was being unloaded of steel beams. Seratono came towards him drying his hands on a dirty rag. Clement could tell his presence was not celebrated.

'This about Mitch?'

'Yes.'

Seratono went to put the rag down but there was nowhere for it but the ground. He gestured to the shade of a gum. They ambled over. A forty-four gallon drum was the makeshift table, crushed packets of cigarettes and a paper cup with remnants of Coke or some other gooey drink for decoration.

'I know you gotta do your job but he's a good bloke.'

'He bought grass off Schaffer.'

'So did I. You gonna bust me too?'

'He has a record.'

'A long time ago. You wanted to ask me about him, you could have done it before you pulled his place apart.'

'I understand he's your mate but he had no alibi and he wouldn't invite us in.'

'He doesn't trust cops. What do you want to know?'

'You don't think it's possible he'd kill anybody?'

'No. Not like that. I mean, maybe he could get into a fight, you know, accidentally hurt somebody but he's not ...' He tried to find a word that wasn't too damning but abandoned that. 'Look, I know him better than I know you. You could be a killer, how would I know? Mitch, no, no way.'

'Has he ever had any bikie connections?'

'What? Like the Dingos or Hells Angels?'

'Yes.'

Seratono smirked. 'No. He's a fisho not a biker.'

Clement pulled out a police photo of Arturo Lee. 'You ever see him with this man?'

Seratono shook his head as he studied it.

'You recognise the guy?'

Seratono continued to shake his head. 'He a suspect?'

'We're trying to find out about him. Mitch ever do any harder drugs? Speed? Ice?'

'Not that I know of. Hey, he's a fisherman who smokes a bit a pot. That's it. Why didn't you speak to me yourself? Why did you send the other bloke?'

'One, I couldn't compromise the investigation. And I had to fly to Albany. My dad had a stroke.'

'He okay?'

'We think he's coming good.'

'I hope so.'

'Thanks.'

Clement put the photo away. 'I'm sorry about all this. He's your friend, I know. You remember we used to ride our bikes all around bloody hours on end?'

Seratono chuckled. 'How fit were we?' The coil of old friendship still wrapped them despite the years. 'When did you decide to become a cop? How did that happen? You were pretty smart at school.'

The implication being that nobody smart would want the job. Based on his experience since, that now seemed to Clement a reasonable sentiment.

'I kind of fell into it I suppose. We left here right after I finished high school, went back to Perth. I wanted to do engineering but I didn't get the marks. I was living at home. Everybody else I knew had moved out of home. I felt, you know, pathetic and my old man was on at me all the time, "Don't think you're going to lounge around here." I was playing indoor cricket and a few of the guys in my team were cops. I wanted to get away, that was it.'

That was the answer, convenience really. All he knew for sure was he had no epiphany moment, no burning vocational call to fight on the side of good against evil.

'You marry a local girl?' Clement said.

'Abigail. From Queensland. You did alright for yourself I heard.'

Clement put on a half-smile. 'Marilyn and I aren't together.'

'Oh. Shit happens.'

'Yeah. We've got a daughter. I came back to see more of her. Marilyn moved back here with her mum.'

Bill looked him up and down, nodding slowly like he got it. 'I better get back to it.'

'Sure.'

'What I said before. If you want to come out on the boat someday, the offer's there.'

'Thanks.'

Seratono walked slowly back towards the semi.

...

Clement drove wondering if he had any real friends and decided he wasn't sure. Colleagues, yes, but not like Bill and he had been back then, lying in the dirt staring up into the sky, saying what you would do if you won a million dollars, arguing the merits of a Polly Waffle over a Kit Kat, modifying bikes, testing how far you could walk in bare feet over hot sand. That stuff you never found again, you thought you would, that it was just a matter of getting to know somebody, but it wasn't.

It was never that easy with women, at least for Clement it hadn't been. If you were yourself, you got crushed. You learned early you had to be a schematic only, give a hint of something within, the music you liked, or what kind of dog. Then you might test the water with a bit more, ready to retract at the first sign of trouble. A word he had heard all the time growing up had been 'détente'. Clement couldn't think of the last time he heard it but he thought now that successful marriages were those that employed détente. By learning to withhold so much through those late teens and twenties he had effectively become a kind of clone of himself with all the interesting bits of the original trimmed away. So actually Marilyn had never fallen out of love with him because she'd never been in love with the true him. He supposed he could have opened himself further to her but the risk ... rejection would have obliterated him. Anyway by then neither of them wanted détente, just unconditional victory.

Only as a homicide cop was the original Dan Clement unsullied. He looked at clues the way he'd studied birds, listened to the cadence of a voice and in it heard truth or lies just as he used to be able to tell how high gums were from nothing but the rustle of their leaves.

Maybe he should have given everything to Marilyn but he didn't trust himself, and yes, he didn't trust her. And here's the wicked thing, he still didn't because he knew she had done the same thing, was still doing the same thing. The Marilyn with Brian, come on, was that Marilyn? He didn't believe so.

But maybe he was wrong and there was no real me or real you. Maybe, he surmised, we reflect the qualities our partners desire in us. As we change partner we shed one skin and grow another; different but not a fake, just a different truth. Your life was therefore a series of different yous. The young Daniel Clement who rode with Bill Seratono was no more true than the older one with Marilyn, simply the first; and the Marilyn he'd come to know no more or less genuine than the one now with Brian.

•••

He walked into the detective room to news from Earle that there were no matches between Karskine's time in jail and any of the Dingos.

'I think it's a dead-end,' Clement told Earle.

'There's Darwin and Adelaide still.'

But Clement was sure as he could be that Karskine was not their guy, nor for that matter any of the Dingos, though Mal Gross had arranged for every single member to present himself for interview. That was something Clement would divvy up between the team.

In his office he stared at the board looking for inspiration, feeling the pressure build like a wave behind him. Now he had done the local paper it was inevitable Perth would get involved, television especially. With a second murder now, Eastern States media would inevitably follow. It irked that he still hadn't spoken to Schaffer's sister. He was about to call Perth HQ and ask for a translator. Bugger it. He may as well give it a go himself. Hamburg was six or seven hours behind, breakfast time, a good time to find people home. He called the number for the sister's former neighbour, Frau Gerlanger. It rang for a few seconds and a woman answered, in German naturally. She sounded elderly.

'I'm Australian. Do you speak English by any chance? I'm trying to reach Christiane Hohlmann.'

'Moment.'

The single word was heavily accented. There were sounds in the background. A man came on. He sounded youngish. His English was excellent.

'Can I help?'

'Yes, thank you.'

Clement repeated what he had just said, explained who he was and where he was calling from. 'I believe Frau Gerlanger might know how to reach Frau Hohlmann. Her brother has died and we're trying to notify her.'

'I'll ask my grandmother.'

Clement waited during the exchange. The grandson came back on.

'My grandmother says Frau Hohlmann died two months ago.'

Clement felt a pang of frustration, then immediate guilt for it.

'Could you ask your grandmother if Frau Hohlmann was in touch with her brother much?'

Again the action played off stage.

'She says they hardly had anything to do with one another. Christiane left Hamburg when she was young and settled here.'

With more to and fro Clement filled in a picture of Christiane Hohlmann. She had been single till quite late in life, at least for that generation. As Christiane Schaffer, she married Bernard Hohlmann in her late thirties but had no children. Her husband died quite a long time ago and she had lived at the apartment complex until health issues had made her move to a retirement village with medical staff. Her brother would occasionally ring her or write to her but they were not close. She had liked her brother's wife but the marriage had not lasted long and Christiane Hohlmann had sounded like she was not surprised, she blamed Dieter. According to her he had a gambling problem and had nearly lost the family home at one point. As far as Frau Gerlanger knew, her late friend was comfortably off without being wealthy. She had owned her apartment and sold it when she moved but was worried the money would not be enough to last her the rest of her days. Sadly it had been more than sufficient.

'Could you ask your grandmother the name of Dieter's ex-wife and whether there were any children?'

Dieter's ex-wife was Maria. Frau Gerlanger believed she had remarried but still lived in Hamburg, she did not know her new name. There had been no children with Dieter but Frau Gerlanger did not know if Maria had children of her own with her second husband or stepchildren. Clement obtained the address of the retirement village. Before he hung up he tried another pot shot.

'Frau Gerlanger wouldn't know the executor of the estate would she?' He had to elaborate and expand on 'executor' before the grandson understood.

'Yes. Christiane left a favourite painting of hers to my grandmother.'

'Would she have the contact number?'

'I have it here.'

The grandson read off the contact number and address for a Munich solicitor. Clement thanked him profusely and rang off. Feeling pumped, he tried the solicitor's number fully expecting to strike out but once again fortune favoured him.

'Do you speak English by any chance?' he asked of the pleasant sounding young woman.

'A little bit.'

Her English turned out to be perfectly adequate. Clement explained the situation. He was hoping somebody might be able to tell him if the late Dieter Schaffer was to inherit something. The young woman cautiously told him he would need to talk to her superior Herr Broden. He was currently with a client. Clement gave her his numbers and said he would greatly appreciate Broden calling at his earliest opportunity.

'Does he speak English?'

'Yes very well, much better than me.'

They laughed. Clement imagined the young woman way across the other side of the world, her conditioned hair bouncing, nice perfume, a tight turtleneck—why he imagined a turtleneck he wasn't sure, some sort of cultural stereotype. A lifetime ago it would have been inconceivable they could have had this conversation. Now it was possible that they could be on a date in thirty-six hours; earlier, if Skype counted as a date.

'Thank you again.'

'My pleasure.'

The buoyancy he felt after the conversation with the pleasant girl and his information from the Gerlangers was quickly punctured by his tooth suddenly aching again but he sidelined the pain and called Shepherd for an update. He and Taylor had done every shop in town and the Roebuck Hotel. Nobody had seen Schaffer and Lee together. They had re-canvassed most of Dieter's former customers for another duck egg. None were admitting to having supplied Lee with a joint but Shepherd thought they were all shady.

'I reckon they're worried about dobbing on bikers.'

'Try the Cleo.'

Shepherd rang off with a grunt.

Just when Clement had hoped that there might be new momentum from Lee's murder, it was developing into a grind again. He wanted a coffee but wondered if that would exacerbate the toothache. He poked his head outside. Earle was yawning and stretching.

'Lee's so-called girlfriend turns out to be an occasional bonk,' he informed Clement. 'She didn't have anything useful on him.'

The phone in Clement's office was ringing again. He moved back inside swiftly.

'Detective Clement, Kimberley Police.'

'This is August Broden. You telephoned me about Christiane Hohlmann.'

'Yes, I did. Thank you for returning my call. Do you want me to call you back?'

'Will it take long?'

'I don't think so.'

'Then please, proceed.'

Clement told him the basics. Broden was suitably alarmed to hear his client's brother had been killed, possibly murdered.

'You think it could be for the estate?'

'That's my question, was her brother a beneficiary?'

Christiane Hohlmann had left her brother virtually all her estate, over one hundred and sixty thousand euros.

'And you had communicated this to him?'

He had. He had sent Schaffer an email at first and then Dieter Schaffer had called him. All the relevant forms had been emailed. Schaffer had signed them and posted them back.

'You don't know this? There is no record?'

The German seemed offended by the slackness of Clement and his cohorts.

'His computer was stolen and we found no paperwork.'

Clement ascertained that Dieter's payday was scheduled for about four months hence. The last time Broden and Schaffer had spoken was about three weeks earlier.

'What happens now?' he asked the solicitor.

'If Dieter Schaffer left a will, it would go to whoever he nominated.'

'We found no will.'

'Then if he has no family I suppose it gets put in trust until somebody claims it, a cousin, a relative somewhere.'

'Dieter Schaffer had an ex-wife. Was she mentioned in the will at all? Her name is Maria but she has remarried.'

Broden said the only other person receiving anything was Frau Gerlanger. She had been left a painting.

'And Frau Hohlmann's personal effects?'

Disposed of by the retirement home.

Clement thanked him for his assistance and mentioned it was possible he might need to speak to him again. Broden said that was fine and wished him well.

...

'Dieter Schaffer's windfall probably had nothing to do with drugs.'

Clement stood outside the rear door of the station with Earle who was blowing a stream of smoke into a sky dark and unsettled like a room before an argument. The scent of wild flowers had been hovering until Earle's smoke stream obliterated it.

'You think it was the inheritance he was talking about?'

'Yeah. Over a hundred and fifty thousand euros.'

Earle wondered if somebody might have killed him for it.

'There's no other beneficiary, no relatives.'

'And Lee?'

'Could be exactly as Marchant said. Somebody hands Lee a joint ...'

Mal Gross, covered in the fug of tedium, joined them.

Clement didn't stop. '... "Wow, great grass where did you get it?" He approaches Dieter. Dieter says fuck off. He doesn't need to sell speed, doesn't even need to sell his pot. He's got a fortune coming. You saw how he lived.'

He turned to Gross and explained Dieter's windfall.

Earle ground out his cigarette. 'So the argument was just an argument. But the murders have to be connected by something. It can't be coincidence that we're investigating Dieter Schaffer and his dope and the next person killed is a biker he argued with, who was at his place the night after his death. You don't think that?'

He didn't. And yet something wasn't right, wasn't natural. He wished he could figure it out but his brain was tired. Earle was still spit-balling.

'Could it be somebody with a grudge against drugs and people who sell them?'

'It could, *if* somebody knew Lee was here to make and distribute drugs but that was secret.'

'Not totally. The Dingos could have leaked, or Lee's mob.'

Mal Gross shuffled. 'I've been at it for hours. I can't find anything linking the victims. If the killer is somebody connected with the Dingoes then the reason they are doing it is because they want all the action for themselves but I don't think the Dingos have anybody smart enough or ambitious enough for that.'

Clement was inclined to agree but they had to pursue it. 'Maybe there are factions within CZG. When is our first Dingo turning up?'

'Ten minutes, Marinovic the landlord.'

'They say there's a cyclone heading our way.' Mal Gross kept in close contact with all the Emergency Services.

'How big?'

'A big one, a cat four maybe.'

'When?' Earle and Clement spoke simultaneously.

'They reckon Wednesday or Thursday.'

'That's all we need.' Earle had spoken what they were all thinking. Normally cyclones bypassed Broome. Onslow was more likely to cop it. But if a cyclone did hit it would mean a shutdown of most everything, communications, airports, shops. Even a small one would see the available uniforms diverted to emergency business. If it was a big one, they could lose buildings. He would have to make sure all evidence was totally secured.

'Put that on top of a serial killer, I don't like the chances of a big tourist season.'

26

Over the next four hours they interviewed Marinovic and seven other members of the gang. Not one of them produced even the faintest spark in Clement. Some admitted meeting Lee, none put Lee and Schaffer together, none put Lee with any other members of any other gang. In between interviews Risely updated Clement on the steady stream of media requests. When the last Dingo had thudded his way from the interview room down the corridor to the exit Risely cornered Clement again.

'You'll have to speak to them sooner or later. They know I'm just the desk jockey. They want the operational head.'

'Tell them I'm busy.'

'Perth is getting restless.'

'Then the Commissioner should do the interviews. We've got nothing: no murder weapon, no motive, one pathetic piece of CCTV. We can't put Lee at Jasper's Creek with Schaffer, we can't put Lee together with anybody else who might have been at Jasper's Creek. If he wasn't a bikie we'd probably not be looking for a connection.'

'But he was a bikie, right? So we need to go down that path.'

It was true and there was no point taking out his

frustration on Risely. Clement retreated to his office and slumped in his chair. His phone buzzed and given the time of night he automatically assumed it was his mother, and in his current mood, bad news. The ID told him he was right about the first thing.

'Hi Mum.'

'Hello? Daniel?'

She was on her mobile and clearly not sure where to speak. 'Just put it to your ear. It will work fine.'

'That better?'

She was loud and clear.

'Much. Everything okay?'

'He's improving.'

Clement's body relaxed.

'They've moved him from intensive care to a ward. He's in with two other men.'

His mother ran down the condition of the others. Clement had little interest in them but he let her talk. Eventually she swung back to his father.

'His lucidity comes and goes. One moment he is talking quite normally and then he's off in his own world. I think he thought he was back in Broome at one stage. But they say he should gradually return to normal. He's eating well and he's able to move everything. How was your trip?'

'It was fine.'

'Phoebe rang. It was so nice to hear from her, poor little thing. And Marilyn, it was very nice of her.'

Clement never knew quite what to say when his parents brought her up. He suspected they thought he was the prime driver in the break-up. He did not have the kind of relationship with his parents where one shared deep emotions but one time his mother had looked reproachfully at him and said something about how you don't realise what you have till it's gone. Well his mother hadn't had to live with Geraldine conducting Marilyn like she was lead violin in her orchestra. Clement and his mum talked the inanities of life—plane capacity, hospital elevators, weather—and both felt better for it.

'I'll call you tomorrow. Bye Mum.'

It was no use just sitting on his arse. He walked back out to the main area and caught Risely about to head home. He offered an olive branch.

'How about I speak to local radio, ask if anybody saw any vehicles near Blue Haze or Jasper's Creek on the nights in question.'

Risely was enthused. 'I'll set it up for tomorrow, say seven thirty? That way we'll get the breakfast and most listeners.'

Clement okayed that but his brain was still mired in cul-de-sacs, and obviously it showed. Risely's demeanour changed to pity. 'Hey, it'll come good.'

Shepherd was still out chasing down probably fruitless leads, Gross and Earle looked dog-tired. Clement saw no point keeping them here.

'Unless you've got something special you're chasing up, you guys may as well go home.'

Mal Gross was handing over to the night crew and said he'd head as soon as it was done.

Earle shoved back in his chair. 'You want to come to our place for a bite to eat?'

It was kind of Earle to ask but Clement needed his own company.

'Nah, I've got a few things.'

Actually he had nothing on but right now he needed to be alone. Clement went to grab his jacket from his office but stopped at the threshold. Something inside was flashing. What the hell was that?

In the centre of the meeting table was the child's watch in the evidence bag, pulsing evenly. He guessed Lisa Keeble had left it for him, thinking he'd return it to evidence, but she had been so busy she had forgotten to mention it. He scooped it up and was about to call Phoebe but decided it was too late and drove to the Cleo wondering if Shepherd and Taylor might be there following up on Schaffer's customers.

There was no moon. It felt like the air was slowly closing on him from all sides, squeezing the juice from him. He had the window down as he drove along the coast but the ocean offered no succour as if too busy brooding on the inevitable pain that would come with the cyclone. The Cleo carpark was thinly populated. Perhaps news of the second murder had spread and people were already staying at home.

...

'It is a bit freaky,' admitted Michaeley the barmaid handing him his fish burger. She said the only clientele had been hard-core regulars, nearly all men.

'You can't help looking at them wondering, you know, are you the one?'

Clement had established right away Shepherd had been in earlier asking whether anybody had seen Schaffer and Lee together. Neither Michaeley nor any of the other staff remembered Arturo Lee. Michaeley wiped a glass that was already clean.

'Shep offered to drive me home if I was worried.'

Of course he had.

'Do you know if he's single?' She sounded hopeful. Lisa Keeble would be pleased she might finally be off the hook.

'Very.' Clement thought he saw a small smile appear.

'He said he had to chase down a few more things and then he'd come back before closing.'

Shep doing his civic duty. Michaeley slid down the bar to serve a thirsty patron and Clement took the opportunity to edge away to a high bar table. He began eating the burger. It was not as good as the previous time. The expectation had been too high or maybe it was that the kitchen had closed by the time he'd arrived and Michaeley had prevailed on the cook to fix him up as a favour. But he was hungry and it was better than anything he could have put together at the flat.

By the time he finished the burger the bar had thinned even further and he had no desire to bump into Shepherd so he carried his plate over to Michaeley and wished her well. He drove back to his flat, dwelling on Dieter Schaffer. Had Schaffer been referring to the money from his sister's estate when he said he'd be rolling on it? Was he planning to use his inheritance to buy into the drug operation of Lee's or start a rival one?

Clement parked and climbed the stairs to his apartment which was baking and airless. He left the front door open and pulled the sliding glass door that gave onto a tiny balcony overlooking the harbour but there was no breeze. It was like being buried in compost. He put on his Kmart articulated fan, clicked on The Cruel Sea and lay back on his bed knowing he wouldn't sleep for hours and worrying about the interview he would have to give in the morning.

27

Standing in his kitchen, Gerd Osterlund gazed over the Indian Ocean, this morning the blue-grey colour of a revolver. It had threatened to rain in the early hours, distant rumblings, air so dense you could feel the moisture in your lungs with every breath. He loved the humidity, so different from where he had grown up. The sky this morning was remarkably similar in shade to the dark grey trousers he remembered on bus conductors of his youth, trousers that always matched the sky overhead. If it were purely a visual world you could momentarily forget you'd ever left Germany but even now at five thirty a.m. it was sticky, the air holding you close like a lover who had stayed too long. In Germany if you saw a sky like this, you could expect cold that gnawed your bones.

Osterlund watched coffee drip into the small silver cup. He thought of Dieter Schaffer. It had been almost a week. At first he'd been very concerned but now it seemed likely Schaffer had simply got himself into trouble with bikers. It was bound to happen. He picked up the cup, sipped, and placed it back on the saucer. He'd already dressed in preparation for his walk. Resting on the bench his phone plinked, its signal for a text. He wondered which of the territories might be contacting him at this time: surely too early for Europe?

He guessed North America and opened his phone display.

A photo filled the screen. The cup and its chrome saucer leapt from his hand. Coffee splattered over the tiles. His eyes remained fixed on the screen. His heart pounded through his chest. One text, a number not recognised by his contacts list.

Who had sent this? The detective? Did he know more than he let on? But why? Surely he would just come right out—

'Are you alright?'

Astuthi had appeared at the top of the stairs, hair wild, a white camisole over her dark skin.

'It slipped out of my hands.'

She was looking at him acutely. Her eyes strayed towards the phone. He clicked it off.

'I wasn't properly awake. I'm sorry, go back to bed.'

'I'll clean up.'

'I can do that.'

'I'm awake now. It's fine, you sure you're okay?'

'Yes, I'm good. I was just about to go on my walk.'

'Well you go, I'll do this.'

He hesitated but knew if he did not follow his routine she would worry. Still shaken he descended the stairs to the bedroom where his heartbeat slowly returned to normal and his brain unclogged. At first he had been on alert over Schaffer's murder but the news of the bikie killing had relaxed him, made him think it was something to do with the crowd that Schaffer hung around. Schaffer had always been a problem. He cursed himself for his own stupidity in not taking action himself. He needed time to think. He could hear Astuthi moving about above; it would be easier too without her at his shoulder.

Exiting the house his eyes scanned the low scrub that led to the beach. It was not possible for anybody to hide there without being seen. All the same he diverted to the barbecue, armed himself with the sharp knife he used to slice steaks and placed it in the long side-pocket of his shorts. His mind was racing. He forced himself to click his phone back on and look at the photo again. No, it was not a prank; somebody wanted him to feel their breath on his neck. Reflexively he swung around. As far as the eye could see was pristine white sand, not a person in sight. He started south as usual. Going to the police was not an option. Who the hell could it be: one of Schaffer's old police colleagues? Would they really have done that to Schaffer? He'd dismissed Schaffer's concerns about the Edershen murder but now it seemed he should have paid more attention. Where did the biker fit? The logical thing to do would be to leave for a while, see if the police got anywhere. Bali was too close. Europe made more sense, a working holiday. Or he could stay here, tough it out, hire some muscle. In Bali he'd kept a revolver. He regretted he'd left it there.

Normally, thongs in hand, he liked to walk along the strip close to the water's edge, where the sand was soft but not sloppy, enjoying the feel of wet sand on his soles. He could see a lone fisherman about a hundred metres south and decided to give him a wide berth even though he was pretty sure it was the same one who had been there most of the week. He had been tempted to strike up a conversation but he had told the detective the truth: he had little interest in fish other than when served on a plate with crisp potato wedges. Think calmly, he told himself. He knew people, ex-cops, other thugs. They could probably do a better job than the police here. Find whoever was responsible and stop it. But did he need to stay for that? He and Tuthi could enjoy a holiday anyway. His travel agent—

The thought stopped in its tracks. A distant shape appeared heading towards him fast. He planted his feet.

His hand gripped the handle of the knife. The figure was close enough now to make out: a man running with his dog. The dog was a red setter or something like it. The man was pumping his arms, no sign of an axe. Perhaps he had a gun. Osterlund was already regretting his decision to leave the house. Then the angle of the man's run changed sharply, away from him up towards the road. The setter followed. Osterlund edged the other way towards beach and the man and the dog passed a good thirty metres away. Osterlund turned back and watched as they continued on their course, travelling fast. Soon they were a dot behind him. Up ahead, as far as the eye could see, there was nobody. That was it then, settled, he didn't want to have his blood pressure hit one-eighty every time he passed somebody. Soon as he got back he would organise a long business trip. The police could hardly find that suspicious. He'd put somebody in his house who could find the source of his problem and make it go away. Something fizzed through the air behind him but before he could turn, a burst of pain exploded in his knee. It was sharp, as intense as any he'd known. He tried to walk but toppled into the sand, recoiling at the sight of an iron arrowhead poking through the front of his knee.

28

He was terrified. There was nothing firm under his feet. Gravity was pulling him down, water rushing into his nose and mouth. It required all his energy to try and keep his head clear but his arms had lost almost all their strength and felt sewn on, sodden, as if they belonged to a dummy. His father watched on, bending down towards him, hairy legs, blue bathers with green trimmings, the kind that looked like shorts.

'Help me,' he tried to scream but his father just kept gesticulating with his arms and exhorting him with words that were lost beneath the terror of his pumping pulse. The bitterness of the chlorine was in his mouth at the back of his throat, coming in gulps now. With his last effort he reached out and felt the tips of his fingers contact the solid wall of the swimming pool. Clapping him like he was some hero, his father reached down and rubbed his hair but he could still hear nothing, his ears blocked as he gasped for breath.

A burst of music slammed into him but not Neil Diamond, his father's favourite. The image pixilated, the swimming pool and patio gave way to the dirty white ceiling of his flat.

His phone was ringing.

He reached for it, the dream lingering. He had been six years old, late for a kid to start learning to swim in

Australia. He couldn't remember if he was angry with his father, he supposed so. Why wouldn't he be? The phone number on the ID seemed familiar. He pressed answer and put the phone to his ear.

'Clement.'

'Detective, it is Astuthi Osterlund.'

Her transparent anxiety made him alert. A bad feeling was already oozing under his skin.

'Yes, Mrs Osterlund.'

'I'm worried, my husband has not returned from his walk.'

'When did he go out?'

'Just after five thirty. I went down to the beach and searched. I couldn't see him. He's not answering his phone.'

It was six fifty now. For once he had overslept.

'It's not seven yet.'

Her words came in a jumble and Clement had to pick his way through them. Gerd Osterlund was always back from his walk by six thirty. Earlier this morning before he went on the walk he received a phone call or text. He dropped his cup on the kitchen floor which had woken his wife. He told her it had slipped but she could see him looking at the phone and he was concerned, scared, even though he was trying to hide it. When he didn't arrive back by six thirty she had started calling his phone every couple of minutes. It went to his voicemail.

By the time Astuthi Osterlund had reached this point in her narrative Clement was heading to the shower.

'I'll be there in ten minutes. Call me if he turns up.'

...

It was closer to fifteen minutes before he swung into the driveway. He'd lost time calling Risely to explain why he would not be doing the scheduled interview.

'You think there's anything in it?'

'I hope not.'

Whatever Risely was thinking he kept to himself and said he'd take care of the media. Clement drove to where Astuthi Osterlund waited anxiously by the front steps. She wore a brilliant batik wrap over her slender body. Her face was lined with worry. He climbed out.

'No sign?'

'No.' She was trying to restrain her panic. 'After Dieter ...'

The image was too disturbing for her to complete the sentence.

'Does he ever take longer on his walk? I mean we're talking what, forty-five minutes?'

She was shaking her head.

'I thought first maybe he met somebody he knew and they walked around the point to the Mimosa for coffee but he would have called me.'

'His battery might have run out or he could have lost his phone.'

'He would borrow one. And this morning, I could tell he was worried about the phone call.'

'He didn't say who called or texted?'

'No.'

Clement was already running scenarios: the unfaithful husband having an affair, promising he'd leave the wife, his lover saying enough is enough, threatening blackmail. On another occasion in a different situation he would have gone with that but he had a potential serial killer out there, Schaffer was known to Osterlund, and they were both German. There was enough to set alarm bells ringing.

'Why don't you take me on his usual route?'

'This way.'

He followed her through the house and down a staircase to a bedroom and bathroom below, modern, nicely furnished but without the wow factor of the living room. A big sliding glass door opened onto a patio which ended in low brush and white sand.

'I'll leave it open in case he comes back.'

Normally the salt air was invigorating but today it was a suffocating damp cloth.

After about twenty metres they hit low dunes and very quickly the beach itself. Clement realised he needed to remove his shoes. As he peeled his socks he called the station. Mal Gross had arrived. He filled him in. 'Tell Graeme to stay there and interview the rest of the bikies unless I call to say otherwise. Anybody else around?'

'Jared.'

'Can you send him here?'

A pause, then Gross said Jared was on his way.

It was hard going through the sand and Clement angled inevitably close to the water. There were a handful of people scattered along the beach.

'How far does he normally walk?'

'He leaves at five thirty, back at six thirty. He was a few minutes later today.'

A creature of habit. That could be a bad thing if you had enemies.

'Straight along the beach?'

'Yes, always this way.'

That meant thirty minutes south then the same back.

'Last night everything seemed fine?'

'Yes.'

'Tell me about this morning again.'

She told him how she'd woken as she usually did when Osterlund's alarm went off at five fifteen.

'Normally I stay in bed. He has a coffee and then goes on his walk. I was drifting back to sleep when, I think it was his text sound, then a crash. I ran upstairs.'

She explained how he looked, pale, not right, the cup was on the floor, coffee everywhere.

Clement wondering now if it was a medical thing, whether Osterlund may have had a stroke or something similar, then wandered off disoriented. Even if it was just the shock of whatever that text may have been, he might be taking his time coming to grips with it.

'So you didn't actually see him start on the beach?'

'No. But he didn't come up through the house.' She was very anxious.

'It's alright, just trying to cover all bases.'

'His flip-flops were gone. He always takes them.'

'Is it possible he might have gone around the house back to the front? That somebody could have arrived?'

'I would have heard them.'

'You said you came out to look for him?'

'I ran out and looked to see if he was coming back. Then I called you.'

'Did you speak to anybody on the beach who might have seen him?'

'There was not many people around. Two backpackers, you know? They hadn't seen him.'

'What's his number again?'

She rattled it off. He dialled it and got a voice message. If the axeman had got to Osterlund, he could have dragged him into the ocean. After all, he'd stuck Dieter Schaffer in the creek. Clement plugged on through the sand trying not to betray his growing concern. He was already sweating freely.

'Does he have any other family? Were you his first wife?'

'He wasn't married before. He was never going to get married till he met me. His parents are dead. He has no brothers or sisters.'

'When did you meet?'

'Six years ago. My family have a restaurant in Bali.

Gerd used to dine there. I knew him for two years before we dated. He taught me German, I taught him Indonesian, that's how we met.'

'What did your parents think?'

'My mother was worried I would want babies later and Gerd was too old, but they like Gerd. He is respectful to them. He is two years older than my father.'

Clement's phone rang. It was Jared Taylor. He had arrived at the house. Clement told him to drive the streets from the house to the beach in case Osterlund had for some reason taken the road back instead of the beach. He remembered Osterlund entering from the front of the house the other day after his walk.

'Check whether there have been any accidents. If you see nothing, park and walk the scrub alongside the beach. He usually walked for around thirty minutes south before turning back.'

The sky seemed more troubled by the minute; pent-up anger would be unleashed with force. They would need to make progress quickly.

Clement was no match for Astuthi Osterlund, she seemed to glide over the sand. He struggled to stay with her.

'Your husband said he thought Dieter Schaffer used to ring just to speak to you.'

She managed a smile that might be called wry.

'Gerd might say that but it's not true. Dieter liked talking to Gerd, he wanted to talk to someone from the old homeland and I think he looked up to Gerd.'

'Did you like Schaffer, apart from him being a drunk?'

'He was fine. He used to talk about his ex-wife, how he messed things up and missed her. Gerd was harsh with him.'

'How?'

'You know, he'd not really want to listen to him or

share with him, in case he started hanging around, like Dieter was…' she pondered the right word, '… an intrusion. I don't think my husband liked his life in Germany much and Dieter would remind him of it.'

Clement could relate. He felt uncomfortable around Bill Seratono because Bill reminded him of what he had been, of times past, of confided dreams. There was that unspoken accusation he felt when he was around Seratono: you shouldn't have left, you're a turncoat and so on. The worst thing was he could not be sure if it was really there or it was simply his own guilty projection. Maybe Schaffer made Osterlund feel guilty because he was successful and Schaffer not.

'Have you tried all his friends?'

'No. He would answer his phone.'

'Maybe a friend had some emergency and Gerd went to help.'

This gave her hope. She took to the task feverishly, making half a dozen calls in as many minutes. Nobody had seen or heard from him but they all promised to ring around and keep an eye out. Clement had no choice but to pile on her misery.

'I have to ask you this: is your marriage good?'

'Yes, of course.'

'You don't think your husband has some other relationship?'

'Gerd doesn't have relationships except in business. You ask me if he has other lovers, possibly, probably. He's a man. He does business overseas. I'm not foolish. But if he got a phone call that worries him, it's not from a woman.'

'You're sure?'

'If Gerd wants to leave, he'll tell me. If I can't keep him, that is my problem. But this morning he seemed … afraid.'

She spoke the word as if testing its efficacy, then nodded like she'd nailed the emotion.

They walked on beyond the usual distance Osterlund travelled, passing in total only five groups of people on the way. Clement asked each of them had they seen Osterlund. All responded in the negative. He phoned Taylor who was now on foot, around a quarter of the way through the scrub heading in the same direction. He'd found nothing so far. Clement said he would turn around and come back through the scrub from the south towards Taylor. He called Mal Gross again and caught him halfway through a coffee.

'The bikers are in with Graeme.'

'Good. Listen, I'm going to need some help to search the area. There's no sign of Osterlund.'

Gross promised to get some uniforms onto it immediately.

'Tell them to call me when they have reached the house.'

Clement guided Astuthi Osterlund up towards the scrub area. She was growing more dispirited by the minute. They picked their way back north. It was not as easy to see the ground ahead as it had been on the pristine beach. If Osterlund's body was lying flat they wouldn't see it until almost upon it. Clement couldn't help thinking about the similarities in the attacks on Schaffer and Lee. Both had happened in remote locations. And at six in the morning here it would also have been deserted. A moment later he was back on the line to Gross.

'The IT guy, Manners: can you get him onto Osterlund's provider and find if there was any communication this morning?'

'Sure. The boss is asking if he should be worried.'

Clement was conscious of the woman with him. 'He should be thinking about it.'

As he ended the call he saw Astuthi Osterlund get off her phone.

'Our neighbours, the Lucases, are going to drive around and look for him.' She was near tears. 'Why would somebody want to hurt Gerd?'

Clement's phone rang. Astuthi's eyes filled with dread. It was Jo di Rivi. She and Restoff had reached the house, Lalor and Hagan were right behind them.

'I want you to start searching all that bush around the house.'

Astuthi Osterlund's fear ramped up. 'Why are you looking in the bush?'

He did not want to say, 'In case your husband's body is there.'

'We need be thorough.'

She let that sink in as they walked on without conversation. Eventually they got close enough to make out Taylor heading towards them. He pointed behind him.

'Nothing. There's a couple of lay-bys just back there where vehicles drive off the main road to get close to the beach but they're empty.'

'You keep going, double-check the area we just covered. We'll go back to the house.'

It took them about ten minutes to reach the first of the areas Jared Taylor had described as a lay-by. It was little more than a sand track off the main road that ran up through scrub and stopped about ten metres behind dunes. Clement scanned around. There was broken and flattened scrub where a vehicle or vehicles had turned but it was now empty. He was vaguely conscious of Astuthi Osterlund trying her phone again as she had done every five minutes or so. Then he heard the sound of a phone ringing. She hadn't heard it and was about to hang up.

'Don't.'

For a second she was confused but realised what this sudden command meant. Clement was already past her heading towards the beach. She ran after him. The beach was still bare but the sound pulled him to an area ten to twenty metres in. A phone lay on the sand, pitted by wet dark spots. Blood?

'Stay back,' he yelled to her. He slipped on evidence gloves and picked up the phone. The screen was opaque. He pressed it and a photo filled the small screen, a photo of Dieter Schaffer at Jasper's Creek, lying stretched out on the ground in his pristine t-shirt, his head split, grotesque and bloody.

29

Clement felt like the kid in the school play whose job it was to stand there with a crown and cape looking important while the other kids sang and danced and did all the stuff that actually required talent. He was immobile in the centre of Gerd Osterlund's lounge room as a variety of techs in full crime-scene clothing moved about dusting, photographing, cataloguing. Even Graeme Earle had something to do. Having cancelled the interviews with the remaining Dingos he now sat at the kitchen bench methodically combing recent emails on Osterlund's computer.

'They're not on Facebook? Twitter?' he asked Clement.

'Mrs Osterlund says not.'

The crime scene now spanned the beach and the house, the beach having been sectioned off from a hundred metres north of the house to the lay-by south where they had found the phone. Despite the photograph on Osterlund's phone, it couldn't be absolutely determined Astuthi Osterlund hadn't killed her husband, been involved in his abduction, or colluded with him to stage it. Clement did not believe any of these things but decreed nonetheless the house be treated like a crime scene. He had to balance potential contamination of the scene with the possibility that somebody would call the house and make ransom demands, so Mrs Osterlund was still inside being shadowed by Jo di Rivi. They were currently downstairs in the bedroom which had already been processed. Lisa Keeble had nowhere near enough bodies to work the case so more techs were flying in from Perth.

Scott Risely entered the house in an obligatory crime-scene suit. His fingers raked back through his cropped grey hair.

'Perth is sending a media liaison person and three more detectives.'

'You know who?' Clement hoped it would be people he'd worked well with before.

'Not yet. You think he was abducted?'

'That's my best guess.'

'Why different this time? If it's our guy why not just kill him?'

'He might want to know something from Osterlund. He may want to just draw it out.'

'Or it could be a ransom. Osterlund is wealthy, right?' Risely automatically lowered his voice. 'Where's the wife?'

'Downstairs. Di Rivi is with her.'

'I'll get the phones monitored.'

Clement scanned the empty beach through the glass. No birds. Something bad was coming. 'I don't think this is a ransom situation. The abductor has had time to call her. He must know her next move would be to call us.'

'We still need the phones monitored.'

'I agree.'

Risely leaned back in to keep it confidential.

'Are we sure this is the same guy? I mean, maybe the wife wants him to disappear and it's a good opportunity.'

'What about the photo of Dieter Schaffer on his phone? She'd have to have something to do with that.'

Risely remained suspicious. 'If Osterlund isn't involved in something, why didn't he call us when he got this disturbing text?'

'It was very early, maybe he thought too early, went for a walk to kill time.'

'Or he is involved.'

Sound logic. Clement was already planning ahead. 'We need whatever CCTV we can get: coast road, town, service stations, anything between say five a.m. and seven a.m.'

Risely moved off to get it in train. Clement considered their killer-cum-abductor. This was the most dangerous of his crimes so far, with a much higher chance of detection. Either he was becoming bolder—not uncommon in a serial criminal—or Osterlund represented some much bigger prize than the others had. Maybe Risely was right and there was money involved?

Jo di Rivi appeared from the stairs. 'I'm getting her a cup of tea,' she explained.

'What's your take?'

The constable looked surprised to be asked. Clement pushed. 'You think she's genuine?'

'Yes, I do.'

'Me too. How's the dog?'

Jo di Rivi smiled proudly. 'She's good but she's hardly seen me.'

Even our pets suffer our vocation, thought Clement. 'You got a name yet?'

'Working on it.'

Clement's phone buzzed again and di Rivi headed to the kitchen bench.

'Clement.'

'It's Brett Manners. I thought that phone number was familiar.'

'Which phone number?'

'The one that sent the text to Osterlund's phone. It's the phone we were looking for, Arturo Lee's.'

...

Risely slapped his fist into his palm in emphasis. 'The photo of the dead Schaffer came from Arturo Lee's phone. Lee is on a slab in Perth. Well, that's it, that's our connection.'

Clement had called his boss and Graeme Earle outside to the front veranda. The uniforms were assiduously going about their business, processing the surrounding bush.

Risely ran like a marlin. 'Lee and some associate kill Schaffer, take his photo for some reason. Extortion maybe? They're going to scare the shit out of Osterlund so he'll pay up. The unknown associate gets greedy, kills Lee.'

Clement felt the need to haul in his boss.

'Actually just because the photo was sent from that phone doesn't mean it was taken on that phone. It could have been taken on a camera and downloaded to the phone before being sent. It could have been blue-toothed from another phone. All you can say is it was texted from that phone.'

Earle soaked up this revelation. 'So Lee may not have been at Jasper's Creek?'

'Exactly. It could have been transferred to his phone after he was killed.'

Risely was unfazed. He checked his watch. 'There's a strong connection somewhere, even if we don't know exactly what. I've got a radio interview in ten. I'll ask for anyone who was on the beach this morning around five thirty to six thirty to call us. I've got the phones and the CCTV stuff underway.'

Earle said, 'Schaffer and Osterlund are both German. You know what these dickheads are like, most of them are clueless. Maybe Osterlund was the target all along, "the rich Kraut", but they screw up and go after the wrong one.'

It wouldn't be the first time something like that had happened but Clement couldn't see why the abductor would give Osterlund a heads up. Why not just snatch him? Clement made himself look at the photo of Schaffer again. There was something about it he should be seeing. Clement's phone rang. Lisa Keeble was overseeing the evidence collection from the lay-by, run off her feet but holding it together.

'Definitely signs that a vehicle was there recently, and I think we can say it's not a small car and it's not a truck but there's no tyre tracks to speak of. Just got off the phone from Rhino, too, nothing in the samples I took from the undercarriage of Karskine's car that matches any vegetation or soil from Jasper's Creek.'

The trouble with the science of a case was it was always two or three steps behind where the case was heading. Clement mentioned to Keeble the wet stuff in the sand where the phone had been found.

'Was it blood?' he asked.

'Yes. I'll let you know if it matches Osterlund's.'

'There didn't seem to be much of it.'

'There wasn't. I'd say it wasn't a big wound.'

'Could he have been shot?'

Keeble spoke off the phone, giving one of the techs a direction before returning to him. 'Normally I would expect more blood.'

'Small calibre?'

'Possibly. We've got a metal detector down there just in case there's a spent cartridge. We found an area that looks like the primary location of the attack on the beach about twenty-five metres in, equidistant almost to the ocean, slightly to the north-west. Then it's essentially clear until those drops where you found the phone. None on the grass where the lay-by borders the dunes so I think the vehicle was backed in and whoever was bleeding went straight into the vehicle.'

'Okay, keep me posted.' Clement felt sweat pooling on his collar, excitement or humidity, he wasn't certain. He ran Keeble's info past Earle. Earle's brows knitted.

'Osterlund was a fair size. How could one person have carried him? Are we looking at two?'

'Maybe. Osterlund gets a photo of his dead mate at five thirty. For whatever reason he doesn't call us or tell his wife about it. I don't know about you but I'd be very wary. Yet he still goes on his walk.'

'To meet someone?'

'He'd have to be cautious. Maybe he armed himself?'

...

Clement went back inside and took himself down the staircase to the bedroom. Jo di Rivi was sitting on the bed, Astuthi Osterlund staring out the window sipping her tea. She swung at his footfall, anxious. Clement got in quickly.

'We're still trying to work out what may have happened. At this stage we believe he may have been abducted.'

'You think they will ask for money?' She was hopeful.

'It's possible. Did you have any problems with neighbours? Friends?'

She shook her head. 'We don't see many people. They are all nice.'

'It seems somebody must have known Gerd's movements. Did he mention meeting anybody regularly down the beach?'

'No.'

'Have you had people through the house lately, besides your friends, any tradespeople?'

'Not for a long time. We had the dishwasher person last year.'

'Gerd went for his usual walk even after he had that text. I would think he might arm himself. Did your husband own a gun?'

'In Bali we had one. Some Europeans were attacked. He left it there.'

'Would you know if there are any knives missing?'

'I'll check.'

She started up the steps. Jo di Rivi was about to follow when Astuthi Osterlund stopped and turned back. 'He keeps a knife out here.'

She stepped out of the sliding doorway. Clement followed her to the barbecue, a luxury model shining like the skin of a formula one car. She picked up an empty self-sharpening scabbard from a sideboard.

'There was a knife here he uses for the barbecue.'

'You sure?'

'I washed it and put it there ready for the next time.'

Like Arturo Lee, Osterlund had armed himself. Like Lee it had made no difference. Clement looked at di Rivi. 'Credit cards, bank cards?'

'I got all the details and rang them through to the Sarge.'

One less thing to chase up but somehow he didn't think the abductor was going to make the mistake of using Osterlund's cards. The policewoman went back inside to stick with Astuthi. The air around Clement was seething. Osterlund had been on alert from the photo. In his mind Clement saw the carcass of Dieter Schaffer stretched out. A switch in his brain snapped on. Once more he studied the photo. He knew what it was that bugged him. It was posed. There was Dieter Schaffer stretched out on the ground, head bashed in but the focus was the pristine t-shirt, Hamburg 1979 right across Schaffer's chest. That was the message this photo sent, and now Clement understood why the t-shirt did not fit. It was not Schaffer's. The killer had brought it with him specifically to take this photo.

30

'Daniel?' Mathias Klendtwort's voice was croaky. Clement's call had clearly woken him.

'Mathias, I'm so sorry for doing this.' And he was, four a.m. was a helluva time for a phone call but Clement had felt it was urgent.

'It's okay. Hold on.'

He imagined Mathias getting himself up, clicking on a light. Clement trudged a little further towards the grey ocean. Nature's colours were merging, the sky and ocean one ominous grey.

'It's freezing here. I have to get the heater on. So?'

Klendtwort waited expectantly. Clement sketched the details of the second murder and the abduction of Osterlund. The German loosed a low whistle. Clement got to the point of his call.

'Did something big happen in nineteen seventy-nine that involved Dieter?'

'Yeah, real big, what we talked about before. We lost a colleague.'

'The drug czar business.'

'Yeah, the Emperor.'

'Tell me about it, can you?'

'You think this might be relevant?'

'It could be.'

'My whole time as a cop, it's the worst thing. Okay

it's Hamburg nineteen seventy-seven, seventy-eight, around there, and heroin is everywhere. I mean it was easier to get smack than icing sugar to pretend was smack. Nobody can find out exactly where it's coming from and we've got teams all over the city looking.' Clement heard the shuffling of a packet of matches and the subsequent strike of the match head. 'Al Quaeda have nothing on this group, they are smoke. So our superiors set a bunch of us up full time, Kripos that's what they call us, as a special unit with a couple of guys going undercover. I'm on the unit, Heinrich, Dieter and a really cool guy Pieter Gruen, he's the—how do you say it?—the golden boy, a great guy. We're looking, looking, following down leads, putting pressure on junkies, tapping phones. Nothing. Finally we get a break, a ship bust. Somebody talks. Pieter Gruen goes undercover, like deep cover, and follows the trail for a whole fucking year and we find it all leads back to this porn shop right in the middle of the Reeperbahn, right under our noses where we are stationed. That's the distribution centre. Most of the heroin in Hamburg is coming from a porn dealer they called the Emperor. I'll think of his name in a minute. He had a string of peepshows ... that's what you call them?'

'Yeah, that's right.'

'Is this too long?'

'No, please.'

'The Emperor ran peep shows and strip clubs and porn magazines and movies all through the Reeperbahn.'

Clement was remembering the photo of him they had found among Schaffer's printouts.

'The girls, the prostitutes and the strippers, they would do their shows and get a hit without having to leave where they were. There were loads of dealers and Gruen, he infiltrated there ... Donen, that was the guy's name, the Emperor—Kurt Donen I think—definitely Donen. He was like a phantom, this Donen. We had one photograph of him ever that Gruen got just before he disappeared. Nobody except his inner circle knew him and nobody knew them except the highest ranked dealers. Me, Heinrich, Dieter and a couple of other guys, we were the squad running the operation. Dieter was Gruen's control, he was the point of contact, the only one who would meet with him. I spied him once or twice around town but never acknowledged it. For his own security, we didn't even know where Gruen was living, not even Dieter.'

The German took a long drag on his cigarette. Above Clement a lone gull had appeared looking wary of the brooding ocean. Was it a brave scout or a scared straggler, he wondered. Klendtwort coughed then came back on.

'Anyway more than a year after we start this operation we have this bust finally going down. Gruen is in, it is all set up. We're ready to take down the Emperor in his porn shop. Gruen is going to call us in on his last visit, that's the plan. We never get the call.'

'What?'

'Gruen vanishes, disappears and the Emperor too. And for a while everybody is pointing the finger at Pieter, saying he has gone over to the dark side and we have internal investigators checking our bank accounts and up our backsides. A week or two later body parts start turning up in the river wrapped in porn magazines. It was Pieter Gruen, cut apart by a chainsaw. We were devastated all of us, you can imagine, especially Dieter. Pieter had a boy he loved to death, a wonderful wife. This guy Donen was a monster. He killed anybody in his way. Somehow he found out about Gruen.'

Clement felt his skin tingling. This could be something. The brutality matched.

'What did you think? Did somebody leak?'

'Maybe one of Gruen's old buddies saw him on the job and told the wrong person and it found its way to Donen. And of course there was corruption, somebody in administration could have found out. The internal people looked really hard at us all. Some junkie, I don't remember his name, he came in to us off the street—this was weeks later—said Pieter had been his friend and they had both been dealing for the Emperor. He claimed Pieter was ready to take down the Emperor and nobody else knew. He said Pieter told him to scram because it was all going down and one of us must have given him up because nobody in the Emperor's organisation had a clue.'

'Did you find him credible. I mean, did you believe him at all?'

'For a minute. The guy came to us, we didn't bust him and he was scared, you know, that was real. But we showed him a bunch of photos and he couldn't identify Donen so we figured he knew something second-hand but was making the rest up, maybe hoping for a reward. In the end they cleared us all. It left a bad taste though and Dieter didn't want to do Narcotics or Vice anymore. He went to work on stolen automobiles. It kind of ended it for him, I think. And he wasn't with his old pals so much. I stayed in touch with him the most.'

'How did you identify the Emperor as Donen?'

'Pieter Gruen somehow got the Emperor's fingerprints on a cigarette lighter. We had a dead letter drop, a locker at a swimming pool. Pieter could leave messages there or anything else interesting. It was Heinrich's job to clear it out. Anyway, we got the lighter in an evidence bag with a note from Pieter that the Emperor's prints were on it. It was a big breakthrough. The prints matched a juvenile case. It never went to trial but somebody kept the prints and they matched.

Donen's parents were dead, the relatives had never seen him since he was fourteen, there was no photo of Donen at that time but now we had a name.'

'What happened to Donen?'

'He disappeared before we rounded him up. We got the minnows. My pal Heinrich, he kept looking for him. There was a rumour he got involved with Sardinians and was murdered.'

'Do you recall the name Gerd Osterlund in connection with any of this? Tall, slim, balding but fair. Back then he probably had a good mane of hair.'

'Not offhand. How old is he?'

'Early sixties.'

'Right age I guess. My mind these days, pfff.' He didn't need to elaborate. 'I'll ask Heinrich, call you if it rings a bell with him. Two Germans, same age. There feels like there's something there but it doesn't add up, right?'

'Yeah.'

'I know that feeling.'

'Thanks anyway. If anything occurs ...'

'We'll call you, don't worry. I'm still angry about it, I still feel guilty.'

Clement ended the call frustrated. He was sure the text sent to Osterlund was a specific warning, a threat. The only seemingly significant criminal event that might be related had been the murder of the undercover officer. Could Osterlund have been involved with the Emperor? It had to be possible. But there was no evidence of Osterlund being involved in narcotics here. They would have to look deeper, ask the Germans for support too. Time was running out. The case felt schizophrenic. One half pointed to Germany and a near distant past, the other pointed to bikies and the present. He rang Graeme Earle and asked him to join him outside.

'Something?'

Earle laboured over the sand in his leather shoes. Clement ran through his theory of the photo. 'If it was about a ransom he wouldn't send the photo and then snatch Osterlund half an hour later. This was a message, "This is what I did to Schaffer because of Hamburg: you're next". The t-shirt was original, never worn. But I don't think it was Schaffer's. Even in the early photos he was a big guy and the t-shirt is clearly too small.'

'You think his killer brought the t-shirt with him. You reckon we're looking for a German?'

'Probably.'

'Where does Lee fit?'

'I don't know. But I'm sure this is what the photo was all about. He wanted to make Osterlund squirm.'

He explained what he'd learned of Pieter Gruen and the Emperor. 'Dieter Schaffer was Gruen's contact.'

Earle digested that. 'Could he have seen the Emperor out here, you know a chance meeting?'

'It's possible I suppose. Drugs are involved via Lee and maybe the Emperor is still in the game.'

Earle was thinking hard. 'Maybe Osterlund witnessed something. Say at a German function. Something he hadn't realised was important.'

It was a sound point. It didn't really explain why the abductor would send that photo to Osterlund though.

'I need you to try and find out every German living or staying in the Kimberley or greater north-west. There's a German club and society in Perth. They'll have a list and you can follow that up. Each of those people on the list will know somebody else and so on.'

'Ellie, my German friend, should be able to give me a rundown of locals.'

'Even better. She must know Osterlund. Check if he was hanging with anyone, or anyone seemed interested in him.'

His phone buzzed. It was Shepherd. Clement had

sent him to check on Mitchell Karskine's movements that morning. One of the techs was moving around taking photos and sifting sand. It looked like a scene from a sci-fi movie.

'How'd you go?'

'Just left him. Says he was home until seven fifteen when a mate picked him up for work. Reminded me he hasn't got a car at the moment. Mate confirmed the story.'

Clement's phone indicated another call. His tooth had begun to throb again.

'Hold on a second.'

Mal Gross this time. 'Right after the boss went on radio we got a call. Guy walking his dog says he's pretty sure he saw Osterlund on the beach this morning around six.'

'I'll send Shep. Call him with the details.'

He went back to Shepherd and gave him the good news. 'Interview him and pay particular attention to his car. We can't rule out anybody at this stage.'

'Gotcha.'

Lisa Keeble appeared near the barbecue area and held her iPad up like a tour guide. 'Got something I think you'll want to see.'

Earle and Clement huddled to look at the screen.

'This is from the area just a few metres the beach side of where you found the phone.'

The entire screen of the iPad showed a video tracking some impressions in the sand.

'Footprints?'

'Yes and see these lines here? They are very faint.'

She paused the image. By peering very closely Clement could see two parallel lines in the sand about a metre apart extending for around ten metres towards the lay-by.

'What I am looking at?'

'I think your guy might have used some kind of sand sled to transport Osterlund.'

Earle said, 'I've seen things like that. Some of the guys take them when they're beach fishing remote spots. You can bung on a full esky, all your gear and drag it through the sand.'

Keeble ran on. 'I think the victim, presumably Osterlund, was incapacitated then placed on the sled. Your perpetrator then pulled it up towards his vehicle. At the secondary point where the tracks are visible the sand is fractionally harder and there are some rocks. I'm guessing there was a bump and the phone dropped out of a pocket a few metres further up because it had been dislodged.'

Clement went with it. 'If that's anything like what happened, our guy was totally prepared and knew Osterlund's movements. He's been watching the place. It wasn't an accident he sent that text at five thirty, he knew Osterlund would be up. Lisa, I want your guys to pay particular attention to any areas front or back of this house that somebody could spy from.'

Earle said, 'If there wasn't much blood does that mean he wasn't dead?'

'If it was a fatal stab or head wound you would expect much more blood but he could strangle him, lots of other ways to kill somebody.'

Clement observed that if Osterlund was placed on a sled, one way or another he couldn't walk.

'He could have been tasered,' offered Earle.

At that moment the tech Briony joined them from the bedroom. She was in her forensic suit holding a laptop in her hands.

'We found this in the boot of Gerd Osterlund's car.'

Clement took one look at the very used, old-model laptop and had no doubt it was the missing computer of Dieter Schaffer.

31

'Is your husband involved in drugs?'

Clement sat in the same position he'd occupied that first visit to the house, under the fan. This time he wasn't looking at the ocean. Astuthi Osterlund shook her head vigorously.

'No. That's crazy.'

Earle sat at the other end of the sofa observing. Jo di Rivi was up in the kitchen area giving them space. Lisa Keeble had gone to supervise evidence collection and ensure fingerprinting and DNA testing was carried out on Schaffer's computer. They had already established the hard disk had been wiped. Clement recapped.

'Dieter Schaffer grew marijuana plants. Arturo Lee was a bikie looking to distribute drugs. Arturo Lee was at Schaffer's place the night after Schaffer was murdered. Quite likely so was your husband. The computer we retrieved, which you confirm you have never seen before, has been completely wiped. We believe it is Dieter Schaffer's. Gerd must have had something to hide.'

'Gerd was here that night.'

Clement wanted to make sure there was no mistake.

'Not the night Schaffer was actually murdered but the next night.'

'Yes, I know what night you mean. Gerd was here.

We ate fish and we talked about Dieter. It was the day you visited. Gerd has never taken drugs, not in Bali, not here, ever.'

'What were your husband's movements earlier that day? Can you remember?'

'Gerd went for his walk as usual. At least I don't remember any different, he does that every day. We'd had guests for dinner the night before.'

'The Lucases across the road?'

'Yes. After his walk he came back and relaxed I suppose. He must have got your message and waited for you.'

'Did he tell you he had received that message?'

'No. He doesn't talk about his business.'

'But it involved you. Dieter Schaffer was your friend too.'

'You called Gerd's phone, that's not my business.'

The tenet of the relationship had seemed pretty clear from that first visit. Clement was learning nothing different. 'After I left?'

'He went for a round of golf.'

'Whereabouts?'

'The Mimosa.'

If Osterlund played golf it would have to be the Mimosa. The public course wasn't much chop. Clement couldn't imagine Gerd Osterlund hacking around there.

'With anyone? A friend?'

Astuthi Osterlund's hands were moving nervously. 'Sometimes he plays with John Sherwin, sometimes by himself.'

They got Sherwin's details and Earle broke away to call him.

'What time did he come back from golf?'

'I don't know, four o'clock maybe. I'm not sure.'

Osterlund could have driven to Schaffer's that afternoon while Clement was at the Anglers and the

Mimosa interviewing the witnesses. He could have removed the computer, missing the patrol Mal Gross had sent around. If that were the case it implied Osterlund had no idea Schaffer was dead until Clement had turned up here. Otherwise he'd likely have removed the computer before or after killing him. On the other hand, Arturo Lee could have retrieved the computer and have been about to split when Clement had arrived, so he clocked him. But for Osterlund to have it now it meant either Lee had given it to Osterlund, which suggested some financial transaction somewhere, or Osterlund killing Lee to take it from him.

'The night before last, where was your husband?'

'He was here with me.'

'The whole night?'

Astuthi cast her mind back.

'We had dinner in Chinatown, early. We came back about seven. I don't think he went out after that ... no, we just stayed in, then went to bed.'

'Are you sure your husband and Dieter Schaffer weren't involved in anything illegal?'

'I told you, we barely saw Dieter, my husband didn't even like him much. Maybe somebody put that computer there.'

'Where are the car keys?'

She pointed over to a ceramic bowl on the table.

Clement said. 'Somebody would have to get the keys and put them back without you knowing.'

She looked crestfallen. Clement pressed.

'You said Gerd has no family. What about friends, business colleagues?'

'No close friends. The person he speaks to most is his accountant Werner Helstag.'

'Did your husband or Dieter Schaffer ever mention a man named Donen or "the Emperor"?'

She looked completely at a loss. 'No.'

Clement showed her the clipping of the drug lord's photo.

'This man.'

She looked closely but shook her head.

Earle joined them. 'Sherwin did not play golf with him that day. I called the Mimosa. The guy there doesn't remember him playing by himself or with anybody else.'

Astuthi Osterlund looked confused. 'Maybe the man missed him.'

'It is possible. But these things just don't add up. Are you sure Gerd never lived in Hamburg?'

'He told me he didn't. He doesn't talk about his past.'

'I need the oldest photos you have of him.'

She thought about it. 'In the bedroom, in the closet.' She disappeared downstairs.

Earle admired the view like a man who knew he'd never own it. 'Schaffer and Osterlund had to be mixed up in something, drugs, kiddy porn, something.'

Clement was thinking blackmail could be involved: Osterlund the successful businessman, Schaffer a cop who might know a few secrets. Astuthi Osterlund said her husband 'tolerated' Schaffer, which could suggest that kind of uncomfortable relationship. When he learned Schaffer was dead, Osterlund would be keen to retrieve the computer and wipe whatever shameful thing it was he was concealing.

Astuthi emerged, carrying the kind of photo album made obsolete by the digital revolution. 'This is the earliest. Nineteen-nineties I think.'

Before he met her, then.

Clement flicked through the shots, his guess, a Balinese holiday. Her time frame seemed about right on these, early to mid-90s, Osterlund looking relaxed by temples and at the beach, but unsmiling, impenetrable. Interestingly he was never with anybody in the snaps, always by himself. If he was with some companion he had discarded any snaps revealing their identity. Perhaps he'd had a guide or passer-by take them for him?

'We'll take this with us. Please, if you can think of anything that seemed odd or unusual, you must tell us.'

'He wasn't into drugs. I'm sure of that.'

They prepared to leave. She seemed suddenly small, timid. 'I'm scared for him,' she said.

What could Clement say? She had every reason to be.

32

There was only one way to express the elation he felt. He danced. The hot earth scorched his bare feet but he welcomed the pain as a spirit flowing into him, coursing its way through him, sanctifying him. Despite his preparations there had been more than a small element of risk to this endeavour. There was no guarantee Osterlund would follow his morning ritual. It was just as likely he would stay in the house, make a run for the airport. He could have waited until Osterlund was actually on the beach to send the text; that was in fact his original plan; but he wanted Osterlund to experience for as long as possible the terror of knowing he was a target and why. The gamble had paid off, Osterlund had kept his distance thinking he'd be safe. But he had outsmarted Osterlund, hadn't he? It was much more difficult to abduct than just kill him on the spot. He had to get him off the beach and into the car and at any time somebody might come running by or decide to park beside his car at the track. In the end he had decided to leave all this in the hands of the Great Power. If It wanted him to succeed he would.

Even now he was not certain somebody hadn't seen the car, either parked there or on the way out, that was the critical window. Once he was on the open road, he was just another vehicle. He had carefully avoided town or anywhere there might be cameras. He knew one of the first steps the police would take would be to look for vision. If they got a strong tip they'd come looking for the car, maybe interview him but he had a good feeling he'd be gone before it reached that stage.

The growing press speculation over the murders would be accelerated by the even more sensational abduction, yet he was indifferent to the coverage. This was a private matter. Had Schaffer been devoured by a crocodile as planned, it may well have stayed that way, but the Great Power perhaps had reason to direct things differently, thereby necessitating the execution of the biker. This is not to say he did not enjoy a pinch of pleasure from the puzzle about what might have become of Osterlund but underneath all that was the perpetual sadness of times missed, of what might have been in his life. Perhaps he should dance again? He did feel alive at that moment as if his life had been on hold and now the pause button had been punched off.

The muffled cries of the unclean reached him from below. He had been appointed the gatekeeper to hell. It was a position he did not take lightly. There were those who mistakenly thought hell an outdated, theoretical concept. He knew the exact opposite was true. Hell was real and happening right now, presided over by him alone.

33

Two of the three additions to his detective team, Paxton and Whiteman, had been colleagues in Perth, good thorough detectives. He didn't know the third detective, a younger man, Ryan Gartrell. It was an hour since the discovery of the computer and all were assembled in the Major Crime area of the station. Introductions had been made so, setting aside the increasingly nagging but still distant throb of his tooth, Clement wasted no time.

'No need to explain we are in a shit-storm, two homicides and a possible third, at the very least an abduction.'

Risely emerged from his office ushering a young woman in a sharp suit. 'This is Chelsea Verschuer, she's our media liaison person.'

Clement shook her hand and introduced himself. She was attractive, well groomed, her hair freshly shampooed. He guessed she had it cut frequently at an expensive salon.

'However I can help you, I'm here.'

'Thank you, Chelsea. The first thing I want you to do is put out some press release asking all landlords to check any vacant properties.' He looked to Risely. 'And we need all our spare uniforms checking too.'

Risely made a note. 'Got it.'

Chelsea Verschuer had her own checklist. 'Has a recent photo of Gerd Osterlund been sent to media?'

'Yes, they should all have it and Manners, I believe, has texted a copy to all our phones so we have that at our disposal at all times. Gerd Osterlund is the immediate priority.'

Clement indicated Shepherd. 'Shep interviewed a witness who saw Osterlund on the beach this morning, probably not long before he was abducted.'

He recounted what Shepherd had told him immediately before the Perth detectives had arrived. The witness, twenty-eight year old Jed Steven, had been running with his dog and passed Osterlund about halfway on Osterlund's walk south. Osterlund had looked anxiously at him and Steven, guessing the guy might have a problem with dogs, ran wide. From the position Steven described and what they had later found it seemed that the abduction must have happened within minutes of this encounter. Steven remembered only a few other people on the beach at that time, a couple mid-twenties jogging to the south and a fisherman to the north, close to where he passed Osterlund.

'Obviously identifying this fisherman and the jogging couple is a high priority. If not suspects, they could be witnesses. Mal, could you call all our uniforms in the area and get them to specifically ask anybody who lives near there or is on the beach if they might know who these people are?'

Mal got right onto it.

Chelsea Verschuer held up a hand. 'I'll get the media to highlight it unless there's a problem?'

'No, that would be useful.'

Whiteman spoke. 'This witness, Steven, no bells?'

Shepherd shook his head. 'No, he was open, his car was right there, an old hatchback, not the sort of vehicle you'd take someone in. He pretty much called in right away. Unfortunately he parked in the lay-by to the south of the one where we think Osterlund was taken. He didn't see any other cars in the area at the time.'

'Did he give descriptions of the couple and the fisherman?'

'The couple are late twenties. The girl "cute, dark hair, neat body", the guy "balding, hairy, fit". The fisherman he saw only from the back. Couldn't give an age and was "pretty sure" he was a he.' Shepherd used his fingers as quote marks.

Clement said, 'There's got to be some association between Osterlund, Lee and Schaffer but it's unclear at this stage what.' His tooth suddenly kicked in again, much worse this time. 'So far we haven't found a connection between Schaffer and Osterlund other than they were Germans living here who were in touch. Osterlund has been here the last three years. Prior to that, he lived in Bali for three years and before that Frankfurt for six years. Anything earlier is unknown. Graeme spoke to his accountant who has been working for him the last twelve years. He says before marrying, Osterlund was a dedicated businessman involved in IT who he knew slightly socially. He's given us some business associates to follow up. We're onto all drug enforcement agencies to see if he rings a bell. We've checked phone records of all three and there's no link we can see but the framing of this photo sent to Osterlund is curious.'

Clement ran them briefly through the potential significance of Hamburg 1979 as it related to Dieter Schaffer's police career.

'It may be some incredible long shot that this guy,' Clement held up the photo of Kurt Donen, 'crossed paths here with Dieter Schaffer and that Osterlund became aware of the fact or didn't realise he knew something important, but we have to consider it. Could Osterlund have been abducted to see if he'd told anybody anything? It may be remote but we have to consider that too. Graeme is checking on all Germans in the Kimberley and Pilbara regions but I want you paying particular attention to anybody of German or Austrian origin who surfaces in your quadrant of the investigation. Questions and suggestions?'

Paxton raised the question of CCTV cameras.

'We're collating all CCTV footage for the town between five and seven this morning. There's very little anywhere else in this area. If the abductor used the coast road and circumvented town there's basically nothing except servos where we might get something. Shep, you have some vehicle sightings from residents around six a.m.?'

'A dark blue van, probably ten years old, maybe a Suzuki. Also a grey sedan, described as old, make unknown. Both of these vehicles were seen heading south along the coast road. Also two different, later model Mazdas: one white, one blue.'

'Packo, you help Shep on this. Obviously the van sounds the most promising. I want you to check these vehicles against any owned by Dingos or their associates. Also anybody on Dieter Schaffer's list of clients, or the contacts we have for Osterlund from his phone and computer. And ask Mrs Osterlund if any of those vehicles sounds familiar. Ryan, I'd like you to help Sarge on any intel on bikers who might have wanted to move into the territory. Whitey, I'd like you to work out of here as fresh eyes on anything we might have missed. Start with Schaffer, then Lee, then Osterlund. Graeme, you're on the German angle. That's it for now.'

'Do you want me to put anything out about these vehicles?' Verschuer's exaggerated red lips were oddly distracting.

'Not yet, just a general appeal for information on people out walking or driving at the time and what vehicles they saw on the road. Okay, people, let's get to it.'

Chelsea Verschuer approached him. 'The networks are screaming for a briefing.'

It was the last thing Clement wanted. 'It's a critical time in this investigation.' He tried to sound apologetic though he wasn't in the least.

'Stan Le Testa and Sharon Nistrom say they've liaised with you before.'

They were Perth television journalists, crime reporters. Neither had taken the trouble to send him so much as a farewell text when he'd left town. Obviously they believed they'd not be needing him in the future. Thank God he'd changed his mobile number when he'd left, they would have bombarded him.

Chelsea pulled her most appealing face. 'It wouldn't be more than ten minutes.'

'Not right now, Chelsea. Got a murderer to track down.'

34

The day of the wasp, as he catalogued it, played on a YouTube loop in his memory. It was a Sunday and for once the skies over Manchester were bright blue with a few wisps of white cloud immobile, as if they had been stuck on. He was to be found as always on such a day in the back garden, his personal zoo, big enough to smother him in its wonders, even at the ripe old age of nine. The scent of flowers wrapped around him like a flag in a light wind. The roses were particularly pungent but they weren't alone. Pansies in bright contrasting colours matched the butterflies that seemed to crouch and quiver on their leaves. He always thought they looked scared as if waiting for some horrible force to come bursting in, shouting at them.

He knew how that felt.

His favourite were the spiders. Lying on his tummy as close as he could get to them he would watch them spin their webs, or climb over to the tiny flying bugs trapped within. Spiders were clever, he decided, perfect hunters. They would stake out the territory of high insect traffic and then find two branches or posts to hold their web. Only rarely were they foolish enough to waste energy on a web that would be torn apart by humans, setting them up above head height. The trick he saw was in their preparation, for once the web was set the spider could essentially sit back and relax. It seemed the spiders were in no hurry to eat their victims and he wondered if the spiders actually enjoyed watching the plight of those trapped and struggling beetles and gnats.

This day, however, was different. He was lying on the lawn drowsy, smelling his skin as the sun warmed it when something dropped right close to his arm. It was a fat black spider, inert. As he propped himself up a wasp landed beside it and wasted no time latching on to it. The hunter had been felled, presumably stung by the wasp, which even now was dragging the spider's large carcass along the trimmed edge of lawn. He watched fascinated as the wasp reached the base of the small garden shed and began to hoist itself up carrying the spider. What incredible strength and resolve it displayed. At one point it hit some impediment which on close inspection turned out to be a spider web. In trying to shake itself free the wasp fell all the way back to the ground with its booty. It instantly resumed its climb with the stunned spider towards its own nest under the eaves of the shed. It was around this point that he became aware of an unusual sound hovering beneath the twittering of the birds, a kind of hum. His first thought was it might be the lawnmower but he almost immediately dismissed that for it was too even, not cackling and popping. He edged towards the house and the sound got stronger. Now he identified it as a motor, more muffled though than he would have expected. A narrow concrete path led up the side of the house, a sizeable two-storey. He had expected to see a car idling out front in the quiet street but there was no car. His mind grappled with the quandary: no car, yet the sound was still near.

He swung and found himself facing the garage door.

...

The day of the wasp dashed. Once more he was in the present, the cement sky pressing down upon him. The sand was still warm on his back. He sensed something, a warning in the air. Was it just a human's in-built radar alert to an approaching cyclone, a sophisticated development of the 'flight' instinct? Did we react to air pressure in the way we might if some giant animal with sharp teeth ran towards us? Or was this just for him, the Power who had guided and protected his every move whispering to him that it was time to go?

There.

He sensed its breath. He had stayed too long already. All things must come to an end. It had been a long, long journey but from the first moment he had held the letter in his hands he knew his life was forever changed. The hand that had penned the words had been unsteady, untidy, making it difficult to read but no less potent.

> *... I knew your father, he was my friend, the best friend I ever had but it did not begin like that really. We were different, from opposite walks of life. I was the worst kind of man, hardly a man at all, perhaps more like an animal. I would like to think I changed, and if it is true that I have, then all credit goes to your father. I feel I owe it to you to tell you all I know. Back then I was a pitiful excuse for a human being, a junkie who sold ...*

He saw Wallen's face before him now.

'I could not have done it without you, old friend,' he said, then looked back across to the pit and felt a swelling sense of pride. Almost done.

35

The news crews had arrived and set up around the station. Inside the station the mood was one of frustration. It was more than five hours since the computer had been found and the investigation had not advanced a metre. Every available police officer was searching vacant buildings. One promising lead—a Dingos member owned a blue van—died in its crib. An independent witness said the van had not moved all morning. The jogging couple had been located and cleared. They had never really got close to the area of the abduction, staying further to the south. Their vehicle, however, a new Mazda, was one of the ones reported as being in the area so at least something could be eliminated but it was more than compensated for by the number of vehicle reports coming in. Osterlund was not on the radar of the Australian Federal Police or any agencies with whom they liaised. Graeme Earle was busily constructing his list of Germans who might be resident or visiting the area and Whiteman had been delegated to help him. The Hamburg Police had sent the complete files on Kurt Donen, Dieter Schaffer and Pieter Gruen, and Clement was alone in his office using the computer translator on them. Born in Essen in 1947, Donen's criminal career was first recorded when, as a sixteen year old, he bashed a pimp in Essen. The police report indicated Donen's motive was financial: he was running his own string of girls and wanted to discourage competition.

There were references to Donen's progress in brothel ownership and later pornography publishing. Donen was prime suspect in at least six suspected homicides. Two were drug rivals, two his own distributors, a prostitute who was a casual informer, and Gruen. Reportedly a chainsaw was Donen's weapon of choice. Until Gruen, the police had found it impossible to penetrate his operation and very little was known of Donen other than what came as hearsay from lower-level drug mules.

Copies of his fingerprints and photo were included. It was the same photo as in the article Schaffer downloaded but clearer. Donen was wearing an overcoat and sitting on a railing perusing a German newspaper. Somebody had printed the date on the file so it could be read more easily. Checking across at Gruen's file, Clement saw the date was nine days before Gruen had gone missing. The name of the drug dealer who had presented himself to the police and claimed to be part of the organisation had been noted, Michael Wallen. After some unconfirmed reports in 1981 that Donen could be in Amsterdam, there was nothing on him. He had vanished. Clement had just started on the file of Pieter Gruen when his door opened.

'Dan?'

He looked up. A fatigued Risely entered, closed the door and said with gravitas, 'The AC is talking task force.'

Clement knew that was inevitable but even so a sour feeling in his mouth welled. 'I won't be running it, I presume?'

'Probably not, they need to make it look like they're doing something.'

'How long?'

'Twenty-four hours max. They're panicking there'll be another death or abduction. Frankly, so am I.'

'We've got some promising stuff.'

'We've also got an abducted person and we're hitting twelve hours in, not to mention a week since Schaffer was murdered. This is a tourist town. Murder and a cyclone is a big sign saying stay away. Our Minister has been copping it from the Treasurer. Nothing to do with the fact he's Minister for Tourism as well! Look, it's not personal. It's all about bad press and votes.' Riseley fixed him with his gaze. 'You've done a good job, Clem. Nobody thinks otherwise.'

Somebody did.

When Risely had gone, he sat there soaking up the disappointment for a long moment, wondering if he should tell the others. In the end he decided it might look like self-pity. He'd find a good time and inform Earle and it would seep out from there. He went back to the files; he scanned but felt he wasn't taking in anything. Dumped, that's how he felt. He closed his eyes, tilted his head back and let random questions fizz past. How did the abductor pull this off? What was the significance of Schaffer's life as a police officer? Was he bent? Why the biker? No answers.

His phone rang. He opened his eyes and was surprised to see it was Marilyn.

...

The stretch of road was empty and dark. In this part of the world, man still only had a toehold on nature. He was fairly sure Marilyn had had an affair; or if not an affair, at least sex with another man in those months before they split. Perhaps nowadays he wasn't so sharp but back then he was at the height of his game. He never accused her, not once, in truth he didn't wish to know the answer. Probably her lover was on that museum committee, an intellectual who frequented foreign films and enjoyed cos lettuce. Nobody would ever know her as he did though. He knew every pore of her body that in some way he failed to satisfy, every lost aspiration that was slapped down by the moisturiser ritual prior to bed, every doubt that landed like a butterfly about her brow as she sipped her Darjeeling and studied him over the rim on her favourite cup, the one with the tiniest chip on the opposite side to the handle. If you want to know somebody, really know them, he thought, you must first disappoint them, and he had disappointed Marilyn in spades. And despite that, tonight she had called him and mentioned that Phoebe was scared about what was happening and wondering if he could reassure their daughter.

As Clement swung up the long driveway, lightning shimmered over the ocean. The radio was suggesting a potential category four cyclone: that would be a monster if it hit but they generally talked up the size and began reducing as countdown approached. Clement would gladly take a small cyclone to rid the heavens of the humidity.

His arrival was greeted with the faint grumble of thunder. Marilyn met him at the door. She looked good. Too good. A slim patterned frock clung to her body, a bead of sweat on her neck. 'She's just finishing off her bath.'

It was a strange sensation entering a house that had been so familiar and welcoming but where he was now considered an alien. He followed Marilyn's slim ankles along polished wood into the parlour, a formal room old Nick never enjoyed. It was all Geraldine's taste, the kind of style private schoolgirls of the 1950s aspired to, rosewood sideboards polished to high gloss, a chintz lounge suite, a slim-legged table with a large vase of fresh flowers, the colours complementing each other and the room. Nick used to prefer an old wicker chair on the back lawn. Sometimes Clement thought this was the essence of Marilyn, she was forever torn between the personalities of her parents, and instead of finding a happy medium she was either wholly one or the other. Tonight the easygoing nature of her father seemed to have the upper hand, much to Clement's relief. She slipped off her sandals and sat on the sofa, curling her bare legs and feet under her bottom. He sat at the other end of the sofa. His eyes travelled over the oils of old luggers and early Broome. Some of these paintings were near a hundred years old. They were the only thing in the room he responded too.

Besides her.

His gaze rested on her now. With what seemed genuine sympathy she said, 'You look tired.'

He almost said, 'You look good,' but she knew that, knew he was thinking it too, so he stayed safe. 'Thanks for calling Mum, she appreciated it.'

'I love your mum. And your father. They weren't the problem.' Implying he was. 'Any news there?' she asked.

He told her his dad was improving, hopefully he would return to normal.

'The murders. You have any idea who it is?'

'No. But I think we're getting closer.'

'Is it some psycho?'

'I don't think so but I can't say that. I don't think you're in danger. I think there's a reason for it but I can't see it yet.'

'We used to talk about your cases once upon a time.'

When he was young, looking to impress, before he realised all that was temporary. 'You resented it.'

'No, I resented being shut out. I resented your work being an excuse for what wasn't happening between us. But I was always interested.'

Maybe that was right, but it would take a lifetime to unravel the knot. He jerked his head to indicate Phoebe hidden behind walls and corridors.

'So she's scared?'

'Not scared exactly, concerned.'

Seeing her like this on the sofa, so less formal than usual, girlish even, stripped away the years. 'Not long after we first met, you were teaching at Geraldton and I used to drive there every weekend unless I was working.'

The trip from Perth to Geraldton was long, four and half hours, and his old Corolla used to overheat badly, necessitating many stops.

'I remember. I had a single bed you kept falling out of. Why?'

'On the way here I had this memory, sensation, whatever you call it, that I've spent most of my life driving towards you and never reaching you.'

She looked at him oddly. It wasn't the sort of stuff that ever found its way out of his mouth but there was no artifice left in him now.

Finally she said, 'The thing about driving to someone is that they're spending that time waiting and then eventually after a short interlude, you turn back around and drive away again and they have the waiting to do all over again.'

There was the sound of a door opening at the far end of a long hallway, voices and then feet moving fast. Phoebe entered in satin pyjamas and ran to him for a hug. Her hair was wet. Geraldine followed but without any intention of offering him physical contact. Even at bath time she looked like a head librarian but tonight at least she was civil.

'Hello, Daniel.'

'Hi Geraldine.'

'Good luck getting this maniac.'

She turned on her heel and left for other regions of the house. Clement smiled at his daughter. 'How did you like the boat?'

'It was really good. We saw so many fish and a sea turtle.'

'A turtle hey? That's great. And you weren't seasick?'

She shook her head, little droplets scattered.

'Ashleigh was one day. That might have been because she ate too much chocolate.'

'Mum tells me you're worried about this bad guy out there.'

Her big eyes turned on him. 'Is he going to take kids?'

'I don't think so.'

'Why did he take the man?'

'I don't know yet. We're working on that.'

'How are you going to stop him if you don't know who he is?'

Marilyn piped up. 'Your dad is really good at stopping bad people.'

The vote of confidence caught him off guard. Phoebe wasn't convinced.

'But if you don't know who he is, how can you?'

'Well that's what I do. It's called detection.'

'Are you going to shoot him?'

'I hope it won't come to that.'

'I'd shoot him and then cut his head off just to be sure.'

Marilyn and he made eye contact. At least she couldn't blame that on him. Or could she?

'Can you stay tonight?' Phoebe pleaded. He glanced sideways. Marilyn's eyes were shutters.

'Look, sweetheart, I can't but your mum is right. We'll find this person and stop him.'

'I don't want him to hurt you.' She hugged him tight.

'He's not going to.' He tried to divert her. 'What have you been learning at school?'

'A story. Do you want to hear it?'

'Of course.'

She made herself comfortable between them found her book and read easily. The story was about a fish called Marvin who was always 'starvin' and never 'laughin' till one day he made a friend of an anemone. The theme appeared to be that what you think are your 'enemies' can turn out to be your friends. Clement's experience had been that it worked the other way. When she had finished and Clement had praised her enough Phoebe suggested a game. Marilyn intervened.

'Next time. Okay, Miss P, bed.'

Phoebe kissed her father on the cheek.

'Good night, Daddy.'

'Night, sweetheart. You okay now? You're not worried?'

She did the right thing and shook her head but her eyes kept sliding away. He gave himself a five out of ten. 'You sure everything is okay, now?'

She'd been grappling with something. 'Detectives find things, don't they?'

'I guess so.'

'Well, I know you're busy but I really need my watch. It's my favourite.'

Marilyn said, 'I'll have a look after you go to bed. I'm sure it will turn up.'

Phoebe looked hopefully at her father. He felt obliged to reassure her. 'I'll keep an eye out for it. What's it look like?'

'It's about this big and it glows. It's a turtle.'

36

His daughter had just told him she had lost her watch, the same kind of watch found near the second murder victim, Arturo Lee. He forced himself to stay calm.

'What colour is the band, sweetie?'

'Blue.' There was a beat. 'I think.'

Clement was pretty sure the watch they had found had a black band.

Marilyn said, 'I'll find it okay?'

Clement leaned in to his daughter. 'When did you last have it?'

Phoebe thought hard. 'I'm not sure.'

Marilyn tried to soothe. 'Maybe you left it on the boat?'

The child screeched at her mother. 'No I lost it before then. I told you. Because when I saw the turtle I went looking for my watch and I didn't have it.'

'That's enough, off to bed.'

'Just a second.'

Marilyn caught her husband's tone and shot him a look. Clement's gaze encouraged her to let him continue. 'You had it before your trip?'

'Yes, I remember I had it in the car the morning before when we went to get some bathers.'

Marilyn seemed to feel it necessary to explain. 'Her old ones were falling apart.'

'So you went to town?'

Marilyn answered. 'Yes,'

'And you haven't see it since?'

Phoebe flubbed her lip and shook her head.

'I'll help Mum look for it, okay?'

Marilyn, uneasy he could tell, went off to put Phoebe to bed. As soon as they'd left the room he went outside to the car. He'd put the watch in the glove box meaning to hand it over to Lisa Keeble to secure in the evidence locker but the Osterlund business had derailed everything. He pulled it out and stared at it in its evidence bag. Was it the same watch? The wristband was black as he had thought. How many of these watches were there? Somebody said they sold them at servos. There could be lots. He hadn't wanted to ask Phoebe if it were hers. That would lead to explaining why she couldn't have it back. What if it was hers? Had she lost it and the killer simply found it by coincidence? Or did the killer know Phoebe was his daughter? How would he have got the watch, actually stolen it off her hand? Or had he been here, on these grounds, taken it from her room?

'What's going on?'

Marilyn was walking towards him. In the glow of the car's interior lamp she seemed fragile now, and very scared.

'Is this the watch?'

She looked at him, asking silently what it was doing in an evidence bag. While she put it under the light and examined it closely, Clement told her where it had been found, then prompted again, 'You think that's it?'

'It looks just like it. I'm not sure about the band.' Her mind was working fast over the same ground his had covered. 'If it is, how did it wind up there?'

The awful possibility dawned. Her voice was a whisper. 'Has he been here?'

Clement deflected. 'Have you checked the car for her watch?'

'Yes. But quickly.'

He followed her across to her car and they both searched thoroughly. There was no sign of a watch.

'Do you have any photos of her wearing it?' he asked.

Marilyn thought she might have some on her phone. They went back inside. Marilyn found her phone and began scrolling through photos. Snap after snap of Marilyn and Brian, or Brian and Phoebe, at dinner, on the beach, with horses. Every photo delivered its own vicious little sting. None of the photos showed Phoebe with the watch. Marilyn was starting to lose it now.

'He could have been in her bedroom. He might want to hurt you.'

And his family to get at him; there it was, the inevitable accusation. Clement did not defend himself. After all he'd surmised as much. Instead he remained the policeman.

'I don't suppose there is any chance you or Phoebe were out near Blue Haze around that time?'

'No. I don't know if I've ever been there.'

Clement saw Geraldine drift past, copping a look. She would have wanted him out by now. 'And you don't remember being near a biker?'

Marilyn snorted.

Clement said, 'Take me through the trip to town to get the bathers. Where did you park?'

Marilyn recounted their movements as best she remembered. They'd parked on Carnarvon Street close to the shop in Jimmy Chi Lane. They'd bought the bathers.

'Did she try them on?'

'No. I know her size. We just bought off the rack. Phoebe was pestering me for a milkshake so we strolled down to the Honky Nut.'

She saw Clement's reaction. 'What?' she demanded.

'One of the victims used that café.'

Marilyn's hand flew to her face. Clement pushed. 'What then? Where did you sit? Who served you?'

They'd sat outside. Marilyn couldn't recall who'd served them.

'After the milkshake, did you go anywhere?'

'We went back to the car. There's an exhibition of photographs at the Boab Gallery I wanted to see. We parked out front, did a quick look. I stopped at the fruit shop bought some fruit and veggies and we came back here.'

They hadn't gone out again. The next morning they'd got up at six and Marilyn had driven to the private jetty Ashleigh's parents used. Clement was thinking there were not that many places the watch could have gone missing. And one of them was the Honky Nut.

Geraldine had begun pointedly lingering.

Clement said, 'Could you ask the Porters if they happened to find it? Is Brian here tonight?'

'He's in Queensland for a couple of days.'

The silence swung between them.

'I could come back, stay the night.'

Her glare hit him between the eyes. 'And if he's after you?'

Clement hadn't told her about how he'd been hit over the head. He would not reveal that now, petrol on flame.

'I can get a uniform,' he said.

Marilyn thought about the offer. 'I don't want to scare Phoebe more.'

'Better she's scared than harmed. You too. I'll organise it.'

'I'll have to tell Mum.'

There was that. Unfortunately it was inevitable. Clement dialled the station. Mal Gross was still on. He told Mal what he wanted. Mal knew better than to ask why.

'I'll send Parker.'

'Thanks, Sarge.'

He turned back to her. She looked vulnerable but determined. He said, 'Keep your doors locked, don't go wandering outside.'

He hung there waiting for the touch of her hand on his arm, a sign that said 'we're still intimate even if we don't have sex'. It never came.

As he left the porch he watched her silhouette in the doorway behind a screen door. Then the main door closed. He was barely back in the car when lightning split the sky, much closer now. Tonight there had been so much of the old chemistry between them he could almost think it could work again. He killed the idea. No, tonight was just like that last flash of lightning, a moment of brilliance before everything returns to black.

...

By the time he made it back the TV crews had settled in for the night. A camera even filmed him entering the carpark, part of some stock footage he guessed. The whole way he'd been thinking about the potential danger his job brought Phoebe and Marilyn. You were dealing with desperate demented people, people who would hurt you given half a chance. It had been wrong for him to come up here, selfish. Marilyn hadn't quite accused him of that, hadn't said that their lives would be simpler and better if he'd just quit, stayed with Skype, but both knew it was true.

The incident room was wilting. Earle's progress on compiling his list of Germans was glacial. The others were each methodically following their instructions. Almost every case Clement could remember went in rushes and lulls. Now, after a brief spurt they had been becalmed. Clement knew this was typical but that was cold comfort. A man's life was at stake and it was sickening to think he was at the mercy of anything other than his own wits. Mal Gross intercepted him.

'Parker called, he's at the house now.'

Gross did not ask why the request had been made. Clement felt obliged to offer something.

'The watch we found at Lee's murder ... my daughter had one just like that, went missing on the weekend.'

Gross got it. 'You can rely on Parker but I can send another?'

'Not yet.'

'I've arranged for the last few Dingos to be interviewed starting at eight tomorrow morning.'

Gross moved off. Clement's brain felt clouded, his head was still sore, somewhere dimly his tooth ached, Marilyn's presence still lingered. Clement girded himself. He had to put any question of Phoebe's safety on hold, tell himself she would be fine.

He had to locate Osterlund.

37

A steel arrowhead poked out the front of his knee, its shaft extending behind. The pain had been excruciating at first, then ebbed, and was now pounding again. He guessed some ligament had been severed. His throat clawed at him like a wild cat. He'd had not a drop of water since morning. For the thousandth time he cursed himself for venturing onto the beach. Once he'd been brought to ground he'd been helpless. He'd waved the knife around but there was an arrow aimed at his throat, so he surrendered, was bound with plastic strips, first his legs, then his arms behind his back. His assailant had said nothing. He was dragged across the sand and bundled in a vehicle under a tarp. It seemed they drove for half an hour at least before he was again dragged out under dark grey sky, the bush somewhere, gagged, rolled down into an earthen pit.

He tried to talk, to plead but his words died in the gag. Why was this happening? Was it money?

His captor squatted on the edge of the pit and spoke for the first time, clearly and calm.

'I know you hope the police are going to find you in time. They're not. They're busy looking for a connection between you and bikies and Herr Schaffer. You know what it's like to grow up without a father?'

Osterlund tried to speak, to ask him what he wanted

but what wasn't muffled was obliterated as thunder rumbled, very powerful, closer than before.

'God is angry tonight. And why wouldn't he be? One of his children held down, sliced apart with a chainsaw, butchered. A man's heart, his lips, his eyes, wrapped tight in glossy pussy and large tits.'

So that was it. Hamburg. He should have listened to Schaffer, when was it, over a year ago, that Klaus had been killed? For six months or so he'd been on alert but he had become complacent. Klaus had numerous enemies. A thin smile seemed to play on his captor's lips.

'You understand, I see. Your money can't save you.'

The man turned away, extended his arms to the sky and howled. Literally, howled like a wild dog. To fight the pain in his knee Osterlund bit into his gag, but he could not take his eyes from his captor who had begun to perform some grotesque dance, throwing handfuls of sand in the air. He stomped, he laughed and exhorted into the thunder, mumbling words, most unintelligible down in the pit but one Osterlund caught clearly: 'Wallen.'

And then it was over. His captor stood panting looking down on him.

'You know the expression, to be shat on from a great height? That's what God does to us humans. And tonight, I am your god.'

Osterlund tensed for a bullet, or another arrow. His tormentor loosed his belt, dropped his shorts and squatted over the pit. A huge clap of thunder sounded overhead simultaneous to a white sword of lighting, slicing, bleaching the night.

'Eat shit and die!' the man screamed down at him.

Osterlund edged as far to the other side of the pit as he could. Then the man had disappeared from view. Something was being dragged over his head blotting out what little light there was, centimetre by centimetre.

38

He was sitting in what was normally his mother's position, beside his father in one of the fold-out chairs, staring out at the camp ground. They were drinking beer from small glasses, the kind that were thin and broke easily. His father's glass had a jagged wedge out of it and he was cut and bleeding into his beer but didn't seem to notice. Clement said nothing. He felt it would be foolish to express concern when his father had none. There was a weird duality about Clement. He seemed to be about the age he was now and simultaneously around fourteen. They'd been playing tennis, he saw now. He was dressed in tennis whites and there was a racquet on the concrete stoop.

'One day you'll find someone,' his father said.

'But I have, I'm married to Marilyn.'

His father looked him deep in the eyes and shook his head. Clement was gripped with the same panic as that first time in the swimming pool but before he could ask for an explanation his father was gone and Bill Seratono was there. Bill was dressed as if for some caving expedition with ropes and a little helmet with a headlamp and possessed of the same duality as Clement where he was both young and old at the same time.

'We're ready,' he said.

Clement stood. 'How deep do we have to go?'

'Until it stops.'

They lowered themselves down some hole. It became very dark. Clement felt terrified yet bold at the same time.

'This is how he feels,' he said and knew he was talking of Osterlund's abductor.

Water trickled down the cave walls, glistening.

Seratono's headlamp clicked on right into his eyes. The light dazzled him. Clement felt the sensation of something swinging at his head ...

Clement snapped awake at dawn, cramped from being wedged in the car, the dream still so fresh he looked for streaking rain on his windscreen to match the rivulets of the cave. Surprisingly there were only a few drops. Last night, after everybody else had gone except the uniforms on night shift, Clement had returned to his office and tried to get his brain into gear to find something he'd overlooked while trying not to worry about Phoebe and Marilyn. He was successful at neither. He scanned the list of resort staff but nothing leapt out. Like Earle had said, they were all too young to have been around in 1979. It was hopeless. His brain was jelly. Gross had left Parker's number for him. He called and was reassured all was quiet out there. It had been too late to ring his mum so he decided to go home and catch a few zeds. He needed milk and bread but like everything else he'd left it too late. He'd started home through dark streets, his only companion the voice of a radio weatherman warning of the impending cyclone expected to cross the coast about a hundred and fifty kilometres to the north, sometime tomorrow, now today. That's how I spend my life, he thought, hunkered down for some impending catastrophe. And then he'd spun the wheel and started back in the other direction. He had to be at Marilyn's, close to them. Sure Parker was there as protection but the killer had proven resourceful. Clement had parked down the end of Geraldine's long driveway and kept a vigil on the house until around four when he must have dozed off. Despite the physical discomfort he felt quite good. His head had cleared even though the dream still hovered like steam on hot tar.

Nothing in it surprised him. The worries about his father, his relationships and the case were all obvious. Even his wanting to be married still was kind of natural. The exception was that moment where, descending into the deep black hole, he sensed his emotion mirrored the killer's. The killer was scared yet felt invincible, as if he knew he was in a dream. But he was real, he needed to eat, crap, sleep. Where had he spent the night? In a soft bed beside a loving woman, in a cramped vehicle like this, in a tent beneath the stars?

He climbed outside the car now and stretched. The air's wet breath swamped him. It was too early to drive up to the house and what was the point?

Clement called Parker.

'Sir,' Parker sounded tired but alert enough. Clement felt instant relief.

'Everything good?'

'Yes, sir, they are all still asleep.'

'Well done. I'll get the Sarge to organise a replacement for you.'

'He already called, sir. I'm to stay here till ten, then Constable Latich will take over.'

Clement thanked him again. He pictured Phoebe sleeping and was gripped by the terrible knowledge that this part of his dream was all real. In the house he knew so well, he'd felt alien; might he come to experience that same sensation with his daughter? This frightened him. His marriage, his previous life, had been expunged and like some time traveller who changes one thing in the past, it was as if everything in the present never existed.

Before falling asleep, hunched in the car, his reflection visible every now and again when the horizon lit up with nature's lightshow, Clement had been asking himself who might want to avenge Pieter Gruen. He picked up on the thread now.

First and foremost, family. Gruen had a brother and sister. The Hamburg police had been notified and may well have found them by now. Ex-colleagues couldn't be ruled out, not even Mathias Klendtwort and Heinrich Schmidt. Klendtwort hadn't called him back with anything that placed Osterlund in that world. Clement felt bent as a coathanger. He'd sent the others home for a few hours' sleep a little after two. He'd briefed them on the possibilities of the watch. Earle was spent. He'd logged thirty-three Germans or Austrians in the region and narrowed to four those who could be worth a visit. But only one was in Broome. The others were in Derby, Newman and Onslow. Whiteman had checked the Mimosa. It had two current German families as guests, the Panasch family, mum, dad a couple of kids; and the Erdmans, a middle-aged couple who had flown in from Alice Springs four days ago. The Panasch family had only been there two days, which ruled them out. Whiteman had asked the manager at the Mimosa if any Germans had stayed with them in the last month. They had promised to get back to him on that. As for the Mimosa staff, there were a number of internationals, six Brits, two Irish, two Brazilians, two Kiwis, a South African, an Italian, plus Marie Kasprov and Rose Figueroa, the maids Clement had interviewed. No Germans. It had been the same story with the Emerald Bungalows and Apartments. Not all of them knew the nationalities of their casuals but there were no known Germans and none over fifty, which was the most likely age bracket of the killer. Hospitality it seemed was a young persons' game.

The team were all out on their feet. Clement was acutely aware that Osterlund was out there somewhere, possibly being tortured, but there came a point where it was counterproductive to keep the team working so that's when he'd called it a night.

...

He drove back to Broome listening to a weather update. The cyclone had been downgraded to a two but that was still a big storm, wind gusts expected from one hundred and ten to one thirty k where it was due to cross a hundred k to the north. Even so, no one was relaxing. The traffic was thin all the way to the station. News crews were unravelling themselves with tired eyes and coffee after too many drinks at the Roebuck. And what, he wondered, of Osterlund? Was he still alive, gasping the same heavy-lidded air as the rest of us?

The offices had the smell of constant occupation even though only Mal Gross was there bustling around printing up reports.

'If only crims took a rest while we were working the big cases.'

'Busy night?'

'Break-in at the pharmacy, two brawls.'

Gross's night counterpart might have had to deal with the arrests but there was always paperwork.

'The guys have been checking properties every chance they get.' Gross didn't have to add they'd found nothing.

In his office, the first thing Clement did was to call di Rivi. The policewoman sounded brighter than Gross. Mrs Osterlund had been up until around two a.m. retired to her bedroom and then been up again around five. She was still resisting medication.

'How have the media been?'

'Not too bad. A few have called here. I've passed it

onto Chelsea and she's asked them to back off.'

'I'll be over shortly.'

He stopped to fix himself a tea when Graeme Earle entered. He'd been about to head off for the first of the four Germans he had identified as worth a look but thought he'd check first all was well at Marilyn's. Clement appreciated the gesture.

'It's all good there.'

'Did those names of Germans in the region trigger anything?' he asked of Clement.

'To be honest, I only scanned. I'll need to look at them again when I'm compos. Who is this guy you're going to see?'

Lured by Clement's tea, Earle made himself one.

'Name is Liedel, fifty-seven so he's around the right age, worked as a chef in Perth, then in catering on the mining camps but he did time for an assault.'

It didn't sound an overly promising lead.

'They're talking Taskforce. Somebody else will head it.'

Earle was suitably indignant. 'That's fucked. Nobody would have done any better than what we have.'

'Possibly, but that's the way of the world.'

In a small way Clement felt ashamed that he'd had the same prejudice at the start of the case. 'Take care out there,' he said. 'Our man is a killer.'

Earle paused at the door, a mug of tea in his fist. 'I think you've done an effin' good job.'

The flyscreen had barely banged shut when Clement's phone rang.

'Yes Jared.'

'Might have something, boss. Potential witness to a vehicle at the Blue Haze garage.'

The news crews videoed Clement again on the way out. A female reporter in a suit, one he recognised but whose name he could not recall, shot a question that was ripped away in the gathering wind, her hair already a mess. He had nothing against the media guys. Death was their living, and his too.

...

It was a plain brick bungalow, one of a number in a small state housing village about a kilometre from the garage where Lee had been squatting. The wind was increasing. Smoke from a large bonfire out the back of one of the other houses pressed on Clement's lungs as he strode up the gravel front behind Taylor who had been waiting in his car on the corner. Music from the yard of the bonfire was loud here and must have been ear-splitting at the source. Clement only listened to music post-1987 by accident and didn't recognise the artist. A squeal of laughter and shouting from the bonfire yard actually managed to cut through the music, a party which he guessed had been going all night. A small patch of struggling lawn announced the front door, standard mesh security grill. The windows were sliding with aluminium frames. They stopped at the grill, the door behind was open and a light was on somewhere further back in the house.

'It's Jared.'

An aboriginal woman appeared. She had a thin, lined face. Clement put her age at forty but she could have been ten years shy of that. Taylor had explained her name was Bronny Jackson, a single mother with three kids. She opened the security grill for them.

'This is Detective Inspector Clement.'

'Hello Mrs Jackson.'

She pointed a bony finger back to the gloom. 'Tyson's back there.'

Jared had told him that Tyson was the youngest of the three. The father had shot through a couple of years ago. Tyson had been caught wagging school this morning and in the following interrogation by his mother had spilled on more truancy and what he'd seen one day last week. She knew of Jared through his cousin and called him. Jared had not attempted to interview the boy himself but had called Clement. He now led the way down the narrow hallway past a couple of closed bedroom doors to a small living room. It was stifling. The sliding door that gave onto the back was closed. Clement presumed that was to keep out the noise but even so the boom of the bass rumbled in here. The furniture was well worn, a sofa and an armchair that didn't match. A small flat-screen TV, the newest thing in the house, sat on an old pine sideboard. A piece of copper art, a galleon of some kind, was the wall's only adornment. It couldn't have been a bigger contrast to Osterlund's house overlooking the ocean. The boy, Tyson, was small and skinny with black curly hair. His eyes avoided them and he sat hunched like he was expecting to be chastised or beaten. He wore a t-shirt and shorts. Taylor took the lead.

'Tyson, your mum tells us you saw something down at the garage there. You need to tell Detective Clement what you saw.'

Tyson remained mute. Clement sat down on the lino in front of Tyson. His mum hovered in the background.

'You barrack for the Eagles or Dockers, Tyson? Or both?'

'Eagles.'

'Well, I like the Dockers but don't hold that against me. Tell us what you saw, Tyson. It could be important to us.'

Unsure, Tyson looked to his mother.

'Tell the man about the car.'

Tyson told his story in a small, halting voice. Last Monday, Tyson, instead of being at school, was playing in the bush down by the garage. He heard the sound of a powerful motorcycle approaching and watched it swing into the area in front of the garage and stop. He saw the rider lift up the roller door and put the bike in. While he was doing that a car had appeared on the road slowing, almost stopped. From Tyson's position closer to the road but hidden in the bush he could see the car, but the rider, from his position near the garage, would not have been able to. The rider disappeared around the side of the old building. The car drove up towards the village. Then a few minutes later it turned back around and cruised slowly past again.

'What time was this Tyson?'

'I don't know.'

'Had you been there long? Was it morning?'

He thought. 'Probably about lunchtime.'

'Did you see the driver, Tyson?'

'No.' A small voice.

'Can you describe the car, Tyson? Have you seen the car before?'

Tyson was nervous. He shook his head.

'What colour was it? Do you remember?'

He nodded. 'White.'

'And what sort of car, do you know? Have you seen any like it?'

'It was high.'

'A truck?'

'No.'

'A four-wheel drive?'

His mum helped. 'Like Uncle Nicky's?'

'Kind of. Not so big.'

Jared ascertained that Uncle Nicky had a Pajero. Eventually they narrowed the field of cars to some sort of sports utility. The boy was unable to help with numberplate, stickers, roof-racks. They went back over it a few times.

'Have you seen the car around here before?'

Tyson shook his head.

'Okay thanks, Tyson. You've helped us a lot. Make sure you go to school though, right? See you in an Eagles guernsey.'

Bronny opened the door for them. Jared jerked his thumb towards the party which had quietened a little but was still going strong.

'When did they start?'

''Bout eleven last night.'

'You want us to have a word?'

'Better not. They'll get tired soon enough.'

39

With Tyson's information about the vehicle, the main room was invigorated: Shepherd checking all registrations of white SUVs for the region, Whiteman scrutinising the vehicles of all people tossed their way in connection with the cases, Jared Taylor recanvassing everybody in the Blue Haze area to find anybody else who had seen the vehicle. Gartrell and Paxton were methodically confirming Dingos alibies. Only Earle was absent. He'd called earlier. The chef was confirmed as being in Darwin when Schaffer had been killed, so he'd struck out for Derby to interview his second possible German of Interest.

Mal Gross headed to make himself a coffee and broadcast to anybody interested, 'They're saying it's crossing about a hundred and fifty k north but we should still cop a whack.'

Clement called di Rivi and had her put Astuthi Osterlund on the phone.

'Do you or your husband have any associates who drive a white SUV?'

'I don't think so.'

'Have you noticed a car like that hanging about?'

'No. Do you know something?' She was eager for any crumb. He couldn't share though.

'We're following leads.'

He told her to tell di Rivi if she recalled anything then removed himself to the AV room. There was no sign of Manners but the CCTV carpark footage was set up ready to roll so he helped himself to one more look. It is morning, half a dozen cars are visible in the carpark but no white sports utility. The boy said the car he saw near the garage that afternoon seemed like it was following the bike. But the car driver did not make himself known to Lee. If this was their guy and he was working with Lee, why not drive into the garage? Why might he be following Lee?

Clement began threading the needle. Suppose he's following Schaffer, planning when and how he will kill him. Lee is also following Schaffer or waiting for him to ask him about the dope. Lee and the killer spy one another. Is it possible Lee was killed because he may have been able to identify the killer?

Clement sighed, rubbed his eyes. His phone rang. At the sight of Marilyn's ID, every muscle in his body tensed.

'Yes?'

'We found it.'

'Thank God.'

Marilyn was explaining. 'The clothes she was wearing that day were in the laundry. Mum found it in a pocket. I'll tell Constable Latich to go. You were right, it was just a coincidence.'

'I'm sorry I scared you like that.'

'It turned out okay.' Not making a big thing out of it. It was encouraging. Maybe they could be friends.

'I guess you'll be busy for a while on this,' she said.

'I presume.'

'We'll see you when it's done. Take care.'

As if his brain sensed it could now divert its powers elsewhere, the moment he ended the call, his tooth zinged with pain. That was it. He poked his head out of the AV room into the main area. 'Does anybody know a dentist?'

Sometimes it is the one you least suspect. Shepherd looked up from his conversation with Paxton.

'Our centre halfback is a dentist.'

He rang his mate who said he would do Clement in ten minutes. Clement got the details: it was walking distance. He stopped at Mal Gross on the way out.

'They found Phoebe's watch.'

Gross did not need to offer comment, his smile said it all. Clement slipped out the back door and up one of the side entrances. Three news vans were out front, three different crews, no sign of the journalists, which was a blessing. If they were from Perth it was almost certain they would know him but for now he was just another outback cop. The wind had really picked up. Empty soft-drink cans and coffee cups skittered across the roads, signs creaked and banged. The surgery was less than ten minutes' walk and located in a small modern block on the east end of the main drag. An accountant and podiatrist flanked the dentist but were both closed. Nobody wanted to be caught out in a cyclone. Clement pushed into the fresh, well lit but deserted surgery and called out.

'Dan?' The voice came from a room behind the reception desk. Shepherd's teammate appeared in the doorway. He was not your typical dentist. Shepherd's call had found him at the Roebuck on his third lager and he had hastened back to his surgery in black footy shorts, a t-shirt and thongs.

'Everybody cancelled. Cyclone I guess,' he said as he ushered Clement through into the room where the dental chair waited like a predatory monster of the deep. 'I was sinking a few jars at the 'Buck. I told Shep, "If your mate's not gonna sue me I'll do it." Let's take a look.'

Clement lay back, opened wide and stared at the ceiling. Someone had stuck a large print of a Broome sunset up there to soothe. It was the typical one you saw on all the tourist posters, camels in a line on Cable Beach.

'Guess you're flat out right now, eh?'

The dentist, whose name Shepherd had simply given as 'Harry', used a mirror and very gentle probe. Clement grunted a yes.

'You floss?' He pulled the mirror away.

'Sometimes.'

'That lower left molar?'

'Down there somewhere.'

'I'll try and be gentle but this might hurt.'

And it did. The merest touch with the probe had Clement squirming.

'Bad, eh?' Harry pulled the implements out again. 'Fairly extensive decay. How long since you've been to a dentist?'

'Two years, maybe.'

'Do it every six months, you won't cop this. I'll clean it out, fill it, we might get lucky. I don't want to take it out if we can help it.'

Great, now I'm going to be a toothless old man. What next, incontinence pads? Clement already felt the invisible momentum of life shoving against him and now it seemed his own body had defected. After the needle began to do its thing, Clement mellowed, decided it was bearable so long as he did not think about what was happening in his mouth. So he lay back staring at the camels and dwelling on the case. Dieter Schaffer was the key to all of what had happened. No matter how flimsy the evidence Clement could not shake the idea his death was intertwined with Pieter Gruen's murder. Something snagged in his memory: Mrs Gerlanger had said Dieter's sister had written him off because his gambling had cost him his house, but his colleagues glossed over that. He bet small, Mathias Klendtwort said. Was Klendtwort lying? Or had Schaffer hidden from them the extent of his debts. What if the Emperor had found out about Schaffer's debts and offered him a deal to save his home? Was Osterlund maybe an intermediary?

And as he lay there with his mouth screwed open staring at a print of camels on a beach, the puzzle began to take shape. Klendtwort had said Dieter was the only one to have personal contact with Gruen. The locker was used as a dead drop and cleared by Heinrich but only Schaffer interacted with Gruen. There was only one photo of Donen and if it had not come through the dead drop, it must have come via Dieter Schaffer. The answer was dead simple if only they had believed the junkie.

...

Mal Gross was having a smoke in the rear courtyard as Clement strode in.

'Packo and Gartrell have pretty much done the Dingos. Zero,' offered Gross.

The information moved around Clement like air over the wings of a plane but he managed a nod. Inside everybody was working a phone or a file. Shepherd loomed.

'How was Harry?'

Clement gave him thumbs up in preference to talking. Heart pumping he slipped into his office, pulled up the German police file on Kurt Donen again and found what he wanted. He was convinced he was right but needed expert confirmation. He called Keeble, told her what he wanted and asked her to come to his office. He then put in a call to Klendtwort but got only an answer machine.

'It's Daniel Clement. I'd be grateful if you could call me as soon as possible.'

With perfect timing the knock on the door coincided with him ending the message.

'Come in.' His mouth felt lopsided. Lisa Keeble entered but offered no sympathy.

'What's up?'

'You brought the copy of Gerd Osterlund's prints?'

She presented her iPad to him. He spun his computer towards her.

'Look at these.'

She leaned in. He watched her mouth move as if she were talking to herself. Maybe she was, very quietly. She straightened.

'They're identical. Where are they from?'

'Hamburg, ninety seventy-nine, the Emperor's fingerprints. Gerd Osterlund is Kurt Donen.'

40

The apartment Gruen was renting was in a squalid concrete block on the opposite side of the city where Hilda took young Manfred to play on brightly coloured swings. The playground equipment here was broken and the smell of diesel seemed to cling to everything, even the washing strung optimistically on high balconies by women with a skerrick of house pride not yet extinguished. Only a few more days, he told himself. The apartment itself was sparse but he kept it reasonably clean, not so clean it may arouse suspicion if one of the Emperor's people suddenly turned up, which had happened twice. He had his small kitchen table and a black and white TV. His books he kept well out of sight in the drawers of a cheap dressing table in the bedroom. Ten months of this, the highlight being his once-monthly reunion with Hilda and the boy. She knew what he was doing and the danger involved but they could not risk explaining to the boy who regurgitated to his school friends the story fed him, his father was working oil rigs in the North Sea. Gruen was looking forward to shaving off his beard. Last night when he'd finished his rounds, his heroin supply at the tail, he'd headed to Freiheit for a beer but there was no sign of Wallen. A small flower of hope had bloomed. Could Wallen possibly have cleared out as he'd asked?

There was another possibility, a darker one. He tried to dismiss it. He had been foolish to tell Wallen about the bust. It endangered him. He checked his watch. It was time to check in with Dieter.

He locked up the flat and took the rumbling elevator to the ground. Sometimes at night the skinheads would be around but not today. It was a ten-minute walk to the public phone and he timed it well. Dieter picked up on the first ring. Because of the secrecy of the operation he did not know where exactly Dieter had set up the safe house from which he operated.

'Hamburg is going to win the whole fucking thing again this year,' said Dieter.

Football-mad Dieter, his one conduit to the normality of his old life.

'Did you get the photo?' Gruen asked.

Last time they had communicated, two weeks ago now, Gruen had laid out a plan for Dieter to snap a photo of the Emperor. No one had ever managed it and it was impossible for Gruen to take a camera, even a spy camera, into the vault with him. He was routinely searched. He had worked out, however, by careful observation and the occasional chat with Klaus, that a chauffeur-driven old Mercedes was used to ferry the Emperor about the city. Over time he had gleaned some habits of the driver including his favourite bar. If Schaffer followed the driver, he might catch the Emperor. Perhaps it was unnecessary, there would be many mug shots of him soon enough but Gruen always thought of the worst situation, the Emperor getting away.

'Of course I got the photo, a beauty. Everybody is rapt. Listen, we need to meet.'

The first thing Gruen thought was that Wallen had blown the operation.

'What's up?'

'Tell you when I see you.'

'Everything is still go?'

'Yes, it's all fine. Don't worry. There are just a couple of operational things to go over.'

'Usual place?'

'Yes. See you there in an hour.'

Gruen hung up. Thank God for Dieter. He missed the camaraderie of the guys, Heinrich especially. It would be so good to be back with them having a drink, telling them about the last crappy year. He zipped his jacket and walked towards the train station.

...

Dieter Schaffer felt hollow inside, worse than hollow, like it was no longer him at all. Yet what choice did he have now? Once he'd made contact with Donen via the chauffeur, his life as he'd known it was effectively over. Naively perhaps, he'd imagined it was enough to suggest faking the photograph. You can leave, he'd told the Emperor, and nobody will know it's you. He remembered well what the man sitting opposite him now had said.

'You'll know, and so will whoever you have inside my operation.'

That's when he understood what the price was going to be. And still he had not backed away. So here he was now. The room was small and musty. It crowded in on him.

The Emperor was flanked by two of his bodyguards waiting.

Schaffer hung up the phone and said, 'It's done.'

The Emperor stood. Dieter felt a flash of panic.

'What about the money I owe?'

His home was on the line. How could he have lost? He still couldn't fathom it. Hamburg were champions and yet they'd lost at Dortmund, and again when he'd doubled up, at Schalke. Surely they would beat Munich at home? But they had lost yet again and so his team would be champions yet he would be without a home to celebrate in and no doubt a wife.

'You don't owe anything now. The bookmaker understands. Of course, if you displease me ...' He let it hang.

Schaffer's legs felt rubbery as he got to his feet. He left, knowing his soul had been abandoned forever in that cramped room reeking of damp, knowing the ghost of Pieter Gruen would haunt him, and one day, somewhere, rain a terrible justice upon him.

41

The news crew camped outside Osterlund's filmed Clement as he entered, on the phone to Earle who was just arriving in Derby. The crew looked tired already, unshaven and untidy and like angry scammers caught on a current affairs show; the wind buffeted their cameras. One seemed to be a woman but the sexes of news crews tended to merge, only the anchors retained an individual identity. Daryl Hagan and Beck Lalor patrolled the gate and acknowledged him as he passed. Clement parked where he had the first day and walked to the door carrying the Donen file. Jo di Rivi saw who it was. Her eyes couldn't help asking the obvious question: had Osterlund been found?

'Not yet. How is she?'

'She's barely slept. She won't take anything.'

The air was crushingly humid now. Before he entered, reflexively, Clement looked up at the sky but it had nothing to offer him.

Astuthi Osterlund was sitting by the kitchen bench. She looked at him with a mix of intense fear and frail hope. The question was the same as di Rivi's.

'Have you found him?'

And he knew she feared the answer was yes.

'Not yet.'

Her body lost some tension. The vast glass window

reverberated in the powerful wind. It was unsettling, ominous. Lucky the cyclone has been downgraded, thought Clement, a four and the glass would have to be covered though he supposed Osterlund had special protective shutters if needed. Clement sat on the stool beside Astuthi Osterlund and placed the file beside him. The techs had all long gone and the place felt lonely, like a coastal guest house out of season.

'Your husband's real name is Kurt Donen. He was involved in pornography and drugs in Hamburg in the nineteen seventies and he is a suspect in the murder of at least six people including an undercover policeman. The policeman's controller was Dieter Schaffer. It seems likely Schaffer protected your husband.'

She did not throw her hands to her face, nor call him a liar, nor protest her own innocence. Some part of her seemed already resigned to such news. Outside the ocean rippled like a fat man's belly.

'I want him back.'

'You don't seem surprised?'

'I don't know who he was before. He is, Gerd Osterlund, my husband.'

But something was tormenting her, he could see it. Her hands twisted. 'Is he married to somebody else?'

'Not that we know.'

She seemed to weigh that.

'He told me he was never married and had no children. He didn't lie to me.' She said this as if it exonerated him from murder.

Clement said. 'His whole life was a lie.'

'You could say that about many people.'

'But they're not all covering up murders.'

'It's not my job to convict my husband.'

She did not add, 'And it's not yours either.' She would have been right. His job right now was to find him, alive if possible. Sand was whipping off the beach below. He chose his words carefully.

'We have to assume that somebody found out about this, somebody who is out for revenge.'

'They want to kill him?'

'That would seem likely. Gerd is not some intermediary. Your husband may be the end of the line, the one they are after.'

'Maybe they want money?' It was a feeble hope and she couldn't sell it any better with her eyes than her voice.

'They haven't called. This person is very thorough. They prepare. At some point they may have trailed you or your husband, or called at the house on some pretext. Have you seen any strange vehicles? '

'I don't think so.'

'Think hard.' He found an image of a white SUV on his phone and showed it. 'Any car like this?'

She continued to shake her head.

'Like I said before, I don't remember. One of my friends has a silver car like that but she is away in Sydney.'

'Your husband never gave any indication he was previously acquainted with Schaffer?'

'Not at all.'

'The first time he met him here in Broome, were you present?'

She thought back.

'No. I can't have been. The first time Gerd introduced me to Dieter Schaffer it was at a restaurant in town. He said this man is a German from Hamburg.'

Clement wondered how Schaffer had found Donen. Had they been in touch over the years, part of the same operation, or had they ceased to have contact after Gruen's murder?

For the next ten minutes Clement canvassed the same ground with slightly different questions but

Mrs Osterlund could give him nothing that pointed to who they might be looking for. The Germans they had met up here were a mere handful, nearly all passing through. Clement took whatever names and details she could remember. Feeling there was nothing more he could achieve here, he announced he had to get back to the station.

'Are you going to keep looking for Gerd?' she asked, demanding the truth.

It was a pertinent question. Was he going to spend every ounce of his energy trying to save the life of a multiple murderer and drug lord? He was not proud of the answer.

'Of course.'

42

After the blotting of light came the heavy thud of earth being shovelled on top. Was this the plan, to bury him alive? Osterlund fought his panic back down. Levering with his elbows, ignoring the pain in his knee, he dragged himself up from the earthen floor. With hands bound he had to use his head to push up into the tin above him, standing on his toes for leverage. He mustered all his fading strength but he could not budge it. In pitch darkness, he slumped back down. He could not call for help, he could not dig without threatening collapse.

Anger burst inside him like a grenade. Fucking Dieter Schaffer. This was his doing. He should have killed him. And Wallen, he remembered him, that skinny junkie. He was one of the ones who had got away. It was always the weak ones who brought down the strong. Somebody once said no good deed goes unpunished and they were right.

It had been happenstance, Schaffer bumping into him on a rare trip to Hamburg, six or seven years ago. He usually avoided the city precisely for that reason but he was buying out an online competitor and they said the deal had to be done there in person. Schaffer had walked right up to him in the street while he was waiting for a taxi. He felt sorry for Schaffer, an emotion he'd never been able to afford up until a few years before when he began living in Bali. Schaffer was clearly dead-ended in life. He should have just walked away from him but he figured he owed him. Schaffer had tipped him off about the undercover cop and he'd saved Schaffer his home in return, quid pro quo. But it was Schaffer who thought of planting the fake photo. That was inspired and without it he'd have had none of this life. He was set up now. If he'd lost his drug money he never would have been able to buy back into the porn industry, get into online porn in its very early days, make a killing and get out. For the last seventeen years he'd been a legitimate businessman. Schaffer, though, might have saved his home but not his marriage. When they'd reconnected Schaffer was working the docks and living in a rented apartment. Foolishly Osterlund had wired him ten thousand euros. Schaffer hadn't even asked for it. But what did he care? Ten thousand was a drop in the bucket. And then one day here in Broome somebody taps him on the shoulder and he turns around to see fucking Dieter Schaffer. He'd tracked him from the money he'd been sent.

'I've come to join you in the wilderness,' Schaffer had joked. And then Schaffer had seen the fury in his face and begged off with promises he'd never tell anybody, proof of which was his silence all these years. He'd contemplated then and there giving Schaffer a permanent silence but he did not want to soil himself with any more blood and, truth be told, Schaffer's presence was a door into a time when he had been the dark prince of Hamburg, making money hand over fist, a time he enjoyed remembering. Sure, with his publishing he made more than enough but he missed the edge-of-the-seat adrenalin of those days, the keenness of his senses; and he liked sometimes to recall the cold chill of the wind off the river right through his herringbone flares, the smell of tobacco and pils in the basement pubs, the luxury of a car cassette player, the feel of a clutch under his cheap leather soles. He did not want to go back, he was not nostalgic in that sense, but he liked to remember his time on the rise so he would never take what he had now for granted. He decided to let Schaffer be and Schaffer had played his part, never letting on even to Tuthi that they had known each other before. He'd remembered Schaffer's computer and removed it before the police, just in case there had been something incriminating on it. But it was too late by then.

He should have connected Schaffer's death to that of Klaus but when the biker was murdered the same way he had dismissed his concerns. He should have understood Schaffer was a door to the past not just for him but others. Schaffer was the portal, the passageway that had led his persecutor here to bind and tie him and bury him alive in a black cesspit.

He tried to think of other things: Tuthi naked in the morning, the old days in the Reeperbahn when he got his start selling girls to drunk sailors. He was successful because he was fair to the girls, giving them twice what the competition paid, in smack instead of cash but still that's what they would spend it on anyway.

It was all business, nothing more.

Their faces were out of focus now. It had been too long ago. A few OD'd; most just faded away. The early days had been hard. He'd been bashed by chains, cut by switchblades. Somebody hits, you hit back twice as hard. You got smart, employed mercenaries back from Africa and out of work but that only got you so far. The polaroid opened up everything. He could offer pictures to the sailors of the girls they'd paid to fuck. Throw a little extra to the girls for their trouble. There was just as much money in the photos as the sex. He remembered the first magazine issue, his pride. He tried to see the cover in his mind but the thought snapped and he was back in the dark, utterly alone, his hands and feet numb. He would die down here. His tormentor may never revisit. There was air for now but no water. After a tough start, his life had been comfortable, luxurious even. But as death calls you, who is content with what they used to have?

The pain in his knee tore at him. Osterlund bellowed again into the gag, a wail of self-pity.

'A biblical judgment.'

The words came in a voice from long ago, his stepfather's, that mean Lutheran bastard sitting at the table in his braces and rolled sleeves, massive hairy forearms. He sensed him in here now. There, his face glowing, a phosphorescent Shroud of Turin.

'Free me,' he tried to say, but his words were muffled and his stepfather was without ears.

43

The recent impetus had waned. Clement watched his team grinding their way through their various assignments. While he had uncovered more elements of the mystery, time was running out to find Osterlund. The pieces were there, enough of them anyway, but he must look in the right place. That was what he had always been good at.

Before his tooth had driven him to the dentist he had been on the verge of sussing out something. What?

Mal Gross loomed. 'I've covered the road to Derby, Cape Leveque road to the north and a couple of the major tracks east. Traffic's light with this storm coming so if the SUV is out there we should spot him.'

'Okay, good.'

'You think we need to look at station wagons too?'

'The kid seemed confident.'

Mal Gross nodded and went back to his desk. If Tyson had it wrong it was most likely too late anyway. Knowing the interruptions would continue out here, Clement retreated to his office and switched off his phone. He recalled earlier he had been contemplating the connection between Lee and his killer. Now he tried retracing his mental steps. Schaffer's killer knew where Lee was hanging out. Maybe he followed him from town out to Blue Haze?

But Lee was a biker, used to violence, suspicious, on his guard because the Dingos had told him the police were looking for him. If the killer didn't know Lee, how did he manage to surprise him and kill him? Did he just lie in wait in the shadows on the off-chance, or knock on the door and run off and hope Lee would emerge to investigate?

No. He had to know him. Didn't he?

Clement had the sensation of looking across a vast empty desert. He sighed, despairing. His eyes travelled to Phoebe's drawing. He should call her. As he picked up the receiver, the answer he had been chasing fell on him. He gently replaced the receiver.

The flashing watch.

When he had seen it in the dark room the other night his response had been curiosity, 'What on earth is that?' And now he was thinking Lee had thought the same. Lee had been lured to the exact position the killer wanted by that watch.

Clement was certain of it.

...

Clement found Manners gobbling a sandwich and felt bad for interrupting much needed nourishment. Manners had begun to resemble a hologram of himself.

'That liquor shop footage of the carpark ... did we dump the whole hard drive on our computers?'

Manners tried to speak through bread. 'Yeah, got it all.' He slapped his computer to show that was where it resided.

'I want you to go through that footage again, this time I want you looking for white SUVs. Make a note of the rego of any white SUVs or people driving them.'

'It's black and white footage. Yellow, light blue, it might be hard to tell.'

'Do your best. Start on the day of the argument then

work out one day each way, then two days each way.'

'Got it.'

'Did you find Schaffer's Pajero in any other footage?'

'At the shopping centre carpark, just that one day. But HQ clocked it once, remember?'

That was right. They had a shot of the Pajero on the street from when they'd been looking at Lee to see if he'd been hanging about. Clement started to call Perth.

'I'll get a copy sent to us.'

'I've got one, thought we should have that too.'

'Fantastic.'

Manners puffed a little at the compliment.

Clement instructed, 'Look for a white SUV. You never know, if he was tracking Schaffer, he could be on there.'

He left Manners to it and thought of trying Klendtwort again but decided he'd leave it for now. Instead he called Marilyn's. Geraldine answered.

'Hello, Geraldine. Is Phoebe there?'

'What do you think you're doing, Daniel?'

Trying to converse with his daughter? Evenly, he said, 'What do you mean?'

'I mean hanging around here, dragging us all into murder and your sordid world.'

'The watch was a coincidence.'

'It might not have been.'

'Geraldine, I don't have the time for this right now. Could I speak to my daughter?'

'Have you caught him yet?'

'No.'

'Didn't think so.' The phone clunked on a sideboard. A moment later came echoing footsteps.

'Hello, Daddy. I got my watch back.'

'I know.'

'Mummy said you helped look for it.'

Another tick for Marilyn.

'That's true. We need to get together, make up for that lost weekend. I was thinking about the Derby house. '

'Can we take the boat out?'

'Of course.'

'Can I drive it?'

'Yes, you can be skipper.'

That seemed to swing the vote. 'Okay.'

'I'm not sure when this will all be finished but as soon as it is.'

'Alright. And remember ...'

'What?'

'When you catch the bad man, cut his head off, otherwise they can come back to life.'

He assured her he would remember that, told her he loved her and hung up. He'd almost asked to speak to Marilyn but thought better of it, though it would have been enjoyable to annoy Geraldine. His mobile rang. He didn't recognise the number.

'Yes?'

'It's Manners.'

Typical IT guy, using the phone instead of walking five metres across the room. He sounded pumped. 'Come over to the AV.'

Clement made it there double-time. Scott Risely was there too. Manners spoke quickly.

'The footage came from Banton the jeweller. Not a red light camera unfortunately, that would have given us a numberplate.'

They stood at the console and stared at the screen which had been paused. Manners hit play. It was shot from inside the shop focussing on the window display in case of theft. But it was possible to see passing traffic, albeit not in sharp focus. Manners tapped the screen.

'That's Schaffer's Pajero.'

Right behind it came a white SUV. It was impossible

to see the driver. Manners hit pause as the SUV receded. The registration was blurred.

Risely said, 'Can we enhance it?'

'I think so.'

Clement felt himself bobbing with excitement. 'How long?'

'I don't know.'

'Get onto it.'

Risely said, 'The Germans called. They've already spoken to Pieter Gruen's brother and sister. The brother is in Hamburg, the sister in Switzerland. They don't think they are involved. They'll work through ex-colleagues and other associates, anybody who has contacted the department. They are very grateful, rapt in fact.'

He handed Clement a post-it note with a number written across.

'They've given us an English-speaking liaison officer and any help we need.'

•••

They were close now, very close, but Clement did not like relying purely on the physical evidence of CCTV and numberplates. He wanted an additional approach that looked for motive and opportunity. Whoever killed Schaffer had kicked and beaten him as he lay dying. It was extremely personal. Back in his office Clement reviewed Pieter Gruen's file as if it might talk to him. The German police had ruled out Gruen's brother and sister but there might be friends, his best man, a school chum. Pieter Gruen had a boy, Manfred, who had been six years old at the time of his death. Clement searched the file frantically. There was no mention of what had become of Hilda Gruen or her son. He tried Klendtwort again but there was still no answer. He left a message quickly outlining his discovery that Osterlund was Kurt Donen.

'Mathias, I urgently needed to speak to Pieter Gruen's widow, so please call me.'

The more he thought about it the more convinced he became that he could be onto something. Those wounds were gruesome. It had to be somebody very aggrieved about Pieter Gruen. Clement called the Federal Police and Immigration to see if any Manfred Gruen had entered the country in the last three months. The woman he spoke with at Immigration said she would be back in touch. Just before she was about to hang up he had another thought: the mother could have remarried, the boy may have been raised with a different name.

'Actually I'm not even certain about the last name but Manfred is not that common. Can you look up all those for me?'

She said she would 'modify the search criteria' and rang off. Now he felt he was out of the sand and running on firm ground. He left his office and found Ryan Gartrell who was helping run down leads on white SUVs.

'I need to speak to Hilda Gruen, Pieter Gruen's widow. The Hamburg Police might have an address. If not, see if she was receiving any benefits as widow of a police officer, we might be able to locate her from those.'

Clement copied the post-it note Risely had given him and handed it over. 'The Germans have assigned an English-speaking liaison officer to us. Ask for him.'

The door to Risely's office opened and Risely stepped out in a fresh suit. Clement hit him with his theory on Manfred Gruen.

'It's slim but it fits,' Clement concluded.

Risely was feeding off the energy too. 'You've spoken to Immigration? Federal Police?'

'Yes.'

'Good. I have a conference in ten. You want me to mention the vehicle?'

'No. It's our best chance of finding Osterlund alive. Our killer gets wind we're onto him he might kill him ... if he hasn't already.'

Chelsea Verschuer swung in from the back door. 'The wind is too strong. We're going to move it to the library.'

Risely was in agreement.

Clement left them working out the wording of the statement. On hot bricks, Clement took himself back down to the AV room where Manners was hunched over a computer.

'How's it going on that numberplate?'

He shook his head. 'I don't know if I'm going to be able to do this. I'm not getting anywhere. I've tried three programs but it's still blurred. '

'Then ask Perth for help.'

Clement returned to the main room and paced, worried now that he had banked so much on technology.

Time drizzled. He called Earle, found him already on his way back from Derby. The second candidate had been no more likely than the first. Clement gave him the latest.

'You guys have all the fun and I'm battling a cyclone. It's getting nasty.'

Clement told him to take care on the road. He turned to see Ryan Gartrell advancing rapidly.

'That was quick,' he observed.

'It's a police murder. The Germans are desperate to put it away. Good news is we have a name. Hilda Gruen became Hilda Bourke and the pension was sent to a Manchester bank for twenty-five years.'

Bourke? It seemed familiar but it was a common enough name he supposed.

Gartrell continued, 'But they don't have any current

address on her yet. They are going back through correspondence.'

'Okay, good.'

Once more he was becalmed. There had to be something he could do. He looked across at the whiteboard, thought of pieces still missing in the puzzle. Okay, suppose this was payback for Pieter Gruen. How did the killer know Schaffer was bent? How did he know Osterlund was Donen?

It clicked. The drug dealer who claimed to have been Gruen's friend! Clement felt he was getting his groove back. At great risk to himself this dealer had presented at the station to warn the police they had a leak. He had been telling the truth after all when he said he did not recognise the Emperor from the photos they showed. What was his name? Clement was sure it had been in the files but couldn't recall it right now. He would be mid-sixties, he knew what Osterlund looked like and he knew one of the cops was bent.

Clement went through the Pieter Gruen file until he found reference to the drug dealer. There it was: Michael Wallen.

He dialled the number on the post-it and was answered in English.

'Hamburg State Police, Erik Brohlen speaking.'

Clement introduced himself.

The German was polite. 'We are still looking for the information on Hilda Gruen.'

'This is something else, Erik. It might be a long shot but I need to locate the drug dealer, Michael Wallen, who is mentioned in Pieter Gruen's file. If he is still alive I think he might be around sixty, sixty-five.'

Brohlen took down the details. He sounded optimistic.

'If he had a police record we could have his date of birth and full name. I will call you back soon, Inspector.'

True to his word he was on the line in five minutes.

'Michael Wallen: date of birth, eleventh September nineteen fifty-two, owns an apartment in Harburg.'

Clement gratefully copied the phone number. Translation could be a problem but he thought he'd try his luck anyway. He dialled, the phone rang. A man answered.

'Hallo.'

'Do you speak English? This is Detective Clement of the West Australian police.'

The words bounced back soaked in confusion.

'Police? Australia?'

'Yes, you speak English?'

'A little.'

'Am I speaking to Michael Wallen?'

'No. He is my father. I am Rolf Wallen.'

'May I speak with your father?'

'He is not here.'

A flicker of optimism warmed Clement. 'He is away?'

'He is dead.'

It could be a lie. 'I am sorry. How long?'

'Juli.'

July. Six months. 'Was it sudden? Unexpected?'

'No. He was sick a long time.' Rolf Wallen was becoming curious rather than defensive. 'Australia? Kangaroos?'

'Western Australia, yes.'

'This is about what?'

'Did your father ever mention a man named Pieter Gruen?'

'Ja, of course. He is a ... how you say ... Hercules to our family.'

'A hero.'

'Ja, hero. My father say we owe everything to him.'

'Did any of Pieter Gruen's friends meet with your father?'

'No. My father is honest about his life. He is junkie in old days. Gruen give him his life but he is a policeman.'

'And your father never met with any of the police or family?'

'I am sorry. I do not understand.'

'We have a murder case here that may have something to do with the murder of Pieter Gruen.'

'That's a long time.'

'Yes it is. But back then your father told the police somebody in the police was corrupt, informing to the Emperor.'

'My father tells me about this.'

'I believe he was right.'

'Too late for my father.'

It was said matter of fact, not with bitterness.

'Yes, Rolf, but you can help us. I think sometime in the last year or so your father must have met with somebody associated with Pieter Gruen.'

'I don't know this.'

'Did he ever have any contact with Gruen's family?'

'He send a parcel and a letter, I remember. A long time back. I am zwölf.'

Clement went with the word it sounded most like. 'Twelve?'

'A boy, not teenager. I give some of my toys. '

'It was to another boy?'

'Ja. In England. The boy, Manfred. He is my age.'

44

On the way out to the pit for the last time the dark peeled away and dawn shone on the memory of that first meeting with his saviour. He had sat enthralled listening to Wallen's slow plodding words.

'He was my best friend. He will always be my best friend.'

Wallen stirred the sugar through his coffee relentlessly. His fair hair was still thick in clumps though with sparse areas like a well-worn walking track, his eyes were tired and his skin grey. They were in a little café just a street from the railway station, a cheap place where the smell of toast and cooked ham hung in the air, and there was a greasy patina on the check plastic tablecloths. The majority of the customers were men in vinyl jackets that had been long soaked in cigarette smoke and whose razors had not quite done the job on cheeks and chins. It had been an impulse decision to ring from Munich. The tournament was over and the rest of his party were spending their last day sightseeing but he felt he could not let the chance pass. Wallen had offered to come to Munich but he thought he would like to see Hamburg so they arranged to meet here.

Wallen's face adopted its natural line of concern and missed opportunity.

'I was so shocked about your father. I should have tried to contact your family years ago but I was scared. Not just for me, I had a young family. I'm not a brave man. After I tried that first time with the police, I was worried Donen would know I'd tried to talk. For years I ran. And then when I stopped running I couldn't find an address for your family. Finally I rang the police and pretended to be an old colleague of Pieter's and somebody found that Manchester address.'

Yes, that made sense. He would never forget the day the parcel arrived with the letter.

'I bought that t-shirt for myself but never wore it. I know it was too big for a young kid but I thought one day you can wear it.'

'I still have it. I never took it out of its wrapping. And the letter of course.'

He was alone at home reading *Harry Potter*, a boy similarly deprived of family by evil, when the parcel finally arrived.

'At first Hilda didn't want me to write back,' he said. The coffee was too strong for him. He sipped it and put it down.

'I can't blame her. I was a druggie, not then, but before. I've got hep C to show for it. Anyway, I'm glad you did.'

They talked for a long time. About family at first: Wallen in detail describing his own kids and wife, then, asking about his schooling, and Hilda and her second husband. The proximity of the train station meant they could squeeze the juice out of every detail before he climbed on his return train to Munich.

'And you're a sportsman too?' Wallen's eyes crinkled over the rim of his cup.

'We came third out of seven.'

'I never made any team, hopeless. Pieter would have been proud.'

'Tell me about him.'

Wallen recounted how they met, how he didn't have much to do with him at first, how he had saved Pieter Gruen once and how Pieter had in turn saved him from something much more pernicious than a group of skinheads.

'The whole operation could have come crashing down because of me. He put his own life in danger to tell me to clear out. He trusted me. And the worst part is, sometimes I fear—at the end—he might have thought it was me.' Wallen shook his head bitterly.

Hours had passed. Shifts of diners had come and gone.

'Do you know exactly what happened to him?'

'As I wrote you, the man they called the Emperor killed him. I heard that from a very reliable source.'

'Is it true they chopped him up with a chainsaw?'

Wallen did not want to meet his eyes. 'Yes.'

Donen himself had cut Pieter Gruen to pieces while he was still alive.

'The man who told me this heard it from one of the men who was actually there, one of the Emperor's bodyguards, a man named Klaus. I couldn't live with this image of my friend Pieter. I am a coward at heart and I tried to blot it out but I could not and eventually I went to the police. They did not believe me. You understand after that I had to disappear too. Once Donen knew I was prepared to talk...'

'Where is Donen now?'

'If I knew that I would track him down and kill him myself.'

'Do you have any photos of Donen?'

'No. He was too careful. And back in those days it wasn't like now with cameras in phones. But if the cops thought they had a photo of Donen they were wrong.'

...

It was on the train on the way back to Munich that he looked at his reflection in the window and promised he would track down those men and kill them no matter what. He was pragmatic about it though. He was sixteen. First he had to complete his schooling, and he had to prepare himself, be ready to give up his own life. But in the years that took, his desire never wavered. Every arrow he shot was through their hearts, every math problem he solved, the mystery of how to find them, every sentence he wrote, part of their obituaries. There could be no future until the past had been dealt with to his satisfaction, however long that took. And now here he was on the other side of the world and finally it had been done and his life could restart when Donen's ended.

45

The woman from Immigration got back in touch to say there was no record of a Manfred Gruen entering the country in the last five months. They were still in the process of compiling a list of people named 'Manfred' who had entered Australia in that time. Clement had thought the chance of Manfred having his father's surname was fifty-fifty so he wasn't too discouraged.

'You can reduce it by eliminating those under thirty-five and over forty-five. Also please check for a Manfred Bourke.' He could have adopted his stepfather's name.

'I'll email you a list as soon as we have it, shouldn't be long.'

Michael Wallen had been in contact with Manfred when he was a boy. Perhaps they had stayed in touch? Once you accepted that Wallen was not lying and the photo shown of Donen was fake it was a short step to put Dieter Schaffer in the frame. He was the only one who could have substituted the photo. If Clement could see that, Manfred Gruen may have also.

'Look for anybody with first name Manfred up here, caravan parks, vehicle hires.'

He stood in the centre of the room firing off orders. Mal Gross emerged from the AV area and Clement stabbed the question.

'How's Manners going?'

Gross shook his head. Ryan Gartrell slammed down the phone and called out from his desk.

'It's not Manfred Gruen, boss.'

What did he mean? It had to be Gruen, everything fitted.

Gartrell continued. 'The Hamburg Police have records of sympathy cards they sent to Hilda Gruen. Manfred Gruen suicided twelve years ago.'

'You're sure?'

'They're definite.'

The room shrank.

'What about Hilda Gruen?'

'The cards were sent to an address near Manchester in England. They still haven't found her current address.'

'Wallen might have told somebody else.' It was Whiteman.

'Probably, but his son was only aware of that one parcel going off to Manfred.' Clement sucked it up. 'Keep doing what you're doing. Let's find the owner of that white SUV. I'm going out to clear my head.'

Clement fought the temptation to head up to AV and hang over Manners' shoulder again. The guy was under enough pressure already. He climbed into his car and drove back out where the media crews had been assembled a little earlier. None were left. The streets of town were eerily quiet, the footpaths spare of café furniture that could become lethal weapons in a cyclone. A shop-owner was drilling and fixing ply boards over his windows. Clement passed only two cars heading into town as he cruised out, his mind a jumble between the case and the humiliation of being shifted from leading it. On autopilot he turned along the coast road. Sand was whipping across from the beach.

When he saw the entrance to the more northerly track he turned down towards the beach, just as the abductor must have done. Halfway down, crime scene tape, straining and rattling in the increasing wind, blocked his path. There were no vehicles in sight.

He switched off the engine and sat, the increasingly awesome wind emphasising his insignificance and by extension that of any one human being. Yet he was not totally despondent. Hopefully if Manners couldn't crack that plate, Perth would. They were prepared too, roadblocks up, police and emergency vehicles on the alert for white SUVs.

He had been so confident about Manfred Gruen.

He climbed out into the gale, ducked under the chequered tape and walked towards the beach. As if hurled by an angry fist, sand stung his cheeks. He was forced to squint to keep it out of his eyes. Hunching his body he tried to scan the miles of white sand with not a soul on it. The ocean was foaming, angry but not yet psychotic, the sky a grey purple. How had the abductor got close enough to subdue Osterlund? Was he working with an accomplice?

No, Clement felt a single intelligence here. It would be perhaps another trick, more sleight of hand as he had used with the biker. Who are you? You have a beginning like everyone, like me. You were born somewhere, you had aspirations, maybe of being a famous soccer player, maybe that was the thing with the t-shirt, but somewhere along the way they disappeared, didn't they? The only thing that became important was punishing these men for the wrong they did to Gruen, you, or both. That is what sustains you, emboldens you. Nothing can happen to you because you are righting a wrong. That's what you believe isn't it?

His phone rang. He felt it more than heard it in the wind. Automatically he began to retreat to the shelter of the car, the wind blowing him along so his legs had to move to catch up. He pulled the phone from his pocket expecting Manners but it was not a station number. 'Mathias? Hold on.'

He had to yell above the wind. It was a battle to pull the door open. He flopped into his seat feeling more secure out of the gusts. The usual impish tone had drained from the German.

'Hello Daniel. Sorry I missed your calls. We got your message, Heinrich and I. We couldn't believe it. But it had to be Dieter, right? The fingerprints he couldn't get rid of because they came direct to Heinrich but the photo, they just film some schmuck in Belgrade or Prague with a newspaper and they know poor Pieter will never have a chance to contradict them. I can't believe none of us saw through it. I guess we didn't want to.'

Another spray of sand hurled itself at the windscreen.

Clement said. 'I'm sorry, mate.'

'You know why Dieter did it?'

'Just a guess. He got in over his head gambling, it was his way out. I need to speak to Hilda, if you have her number.'

There was a deep, regretful sigh. 'There's something Heinrich and I have been debating. I won't bullshit you, man, this has been very hard for us. Kurt Donen murdered our friend and ruined the lives of Pieter and his boy. He gassed himself, the boy, Manfred, you know that?'

'Yes, I thought ... I thought he might be the one.'

Clement oughtn't feel guilty but he did.

'Tragedy,' was all the German offered before another substantial pause. Clement fought impatience and waited. 'Heinrich remembered something. You asked me about this Klaus Edershen.'

Clement was suddenly thrown back to the clipping of the crime scene in some German park. 'That's right.'

'I looked up the article. It said the victim was a

soldier. And I'm thinking, why did Dieter have the article? There was a rumour passed onto us from Gruen via Dieter, maybe before he went bad, that one of Donen's bodyguards was an ex-mercenary.'

Clement's gaze had automatically turned back to the beach. He was still listening but thinking too about that article. An arrow could have stopped Osterlund, no noise, no shell casings.

'So Heinrich and me work it out, maybe this Klaus Edershen was Donen's bodyguard. Maybe that was why he was killed. The bodyguard, then the informer; somebody is taking them out, right?'

Still Clement did not interrupt. He sensed something was coming.

'Over the years Heinrich was writing to Hilda on and off. In one letter she told him the boy was a junior champion, archery.'

'Manfred was a top archer?' Clement was trying to calculate ages.

'Not Manfred, Manfred's son Peter, named after his grandad. That's why this is so hard. We think you're looking for Pieter's grandson. To be honest we never even thought about him. Last time we saw his father, Manfred, he was just a little kid himself, you forget. Manfred had the boy when he was only nineteen or something—junkie mother shot through. Hilda raised him. This is going to break her heart.'

The woman had lost her husband, son and now maybe her grandson. Clement hated this part of it but could not deny the euphoria building in his veins.

'Peter Gruen or Bourke?'

'Bourke. As a junior he represented his country in archery.'

'England?'

'No, after Manfred died they moved. To Ireland.'

46

They were in a different café this time, by the river, and spring was stirring. It was two years on from that first time when he'd caught the train up from Munich and Wallen's health seemed decidedly worse. It was an effort for him to negotiate the chairs. In this café there were no men in vinyl jackets but women with babies in prams and men with silver hair in suede jackets studying cake menus through their glasses.

'I'm going to kill the men who killed my grandfather.'

Wallen tried to dissuade him. 'You can't do that. If you are caught it will finish your oma.'

'I won't be caught.'

'The only way you won't be caught is if you don't do it.'

The emphasis was on the word 'you'. Wallen had looked at him through watery eyes. Peter understood Wallen was offering to do it himself.

Instead of arguing with Wallen he said, 'I have some money. We could hire a private detective to find Donen.'

'He'll be using a different name. He may no longer even be in Germany. We have no photograph.'

'I thought about that. We could get a sketch artist like the police use to draw him how he looked then and how he might look now.'

Wallen nodded slowly as if this were a credible idea.

'I have an artist friend who could do it. But save your money. The only way we'll find him is through one of the old associates.'

'Good. If they killed my grandfather I want them as well.'

Wallen suggested Peter return to Ireland.

'No. I'll stay.'

Wallen accepted this without argument. Wallen's intelligence was that Donen's two bodyguards had been present holding Pieter Gruen when he had been sliced to death by their boss. The one known as Tank had died of cancer but the other, Klaus, was living in Dortmund.

'I'll find out what he knows and then kill him.'

...

Klaus Edershen had retired to Applerbeck, a quite pretty area in the south-east of Dortmund, where the retired killer blended in with ex-schoolteachers, factory workers and bankers. He was still a powerfully built man and as Peter and Wallen watched him from the shadows on his ritual evening walk with his small dog, Peter could see the fear in Wallen's eyes. Wallen may have had ten years on Klaus Edershen but he was a thin ex-junkie with hep C. Klaus Edershen looked like he could still be manning a machine gun in the Congo.

They had followed him from the small apartment block where he lived alone in one of six units.

'You don't have to do this,' he'd said to Wallen.

'I can handle him. I'll get him drunk and take him from behind.'

The dog, some sort of cocker spaniel, cocked its leg against a tree.

'The dog will make a racket. People will come looking. We'll be stopped before we start. Just find out where Donen is. Find out who the leak was.'

Wallen agreed to do that. 'But if I see my chance, I'll take it.'

'No.' Peter was surprised with the clarity with which he now saw everything. 'You will have to drink with him. They will find your prints. I suppose you are in the system?'

'Maybe. It was a long time ago. Nineteen seventy-five, a dope bust in Hamburg.'

'Assume you are in the system. I'll handle him.'

'You're just a boy.'

'And you're an ex-junkie with a stuffed liver. I prefer my chances.'

Wallen had eventually given in. They had caught a train from Hamburg to Dortmund and hired a car to drive to Applerbeck. They spent the afternoon and evening watching Klaus Edershen's movements, which were those of the retired man: a walk with the dog, a trip to the bar, some shopping and back home for a bachelor dinner. It was pleasant weather though a little chilly in the evening. They waited until nine p.m. and then drove back to the city where they bought bratwurst from a street vendor. The plan was already clear in Peter's mind.

'From here on we can't be seen together or call one another. I'll catch the train tomorrow and kill him.'

'No, wait on.' Wallen held up a hand like a traffic cop. 'Not so fast. He might know who the leak was. It had to be one of the cops worked with your grandfather.'

Peter had already considered that. 'And whoever he was probably told them you turned up.'

'No, I was thinking about that. I didn't go to the police for a month or two. Donen, Klaus, they were all gone by then. When I saw Toro, he clearly had no idea.'

'Toro wasn't so high up.'

They argued. Peter said it was too big a risk to take. Wallen refused to budge.

'You can't have it both ways. We want the men who

murdered your father to pay. You can do the shot, I'm getting the information.'

And that was that. Peter gave in.

'You catch the train tomorrow evening, visit him and find out what you can. I'll meet you back here, eleven-thirty.' Peter felt no qualms about giving orders to a man forty years his senior.

'You're like your grandfather,' said Wallen.

'And don't get yourself killed.'

They split up, booking in separate bed and breakfasts a couple of blocks apart.

...

The next twenty-four hours were the longest of Peter's life. The bed and breakfast place was clean with pink and white wallpaper and a frilly eiderdown, presumably decorated by a woman, but it was cramped and airless so he abandoned it in favour of investigating the city's nooks, crannies and back lanes. Dortmund was a blend of new office towers and gothic spires and might normally have been interesting but he could not concentrate.

Too hyped to eat much, he stopped twice for coffee and sweet biscuits. At five p.m. he watched Wallen board the train to Applerbeck. Now it was in the lap of the gods.

He returned to his bed and breakfast and sat on his frilly eiderdown and tried to watch television but it was no use. He was up and down many times to the toilet even though he had no pee left in him. For something to do he checked and re-checked his bow, assembling it, breaking it down, reassembling. Finally it was close to eleven. He walked out again and sauntered aimlessly this way and that until eleven fifteen. Then he returned to the little street a few blocks from the station where he had arranged to meet Wallen.

Peter built up every conceivable scenario, from Wallen failing to make contact to being strangled by Edershen. He became utterly convinced Edershen had known of Wallen's perfidy. And then as he was imagining poor Wallen sliced apart just like his grandfather had been, he looked up and saw a gangly silhouette weaving towards him out of the mist. He realised Wallen was staggering and Peter immediately assumed injury. It turned out he was simply drunk.

Wallen told his story with slurred words. He had done exactly as they planned, arriving at the station and going to the park at the same time as the day before where Edershen indeed proved a creature of habit walking his dog from seven past six to six twenty-five.

'How busy was the park then?'

'Same as yesterday, hardly anybody: a few dog-walkers, older women.'

Wallen had purchased a bottle of vodka and knocked on the door of Edershen's apartment near eight o'clock. He could smell some sort of cooking.

'Klaus opened the door. He didn't recognise me. I said as much as I lifted the vodka up. Then I said, "Hamburg seventy-eight." But I could see he still needed some help.'

Wallen dropped the name of their mutual contact, Toro, another old drug dealer, and finally the mist lifted from his eyes.

'Wallen!'

'Toro told me where you lived. I was in Dortmund for my niece's wedding, I thought we'd have a drink for old times.'

It was exactly what Peter had scripted Wallen to say and Wallen claimed he had carried it out to the letter. The apartment was comfortable. Two bedrooms, larger than what a single man like Edershen needed. It was neat, sparsely furnished but with good quality furniture.

Edershen turned off the TV. He had just finished dinner and washed up, a good omen for what he might do with the drinking glasses after Wallen had gone. They sat and drank, talking about their lives since they'd last seen one another. Edershen had spent a number of years in Asia but was deliberately hazy on exactly what he had done there and Wallen assumed it was drugs or something else illegal. Wallen lied and said he had been dealing drugs in Italy. Eventually Wallen had steered the conversation to the last time they had seen each other.

'Just before the shit hit the fan. That undercover cop. So many guys got picked up.'

With curiosity bordering on suspicion Edershen said. 'Not you.'

'I got lucky, kind of.'

Wallen adapted the true story of Pieter Gruen, claiming that after his last visit to the Emperor to get supplied he was jumped by some skinhead thugs.

'They beat the crap out of me and took my stuff. I was wondering how to tell the Emperor. You know what he was like.'

Klaus nodded, he did indeed.

'They never got you either?'

Edershen told him a day or two before it was all meant to go down they got word from a bent cop. Wallen threw out the name of a Reeperbahn street cop he knew was bent just to keep Edershen bubbling.

'No, much higher than that fuckwit, the undercover guy's own controller.'

Peter had drilled into Wallen the names of all the cops on his grandfather's squad. He knew who the controller had been.

'Schaffer?'

'That's him. Sold out his own man to pay off a gambling debt.' Edershen shook his head in disgust.

Wallen had tried to hide his excitement.

'You still in touch with the Emperor?'

'Last time I saw him he was about three months after. He was boarding a freighter to Rotterdam, false papers and identity. I never heard from him again. I heard from Tank that he was supposed to be in Thailand back in the pussy trade: bars, clubs; less heat than drugs. You're not on that shit still are you?'

Wallen explained he had been long off it. They talked another hour or so before Wallen took his leave. He'd held up the vodka bottle to Edershen.

'You mind if I take the last bit for the train?'

This had been another of Peter's ideas to make sure Wallen left no prints around. Edershen waved him off. They talked about catching up. Once outside Wallen wiped his fingerprints off the bottle and dumped it in a bin at the train station, then had an uneventful trip back to Dortmund on the train.

A deep sense of release washed through Peter. They knew the name of the traitor: Dieter Schaffer. Finding Donen in Thailand, with his new identity would be very difficult. Not that this would discourage Peter. He would keep looking whatever the chances, but Dieter Schaffer, well he could almost taste his blood.

He said, 'You need to return to Hamburg tomorrow.'

Wallen shook his head. 'No. You have your whole life ahead of you. I'll do it.'

'Don't you want justice for my grandfather and father?'

'Of course.'

'The only way the police get me is through you. You want to help me, go back. I can do this. I am meant to do this. I'll see you in Hamburg in three days.'

He had turned on his heel, giving Wallen no chance to argue.

The next day he hired a car and drove to Applerbeck

making sure he stayed away from anywhere there might be CCTV cameras. He wore a generic cap and rain jacket and had the dismantled bow in a rucksack exactly as it would be the next day. He wanted to make sure there were no surprises. He spent most of his time in the park looking for the best location for the shot, settling eventually for a copse of trees that he could access directly from an adjoining road. He assembled his bow, then disassembled it. For nearly two hours he hid. The park was near deserted when Edershen appeared walking his dog, a little later this time, closer to seven. Edershen walked up a small rise directly towards the copse, placing himself in range for a substantial time. Though the light was poor by this time, the distance was less than twenty metres, which more than compensated.

Peter returned to Dortmund, enjoyed an Asian meal from a small café and turned in early. The next morning he bought a pair of grey overalls from a shop in the backwaters of the city for he thought somebody might remember his outfit from the day before. He retrieved the car but because he could not afford to be lurking in the park for any length of time with a weapon on him, he did not leave for Applerbeck until nearly five p.m. The traffic was dense but he arrived in plenty of time and parked in a shopping centre carpark about a kilometre and a half away.

He walked briskly to the park with everything he needed in his backpack, crossed the narrow road and strode directly into the copse. The breeze was stronger this evening, making the shot more difficult, and the park was busier but to his relief it began thinning rapidly. At six twenty he removed his weapon from his backpack and began assembling it. He was ready to fire by six twenty-four. Of course he had no way of knowing if Klaus Edershen was even in the park, maybe this was the day when he went to the movies or played bocce. Fifteen minutes in, the exercise threatened to turn into a disaster. An unleashed dog, a beagle he thought, came charging up the incline, ran directly into the thicket where he was hiding and stood staring at him wagging its tail. The owner, a slim straggly blonde of forty or so followed behind a moment later and cast about for the animal.

'Jensen?' She called several times in slightly different tones.

Jensen was torn between his new find and his owner's voice. Finally Jensen pulled himself away and ran to her. She scolded the dog playfully before continuing. The archer took a deep breath. He had decided on a throat shot. It was his best chance to kill Edershen but the wind was picking up making it more difficult. While he was debating whether he should aim for the heart instead he saw Edershen's head appearing over the rise. He quickly drew an arrow and took aim. The bow he was using was not a tournament bow. It had been chosen for portability but though it was less accurate, up until now the archer had not seriously considered the possibility he might miss, not at short range. He paused, his arm extended taking the weight of the bow. Edershen's dog must have found the beagle's scent. Instead of continuing he sniffed in a tight circle. Should he fire now? It was tempting: the target was less than twenty metres away.

He held his nerve.

Finally the pooch lost interest and began moving forward fast, perhaps picking up the old scent. Edershen's mind was elsewhere. He had had no idea that less than just a few metres in front of him a deadly arrow was pointed at his throat. Peter felt a great calm as if the anointed hand had laid itself upon his shoulder. He let the arrow go.

47

'Page four.'

Wallen slapped down a newspaper on the bench. This time they were at a coffee shop on the other side of Hamburg, a more bohemian place where would-be film directors and the like might hang out. It was five days since he had killed Edershen. Peter scanned the newspaper article. Police were 'baffled by the killing of an elderly man by an arrow through the neck'. Klaus Eldershen was described as a 'former soldier', a 'quiet man who kept to himself'. Police thought it may have been inadvertent and requested whoever had fired the arrow to come forward.

He looked at Wallen. 'They haven't called you?'

'No.'

'If they had found prints they would have don't you think? I'd say Klaus washed up the glasses you drank from. They are dead-ended. They think it's a psycho or an accident.'

Wallen was inclined to agree but cautioned that they should stay alert.

Caution was foreign to Peter. 'Next, Dieter Schaffer,' he declared.

'He's disappeared.'

'What do you mean?'

'I've made enquiries. He's quit his apartment, no

forwarding address. If you believe his drinking cronies he's in Turkey, Australia or South America.'

'His old police buddies might know.'

'They might but no way am I going near them.'

'Fuck Schaffer. Edershen said Donen was in Bangkok. We'll go there. We'll find the bastard and kill him over his tom yum soup.'

But poor Wallen wasn't up to it. His health was failing and in the end Peter had to go alone, traipsing from sordid bar to bar, through the strident clang of traffic, the petrol fumes and the sticky heat, acting hale and hearty with arsehole ex-pats. He'd had an artist do up a sketch of how Donen might look and he'd worked his way through sleazy bars showing it to bar girls, drug dealers, paedophiles. A couple of older German guys claimed to recognise the man but not as Kurt. 'Gerd' he was calling himself. Three weeks he'd done this until his money had run out and he'd been forced to return.

He had just one slim hope left. His oma. He had not wanted to involve her but what choice did he have now? He played on her sentiment, suggested they do something for grandad's anniversary, contact his old friends. All this took time. Poor old Wallen went into hospital on his last legs. Then from an ex-colleague of Dieter Schaffer she learned he had moved to Australia. She even got an email address.

'But you don't want to push and ask for a physical address because when he's found dead, when the wasp stings the spider, someone remembers, especially old cops. But Australia is a big place, he could be anywhere. How was I going to find him? He wasn't in any phone book, he wasn't on Facebook. How, how, how?'

Peter Bourke paraded back and forth along the lip of the trench. He was shouting only to get his voice above the wind. He was in control, a fundamentalist preacher playing to a congregation of one.

'You know how?' he continued, slyly. 'What obsesses all men? Come on, give it a shot?'

Bourke smiled, it was important his foe appreciated his guile. 'Football. Schaffer was a huge fan of Hamburg Football Club. So, I contact them and say, "I have a friend of my late grandfather moved to Australia, Dieter Schaffer but I don't know where he is and I'm going there for a visit. Is he on a mailing list or something?" Sure enough, next thing I know I am here where the gods intended me all along, part of the earth, and the sky and the wind.' This last word he did shout into the brooding vault above that seemed to grow lower every few minutes.

'See, I play the spider when I need to be the spider, and the wasp when I need to be the wasp. Three weeks I am watching Schaffer, the dog. I sit behind him at the coffee shop, I watch him park his car, offer weed to young women. The wasp is almost ready to sting ... and then one day he calls out to somebody in German and I look across the road and it's fucking you, the Emperor.'

He directed his gaze down at the loathsome one who had ruined his life. Still those eyes appeared to be laughing at Peter, though like the stung spider, Osterlund was inert.

'This isn't the end. The spirits aren't finished with you. They will eat your gizzards from the inside and even when they are done, when there is nothing left, not one glob of fat or sliver of bone they will make you say his name, the last words you will ever hear: Pieter Gruen.'

48

The wind was picking up every second, rocking his car on the exposed coast road so fiercely Clement's forearms ached from fighting the wheel.

'The grandson?' Even via the tinny phone speaker in this hurtling missile, Risely's surprise was clear.

'Yeah. I don't know if he's in the file but I should have allowed for the possibility anyway. Name is Peter Bourke.'

'Now all we have to do is find him.'

'He works at the Mimosa. I remember the name from the staff list. He's served me, an Irishman. He was there when the witness informed me about a biker arguing with Dieter Schaffer. I'm guessing he'd been following Schaffer, spied Lee arguing with him, followed him.'

Risely was digesting this. 'Why'd he kill him?'

'Probably just to divert us. Or maybe he figured we'd find Lee and Lee would mention the young dude following Dieter Schaffer and we'd start to look for him.'

Clement turned off the main road onto the long Mimosa driveway. 'Should be able to ask him in person very soon.' Clement gave him a detailed description for circulation and announced, 'I'm here.'

'I'll assemble a team. Don't approach him till we arrive, unless you have no choice. And well done, mate.'

...

Clement cruised into the reception carpark and pulled into a bay. Pieces of broken foliage were whipping through the air. Clement removed his service weapon from his glove box and checked it. Hopefully he would not have to use it but Peter Bourke had proven he was prepared to unleash any amount of force and use any weapon. Even though he had promised poor Mathias and Heinrich he would do everything he could to keep the boy unharmed, Clement wasn't going to be caught second-guessing with an axe or arrow coming for his head. He forced the door open and stepped out of the car.

The shelter of the Mimosa grounds reduced the wind's power substantially although the tops of the palm trees were shrieking. In the distance maids ran fast as they serviced bungalows. Loose buckets tore off on their own adventure.

When he had entered reception through the automatic doors the gusty wind swirled briefly through the lobby. Clement caught sight of himself in the mirror, a devil from the netherworld bringing chaos and darkness.

According to the concierge Kate, Bourke's shift did not begin until midday. In all likelihood he was in the bungalow he shared with the Brazilian, Arvie, and another young man, Jake Windsor, but there was no guarantee. Arvie was flat out securing the garden from the cyclone so at least he wouldn't be in there but Jake Windsor was a waiter working the same shift as Bourke and there was every chance he might be with him. The same went for any other staff on the late shifts, especially given the impending storm. It was likely they would be jawing together. There was no phone in any of the bungalows. Kate had most of the staff's personal mobile numbers but Clement didn't want to risk trying those. If they were hanging with Bourke and their phones went off he might tumble something was up, so Clement told her to keep staff away from the bungalows and channel them into reception if she could. She could make up some excuse about the bungalows not being safe in the cyclone.

'What kind of car does he drive?'

'A white SUV.' She didn't have the registration. She was nervous.

Clement reassured her, 'Don't worry.'

From her look, it didn't help. He moved closer to the reception door and called Risely again.

'He drives a white SUV, rego unknown but it should be on the list you have.'

'Manners is onto it. We're suiting up. I'll bring you a vest.'

It could not be assumed Bourke had acted alone but that was Clement's instinct. He cursed himself for not considering the possibility of a grandchild as the killer and in the next breath forgave himself. You didn't expect a grandchild to come avenging his progenitors. Nor did he blame his German friends. Even if they were aware of Manfred Gruen having a child, the image that naturally came into their heads was a little toddler chasing butterflies. The world was moving too fast. In a blink Phoebe would be walking down the aisle, or more likely moving into an apartment with some dude who wore his cap backwards.

His thoughts flitted to his father. Clement still hadn't called him. Peter Bourke was just a kid when his own father suicided. Was that the point where his life had been irretrievably shunted in the wrong direction? What was he going to do when he was confronted? Sometimes these people didn't care if you killed them, in fact they wanted it.

Clement automatically gripped the pistol in his coat pocket, its hardness and weight physical reminders of its awful power.

Clement asked himself what he would do if Bourke came at him. They needed him to find Osterlund. Clement had sat under a fan drinking coffee, making polite conversation with the monster who had chopped Gruen to pieces with a chainsaw. Would Clement risk his own life to find him?

He put the question aside hoping he might never need to learn its answer.

49

Daryl Hagan was set up on the Great Northern Highway ten k out of Broome looking for any white SUVs using the road to Derby and the desert. Despite its name, the road actually ran more east than north at this point. The wind had picked up steadily in the three hours he'd been there and now it was whipping through hard. He could smell the rain at its back. Off the top of his head he opined there may be no cars on the road at all with a big storm coming through. His usual partner in crime Beck Lalor disagreed. She reckoned there were plenty of white SUVs especially if you counted cream and even though there was a storm coming she reckoned there'd be a half dozen. Hagan suggested they have a case of beer on it. If between them they stopped more than six white SUVs she won. Being a woman who enjoyed a beer on a hot day, and a bet on any day at all, she agreed. She was set up ten k out of Broome on the road heading north to Cape Leveque. Hagan made her promise she wouldn't be stopping vans or silver SUVs to boost her numbers. As it turned out he was going to skate through easy on this one. Checking in via the radio he'd learned she'd only stopped one white SUV so far. It was not the one they were after but she had taken details just in case. For his part Hagan had stopped only two white vehicles, one of those, a larger four-wheel drive, out of sheer boredom. Lalor was already trying to wriggle out of the bet though, claiming that the cyclonic conditions were keeping people off the road.

'It's a tainted sample,' she said.

'Well you would say that,' he replied. Lalor had done some tertiary studies and she liked to bandy about words and statistics that he kind of grasped without ever being totally sure what she was on about. 'But you knew that when we bet.'

She agreed that was true. 'But I reckon they're going to call us in early, so it can't count.'

She had a point there but Hagan could shoot back some statistical concepts of his own.

'So we were talking four-thirty finish, right?'

That would have been the normal time they would work to before somebody else came to take over.

'Yes.'

'Okay so we can extrapolate the numbers, right?'

'Extrapolate? That's a huge word for you, Hages.'

He was grinning and he imagined she was too. Hagan liked Lalor a lot. If he didn't already have a cute girlfriend he might have considered extracurricular possibilities.

'I picked it up from Manners.'

'The IT guy?'

'Yeah. So what do you say?'

He could hear her mind computing. 'Sure.'

Uh-oh. She sounded confident. Had he miscalculated? He thought he had the numbers falling his way.

'We've done three vehicles in approximately three hours,' she said. It was getting harder to hear her over the wind. 'Which "extrapolates" to seven in seven and a half hours, so I guess I win.'

'No, hang on a second, one of those was a big mother

that I only stopped because I was bored.'

'So you're saying it's actually two in three hours which would equate to five in seven point five hours, meaning you win.'

'Correct.'

'Yes. Unless we get another couple before they call us off, then I win.'

'Has to be any time. This wind is getting very angry.'

'It's worse here.'

'What happens if we get one more?'

'I guess that would be a tie.'

'Take care.'

'Keep your eyes peeled.'

'I will.'

As much as they joked about it both were aware that this was not a job to be taken lightly. The man they were looking for had killed two, maybe three people. If a cop stopped him he might start firing, and they were all on their lonesome, not the ideal situation, but neither was having an axe killer running around a small town.

50

'No car by the bungalow.'

Clement was standing in the small garden at the corner of the last staff bungalow in the set of four before Bourke's. From this vantage he could clearly see the empty parking bay in front of 12. Wearing a headset Risely stood behind him, looking even bigger in his body armour which they were all wearing. It always felt strange to Clement, the way cricket pads felt strange. Whiteman and Shepherd were next in line with Parker and Hathaway, the biggest guys at the station. Graeme Earle hadn't quite made it back yet and was ropeable he was missing out. Paxton had two other big guys working to the back. Ryan Gartrell and Jared Taylor were waiting at the driveway in case Bourke came driving in from elsewhere. Risely called through to the men informing them there was no vehicle out front and warning Gartrell and Taylor to call in immediately if they spotted the white SUV approaching.

The radio crackled.

'Bravo team in position.'

This was Paxton. The bungalows backed right onto bush and though there was no rear door there was always the chance Bourke might try and hightail it out of a window. Paxton and his men would be ready. Risely nodded to Clement, his call.

'Let's go.'

Clement and Risely left cover and started quickly down the narrow path, the others close behind, Parker and Hathaway carrying a door ram. Number 12 was the last of the four bungalows. After talking it over with Risely it had been decided the best approach was a simple knock on the door under the guise of emergency services. As soon as they cleared bungalow 11, Whiteman and Shepherd broke to cover the sides. Clement walked up the step, Risely to his left, pistol ready, Parker and Hathaway behind. Clement knocked loudly to be heard over the wind and yelled.

'Emergency services. We need to clear the bungalow.'

There was no response from inside. Clement guessed the others were no less tense than him. He knocked again.

'Is anybody there? Emergency services.'

Still no response. He tried the door knob and was surprised when it yielded, the force of the wind powering it open, almost off its hinges. Clement and Risely entered, pistols drawn.

'Peter?'

Clement was forced to yell. Risely was running commentary into his microphone. One glance showed the lounge room was clear. The bedroom doors were open. Only the bathroom door was closed. Clement snapped it open. It was empty too. Clement fought deflation. Somebody closed the front door but the walls were still groaning. Clement advanced and studied the bedrooms. One looked cleared out. They were too late.

51

The wind had increased. The desert sand was nasty and careless where it struck. Hagan was forced to shelter his face behind his forearm. Since he'd spoken to Beck there'd been one car, total, tourists getting out of Dodge. His radio went. It was Mal Gross.

'Yes Sarge.'

'We're bringing it in, Hages. It's coming in faster than they thought.'

'You're not kidding.'

'And I hope you told Lalor Corona, 'cause I like Corona.'

The bet was common knowledge. Hagan would have to share. From the case, he'd be lucky to wind up with a brace.

As he was about to open his door to climb into the relative safety of his cabin he saw a vehicle approaching from the Derby direction. This was the opposite direction to where he expected the abductor, that's why he'd set up on the other side of the road, to get vehicles heading out of town. Hagan was good at spotting makes and models from a very long distance, it was his specialty, similar to how some of the indigenous boys could spot a roo and it would look to him like a small shrub. Part of him was inclined to let the car go. But then again the bet would be a tie. Neither would buy a case, and the Sarge and the other cheapskates would have to buy their own beers. He could see the car was an SUV, white. He hit his lights and walked into the road with his sign that read POLICE STOP. He managed to give the driver enough time to slow and eventually pull over. Hagan made sure the road was clear and headed across, his shirt flapping like the sails of yacht. His cap wouldn't make it in the high winds so he left it in his car as he approached the Rav4. There was only the driver, a young guy. Hagan made sure he could see his hands at the wheel. He wasn't taking any chances.

'Everything okay? I don't think I was speeding.'

'No, just checking cars on another matter.'

Hagan used his phone to snap the plates. It beat trying to write anything in this wind.

'You got your licence?'

The young guy flicked through his wallet. Went back and checked again.

'I think I must have left it.'

Hagan's phone buzzed with a text. He read it. It gave the make, model and rego of the vehicle they were after. His training kicked in and his hand went to his gun before he even had time to get nervous.

'Would you get out of the vehicle please, sir?'

52

Clement drove fast, following Risely's car. They'd been standing back at the bungalow, dispirited, watching Lisa Keeble and her team collect evidence. Then Risely's phone had gone off.

It was Mal Gross and he sounded like he'd won lotto.

'Hagan's picked him up. He's bringing him in,' he'd shouted down the line. So now Clement was tailgating his boss, foot flat to the floor through vacant streets. The station loomed dead ahead. The camera crews were battened down God knew where, missing the action. Somewhere a news chief would be spewing.

Risely's car cruised to the electronic gate. It had taken them nine minutes from the Mimosa. The gate seemed to take that long to open. Eventually they slid through and around the back. Clement pulled in beside Risely and got out. Graeme Earle's car was back. The wind was howling, anything not tied down cartwheeling across earth or spinning through air. Mal Gross was waiting for them at the back door. He was no longer excited.

'There's a problem.'

...

Within thirteen seconds of stepping inside Clement saw the problem in the flesh standing next to Earle.

'Who is this guy?'

He pointed at a thin, curly headed young guy of about twenty who stood between an embarrassed Hagan and pissed-off Graeme Earle. He was the one who spoke.

'Says his name is Jake Windsor.'

'I am Jake Windsor.' The young guy seemed confused, not sure whether he was allowed to be angry at cops.

Gross deflected heat from Hagan. 'He didn't have ID and your description went out after he'd already been picked up.'

Earle chimed in. 'Says Bourke sold him the car yesterday for four hundred dollars.'

Windsor was jiggling. 'He did. I got the receipt. I haven't had a chance to register it yet.'

Clement was sure somebody had already asked this but asked anyway. 'Do you know where he is?'

'No. He quit yesterday, said the whole murder thing was too creepy. I haven't seen him since last night. I drove out to Derby and pulled a girl.'

Graeme Earle spoke. 'I called the Mimosa. Bourke quit last night, the night manager hadn't pulled him out of the system yet so they didn't know when you were there earlier.'

Clement fought frustration, turned back to Windsor. 'What time last night?'

'About seven.'

Clement told Earle to call back the Mimosa. 'We need to speak with Arvie.'

Risely cursed softly in the background. Clement was thinking that if Bourke had sold the car he might be thinking airport.

'We have to check airlines.'

Risely was across that. 'No flights out today. All cancelled because of the weather.'

'What about last night?'

Shepherd was a reservoir of trivia, on this occasion useful. 'Last flight out was five o'clock to Perth.'

Clement looked at Windsor but was really speaking to everybody else.

'And you saw him at seven so he wasn't on that flight.'

Earle came over and shoved a cordless telephone at Clement. 'Arvie.'

Clement had to shout so Arvie could hear. The poor bastard must have still been outside somewhere.

'When did you last see Peter Bourke?'

'This morning.'

'What time?'

'Huh? I can't hear.'

Clement shouted the question again.

'When I woke up, seven, around then.'

Clement hung up on him.

'Bourke didn't fly out last night. What time were today's flights supposed to go?'

Again Shepherd was the timetable guru. 'The Bali flight via Hedland usually goes at two twenty. The flight to Perth I think is at three or three fifteen.'

Clement's watch said one fifty. Graeme Earle was already dialling. 'I'll check the airlines to see if he was booked.'

'What about coaches? Any coaches leave today?'

Mal Gross said the coach always went around eight thirty.

Clement asked Shepherd to run that down. If Bourke was on a coach he'd be easy to scoop up at his destination.

Earle swore. 'I can't get through.'

'We'll go out there. Ryan, Whitey, hire cars. He might be trying to drive out.'

Clement turned to Risely. 'Can we keep the roads blocked?'

'In this weather we can't have people working

outside vehicles but we can patrol.'

'There won't be many on the road. Let's just pull over anybody who is.'

Clement and Earle headed for the door.

'Take separate cars, we might need to split up.'

53

Logic decreed he should never have gone back to the pit this morning. Right now he could be on a beach in Bali. But he was the wasp and the wasp did not fly off, it trapped its enemy, it bade its time, it watched it wither. He'd already sold his car to Jake, half what he paid, but he didn't mind, it had served its purpose well. Ana who worked in the kitchen had let him borrow hers to get out to Donen for his farewell visit and then she'd dropped him to the airport, which was nice of her.

...

There everything went wrong. He sensed it when he saw other vehicles peeling away, the place near deserted. Ana offered to wait for him but she was due on her shift and he told her he'd be fine. The only people in the terminal were three befuddled backpackers, one young woman behind the airline counter, a rent-a-car girl who had already turned the lights off in her booth and a couple of terminal trolls who were sweeping up.

The plane he was supposed to be flying out on had never arrived, diverted because of the cyclone. Part of him wanted to abuse the counter girl who was telling him this through overly blushered cheeks. Weren't they supposed to text him? he asked with an edge. She said they had. He checked his phone and found a text sent thirty minutes earlier. She apologised, circumstances beyond their control, blah, blah, blah.

It was at that point he calmed. 'Circumstances beyond their control' was a telling choice of words. This whole enterprise he had long known was beyond his control. Therefore this latest permutation might be seen as a deliberate act by the real Power who guided everything. It may be the Power wanted him caught and punished. It may be the Power wanted him protected. Perhaps, had it taken off, the plane would have crashed in the cyclone. Or maybe he would have arrived safely in Denpassar only to be bitten by some infected mosquito. How could one insignificant person think they could understand the machinations of the universe? It was futile to bother.

This did not mean he should abdicate all thought and just expect fate to carry him where it would. No, he still needed to select what he thought was the best course of action. It would be right or wrong but he must act. The girl said he would be re-booked on the first available flight which she expected would be tomorrow. He was trying to decide what to do when his phone rang. He saw from the display it was Marie. He debated about picking up and finally did.

'Hi Marie. How's this storm?'

'Scary. Listen do you know anything about Jake?'

'What do you mean?'

'Rosa was in town. She said she saw him in the back of a police car.'

'When?'

'About half an hour ago.'

54

By the time he reached the turn-off to the airport Clement had learned that Peter Bourke was not listed as a passenger on the morning coach. That did not mean definitively he had not been on the coach. Nor did the absence of his name from any car-rental lists mean he had not hired a car under another name. Hell, he may even have had a second car he'd organised earlier standing by. The first big splotches of rain slapped his windscreen. He buzzed Earle who had a slight lead on him.

'Why don't you take the charters, just in case?'

'Copy that.'

Earle peeled off at forty-five degrees down a feeder road to a pair of hangars. The rain began to drum faster on the bodywork. Clement pulled up out front of the terminal which looked near deserted. He struggled out and the wind drove him like a rugby pack towards the building. As he reached the door a deep grinding roar snapped Clement up. His first thought was it was the cyclone hitting early, pulling guttering or the roof apart but what he saw was a silver Rav4 powering out from behind the building and up a service road. He only caught a glimpse of the driver but it was enough. Clement fought the wind for his door and got back inside. He fired up his engine, reversed into the kerb behind then turned his wheel hard right and drove up and over a narrow strip of bark chips before slamming down hard again on bitumen. He hammered fifteen metres the wrong way down a one-way strip to the service exit Bourke had taken moments earlier.

The storm hit with a sudden fury. Whatever light there had been was vacuumed out, rain smashing down in a dark blitzkrieg. The rutted service road ran about four hundred metres before dead-ending on Broome Road. He grabbed the two-way and yelled for Earle. No answer. Visibility was almost zero, rain was sheeting and he could not see whether the Rav4 had gone north or south, but south led down to the end of the peninsula so he turned north, hammering as he fumbled for his phone. The phone jumped out of his hands and landed somewhere on the floor. Shit. A car passed on the other side, a blur in the darkness. He hit the headlights. Visibility improved to a few metres. He pushed his foot hard to the floor.

He tried the two-way again. This time Earle answered. Clement spoke fast and loud.

'I just saw Bourke driving out the airport in a silver Rav4. I'm following north. It's stolen or a hire. See if you can get details and call Risely.'

'Copy that.'

Clement hit the Gubinge Road intersection as there was a momentary easing in the rain, and visibility tripled, which took it to miserable. To the left Clement spied a distant fantail of water. Bourke must be heading west, either to double back down towards the Mimosa or give him the slip through the western suburbs. The rain dumped heavier than ever. Clement gave chase, closing rapidly on barely visible tail-lights.

Too rapidly.

His brain was just figuring Bourke wouldn't be driving this slow as he caught a glimpse of the vehicle ahead, a small truck. Shit. On impulse he threw his car into a skidding U-turn. It was a stupid thing to do. Had a vehicle been coming the other way it would have crushed him. Luckily there was none. His back wheels were skating, in this wind he could easily flip. A three-sixty seemed inevitable but the Subaru snapped out at two hundred, he straightened and powered back to Broome Road having lost too much time. The wind was pushing the car across the road. Impossible as it seemed, the downpour intensified. He drove blind. If anything blew across the road there would be no chance to avoid it. Earle came back on the two-way.

'He rented a car. I've texted Risely the details. Be careful.'

'I will,' said Clement but he knew there was no way of being careful at this speed in these conditions. He kept his foot to the floor, headlights were useless. He was Jonah in the pit of the whale.

55

He had caught the Avis girl as she was about to leave. She was not exactly thrilled to write last minute business.

'I only have one available car,' she cautioned as if hoping he'd say forget it but he couldn't shake the warning that was urging him to get out of Broome. Coincidentally the car was another Rav4, a silver one. The forms had taken longer than he would have liked and he had only just climbed into the car when the rain started. He was torn now about where he should head. If he went east towards Fitzroy Crossing the storm would follow and perhaps overtake him. He wouldn't want to be stranded in the middle of nowhere. He could drive south for Port Hedland and pick up another flight there but they'd expect that. It had to be north, try and get to Darwin or maybe find a fishing boat somewhere. As he pulled out of the hire-car area he saw the detective heading for the terminal. The detective looked his way and Peter sensed he had ducked too late. He swung up a service road and pushed his foot to the floor, assuming the cop would follow. The first phalanx of rain hit and everything was suddenly much darker. He swung hard left into a cape of grey, felt the car swivel beneath him as it fought for traction, then right itself. The curtain of rain would hide him from his pursuer. Maybe he'd guess wrong? The cop would radio ahead but it was a cyclone, it would be hard to get out on the road. He had a full tank of petrol and there were lots of places to disappear.

56

Clement drove blind. Randomly a branch or other debris would skitter across the road or thump into the body of the car. There were no other vehicles on the road now. Earle was following somewhere at a slower pace. Risely had people looking for Bourke but the storm was pulling numbers out for emergency situations, limiting coverage. Still the major roads out south and east were covered and he had managed to raise a couple of vehicles to man the road at Beagle Bay which meant if Bourke didn't turn off he had about ninety minutes before his road ran out. The isolation Clement felt was intense, were it not for the crackle of the two-way it might have been an apocalyptic dream. He was a submarine searching a fathomless ocean, his quarry could be two hundred metres ahead or kilometres either side, there was no way of knowing. It had about it the feeling of a moment undecided, of a continuing balance and a resultant stasis, of walking the line between life and death. If he had snapped awake and found himself lying in a bed in post-operative care it would not have surprised him. The image of a hospital immediately conjured his father as if they were in this moment linked in some pervasive heartbeat, as if this could have been his father's dream, just as it might have been Peter Bourke's, as if this landscape and all his thoughts belonged to something bigger than him and his tiny life. The experience ended abruptly when a large branch cartwheeled directly into his path. He swung the wheel reflexively and felt the broken wood thud and scrape into the passenger side of the vehicle but the escape manoeuvre was bought at the cost of any control over the vehicle and this time it skidded into a broadside he could not right. The car skated across the opposite side of the road before leaving the slippery bitumen and ploughing into muddy scrub where it eventually came to rest. He sat for a second or two, his beating heart at odds with what still felt like the tail end of a transcendental state. His foot slammed into the accelerator but the tyres spun impotently, mud churned. Each second meant more bitumen between him and Bourke. He threw the vehicle into reverse and punched down again, urging the rubber to grip. Finally it did, hauling him back out as the rain thumped with the heaviness of banshee fists on the glass. He spun back towards the road and then onto it, at least two more minutes lost. Again he pushed his foot to the floor, gripped the wheel and stared into a river fanning across the windscreen.

How long the next void continued he could not compute, perhaps close to an hour, the two-way his lifeline. The signal varied, sometimes he'd thought transmission lost completely but then Earle would crackle back on. His mind drifted sometimes, to Phoebe then Marilyn and past tensions. He'd followed her once, shadowed her in the best tradition of the KGB. She'd driven to a house and he'd watched from up the street as a man had opened the door and welcomed her in. Clement did not remain to time her stay or see if they'd lit out on some new adventure walking to the car with the easy intimacy of lovers, awkwardness of potential lovers or purposefulness of mere friends. He ran no check on the man. It was her secret.

To reveal what he had done would only condemn him further in her eyes. It cut him she was no longer his. Whether that was love or possessiveness he did not know, semantics wouldn't help but the hurt was true and deep even if none of it made sense.

The orange fuel indicator lit up. He believed that meant he had about twelve k to go before his tank ran dry, a thought that turned him concave until he remembered the cars always carried a spare plastic jerry can of fuel. Running out of fuel on the main road would present a fatal hazard to anybody using it so he was forced to pull over in an area of low scrub. He climbed into the back and found the fuel. It seemed the wind had backed off but it was still ferocious and it took him all his strength to force open the door. The rain continued to bucket, the ground a rice paddy, water to his ankles. Within seconds he was sodden, his slicker threatening to split like a spinnaker. Fortunately the petrol compartment opened with a push, he twisted off the cap and it nearly snapped from the cord holding it. The yellow jerry can bucked in his hands as he fought to shield it with his body. He managed to get the nozzle up and then shove it down into the tank but when it had drained the wind ripped it from his grasp and tore it through the air. It reminded Clement of a James Bond film where the villain was sucked from the plane and spat into the heavens. He fought to get back into the car, the rain smashing into his skin. He called Earle on the radio as he fired up the car and saw the fuel gauge climb.

'I haven't caught sight of him. He could have turned off.'

'So what's the plan?'

'Let's keep going, see if there's any reports. If he sticks to the main road he'll be stopped at Beagle Bay so we can head to there then work back south.'

If he were Bourke he would push his luck, head to Beagle Bay, then assuming there'd be a roadblock, turn off the main road down a track and try and get around it. He doubted he'd go east into the desert. If he got bogged there he'd be a sitting duck. So it would be towards the coast.

About twenty minutes in, the rain having slipped back another notch, he got a report via the station that an hour earlier emergency personnel had responded to a distress call and picked up some fishermen at a creek about ninety k south of Beagle Bay. As they went to turn back on the main road towards Beagle Bay a silver Rav4 passed them at top speed heading north. They swung out after it and a few clicks on a flat stretch of road just managed to spy the car turning west off the main road.

Clement took the coordinates where that had happened and compared his position. It was about twenty k north of him, a no-man's land of mangroves and crocodiles.

57

When the big four-wheel drive had pulled out from the side track just after he passed, he presumed it was the police. A moment later during a gap in the torrent across his rear window he picked out Emergency Service stickers but it stood to reason they were acting as scouts for the cops. He had already decided he would have to turn off somewhere before Beagle Bay. There was an indigenous community around there and the police would almost certainly ask the locals to keep an eye out for him. He had to go now. He threw the vehicle off road into the low scrubby bush to the side of the highway, heading west to the water. The car dipped and bit into muddy ground. Like limbs smashed by artillery on a field of war, pieces of foliage, ripped by the gale, spun through the air lashing the windscreen. The tyres spun and slid, gripping and churning. He expected the bigger vehicle to follow but it didn't, or at least so far as he could tell it hadn't for he could see no dim headlights battering their way through the still sheeting rain. Perhaps it was simply an emergency vehicle on patrol?

There was no way this car was going to get him far in these conditions. You needed a big tank of a car up here. But this was where he had been led so he would make the best of it. He had his bow and a knife, water wasn't a problem. Maybe he would find some fishermen, take their tinny. He wasn't done yet. If it came down to killing the detective to secure his freedom, he wasn't sure what he might do. His grandfather had been a policeman murdered in the line of duty and so he was on the cop's side in a lot of ways. On the other hand, it had been a cop who had betrayed his grandfather. This detective had taken his little girl to dinner and that had touched Peter, that was how it could have, should have been with him and his father.

The car dropped, the suspension jolted, his insides were shoved up to his ribs. He'd hit a gully and he thought it was the end of the line, the little car grunting and digging into mud but then he was up and out of it again and suddenly in bush more dense and dangerous but also offering more coverage from any pursuer.

58

Once Clement left the road, driving became ridiculous. The steering wheel may as well have been an artefact stuck on for show, for control rested in the grooves and angles of ancient ruts. The tyres were a phrenologist's fingers following suggested paths across the terrain's skull by the lightest touch. All the time the water bucketed. This was only the edge of the cyclone which probably barely qualified as a two and he said his prayers it had been no stronger. His chances of finding Bourke were as remote as the location. He slithered and ground his way into denser bush only too aware that a branch could snap and crush the cab and his life. He endured this serpentine rough-ride trying to make radio contact with Earle but this time it seemed they were incommunicado. The last transmission he'd made was that he was turning off to follow Bourke west towards the mangroves but he could only guess whether this was the same track he'd been seen on. Even if it were, Bourke could have left it. In their last communication Earle had estimated he was twenty minutes behind Clement. He'd had his own dramas with a branch smashing the passenger window. Barely perceptibly the rain had eased, the instant of clarity on the windscreen now a fraction longer although Clement was constantly forced to lean out and rip loose foliage from the wiper blades.

It was dark in this denser part of the bush and that meant an orange light shining ahead at two o'clock was that much brighter and caught his attention instantly. He slowed to a crawl to see it better, a regular flashing pulse, a hazard light maybe.

It was more deeply forested here. Slim trees stood like toothpicks on an hors d'ouvres tray, so that he had to drive across, across, then down when a large enough gap presented. And then there it was. A silver Rav4 stopped at right angles, thirty to fifty metres away. Clement edged forward until he was about ten metres shy of it, rain and strips of leaf continued to whip through the air. He scanned intently but could see no movement. He killed his engine, checked his pistol and fought his way out of the vehicle, the wind having abated more than Clement had realised. From what he could see the front left fender had smashed into a low stump, probably locking up the wheel. Through the howling wind the hazard light continued to pulse. It was only when he was close enough to the vehicle to see nobody inside it that Clement remembered the trap laid for Arturo Lee. Instinctively he pushed to his left towards the closest cover. An arrow fizzed past him to his right but he saw the blur rather than hearing it over the rain.

'Don't do this, Peter,' he yelled trying to locate where the shot came from. About three o'clock he thought, but all he could see was misting heavy rain and brush. He doubted Bourke would hear his words beneath the hiss of shaking leaves.

'There's no way out, Peter. We just want Osterlund, we know who he is and what he did.'

If there was any reply he did not hear it. Was Bourke still waiting or had he taken the opportunity to run? Clement was now in the position of waiting for Earle or pushing on. He should wait, but what if Bourke encountered somebody else with a car or a boat that he thought might win him freedom. Would he hesitate to kill another for the chance of escape?

59

Behind a thigh-high bush, squatting on one knee, Bourke had held the detective in his sights from the moment he had left the vehicle. The cop's words were inaudible in the wind, so powerful it was impossible to hold the bow steady. Water was pouring into his eyes off his slicker, forcing him to blink constantly. He was aiming for the thigh but as he released the arrow the target suddenly moved left. The policeman took cover. The angle was tight in normal conditions let alone this tempest. The man yelled out again. Bourke thought he heard his name, Peter, but couldn't be sure. He could guess the man was urging him to give up.

Peter was desperate to get away and live the life of which he had the briefest taste, yet how could he? The storm was backing off but even had he found a small dinghy it could not survive the ocean. They would be looking for him at every airport. He had no money, no false papers.

The policeman suddenly broke cover and ran towards him. This was not how it should be. He loosed an arrow and, though it could not actually be possible in the bedlam, he fancied he heard the thud as it struck its target. The policeman half-ran, half-staggered to a thicket before sprawling into ankle-deep water, where he lay still.

60

Fellow cops who had been shot told Clement it was like being punched by a ball of iron. That was all Clement had as a comparison for being shot by an arrow. And it did feel like a punch but more by a long iron finger than a ball. For the first few strides he was able to power on, aware that some foreign object was stuck inside him, the shaft and tail still protruding from his side, under his right arm near his ribcage he guessed, but no real impediment. But then the rhythm in his stride went wrong like a toddler trying to negotiate a downward slope for the first time, and he was stumbling, unable to straighten. He fell into the water without grace, this was no celebratory touchdown but the humiliation of a fall into muck. He was aware he wasn't breathing so well, he started to feel faint and wondered if he was dying. Because of the arrow he lay slightly on his left, gasping, the water getting colder around him, still splashing with heavy droplets, the gods pissing on him. The leaves above shuffled like the beaters of a cheer squad, he indulged himself with a vision of himself as fallen hero, a generic tombstone and Phoebe and Marilyn sad-eyed in black. He was losing it now, the thought, all thought, it was a fog, he was nothing and nowhere.

61

Peter had not meant his shot to be lethal, but in this gale control was limited. The policeman was lying there slightly tilting up, inert. It was possible he was foxing. He still had the gun so a direct approach would leave Peter a sitting duck. He could not expect the cop to spare him now. The man was his salvation though. The police vehicle was intact. Perhaps he'd left the keys in the ignition. Bourke decided to circle left around to the car, keeping his bow ready. He stopped every few seconds and glanced back at the prone body. The cop hadn't moved.

The police car was a godsend and he meant that literally. Dear Hilda mumbling in the dark room, liver-spotted narrow fingers sliding over her rosary, so long cut adrift by those to whom she prayed perhaps her devotion had been rewarded through this gift to him? The rain was easing but still potent, his feet squelching into pools. He had to travel all the way to the car and pull open the door. No keys. The cop must have them on him. He swung back but could not see the cop's body now.

'Give it up, Peter. You can't get away.'

The cop was sitting on the ground behind him, his back propped against a thin tree, both hands pointing the gun at him, he looked pale and his breathing was laboured.

...

Clement was trying to make himself sound much stronger than he was. A minute before he'd felt water pinging off his cheek and blinked his eyes open again. He had sense of time having skipped a beat and supposed he must actually have passed out. He turned and caught sight of Bourke breaking for cover to the car and realised this was his one chance but dragging himself closer back towards his car had sapped all energy from him.

'Come on Peter, don't make me shoot you.'

'You won't shoot me because you want to know where Osterlund is.'

They were shouting but every word was audible at this close range.

'Where is he?'

He caught it then, Bourke's reflexive glance down. He's buried him thought Clement. He was sure of it.

'Where did you bury him?'

There it was, a momentary look of shock, then Bourke's jaw set. 'That animal cut my grandfather in pieces and chucked him in the river.'

'Don't ruin your life. Think of your grandmother.'

He screamed at Clement, 'Who do you think I did this for?'

'Consider her, Peter. Tell us where Osterlund is. People are on your side. They understand. You can rebuild your life.'

'That's bullshit.'

Clement tried to read him, it was difficult anyway but he was weakening again and he felt control slipping away. 'So what, Peter, we kill one another? Your grandfather was a policeman. You think he'd approve of you killing me?'

'It's too late.'

'Too late to get away, that's all, not too late for another ...'

He wanted to say 'chance' but it stalled like a pool ball stuck in the tray. Clement could hear his own shallow breathing, his words slurring.

'Come on. Let's both get back to our families.'

'You will have to shoot me.'

Clement raised the gun, hoping to instil some urgency, but he could not keep it steady.

'You buried him alive didn't you? Otherwise you'd just kill him on the beach. Where?'

'Sorry.'

His plan was to shoot Bourke in the leg but the gun was waving around. Even if he could just keep him talking a little ...

He felt his eyes closing, he was terribly feeble now. He fought with all his strength to stay conscious and that sucked power from his limbs. His hand dropped to his thigh. Bourke walked forward and gently prised the gun from him the way a father prises a toy from a sleeping child. He could barely keep his eyes open. He felt Bourke's fingers in his pocket and saw his keys dangling like a small fish. Bourke took a step back and regarded him he thought at first with contempt but then realised: no, it wasn't that, it was pity.

62

The policeman had stopped talking and his head just lolled to one side. Peter remembered bringing ice-cream to the little girl who had sat with her father, recalled her face rippling with pleasure. He had not wanted to orphan her. Tears began to muster in his eyes but were they for the girl or himself? For so long he'd had to be strong, at school, managing to avoid the subject of his father with the deftness of a bomb technician disengaging the trigger mechanism. Later as he grew older the questions about his oma, the implicit query of what had happened to his parents, the delicious anticipation of young women wanting to mother him, their red lips circling the straw of a shared milkshake, the way he'd had to bite his tongue when they slagged off their own 'helicopter' parents, a cheap pejorative lingo coined by those who would farm out their children to friends or other relatives while they doused themselves in suntan lotion on a Spanish terrace scanning magazines rather than cramped over a Monopoly board with their children, telling themselves it was really for the kids' benefit, it was making them independent. Well he was independent now. With his bow and axe he had slain the three-headed monster that had devoured his childhood. So what did it matter if he cried? Who was there to witness it?

The car had a quarter tank of fuel. He would drive till it ran out or something presented itself. He had no qualms abandoning his plans for Asia. In fact, he felt he belonged here. There were remote communities, indigenous people he could hang out with, learning their ways. They would have no reason to hand him in.

He drove north through bush cutting over rough ground. The two-way radio buzzed, another cop.

'Clem, where are you?'

He kept on. The bush gave way onto a cleared track, wet and muddy. He decided to take it, hoping it would circumnavigate any roadblocks they had out for him, confident nobody else would be out in these conditions. It had been a long, long journey and he was all of a sudden unbelievably tired but there would be time to rest soon enough. The storm was lightening finally and with it, his mood. He had traversed darkness and had emerged washed by the waters, baptised anew, woken, healed.

63

The world softly faded in on him again. Rain splashing off the bridge of his nose, Graeme Earle looked down at him, distressed, as if he were already dead; Bourke, his gun, the car gone.

I've only got maybe half a dozen words left in me. The thought was surprisingly deliberate, like a thief moving fast but without haste, knowing what he wanted.

'He buried him alive.'

'Where?'

He could only shake his head. Graeme Earle was shouting at him but he was muted.

Black.

•••

The ocean was pale blue, a very small gum tree hovering dead centre, and it struck him as odd but for the first few seconds he couldn't fathom why. No, as his eyes focused he saw it wasn't the ocean it was a wall and at its centre was a small watercolour in a cheap frame, no glass. It was the smell, that weird co-mingling of sickly pre-warmed meals and antiseptic that told Clement this was hospital.

'About time, mate.'

Clement turned to his left and through a little fairy-forest of plastic tubes saw Shepherd, beaming, an apple poised half-eaten in his hand. Only then he realised he was wearing an oxygen mask. The clock on the wall indicated it was one ten.

'It doesn't work. It's five thirty in the morning. Welcome, back.'

He tried to smile but wasn't sure if he managed it, the white fell too quickly.

...

Later, the mask off, breathing unaided but with difficulty, his right side aching with every breath, Clement sat alone in his hospital bed listening to faint sounds in the corridor, a trolley clanking, a raised voice, a fading laugh. He had the room to himself, privileged he supposed. Elevated on the pillow he stared directly ahead at the gum tree print. Who chose those paintings, one of the staff here? Or was it an actual job? Somebody in Perth buying prints for hospitals all over the state, matching thematically the region to the print: gold prospectors in Kalgoorlie, whales in Albany. What had been on the wall of his father's hospital room? He tried to remember. It seemed an age ago. That single contemplation prised open a whole cupboard-full of responsibilities that tumbled out: calling his mother back, Phoebe, interviews about how he came to lose his gun and police vehicle. Marilyn had not visited. For that matter she hadn't even called but Shepherd assured him Risely had notified her. His mother had rung a couple of hours ago. Tess was with her now. He'd managed to reassure them he was okay but had told his mum he was tired and would call her back, which was only half true. The fatigue had left him now, it was pure physical incapacitation confining him to bed but he did not reveal that to her, it would only have taken explanation. How he came to be lying in a hospital bed in Derby with a large dressing on his right side instead of the arrow shaft that had been there last time he'd looked, was relayed to him by Shepherd a couple of hours after that first brief phase of consciousness.

Worried about blood loss and hypothermia, Graeme Earle had bundled him into his car and driven hell for leather back to the main road calling for help while debating, should he drive to Beagle Bay where there were some rudimentary medical facilities or try and get all the way back to Broome where he might still need another ninety-minute race to Derby? This was some of the most isolated country in the world, one of the worst places to find yourself at the centre of a medical emergency. In the end, the army came to Clement's aid. The worst of the winds had moved through and though it was still hairy, they'd had a chopper standing by for evacuations. They directed Earle to Beagle Bay where a chopper was waiting on the football oval with oxygen, fluids and drugs. They evacuated Clement direct to Derby. All of this, Shepherd related in his rather high voice with an edge of rapture so that Clement had the sensation of listening to an amateur calling a football game.

From his surgeon Clement had learned he'd been rushed straight to surgery where for more than two hours they had worked on him, removing the arrowhead, repairing his right lung and then stitching him back up.

'The main concern was blood loss and infection. We've got blood into you and hopefully there'll be no infection. You also have a fractured rib from the arrow; can't do much about that except tape you up, I'm afraid.'

Graeme Earle had been forced to stay at Beagle Bay to pursue Bourke. To Shepherd's annoyance, the three Perth detectives had been sent off to join him.

'All the glory to them, us locals get to look for Osterlund, probably drowned by now if he wasn't dead already,' he offered without cheer.

Risely was overseeing the Bourke operation but it would be another three or four hours before the weather permitted aerial surveillance. Earle was at Beagle Bay and the detectives on their way to join him.

'So what happened? How'd he peg you?' Shepherd asked it with complete insensitivity but Clement preferred that to somebody pussy-footing around. Clement told him as he remembered it but his mind was already moving forward to the question of Osterlund and he ended the story about himself abruptly. 'Lisa must check Bourke's car for soil, anything that might tell us where he went.'

'She's onto that, been onto it pretty much since they brought it in.'

'Keep looking for CCTV footage of his car. He's probably been out to wherever he buried him since he snatched him. Check the records, when he wasn't working, when his roommates say he was out, that's when he would have been on his way to him.'

His mind was running now. Shepherd dutifully took notes.

'It can't be too far away because he'd have to drive out and back. I bet he filled his tank on the abduction day. '

'But his mate bought the car and took it to Derby, that'll screw up all the kilometres and fuel and everything.'

'Find out how much petrol was in the car when the mate bought it, if he filled up, when, where, calculate the ks. Most likely Bourke headed into the desert, far enough for privacy but not so far he can't get back. Forty minutes to an hour, plot it out on a map.'

He sent Shepherd off immediately to work on it.

...

That was two hours ago. Not long after Shepherd had gone he'd called Risely who was genuinely pleased to speak to him. No sign of Bourke yet. The search for Osterlund was continuing as best it could in the circumstances. They'd tried calling Bourke on the police radio but he was not responding. Manners and two others were checking CCTV footage for any signs of a white Rav4 since the abduction.

'You might want to go back a few days before. He might have prepared somewhere,' said Clement grimacing. He was still investigating the positions in which talking was possible without inflicting pain on himself.

The cyclone was through, said Risely. Rain was still spitting from its tail but choppers and fixed wing would be up soon. He saw the only hope of finding Osterlund alive now was locating Bourke. Astuthi Osterlund had finally fallen apart and was being medicated so she could sleep.

Clement ran his theory of a desert burial.

'Even so, it's too vast an area.'

'Maybe not. They've had choppers and whatnot out the last few days reporting on the weather, maybe one of them saw a white car stuck out in the middle of nowhere.'

Risely said he would try but Clement could sense doubt seeping down the line.

'How about Lisa?' he asked.

'She's processing the car but the roommate contaminated it driving it around Derby.'

'Has anybody spoken to the grandmother?'

'I think Perth might have.'

'You should get her involved. He said he did all this for her. Maybe he's listening to police radio. Get her to ask him to give up Osterlund's location.'

'That's a good idea. I'll get onto it. Take it easy, Dan,

I mean it, you've done a great job but you need to rest. I've told the internal guys to give you forty-eight hours. Rest, mate.'

And that's what he had done since, going on for two hours now, nothing. It was driving him nuts. There had to be something he could do except just wait.

Think, he commanded himself. His phone rang. It was Marilyn.

'Hi,' he said, easing himself on his left side.

'How are you doing?'

'I'm pretty good. Sore, sore as hell actually on my right side, and a bit weak but I'm alright.'

She asked him the details. He recounted what he could remember and what he'd been told had happened after it went blank. While he was talking he was thinking about Bourke planning this thing. Did he just bury Osterlund in a box and then bury that?

'Is Phoebe there?' He wanted very much to speak to her.

'No, I thought I better wait till she was out just in case ...'

Just in case the news had been real bad.

'What's he like, Peter Bourke?' Her question caught him off guard. He didn't actually recall anybody else asking that. Risely had questioned whether Bourke was injured or psychotic but not what he was like.

'Probably would have been a nice kid but he's damaged. He could have killed me, he chose not to.'

He could feel her on the end of the line, her presence, he could almost smell her. They were one and indivisible, they were divided and apart, they were sympatico and discordant, they had a relationship that needed a theological mindset to explain because it was all contradiction, they had no relationship at all except what held by a gossamer thread in a single moment.

'You're very special, Dan, you always will be. I'll get

Phoebe to call when she's back.'

What did that mean, very special? That I love you but can't stand you? I loved you once but not now?

'Is Brian special too?'

He couldn't help himself and felt the immediate emotional disconnect on her part. He was stupid. He had learned nothing.

'I'll get Phoebe to call you when she's back. Take care.'

He sat there, the light weight of the phone in his hand. It reminded him of the heavy gun he could no longer hold, the pistol that Peter Bourke stripped from him. Thoughts of Marilyn evaporated suddenly. There was something about weight, the arithmetic of subtraction, the use of absence to deduce past reality, omission as a dynamic principle.

He saw it now, a way of tracing Osterlund, well, an aid to tracing him. And something else he should have spied an eon ago. Bourke had to have known the cyclone was closing in, even a deaf mute living in Broome knew that. So why didn't he fly out the previous evening after he'd quit his job and sold his car? Because he wanted one last triumphant moment with his captor. Clement dialled Shepherd: engaged. He waited, worked it through again in his head. Bourke had already sold his car, so how did he get there? He dialled again. This time Shepherd was free.

'Shep, you need to find out if somebody loaned Bourke a car Tuesday night or early Wednesday.'

'Why?'

'Because he went out to wherever he buried Osterlund. And there's been a mini-cyclone so if somebody did loan him the car they probably haven't driven it since. You can check ks travelled, fuel consumed and Keeble can check soil on the inside of the vehicle and compare it to the car Bourke sold his mate. Also, Bourke might have had to fill up on the way out or back and he won't have been careful, he thought he was going to Bali, right, so there might be CCTV of him with that car. Are you getting this?'

Shepherd said he was.

'Okay, now what you do is, you work out the arc of where he might have travelled and you eliminate every direction where he would have been captured by camera, you understand? If we work out all the routes he didn't take we are left with the few he must have taken and if we catch him coming in or going out with the other vehicle, we know where to concentrate the search.'

He asked Shepherd again if he got it. Shepherd claimed he had. But he knew what Shepherd and Risely and everybody else was thinking. What does it matter if some murdering drug dealer, pornographer is found dead? We are safe, the good people of the Kimberley are safe; or most of us at any rate, because we know now who the killer was and he wasn't after us. As Shepherd had said earlier, Osterlund was a side-issue, Peter Bourke was the main game, Peter Bourke was the glory.

64

'Please Peter, give yourself up. I still love you. But it's time to stop this, please, for me.'

The woman's accent, a weird mix of German, English and Irish, sent by the wonders of technology via satellite into a receiver in far-off Perth was further distorted by the crackle of the two-way radio. She persisted over and over. 'Please, Peter, speak to me, pick up.'

At the radio itself there was no response but the chatter so organically different from the slow drumming of rain on spare earth, the default sound for hundreds of ks, was caught by the tall skinny man who had ventured out today to see if anything of his family's fishing hut remained. He was not confident. The hut was just a few sheets of tin over a wooden frame, no more than a shelter, really. The sound of a small plane buzzing above had persisted for more than an hour now, since he'd started walking from his cousin's. Just when it's too wet for mosquitoes you get a big one buzzing over your head, he thought to himself. He assumed it was to do with the storm, maybe taking photos for TV. He hadn't seen TV for a couple of days and his radio needed batteries but his experience told him it would all sort itself out soon enough. All he was thinking about was any of those big tides washing crocodiles in closer. Little dry gullies become creeks overnight, you had to watch yourself. That's when he heard the crackling sound and diverted to investigate. Campers, is what he was thinking, and laughed. They picked a bad time for a camping holiday. The sound was stronger now, sounded like an old woman's voice but all distorted. He stopped and once more there was only drumming rain and that electronic scratch. The police vehicle was ten metres away from him. He was looking at its rear. Seemed to him it might have been on one of the narrow walk tracks here and then, wham! A big branch had fallen right across the cabin, crunched it down like a soft-drink can. He jogged over, his old runners squelching with every stride. He approached cautiously from the driver side. The young man at the wheel, a policeman he guessed, was twisted, looking away into the distance with eyes of a dead fish in the bucket on the way home. The cabin had been pushed down right onto his neck by the big branch on top of it. Not a mark on him, but he was dead for sure. The old woman's voice crackled through the radio again.

'Peter, please answer me if you can hear me. It's not too late, love.'

65

When the call came, Clement, with great difficulty, was edging his way out of the bed for a pee. It was Graeme Earle.

'One death from the cyclone and it's our multiple killer. Is that what you call karma?'

Clement did not feel sad for Peter Bourke, not really, but he did feel a great hollowness and a sense of loss of what could have been. Earle was heading back from Beagle Bay now. He fed Clement what he knew of progress on Osterlund. Peter Bourke had been carrying phones and camera but none of them contained obvious pictures to point them to Osterlund. But he had indeed been captured in the borrowed vehicle filling up to head out to his dungeon. The girl who had loaned him the car had warned him it was near empty and she had only driven him out to the airport since. This had allowed them to calculate the distance he had travelled in a round trip to about thirty-five k. The service station gave them the rough direction. Planes and choppers were out looking.

'It's got to be bush or a clump of trees. He would have needed cover.'

'Imagine if we found Osterlund alive? That would be ironic.'

...

Irony however had run its course on the case. Six hours into the search a chopper spotted the partly collapsed pit and a little over an hour later Osterlund's body was hauled out. He was still bound, an arrow protruded from his knee. Rhino send word later that drowning was the official cause of death but that the autopsy showed he was likely already unconscious and probably would never have regained consciousness anyway.

'Drowning in a desert, that's ironic,' said Rhino.

...

On Monday, the day of his hospital discharge, two experienced detectives from Perth were sent to interview Clement, a man and woman, Eastaway and Chapman. He knew them both: good people, efficient. He was reconciled that they had to ask questions about how he'd lost his weapon and car and after the introductory stuff they got down to where they all knew it was heading.

'You decided not to wait for Detective Sergeant Earle but to pursue alone. Why?'

It was Chapman. She was in her forties now, originally Fraud squad.

'We had hopes of finding Osterlund, every minute counted.'

'And when you found the damaged vehicle?'

'The same. Plus there was Bourke's welfare to consider. For all I knew he was in trouble in the vehicle. It was raining so hard you couldn't see inside until you were on top of it.'

'You sensed an ambush, I think you mentioned to your colleagues?'

This time it was Eastaway. Pushing fifty he had a bulbous nose with huge pores.

'Yes. He used the same technique with Lee the biker and it helped me avoid his first arrow but then I had to decide whether to wait or go after him.'

'And that's when he shot you?'

'Yes.'

'In retrospect would you have done things differently?' Chapman this time.

Clement dwelt on the answer. 'I don't know that I could have. I couldn't wait for DS Earle. Bourke had the advantage and he took it.'

They wrote notes. Eastaway was the one who spoke next. 'You got the drop on him though, later, is that correct?'

He explained how that had happened. He relived the moment, he had Bourke cold.

'You could have fired.'

He wasn't sure whether Chapman was offering a statement or question.

'I tried to but I just ... fainted I guess.'

'Before that though. You could have fired.'

He nodded. 'Yes but I was trying to get him to tell me where Osterlund was.'

And in the end they had both died hadn't they? In the end, despite all his efforts, he had saved nobody and nothing. But then his eyes fell on the large card signed by every one of those he'd worked with. Graeme Earle who had proved himself a rock-solid deputy, Lisa Keeble thorough, clever, Scott Risely had walked the line between keeping the powers happy without selling him out, Jared Taylor was a humble student and quiet teacher, Mal Gross provided the humour and glue, Manners had come through, and even Shepherd for all his cheap footy cant had the makings of a good detective. He looked from Eastaway to Chapman.

'Sorry, lost it for a minute. I'm ready again.'

66

They drifted in slowly darkening air, the sunset as pink as a matador's cape. Bill Seratono handed him another freezing beer. Clement could now lean forward and take it without the movement causing a stabbing pain. His right half must have mended, he supposed, or the three earlier beers had anaesthetised it. Far in the distance, shoreward, the Derby jetty loomed like the black skeleton of an animal that had died drinking in the ocean.

'And your father? He's okay?' Bill punctuated his question with the gentle *pfut* of his can being opened.

'No lasting effects, touchwood, but he has to be careful, medications, all that. Phoebe and I are visiting them in a few weeks while her mum's in Europe with her boyfriend.'

Clement wondered idly if fiancée was the more correct term.

'So are we going to lose you a second time?' Bill trawled his line easily and reset it.

Di Rivi's dog popped into his brain. He wondered if she'd named it yet.

'Not just yet.'

The Assistant Commissioner himself had called, peeing in his pocket. 'Outstanding police work' and 'copybook restraint' being two of the phrases bandied about. HQ loved the idea of a wounded hero. They wanted him back on public display in Perth, a stone's throw from the TV stations.

'In your own time,' the AC had added, code for the sooner the better. But how could you trade this, or the fishburger at the Cleo, or a dentist who worked on your teeth in his footy shorts for free?

'Is Mitch ever going to talk to me again?' he asked, enjoying the breeze on his face.

'Who knows? I told him it was his own bloody fault. He should have been upfront.'

Clement spared a thought for all the innocent, disconnected people crime touched along the way: Karskine, Astuthi Osterlund, young Tyson. Crime, especially murder was a muddy boot traipsing through your living room. Bill spoke again.

'Guess what I heard just before we came out, been meaning to tell you.'

Clement was at loss as to which of the many billion gigabytes of possibilities in the universe he should select, so he waited.

'Wildlife boys trapped a great big croc in Jasper's Creek. Mate, you are dead lucky.'

Yes, thought Clement. I am.

ACKNOWLEDGEMENTS

I would very much like to thank Professor Ian Dadour of the Forensic Science Department, University of Western Australia, for his feedback on the forensic components of the book, Elli Roeder for checking the German perspective, and Bruce and Alison Brown for Kimberley consideration. A huge thank you is in order to my editor Georgia Richter for her detailed and insightful assistance from start to finish. I would like to thank all those at Fremantle Press who have helped in some way into getting this book up and about, with especial gratitude to Clive Newman. Clive was there for my first novel all those years ago and it was pleasing he could be involved in the early stages of this one before retiring. A very big thanks also to my network of family and friends in Perth—Jude, Muffy, Chris, Simone, Dette, Mable, Rob Mak, Johnny and Shevaun—who always keep the home fires burning.

ABOUT THE AUTHOR

Dave Warner is an author, musician and screenwriter. His first novel, *City of Light*, won the Western Australian Premier's Book Award for Fiction, and his ninth novel *Before it Breaks* the Ned Kelly Award for best Australian crime fiction. A sequel, *Clear to the Horizon*, features the lead characters from these books. Dave Warner originally came to national prominence with his gold album *Mug's Game*, and his band Dave Warner's from the Suburbs. In 2017, he released his tenth album *When*. Dave has been named a Western Australian State Living Treasure and has been inducted into the WAMi Rock'n'Roll of Renown.

Dave's next novel, *River of Salt*, will be published by Fremantle Press in 2019.

www.davewarner.com.au

ALSO BY DAVE WARNER

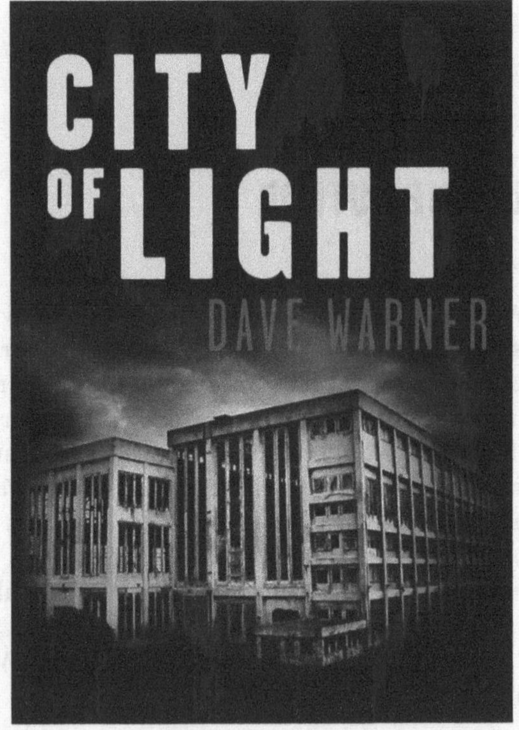

ISBN: 9781925591392 (PBK)

'Jesus Christ. I found one.' These words are blurted over the phone to Constable Snowy Lane, who is preoccupied with no more than a ham sandwich and getting a game with the East Fremantle league side on Saturday. They signal the beginning of a series of events that are to shake Perth to its foundations. It is 1979, and Perth is jumping with pub bands and overnight millionaires. 'Mr Gruesome' has just taken another victim. Snowy's life and career are to be forever changed by the grim deeds of a serial killer, and the dark bloom spreading across the City of Light.

AVAILABLE AS EBOOKS

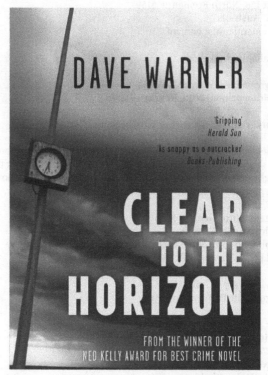

First published 2015 by
FREMANTLE PRESS
25 Quarry Street, Fremantle 6160
(PO Box 158, North Fremantle 6159)
Western Australia
www.fremantlepress.com.au

Also available as an ebook.

This edition printed 2015. Reprinted 2018.

Consultant editor Georgia Richter
Cover design Ally Crimp
Cover photograph 'Cape Leveque Road', Red Dirt Photography
Printed by McPherson's Printing, Victoria, Australia

National Library of Australia
Cataloguing-in-Publication entry

Warner, Dave, 1953–, author
Before it breaks
ISBN 9781925163797 (paperback)
Detective and mystery stories
Broome (WA) – Fiction.
A823.3

Fremantle Press is supported by the State Government through the Department of Local Government, Sport and Cultural Industries.

Publication of this title was assisted by the Commonwealth Government through the Australia Council, its arts funding and advisory body.